ENTRAPMENT.

T G Hancock

1ST Edition 2017

PAPERBACK

Entrapment.

© Copyright 2017

Thelma Hancock

The right of Thelma Hancock to be identified as author of this work has been asserted by her in accordance with the Copyright, Designs and Patents Act 1988.

A CIP catalogue record for this title is available from the British Library.

ISBN 978 1 9997425 6 0

This edition published in 2017

Printed and Bound in Great Britain

i

1

Friday.

'OFF ALREADY, DOCTOR KEGAN?' Hugh offered a smile, his teeth gleamed. 'Duty visit to my mother, Fraser. You know how they nag.'

'Don't I just! 'Don't forget to ring me. Have a proper meal, eat some veg. Is she a nice girl?'' The young man grinned at Hugh as he spoke in a high falsetto voice. He revealed a gap between his top teeth and the fact that he'd been eating something green for his lunch.

Hugh, reflecting that Fraser obviously listened to some things his mother said, grinned back. 'And is she a nice girl?'

The grinned widened and took on melon-like aspects. 'No, thank God.'

Hugh gave a grunt of laughter, picking up his briefcase which had spent the day outside the door, next to the telephone table. He absently placed the loose sheets inside and snapped it shut as he said, 'Have a good weekend. I'll see you Tuesday.' He strolled away, out into the late afternoon sunshine.

The sun was warm on his back. The street smelt of heat, hot tarmac and hotter metal, a hint of onions from the takeaway, and antiperspirant thick enough to create London smog. He could hear the birds, coughing in the updraft of car fumes, the tinny sound of someone's headphones, played too loud and guaranteed to leave them deaf, if they lived that long. The revving of the cars and panting of buses just part of the general cacophony.

He strolled along, the late afternoon sunshine casting his shadow before him. His eyebrows raised and his lips pursed as a pair of grapefruit in a string bag, cunningly disguised as a woman's bottom, wobbled past. He was making his way to a café with outdoor seating. This novelty of foreign shores spilled across the pavement and allowed one an interrupted view of passing traffic, birds in the gutters, and leaves bent on suicide under car wheels. It also allowed him to look across the roadway at the red and grey brickwork of Carlisle Cathedral.

The Cathedral was small compared with the Norman buildings down south but it made up for it in beauty and proportion. The foreshortened nave adding a hint of mystery, the buttresses telling of the weight and power of the church in the twelfth century.

'Espresso, latte, black, white.' The girl behind the counter gave a gentle sniff as Hugh went inside. The room appeared dark through the reactolite of his sunglasses. He strolled over to the counter and before, he could shape any words, she continued, 'Regular, large, to take away or drink here, and will you want cinnamon or chocolate on that.' She looked at him expectantly.

'A mug of plain black coffee, which I will drink here.'

She opened her mouth to start the spiel again.

'That mug. That coffee, no flavouring.' Hugh pointed

at a plain pottery mug and a glass jug of what he sincerely hoped was coffee lurking in its murky depths.

He prayed for patience, or at least to keep his hands away from the girl's throat, the, albeit regrettable desire experienced by vampires and homicidal maniacs, when confronted with the apparently inane. He had been coming here for coffee for the last couple of weeks. Always the same order, and still she gave him the list every day. He offered her a smile of pure saccharine, as she poured out his coffee and handed it over with an offended manner. He could almost read the words she wasn't saying. 'And a good day to you too!' He murmured as he walked away after leaving the price on the counter.

He was wending his way through the tables outside towards a seat in the shade, holding his mug in one hand and the briefcase in the other, when a blonde came teetering along on red heels and waving a matching handbag the size of a small European principality. It had about the same number of electronics gadgets in it too. Her Kindle jostled for bottom position with a digital camera and three mobile phones. There was also a miniature dog, or possibly tame rat, sitting taking the air in the top of it.

Like a baseball bat going for the plate. She swung the bag off her shoulder, catching passing mugs in the process, and sent him spinning as she prepared to sit down. Lattes rained down on the white of his t-shirt and turned it eau-de-nil and the world did a slow-mo. He watched dreamily as the mug went up in the air and turned three times before falling into the lap of an elderly woman who screeched like a parrot sighting a particularly fine pineapple; which her hair somewhat resembled.

He waited for the inevitable spinning plate to roll out

into the roadway and be narrowly missed by a car's tyres and then he gently folded like a five pound note and lay, dazed, among the remains, trying to gather his wits and tuning out the high pitched squeals of some fashion model who was exclaiming about the ruination of her hair style and shoes. He was more concerned with the ruination of his bodily organs.

FRASER, MEANWHILE, WAS HAVING troubles of his own. His rosy dreams of getting away for a date with a girl who 'wasn't nice' were fading. His boss spoke in the tones of one with a mouthful of marbles and an agenda that he knew was right, because it was His agenda.

'And how was Dr Kegan today, Fraser?'

Fraser looked at the thick mane of white hair, the hawk-like nose and the Saville Row suit and thought, not for the first time, that all this man needed was a large white cat to stroke. However, his elegant white fingers were gently stroking a grey parrot of moth eaten appearance perched on his left wrist.

'He was going to visit his mother, he said, sir.'

'And what did he require from our manuscripts?'

'He was looking at the rolls from King Edward's time, sir.'

'Ah, yes. Part of the hundreds for the area. And did he seem pleased with his research, Fraser?'

'Seemed just as usual, sir. Said he'd be back on Tuesday.'

'Good. Go and speak to James about your duties for

the rest of the day then.'

'Yes, sir.' Fraser pulled a face as he walked away; he'd had what he thought of as a cushy afternoon sitting outside the door while the good Doc Kegan read the manuscripts. He didn't really see why he had to sit there. All Hugh Kegan did was read and make pencil notes. But his orders were to watch, so watch he did. Or rather half doze, he'd hoped to get off a bit early, but James would find him something that was bound to take him into overtime, and he never got paid for overtime.

Mr Henry James Ratcliff nodded to himself as Fraser walked away. Then, as he pushed open the door to the library, he spoke quietly to the parrot who had sidled up to his left ear and was quietly squeaking into it. 'Yes, Polly, he's very naïve, but he's very young as well and will train up nicely. Now, let's have a look at what the good doctor has been viewing today. He allowed the parrot to sidle onto the back of the chair that Hugh had lately rested his backside on, and relaxed onto another similar seat for himself. He pulled forward the pile of books Hugh had left behind neatly stacked on the table and settled to his own private game of 'guess what the historian is writing about.' At one stage he frowned and gently pulled at his hawk-like nose there should have been another sheet of parchment there.

Fraser meanwhile, was speaking with James. James Dove was Henry Ratcliff's general factotum. He had served in that capacity for over fifteen years and, in Fraser's opinion, had a face like a meltit welly. When Fraser appeared in the kitchen he was sitting at a large pine table covered in newspaper, with several pieces of silver resting upon it. He was polishing a silver plate, the air redolent of sulphur as the cleaning mix worked on the metal. Fraser pulled a face not unlike a melted wellington himself.

'The boss says what can I do for you.'

'You can make sure the tyres are clean, I don't know what you did this morning but it wasn't cleaning the car properly.'

Fraser opened his mouth and closed it again. He had cleaned the car this morning. The bodywork and the inside. It hadn't occurred to him to wash down the tyres. He nodded and kept walking, going through the outside door and into the back courtyard. If cleaning the tyres was all that was required he might get away on time yet. He would stretch the job out as long as he dared. He liked working on the car anyway and working with cool water in the warm sun was a delight for children and quite a few adults, Fraser included.

The Daimler sat like a squat toad in the centre of the cobbles. It's black coachwork pristine. The chrome gleamed in the sunshine and the windows reflected back the image of a typical young man in his very early twenties, the ubiquitous uniform of jeans and t-shirt enhanced by the addition of a small gold earring in the left ear poking through blond locks. A tiny St Christopher round his neck on a short chain peeked out when he engaged in anything energetic, as was going to happen now.

He looked at the tyres, they had small amounts of mud and grit in the Goodyear treads. He walked over to the small lean-to shed and got a bucket and sponge, setting them down next to the car before going away whistling to attach the hose to an outside tap. He liked this job, he liked Mr Ratcliff, what he knew of the man, and if it wasn't for James he would think himself lucky indeed.

HUGH'S BODY MEANWHILE HAD decided it too wanted a rest. The screams of the young woman faded out. He came round to someone saying, 'Mind his head.' He blinked, it was better than 'what's he got in his pockets', or 'tell me the secret code', he supposed. Outlying parts of his body registered their protest at being ignored and he gave a nice theatrical groan and opened his eyes properly. 'Agh! The light!' Maybe someone did want the secret code.

'Sorry, sir. Just checking your responses.'

The medic waved the pen-torch in front of him again. 'Just follow the light, sir. You've had a nasty crack on the head. Its lucky Bill had stopped off for two coffees, meant we were on the spot so to speak.'

Hugh followed the light. At least his eyes did; the rest of him was just whistling in the dark and saying, 'Who me, nothing to do with me, guv.'

He faded out again.

The medics, ignoring the prior claims of the buxom wench with the spoiled hair-do who thought she needed urgent treatment for minor splash marks, loaded Hugh's body onto the waiting ambulance and took him off to the Cumberland Infirmary. Bill collected the ordered coffee first.

Hugh's brain was running a reprise of the day's events and trying to make sense of the situation, his brain knew it was a reprise but his body was trying to gain attention about the current situation.

He was looking at a manuscript. An ink blot marred the smooth, soft vellum in front of him. He cocked his head on one side looking not unlike an inquisitive sparrow, if sparrows came with over-long black hair and a droopy moustache. He looked at the brown stain, why hadn't the scribe scraped it away. It wouldn't have taken long and was common practice, for monks anyway.

He shifted on the hard chair, his denims rasping against the wood, and looked about him carefully, before gently using a fingernail to scrape a tiny corner of the ink. He couldn't be sure, but it could be a deeper brown underneath. A bloodstain? Oh! wouldn't it be great if he could have an adventure? Only analysis would tell him, and there was no way this private library, in this very private house, was going to allow him to remove a fragment of precious parchment for that kind of speculation. But it would be nice to have an adventure, like that guy searching for the Templars or Indiana Jones or someone. He shrugged; he was just a boring teacher trying to inspire an interest in history.

He should have listened to the Templars instead of writing about them, among other things they warned about being careful what you wished for.

He moved back and picked up his pencil to make a note of the text. The ancient and beautiful calligraphy wore its measured way along the lines to the bottom of the page. Except for that fifty pence piece sized blot at the outside edge.

Having made his notes he sat back. The solid chair creaked under his weight and the guardian glanced in through the glass door. Hugh, with impeccable credentials to his name and a good Oxbridge accent to back them up, plus money to pay for the privilege, had been accepted. He had been coming to this quiet, and private, library, for nearly two months now.

Hugh grinned his over active imagination wove a story about ancient blood, spilled by Viking raiders. He gave a muted snort of laughter; it was probably some ancient scribe cutting himself as he sharpened his quill. Some careless owner dripping blood from a high born nose? Maybe something more sinister?

He glanced at his wristwatch, the thin gold glinting among the dark hairs. It was a little earlier than he normally stopped work but he wanted to think about the new information he had read that day. It was jostling in his mind like women at a new year's sale. He stood, a tall lanky man in his middle forties. The ubiquitous jeans and t-shirt hiding a six-pack of which he was secretly proud.

He gathered the loose sheets of paper and the two pencils and went over to the door, lifting a hand to knock, but his guardian was already unlocking it and sliding back the glass panels.

The air conditioning hissed, maintaining a steady humidity and temperature, the better to preserve the ancient manuscripts. Nevertheless, Hugh thought he could feel the sweat running down his back, he surfaced to realise the hiss was from an oxygen mask and the sweat from shock.

'Mind how you go, Bill, get him onto the bed, and we can hand him over.'

'Yeah hand me over.' Hugh thought and went back to sleep.

HER NAME WAS HELEN McKenzie she was dressed in tight jeans which rested on her slim hips, a tight, white t-shirt which showcased her bust and a black apron which did absolutely nothing for her figure. She had served the coffee, but, she really didn't want to do this job. She was bored out of her skull, which technically is better than having your skull bored into, but is still a painful experience she thought. She was a trained police officer for heavens sake! Why couldn't one of the men serve coffee to tourists? It really wasn't fair, just because she was female she had to dress in uncomfortable clothes and be polite to impolite people.

She frowned as the young woman who had caused the accident finally stopped standing in a daze and gazed at the space where Hugh had been. She looked under the table as if expecting him to be under it, and then she plopped down onto the seat adjacent, rocking the crockery dangerously on her table as she leaned back against the woodwork.

Helen cocked her head on one side. It could have been a diversionary tactic. They had been watching this area, trying to catch what they presumed was a well organised group of pick-pockets. When the Blonde Disaster Zone stood again Helen looked across at her male college and gave a slight nod. Instead of heading away, however, the woman approached the counter.

'He's left his briefcase. Should I take it to the police? Or go up to the hospital?' The blonde spoke with a husky voice like Miss Monroe with a thirty a day habit.

Helen offered a faint smile; she certainly didn't need to break cover for this young woman. 'I can put it under the counter for you.'

The blonde stood uncertainly for a minute, shifting her weight from one leg to the other and swaying, displaying her charms in the red summer dress. She shook her head. 'No. He might need it and I caused all the chaos. Didn't I, Suki?' The little dog peered over the top of the bag, maybe checking for vicious sparrows. 'No. I'll take it up to the hospital. Thank you, anyway.' She stepped back, landing on the toes of the plain clothes copper behind her. Her stilettos, living up to their name, gauged into his foot. All three winced.

'Sorry.'

Helen shook her head slightly at him. He stepped back smartly as the blonde bombshell swung around, nearly catching him in the groin with the handbag and managing to knock a glass off a nearby table as she completed the turn.

'I'll go up to the infirmary.' She repeated and moved away, unaware of the further chaos she had just perpetrated.

The two police officers exchanged a glance. She might be a disaster waiting to happen, but they didn't think she was one of their pickpockets. They certainly weren't going to reveal who they were to help her. In fact the male partner was giving her a wider berth than he would a maniac with a knife.

'Yes, that's what we'll do, Suki.' She smiled a bit absently at the policeman and wandered off, leaving a minor trail of devastation behind her. The briefcase in her left hand, the handbag over her right shoulder, with both swinging near people's heads and drinking vessels so that they made frantic and sudden grabs as she passed.

The police watched her progress. Michael, the male partner, spoke quietly. 'God help him if they let her anywhere near him in that hospital.'

'You're not kidding! Another coffee, sir? Certainly,

sir.' She raised her voice as a further customer came up behind Michael, beginning her familiar spiel.

HUGH, HOWEVER, WAS BEING carted, in the manner of a recently bagged animal trophy, into the bedlam of A and E. His eyelids had gone on strike and his brain was debating whether to come out in sympathy.

He was dimly aware of the medic talking to someone, then a soft female voice speaking and soft female hands touching the bump on his occiput. He would have winced, but it seemed like too much effort.

'I think an x-ray and scan, ASAP, Nurse. Then let's see if there's anywhere to ward him for observation for twenty-four hours. While you get that organised I'll pop a couple of stitches in here.' The Doctor nodded at the young nurse and walked away to arrange for a few tools of her trade to be provided.

Peace reigned and Hugh cautiously opened one eye after a few minutes of blissful enjoyment. He appeared to be alone in a curtained cubicle. Institutional green met his eye. Then, like something out of a Hitchcock movie, a hand gripped the curtain. And remained gripping it.

He opened the other eye and watched it with a mixture of suspicion and slight horror as a voice said, 'We'll just leave it here, Suki. It's not like it's an airport; they don't check for bombs and things.'

There was a piercing 'Yip!' before the hand let go of the curtain. Events became somewhat confused about then.

A male voice said, 'Oi, get that dog outta here.'

An elderly female voice said, 'She was talking about bombs!'

Another said 'I'm calling security.'

And the author of his troubles slid inside the curtain, managing to tangle a burly male specimen in their folds as she retreated backwards towards the solid examination couch upon which Hugh lay watching the activity with dread. He recognised her now.

She landed on him with sufficient force to remove the air from his lungs and wonder about the state of his solar plexus. She tried to right herself and managed to hit his nose with the handbag before standing and backing into a corner, sending the BP monitor on a private ride into the other corner, the couch off centre, and his light blanket slithering onto the floor. Being male, and not yet dead, Hugh watched her chest rise and fall a few times before transferring his attention to her face. She was shaking her head, panting slightly, and looking towards the gap in the curtains.

A hospital worker of large size and ugly mien was glaring into the cubicle. A female, clad in nothing but a hospital gown and a grim expression, was advancing towards the couch in a militant manner, somewhat spoilt by the fact that she was trying to hold the gown together at the back and prevent anyone observing something better ironed, then hidden. It produced a strange sidling walk.

'I was only bringing his briefcase; He left it at the café. I thought he might need it.' The blonde stood holding it out like the head of John the Baptist on a platter. 'Um! I'm sorry. I didn't mean to upset everyone.' Everyone continued to look at her. Hugh was admiring the figure, as was what he presumed was a porter of some kind. The elderly lady had come to a halt next to a side curtain and was still scowling, but given the figure before her that wasn't surprising. The two women looked like one of those before and after pictures for a miracle cream he thought.

A uniformed giant shouldered his way past the porter and looked around. 'I'll have a word, if those not involved would like to go about their business.' He waited with monumental patience for the room to empty of the more mobile of its occupants, before looking at Hugh. 'Is this young woman bothering you, sir?'

Hugh, who had closed his eyes, opened them again along with his mouth, but he was forestalled.

'I'm sorry, I'm really sorry. He left his briefcase at a café in town when I knocked him down; I thought I would bring it here so that he didn't have anything to worry about. The staff said this was his cubicle.'

'And who are you, Miss?'

They watched with some fascination as her cheeks pinkened. 'All my name?'

Security nodded in a magisterial manner.

'Oh dear!' Her voice dropped and became even huskier. 'Maybelle Harriet Branwell. But most people call me Harry' She watched with a resigned look at the familiar expression crossing the two men's faces.

'And why did you knock him down, Miss Branwell?' The sang-froid of the security man was becoming a trifle congealed.

'Um! It just sort of happened.' She shrugged and tried a half smile on both men.

'And does the briefcase contain a bomb?'

'No. I don't know. I didn't look, maybe. Ask him, he left it at the café.' Harry looked desperately at Hugh, before setting the case on the bed and backing away as if it was indeed an unexploded bomb.

'Sir?' There wasn't just a query, but slight desperation in the voice this time.

'No.' Hugh scanned the male chest, found a name tag, and nodded. 'Dave. It contains some harmless notes and a half eaten tomato sandwich which has gone a bit soft.' He sighed slightly and was just about to expand when Harry smiled properly. Both men gave the smile the attention it deserved for a second before a mounting confusion invaded their faces as she started to speak.

'You should put it between two lettuce leaves. It stops the juice leaking; even better slice it on the round.'

'Eh!'

'The tomato, if you put it between t...' Harry stopped and looked at them. 'Look, I'm sorry I knocked you over. I thought you might need your briefcase and I didn't want you to lose it, so I brought it up to the hospital for you.' She looked about at the minor chaos and bent to pick up his blanket, managing to empty the contents of the water jug as she did so, the cover ended up dripping water as she lifted it.

Hugh winced and swung his legs round so that he was sitting on the side of the couch. He took the blanket off her and laid it on the end of the couch, glanced at the security man, Dave, and exchanged a wry smile before pushing himself to his feet. Taking an elbow he settled Harry on the couch.

'I don't think she has any intention of hurting anyone.' He laid stress on the word 'intention' and Dave offered a smile of his own.

'Right, sir.' He backed out, leaving the odd couple alone.

Hugh sat down gently next to her. Silence reigned again, indeed it poured into the room for a whole minute. His head was pounding; there was no room in there for pensiveness. There wasn't any change about his headache, but he did his best to concentrate on the young woman sitting beside him.

'I'm...'

Hugh reached out a hand and stilled the hands waving about and threatening his person. 'It's OK. Accidents happen.'

'But they're always happening to me.' She sniffed. It wasn't ladylike, more a snort, and she fumbled for a handkerchief in the bag.

The dog gave a small 'Yip' and moved quickly out of the way.

Hugh hastily found a piece of tissue in a trouser pocket and handed it over before the poor animal suffered any further.

She dabbed her eyes and wiped her nose.

He watched her pulling herself together. It wasn't exactly a strain on his eyes, even if said eyes showed a tendency to blur around the edges. The entrance of the doctor rather cut short that pleasure, but did provide him with other joys. The doctor had a plastic dish in her hand such as he might have used for the microwave. Its contents weren't quite so appetising.

'Oh, hello, are you Mr Kegan's friend? I've just got to pop a stitch or two in and then we'll send him for a scan. We're a bit short of beds so; if it looks good you can take him home and keep an eye on him. We're rushed off our feet today. Nurse will give you a leaflet telling you what to watch for.' She smiled nicely and nodded at the curtain. 'Unless you want her to stay?' She looked at Hugh.

Hugh shook his head and wished he hadn't.

'I'll be outside.' Harry removed herself. This time without knocking anything over, and went to sit opposite the curtain on a hard green chair.

2

'MY GOD SHE'D BE worth a fortune to us. Did you see the chaos she caused?' I'm soaking wet from that coffee, she pulled a face and her top away from her bust. The speaker was a well dressed woman in her late forties. Her grey coiffure had that 'just from the saloon look'. This can be interpreted as so thick with hairspray it appears to be made of shiny plastic, or bounces so much it makes you feel seasick. The make-up was beautifully applied, and the clothes a tribute to a local costumier with a good knowledge of engineering as applied to tensile strength.

She was talking to another woman who was equally well dressed and groomed, though her costumier had been more concerned with the application of lycra as it pertained to lifting and separating.

Both spoke quietly as they sipped coffee and dabbed genteelly at their rouged lips. The first speaker, a Mrs Giles Skeat, glanced casually around. 'Did you...?'

'Oh. Yes, two wallets and a card case.'

'How nice! Drink up, dear, and we'll go and look at the spoils.' They finished their coffee in a leisurely manner and gathered up various plastic shopping bags. They glanced at Helen, busy at her counter. 'Thank you, my dear, a lovely cup as usual.' Mrs Skeat nodded in a gracious manner, and they made their stately way out of the café and walked down the street like two galleons before a force seven.

'Your place or mine?'

'Yours I think, Jane.' They turned off and walked along Paternoster Row heading out along the old city walls and down into a small area of rather nice Tudor houses.

Once inside Miss Jane Wilson's front door, both perceptibly relaxed. The *haut monde* both had adopted fell away as cleanly as the coats they removed and Jane said, 'I'll put the kettle on shall I?' Her voice dropped several degrees down the social strata, like a spider abseiling down a pipe.

Mrs Skeat, Dot to her friends, nodded and went into the small front room, sitting carefully down as one whose foundation garments really did have a hint of steel reinforcing in them. And, leaning back in a soft chair, she closed her eyes. She spoke as she heard her friend returning. 'How's your son getting on?' Her voice remained well modulated.

'Oh, Fraser says the job is great. He's looking after an old boy on the other side of town. Acting as security and chauffeur. He wasn't sure at first, said he thought they'd look down on him, but now he's got to know the butler type and the cook he reckons they're just the same as him, so it's OK.'

'That's nice. It's so hard for the young ones to make a decent living, with jobs so scarce.' She opened her eyes and grinned at her friend. 'And if they don't earn, we can't.'

Jane's lips twisted, then she giggled. 'Yeah. That'll teach 'em to ignore us.'

'I told you, Jane, once you turn forty you become invisible to the bulk of the population. So long as you don't look like mutton dressed as lamb, or behave in an eccentric manner, no-one sees a woman in her prime.'

'What did you make of the klutz?'

'I think she was a ditzy blonde.' Dorothy raised her voice as her friend went into the kitchen and returned a minute later with a tray with tea things upon it. 'But she was good for us wasn't she?'

Jane nodded as she came round a chintzy sofa and set the tray down on a coffee table in front of the fireplace. The room had a slightly damp and unlived in feel, as if someone had read about front rooms but wasn't quite sure how you lived in one. Various pictures adorned the walls. They were very eclectic, looking as if they'd been acquired at garage sales, from very different levels of society, which indeed they had.

Jane was an avid and indiscriminate buyer at garage sales. The Monarch of the Glen rubbed shoulders with a rather kitsch chocolate box picture of a pair of kittens. Both faced a piece of art in the style of Picasso, but only the style.

Dorothy didn't raise her eyes to these excrescences. She was fishing in one of the plastic shopping bags handed to her by her friend, pulling out two wallets and a card-case as Jane said, 'Here, see what we've got while I see to the fire.' She knelt down at a ready laid coal fire, and struck a match, watching with satisfaction as the paper and firelighter caught with a soft whoosh.

Dorothy set the case aside and flipped open the first wallet. 'Tourist.' She announced. 'Still he'd changed some of it into British and Euro's. I wonder...'

'No, we take the cash but I'm not touching anything else.'

Dorothy shrugged. 'Yes, you're probably wise.' She handed over the traveller's cheques and began to look in the other pockets of the wallet while Jane fed the small sheaf into the flames.

'Nice family.'

Jane turned away and became busy with the teapot; she glanced over and spoke, 'I'm supposed to be the big softy around here!' Dot laid the photo down on the side and extracted a driving licence and several printed cards. She cast an intelligent eye over them. 'He was B negative. Gave blood regular. Member of the Shunters and Wheeltappers Association. Lapsed. Works in computers. Oh! Train tickets.' She held them out to Jane.

'London, and enough for the whole family. Now I feel bad too.'

'Softy!'

'Put them on the fire, Jane. We can't do anything without incriminating ourselves.'

Jane sighed and flicked through the contents before offering them to her own private Lares, Roman goddess of the hearth.

Dorothy grunted genteelly and picked up the second wallet and began poking about in the leather dividers. 'Twenty pound note, two fives and a ten. Scottish. I'm not prejudice; I'll spend anybody's money. Anything else in there.' She spoke to herself as she rummaged about. 'Packet of first class stamps, Condom, foil wrapped, and it's left a mark through the leather.' She looked up from peering into the compartments and across at Jane and exchanged a grin, before finally fishing out a gold band, a small passport photo of a woman, and a death certificate, all wrapped in tissue paper which she unfolded completely, and a small lock of auburn hair dropped into her hand. 'Oops!' She held the things out for Jane's inspection.

'Oh!' Jane looked at them and then at Dorothy, before sitting back on her heels. 'No, I can't put that in the fire, Dorothy. I'm sorry.'

'No, me neither. Go and get a duster and a pair of gloves, love.'

Jane rose to her feet. 'What are we going to do? Is there a name and address, or some cards or something?'

'Nothing like that. There's a name on the certificate, but… he must have had a separate card case.' Dot shook her head. 'I'll post them to the police. Anonymously!'

She laid the wallet down and picket up the card case. Flicked through the serried ranks of plastic and tossed the lot onto the fire. Jane came back in with some 'Marigold' gloves, a duster and a can of spray polish.

'Right.' Dorothy put the gloves on and emptied out the wallet, then began to industriously polish inside and out. She picked up the ring, certificate and photo in turn, vigorously polishing before inserting them back into the wallet flap with the re-folded tissue and lock of hair. Jane watched for a minute or two, before quietly leaving the room and returning with a new jiffy bag.

Dorothy picked it up and rubbed over its surface before taking a ballpoint and writing 'For the Police' on the centre of the envelope and stuffing the wallet inside. She tore off the plastic strip, sealed the envelope, and sighed. 'Pair of softies, that's what we are.'

She laid it down carefully. 'I'll take it with me and put it in the box.' She looked at Jane and smiled a bit sadly as she removed the gloves and laid them aside. 'Giles would never have kept my ring.' Then she shrugged. 'So we've made one hundred and twenty five pounds each. That should pay the electric bill.' She took the mug from her friend's hands and sipped cooling tea with a wry tilt to her lips.

'Its interesting isn't it? Looking into the wallets, you find out all sorts of things about people. I can remember their faces. The man with the train tickets was bald and flabby but he carried his children's photos. He didn't look like he would give anything away, much less blood.

'What about...?' Dorothy nodded at the envelope and sipped more tea.

'I didn't notice his face. Just an ordinary man, I think. He'd left the wallet on the . I just slid it off and walked away.' Jane sat back in her chair. 'Do you miss Giles?'

'Nah. Pain in the bum most of the time. I've got more freedom and fewer socks to wash. You never talk about Fraser's father...' She paused delicately.

Jane looked down at her cup and then back up at her friend. 'Nah, like you say, they're a pain in the bum, most of the time.'

The two women settled back in their chairs, pouring second cups of tea and then Jane shuffled around in the chair until she found the remote so that they could watch a quiz programme on the TV.

THE TV WAS PLAYING softly in the background of Harriet's house too. The doctor had sent Hugh home to Harriet's house in a taxi, accompanied by her. Hugh hadn't said much in the hospital but when they'd walked out to the taxi he'd spoken of his plans.

Harry was clutching a sheaf of information on head injury and trauma as she followed him into the car's interior. 'You've got mild concussion; you aren't to be left on your own for the next forty-eight to seventy-two hours.' She settled back against the seat, her cherry red dress riding up and giving him a glimpse of thigh that might have triggered a heart attack in a less resilient constitution.

'Yes, I heard. I shall go home and take it easy.'

'But they wouldn't have let you go home if I hadn't said I would look after you.'

Hugh stifled a groan, he felt that her care could well be dispensed with; it had got him in this fix in the first place. However, he didn't want to hurt her feelings. 'I heard that too. But I can't get into too much trouble in my own flat.'

'No. I could never forgive myself.' Harry sat back with a mulish expression. Well it would have been, if mules came with round faces, eyelashes long enough to tangle over blue eyes and very kissable lips. As it was she just looked like a small child denied a treat.

Hugh closed his own blue eyes and leaned his head back against the soft squab of the taxi, waiting with impatience for the strong pain relief to kick in, he'd been promised it would knock him out, he prayed it would work soon. His skin hurt where the stitches were newly pulling on the skin, there was a dull throb over his eyes, and outlying regions where complaining of GBH by blunt instruments, to whit, chairs, tables and the ground.

'So where do you want to go, love.' The taxi driver, a patient listener to the forgoing conversation, looked over his shoulder and cocked his head on one side, admiring Harry's attributes.

She glanced at Hugh, before giving her own address. The driver nodded and set the car in motion.

'That's a sensible girl.' Hugh slurred the words slightly as he half dozed in the back. He was almost fully asleep by the time they had arrived at the address. Still not with it as the driver helped her with him into the old house on the outskirts of Carlisle, and dropping into the arms of Morpheus with alacrity as soon as they got him stretched out on the double bed.

'You'll be OK now, love.'

Harry nodded as she handed over the fare and a nice tip.

'He just needs to sleep for a bit.' She watched the taxi drive off and went to check on Hugh. He was sound asleep and snoring very faintly. She stood looking at him biting her lip slightly as she thought about what to do next. Finally she nodded and went into the corridor, coming back with a duvet from the linen cupboard which she draped across his recumbent form.

She went off into the next room and switched on the TV as a form of white noise. She took the pile of information that the hospital had gifted her and worked her way through every page, going back to various paragraphs to make sure she had understood all the symptoms to look out for and what to do in case they surfaced.

After that she started to work through the notes she

was preparing for a paper on a recent trip she'd taken. She checked back every hour as the afternoon bled into evening. As nine o'clock arrived she checked on her house guest again. He was still sound asleep. She hesitated for a moment, but decided that he would have to wake soon for sustenance and went into the adjoining en-suite to take a shower.

As she emerged from the steamy room, towels on head and body, she heard her reluctant guest talking. Since she knew they were the only ones in the house this caused her to step back into the shower room and pick up the poker and advance on the bedroom, determination in her stance and fear taking up residence in her mouth like a boiled flannel.

Hugh was still lying on the bed. He was apparently having a conversation with someone behind his eyelids. Harry stood at the doorway, the poker drooping in her hand and her mouth forming an 'o' as she eavesdropped on the strange conversation.

'God, it's hot, Theo, even if it is midnight. This damn boat's as leaky as a sieve. Why didn't you point that out to me, I wonder.' There was a pause in the conversation as if he listened to the answer. Harry thought it was like hearing one side of a telephone conversation.

Hugh gave a grunt of laughter. 'Yeah, I know hell's hotter. I wish the Mamluks joy of it. This tiller's as much use as a sickel in this water. Look at that foam! God, look at those cliffs.' There was a pause and Hugh's face became strained before he spoke again. 'Why did I bring you, Theo? Aye, I know I can swim. And be dashed on the rocks to die and meet Christ with your death on my conscience.' Hugh gave a snort of laughter before lowering his voice and saying, 'Be quiet. Sound carries over water.' Hugh lay still on the bed under the fascinated gaze of Harry.

'I see it. Hold on.' Hugh began to thrash about. Before Harry could move he'd managed to throw himself off the bed and land on the floor tangled in his duvet. 'Theo, where are you. God, don't say you've drowned. How will I face uncle if you're dead? Theo! Thank God, a pulse! Up you come, my friend.'

Hugh tried to stand, still in the grip of this strange nightmare as Harry rushed over to help him. Both ended on the floor again, with Hugh pinning Harry to the ground. She tried to pull herself out from under him, only to end up half under the bed with Hugh's legs across hers.

'Be quiet; be still, a couple of crusaders in our condition would be easy pickings, Theo.' Harry lay still. She hadn't got a lot of option with thirteen stone of healthy male muscle holding her down.

Hugh spoke after a minute. 'Why am I lying on the floor? Why are we under a bed? We are under a bed aren't we, Miss Branwell? Why have you hardly any clothes on?' He began to move backwards wrapping his sore head on the leg of the bed before extricating himself.

Hugh stood up, swaying slightly as he looked around and took in his surroundings. It was a very feminine bedroom. A little on the frilly side as to curtains, and positively foamy when it came to pillows. There was a hint of humidity and a smell of spice emanating from the bathroom next door. Harry grabbed a utilitarian dressing gown from the back of her bedroom door and wrapping, it about her person, had stepped back. Then reached for the poker next to the bathroom door as the towel slid from under the folds of the robe.

Hugh eyed the poker. He looked at the bathroom. He looked at Harry. Then he sat back down on the bed with a thump, so that the springs protested slightly. 'That was weird.' He shook his head and subsided amongst the billowing foam of the pillows, closing his eyes. 'Why have you got a poker in the bathroom?'

Harry looked at the offensive weapon as if amazed to find it in her hand. 'Um! Er! Self defence? Ever since I watched 'Psyco'.'

Hugh opened an eye, looked at her, distrust vying with total disbelief, the eye winked shut again. 'In the bathroom? No-one in their right mind would attack you. You are a walking accident just waiting to happen. So far you have knocked me out, winded me, nearly broken my nose, and...' Here he frowned. 'Why were we under the bed?'

'You were having a dream.'

Hugh frowned some more. The muscles of his forehead were getting a really good workout as he tried to remember what the dream had been about. 'Nope, fading away fast.' He opened the other eye. 'Under the bed?' He sounded incredulous. He closed the eye.

'Well, no. You fell off and rolled under. You seemed to think you were in a boat?'

'I get sea-sick looking at water in the gutters. I never go on boats!'

'Oh! That's a pity.' Harry rested the poker against the bathroom door again and advanced towards the bed. Hugh, hearing the advance, opened both eyes and sat up, holding out both hands. 'Please keep your distance; I haven't recovered from the last assault to my person yet.'

'I'm sorry; I didn't mean to hurt you.'

'Yes, so you keep saying. My mind believes you, my body on the other hand...and leg... and head, is not sure it trusts you.'

Harry stopped a couple of steps away. She had that little girl look again. Hugh winced.

'Why am I here in your boudoir by the way?'

'You fell asleep in the taxi and I didn't know where you lived. Just as well, if you'd been on you're own something might have happened to you.'

'Something did. You!' He regretted the words almost immediately.

'Look, I said I'm sorry. I thought you'd be better off here, than on your own.'

Hugh sighed. 'You're probably right. And I'm sorry too. I have a thirst like a wooden god and a head like a drum player after an all night session. Do you think I can have a cup of tea?'

Harry offered a half smile. 'I'll go and put the kettle on. Your tablets are next to the bed there.' She nodded briefly at the side table where a white packet rested on a pile of books, surmounted by a pamphlet. She whisked out of the room and Hugh sighed some more.

He squinted at the tablets, picked up the packet, and knocked the pile on the floor. He leant down slowly over the side of the bed and scooped up the books, setting them down after a glance at the titles. She was into some really strange stuff. He cocked his head on one side as he silently mouthed the titles. ''Driftwood Architecture', hmm! 'Salvage and Ancient Wrecks', OK, but the 'Great Pacific Garbage Patch'.

What was that all about? He squared the books with a finger and thumb and stood up, heading to the still slightly steamy bathroom.

AT ABOUT THE TIME that Hugh was drinking tea and looking dubiously at a couple of tablets, his actions were being mimicked by Henry Ratcliff, though in Henry's case the dubious look was for the tea not the tablets.

'Cook said you wanted tea, sir. Wasn't that right?'

Henry looked at the proffered china cup, and nodded. 'But I'm not sure that that could be deemed to be called that beverage, James. It has more a look of dishwater to me.'

'Will I take it away and fetch fresh, sir?'

Ratcliff wrinkled his hawk nose, a difficult feat at the best of times. 'No. Leave it. It might taste better than it looks.' He waited until James had left the room on silent feet before murmuring to Polly. 'I personally doubt it, Polly. They don't listen to me, do they?' He held out a wrist and the parrot walked onto it, edged up his arm and muttered into his ear.

'Quite right, Polly.' He shook two tablets out from the small bottle into the palm of his hand and raised the hand to his mouth. The tablets were taken dry and he stood up and walked over to the bay window to look out on the gathering dusk of the summer evening.

'I'm expecting a visitor tonight, Polly. Will you stay and keep us company?'

Polly muttered into his ear but consented to take a peanut from his fist and go onto her perch to eat it. His visitor arrived a few minutes later. Polly eyed the new human and turned her back on him.

The visitor was a small man named Joe Jenkins. His hair was thick and grew in abundance from not just his scalp but his ears and his nostrils giving him a very murine look, a creature he had a lot in common with. Henry expected Joe to lick a hand and run it over his head.

'Joe, how nice to see you again.' Henry Ratcliff held out a hand. 'Would you like a drink?'

'Don't drink on duty, Mr Ratcliff.'

'Very wise. So, what news have you for me?'

'I've got several packets I think you might have an interest in, sir.'

'How nice.' A hint of sarcasm underlay the words; Henry sat down and hitched up his trouser seams. 'Do have a seat and tell me of your travels.'

Joe moved over and perched in one of the deep leather chairs that sat either side of a grate filled with very early golden rod in a brass urn. He unsnapped a briefcase and pulled out several packets tightly wrapped in Clingfilm.

'No trouble at customs, I hope?'

'No, sir. No trouble at all.'

'Is the supply sound?'

'Oh yes, sir, as sound as these things can be.'

'Good.' He watched keenly as Joe took a small knife from his pocket and made a slit in the first packet teasing out some grains and offering them on the tip of the blade. He sniffed delicately and then wet a finger and touched it to the powder, transferring a few grains to his lips.

Joe watched anxiously.

'Excellent. How much can we obtain?'

'Well the Arabs can be a bit...' Joe waggled a hand, 'possessive, as you might say ever since 9/11, but I think I can get us several kilos if you approve.'

'Pounds, Joe, I really can't deal in kilos.'

Joe nodded. 'Will you try the next sample, sir?'

HUGH WAS SIPPING AT a surprisingly nice cup of Earl Grey. His hostess was sitting in a comfortable chair on the other side of the table; she was handling the old and delicate china cup with care as she spoke to him.

'I get involved in what I'm thinking about and forget about what I'm doing. I really am sorry.'

'No harm done.' Hugh shook his sore head and grinned wryly. 'Well, not a lot of harm done, anyway.' They had advanced beyond the, 'my name is' stage and were now at the 'what I do is' stage.

'I'm a structural engineer. I specialise in marine structures.' The frankly incredulous expression on Hugh's face was one Harry was so accustomed to, that she ignored it and carried on, 'Just now I'm looking at the damage caused by gribbles on an old wooden pier up the Solway.'

'How, er! Fascinating!'

'You have no idea what a gribble is have you?'

'Nope. Not a clue.' Hugh grinned at her and sipped more milkless tea, before his brain caught up and he scowled at the pain, lurking like a cockroach under the sink.

'Eat your sandwich and then take those tablets. Then you can lay down for a bit longer.'

'I can't stay at your house and push you out of your own bed, Miss Branwell.'

'Yes, you can. I'm a bit of a night owl anyway.' She sipped tea and eyed him over the rim of the cup. 'So what do you do, to earn a crust?'

'Me. I teach history, and when I'm not teaching it I write about it.'

'Umm!' She set down the cup. 'What period would that cover? Or are you a stickler for the set syllabus?'

'Teaching, I have to stick to what the kids need to know, but personally I like the medieval period.' Hugh took a bite of sandwich and washed it down with tea while he waited for the inevitable.

'Are we talking pre black death, serfs and the oppressed, or post, and Wyatt Tyler and the revolution? Medieval covers a fair few centuries.'

He set the cup down gently. 'Good grief! I thought you said you were an engineer.'

'I am, but that doesn't mean I have to be ignorant about other things.' Harry sighed elegantly and set her empty cup down too.

Hugh nodded and wished he hadn't. He looked at the two white tablets resting like a couple of anaemic slugs in his palm and clapped his hand to his mouth before finishing the contents of his cup in a long swallow. 'OK, when I can think straight we'll talk a bit more.' He felt one eyelid flickering slightly and stood up. 'I think I will take up the offer of your bed.' He looked at Harry and watched as a blush made its way up her cheek bones. 'Er!'

'I do know what you mean.' Harry offered a grin and rose too. She watched as Hugh made his rather drunken way back to the bedroom, following him at a safe distance and pointing out a striped nightshirt which she'd placed on the bottom of the bed. 'It was my dad's. It might be more comfortable.'

She nodded at him and shut the door on his astonished face. Back in the kitchen she cleared the debris of their meal, loaded a dishwasher carefully and made her way into the front room and her books.

Her guest was looking at something which could have doubled as a Bedouin tent. He shook out the folds and was showered in lavender blossom before he could take evading action. He looked doubtfully at the door and then down his crumpled person, gave a shrug, and began to undress.

When he was tucked under the covers and relaxing back against the bank of pillows with his eyes closed, he allowed his mind to dwell on his current situation. It was hardly the stuff of a hero. Harrison Ford didn't take time to recline on feather mattresses clad in a, here he opened his eyes, squinted down his person, and closed the eyes again, a nightshirt! Still it was an adventure of sorts.

3

DOROTHY SKEAT HAD LIVED an incredibly boring life until her husband, Giles, had been knocked over by a bus. She had longed for adventure too. Giles was an accountant. He came home and told her about the long lines of figures he had added up that day. Her life had consisted of washing his shirts and making his dinner. They didn't visit, they didn't go out, and every year they had two weeks in a caravan at Mablethorpe. It always rained there, or seemed too.

He had died eighteen months ago and, once she had recovered from the shock, she'd looked about and realised she was free. The trouble was she didn't know what she was free to do. Just before Christmas she'd picked up a wallet on the street, she'd seen who had dropped it, and given chase. The man had ignored her shouts; in fact she'd been ignored by everyone. Revenge and conscience had a slight difference of opinion. Revenge won on points and dictated that she keep the wallet.

In the New Year she'd met Jane Wilson when she was out having coffee. Jane had been in tears, someone had lifted her purse from the top of her shopping bag and she couldn't pay for her drink. The cashier had looked down his snooty nose at Jane, dismissing her explanation. Dorothy had paid and that had been the start of their partnership and new careers.

They sat now in the comfort of Jane's sitting room; they had eaten sardines on toast and watched Eastenders. 'I must be off, Jane. I'll drop that in the box.' She nodded at the envelope with the wallet. 'Same time tomorrow?'

'I've got the hairdressers first.'

'OK. I'll see you about eleven then.' Dorothy stood up and picked up her coat, pulling on a pair of cotton gloves and picking up the envelope. They smiled at each other and Dorothy went to the door. 'Do you think we should vary cafés?'

'No, like you say, people don't notice us and going somewhere else might just make 'em think.'

Dorothy smiled. 'Yes, you're right there.' She patted her friend on the arm and walked briskly down the path back into town to post the letter. She nodded at a passing policeman, who looked through her, and a couple of giggling girls, who also ignored her. Yes. Jane was right, people didn't see middle-aged women.

HELEN MCKENZIE WAS MAKING the same observation. Her partner looked her over. 'You are not middle-aged.'

'And you, Michael Jorkvil, are a MCP. My feet are killing me, but that's aside from the point. People are generally unobservant. They're so busy talking on their mobiles that they don't see what's happening in real life.'

They were sitting in the Police staff canteen looking over the reports that had come in over their shift. Five more people had reported their wallets lost or stolen in the vicinity of the cathedral that day.

'Take this guy.' She waved the report at Michael.

'Not with both arms loaded down with gold. He was obnoxious.'

Helen sighed noisily. 'This guy, he might have been obnoxious.' She ignored the muttered, 'He was,' from her partner. 'But that's no reason to have his wallet nicked.'

'No.' But Michael contrived to sound doubtful. She swatted at him with the paper before picking up the next report and scanning the details. She laid the paper down and shuffled them neatly together.

'Tell me who you had in your sights and I'll tell you who I noticed.'

Michael grinned, 'One of them is that guy.' He nodded at the report she'd swatted him with. 'He was not just obnoxious; he was being a bit suspicious in my book.' Helen raised an eyebrow, and waited for more. 'He was checking out the ditzy blonde.'

'So were you!'

'Ah! But I'm a policeman.'

'There was very little police and an awful lot of man involved in those looks.'

'Jealous!' He leered at her.

'In your dreams. Michael! Besides my very nice husband is senior to you and he'll protect me from your lascivious ways.'

'Yeah!' There was a great deal of feeling in the comment. He'd met Helen's husband. The man put him in mind of a Doberman, not the slobber or the hair, just the attitude. 'Grr!' He muttered under his breath.

'To get back to the case,' she offered a wicked grin, knowing exactly what her partner thought of both her charms, and her husband's less than charming attitude. 'Who else, are we looking at, the ditzy blonde?'

Michael rubbed his nose with a finger and pulled a flimsy from under his coffee cup. 'She went up to the hospital and caused a bit more chaos.' He pushed the paper across with a finger and grinned as she quickly looked over the typewritten report.

His partner frankly giggled. 'Oh boy! That poor guy.'

'Yeah.' He pointed at the relevant line, 'We have a name, Maybelle Harriet Branwell. She's an engineer, in and out of the country, spends quite a bit of time in America.'

'Quick work.' Helen raised the other eyebrow.

'Application for permits, her name caused a ping.'

Helen nodded. 'Doesn't rule her out, but…'

'Yeah, unlikely. Who else you got?'

'I looked at the trio of hoodies.' She grinned. 'Stereotyping. But they were just lads having a coffee and breaking the copyright laws on their MP3 players.'

'And we ain't out to bust them for that at the moment; we have bigger fish to fry.'

'Yeah. I've arranged for the 'beat' to have a quiet word.' She sniffed. 'I did wonder about the two old biddies, they've been drinking their coffee there two or three times a week since we started this job.' She gave an elegant shudder. 'God save me from getting old. As far as I can make out they shop, get their hair done, drink coffee and gossip.' She shook her head again, shrugged. 'Nah! The guy who got biffed?'

'Teacher, on sabbatical.' Michael shrugged. 'I don't think so.'

'So for ten days work we have nothing.'

'Not so far.'

'They're not going to let you drink coffee much longer and do nothing.'

'Bloody cheek!' Michael shook his head. 'The boss wants these thieves caught; it's not good for tourism, and this part of our Fair Isle needs all the help it can get.'

Helen shuffled all the notes and reports into a file. 'Same time tomorrow?'

'Yeah! I think I'll drink tea, for a change.'

They stood up and made their way to the front of the police station. Helen's husband was waiting. 'Nigel.' Michael nodded as he stepped past his partner and around Nigel.

Helen stopped and took the offered hand of her husband. She grinned up at him as he looked a question at her. To call Nigel handsome was to blatantly lie. He gave the viewer the idea that he was undersized and undernourished. Both false. He wasn't small; in fact he was the same size as Michael. It was true he wasn't handsome, but both men had medium brown hair and brown eyes set in average faces. He was of that build known as wiry, whereas Jorkvil was built on sturdier lines. Helen had been married to Nigel for five years, they understood each other well. She nodded at Michael, who nodded back and went on his way uncomprehending. What did she see in the guy?

HUGH WAS DREAMING AGAIN. It was two a.m. He was watching himself. It was akin to a video of 'what I did on my holidays' in full Technicolor and Hugh was suffering all the feelings of those forced to watch a film when they'd rather be there or wish they were still there, not suffering the acute embarrassment and boredom mix, engendered by watching such films.

It appeared to be somewhere in a foreign land and he had the staring role. Rudolf Valentino he wasn't. It was, however, an action adventure such as he would have taken part in with delight.

Harriet watched cautiously from the doorway, but moved unwillingly towards the bed as his movements became more violent. She was slightly worried that he might fall out, but even more concerned that they both might end up under the bed again!

Hugo reached up to pick a passing blossom and found he was clutching the hand of Maybelle Harriet. He looked at her in a puzzled manner for a minute and then shook his head. 'What?'

'You tell me, you've been mumbling and twitching for the last half hour. I didn't know whether to wake you or not.' She set her head on one side and observed her guest, impartially noting the midnight shadows on his chin and the coal sacks under his eyes. 'It didn't say anything in the leaflets about dreams. Just headaches, and being sick, and double vision and things.' She paused again. 'Who's Theobald?'

'Chap I'm writing about.' Hugh looked at her; she was wearing a rather old pair of flannel pyjamas in faded pink, the top of which proclaimed she was a sleepy-head. Her hair was much longer than he'd imagined and just now a riot appeared to be breaking out all over, with hairs tangling and shooting off in all directions. The figure was just as spectacular as before but she seemed oblivious to the effects it might have on passing or stationary males.

'Do you feel OK?'

Hugh nodded, then considered, 'Thirsty.'

'I'll get you a drink if you'll give me my hand back.'

Hugh looked at the small capable hand he was clutching like a life raft. 'Sorry.'

Harry looked at him. 'You have to let go?' She gave a little wriggle of the hand.

'Sorry.' He said again, and finally released her.

She stood up. 'Hot milk?'

He pulled a face eloquent of his feelings for hot milk, but continued to stare at her.

'Tea, horlicks, coffee, water, paraquat, arsenic, cyanide?' She chanted the list at him with a grin which lit up her blue eyes.

'Eh. Oh sorry. Tea would be nice.'

'I won't be long.' Harry whisked out of the room and Hugh leaned back against the bank of pillows again. He could remember the dream in vivid detail this time. Always before, dreams had eluded him almost as soon as he awoke, but it was like a film he'd watched. He shook his head and lay recalling the events.

Harry, returning with two mugs on a tray, frowned as he spoke. 'Do you think Jung was right, or Freud?'

'Neither and both.' She set the tray down on the bedside table, took a mug and perched crossed-legged and unselfconscious on the end of the bed. 'I think they were both a product of their age; misogynists, Germans, imperialists, moneyed. But,' She sipped at her tea. 'Sometimes our dreams do tell us what we are really thinking about, rather than what is occupying our thoughts.'

'You know you are a very unexpected young woman.'

Harry gave a lopsided grin. 'If you expect the unexpected, does it then become the expected?' Her grin widened at his frown and she continued. 'My parents couldn't understand why I wanted to study. Mum wanted me to fill in some time partying, then give her grandchildren ASAP. She considered it rather an insult that her way of life apparently wasn't good enough for me. Dad wanted a boy to take over from him. I have neither the right figure nor the required taste for tax collecting.'

Hugh ran the sentence through in his mind. He could hardly say the figure currently on display looked more than fine to him. He thought some more while he sipped tea and prevented the words from emerging. Finally he said, 'Past tense?'

''Fraid so. Several years ago now.'

'I'm sorry.'

'It was several years. I manage fine by myself.'

'You and the dog?'

'Suki? She isn't mine; she belongs to the lady next door. I was just taking her to the vet as a favour. She's got a bit of canker in her right ear.'

'Right. So why is she still here?'

Harry looked where Hugh was looking. Suki was sitting on the carpet, looking hopefully at the tray where a few biscuits reclined on a plate.

'Oh dear! I forgot about her.'

'It's a bit early in the morning for returning her.' Hugh raised an eyebrow.

'I told you, I get involved and forget about other things. Men really don't understand that, they get insulted and think I don't like them.'

HENRY JAMES RATCLIFF WAS ALSO gazing at a pet. Polly was sitting on her perch with her head tucked under her arm like Mary Queen of Scots; she emitted the occasional 'peep' which was not something the late queen had been noted for.

'You really are a disgrace, Polly; you look like an overused feather duster.' Polly continued to sleep. James turned his attention to the glass of water in his hand. He took a small sip and set it down with a click on the bedside cabinet, washing away the taste of the tri-nitrate spray. He'd awoken with a small pain in his chest; he didn't want it to become a big pain.

He wasn't exactly disabled, but his heart wasn't as strong as it could be. One of the downstairs back rooms had been converted into a bedroom to save him from climbing the stairs. Stress and overindulgence in his youth had played their part along with a family history of high blood pressure. He relied on the men he employed to serve him well and go where he could no longer travel.

He settled back against the dark-blue oxford pillowcases thinking about the meeting the previous evening. Joe Jenkins was a strange man. He had been working for Henry for a number of years now. Always deferential, punctilious, but remote. Henry had used his usual sources to check out this particular employee. The man had some dirty dealing, but Henry wasn't bothered about that so long as he didn't implicate Henry himself.

He looked again at his pet. Polly didn't like Joe Jenkins and he put his head on one side looking not unlike her for a minute as he pondered the phenomena. Polly was a good judge of character. She hadn't made her mind up about Fraser yet, she liked cook and James Dove but they did feed her. He gave a slight shrug, dismissing Joe Jenkins and nestling down a bit in the bed, pulling the duvet up to his blued chin.

THE MAN IN QUESTION was on a small fishing vessel, he had a net out, but he considered fish to be slimy and tasteless, not unlike himself in fact as far as his crew was concerned. He had spent a great deal of the money that he was paid by Henry Ratcliff, on this small boat, he could use it on his own but it was a struggle. He had company most of the time however. James Dove was his crew. James liked fishing, and would sacrifice a dislike for the opportunities of going out in the boat.

They were anchored at the outlet of the Solway, the bulk of the Isle of Man clearly visible against the night sky. The lights of Douglas, its capital, standing out like a small group of stars that had slipped out of the firmament. The smell of saltwater was strong upon the air, along with the smell of fishing pots drying out.

Both men, looking villainous due to the late, or possibly early, hour, lack of sleep and a shave, and the old clothes that they wore. Ratcliff wouldn't have recognised his rather prim major-domo in his present guise. But then having lived his life being served and accepting it as his due, he rarely noticed those who actually did the serving, his attitude reflected more apparent indifference than arrogance however.

The two men had been sitting aft, drinking tea from tin mugs and occasionally checking for other vessels. Now James spoke above the gentle slap of waves against the hull. 'How was your trip?'

'Successful. Mr R. seemed pleased with the produce.'

'Will you go back then?'

'Oh, yes. I've made a few good contacts there.' Both paused to sip and James pulled his dark blue cap more firmly down. The early morning chill was nipping his ears despite the promise, but only the promise, of summer, from the met office. 'Young Fraser is a bit nosy?' It was a tentative question. Joe wasn't sure he trusted the young man. He liked the status quo maintained. He sipped again from the tin mug and looked under his cap at James, before saying, 'I don't suppose he'll last all that long, the young ones want a bit more than cleaning cars and driving sedately about. When he's got a few pounds in his pockets he'll hand his notice in and go looking for something more exciting?' There was half a question there and James answered that rather than the main thrust of the sentence.

45

He rubbed his chin with a palm against his nascent beard and heard the rasp. 'I don't know, he seems a nice kid. And any job is better than no job.'

Joe shrugged, and then glanced at his watch. 'Nearly time?'

'Aye. I'll haul in the nets.'

'Fish for his breakfast.' Joe gave a slight shudder.

'If we're going to catch it we might as well use it.'

Joe shrugged again, then stood up and moved to the port side as he heard something bumping against the hull. He spoke apparently to the night. 'Money and something for your trouble.' He tossed a small leather case and package over the side, hauling up an oilskin wrapped packet about the size of a shoe box which had been attached to a small rope dangling among the fishing lines.

James looked at the packet and nodded at the ice box. Joe set the packet inside and James tipped the small shining mixed catch of herring and cod on top and flicked the fastenings down, locking whatever fishy business Joe was up to, away from prying eyes.

'Up anchor, James. Let's get back before dawn, bring on the winter nights I say.'

James grunted. He was busy hauling in the anchor and changing the lights from anchor lights to steaming lights. Joe went to the wheel-house and started the engine, casting an experienced eye over the radar screen as he began to turn the wheel. Hardly a blip showed except for a small dot heading away from them and towards the Isle of Man. He spoke to James as James came under the sheltering roof. 'All stowed.'

'Aye. It's a nice night.' James leaned on the side of the door, looking up at the clear dark sky as he pulled out an old pipe and began to stuff it with baccy from a leather pouch worn thin and grey with use.

'If you're going to smoke that, go away.' It was said in a rather prim voice.

James shrugged and grinned, but obligingly went and leaned over the rail instead, watching the bow-wave and the shore-line of Silloth advancing towards them. He sniffed the air; it might be a nice day after all. They had a short drive back to Carlisle's outskirts in Joe's car. He liked night fishing. He didn't enquire into Joe's activities, he was happy to just fish.

He relaxed, planning the work in the house for the day. Henry Ratcliff had a meeting that afternoon at York. That meant he and Fraser would be away most of the day. James nodded to himself; he could grab a couple of hours sleep while they were out. He and Joe had been doing this for six years and he felt he was getting a bit old to be missing his sleep, but he had an investment in the boat now. He'd save some of the housework for Fraser. That might put the young man off a bit more.

4

Saturday Morning.

FRASER WAS JUST WAKING up. He wanted this job and he was determined that he wouldn't be late for the longish drive to York. It was the first time he'd been entrusted with such a long trip in the five months he'd worked for James Ratcliff. He crawled out of bed, hair like a porcupine and breath like a sulphur mine. He really shouldn't have gone to the pub, but it was stupid to have eaten the curry too.

He groaned his way across the landing and grunted as he met his mother coming out of the bathroom. 'Morning, son.' He staggered past and shut the door firmly in her face.

Jane grinned to herself and tightened the belt of her blue dressing gown. She patted her hair and walked downstairs to put the kettle on. He'd never been a morning person, even as a little boy. She busied herself making toast and tea, and was into her second cup by the time he came down trailing aftershave like a Bisto advert. She stood and put two slices in the toaster and flicked the switch on the kettle.

Fraser offered her a bit of a shamefaced grin. 'Morning, Mum.'

'Morning, yourself. You said you had an early start.'

She paused. The tricky waters of teenage angst were behind them, but she still kept a wary eye out for rocks they might founder on, even in the gentle pool of very early twenties. She didn't want to fall into the trap of possessive single mother of an only son. 'I thought I might make an early start too, on the washing. They said it was going to be a nice day.' She paused again. 'If you want anything done just leave it in the bathroom.'

Fraser nodded, busy with the teapot. Good old mum, she'd never gone into his room since he'd turned eighteen. Said everyone needed a private space. Even if they shared a house. Not that that stopped her speaking her mind about girls and such.

'Thanks, Mum. I'll leave it out.' He sat down and began to butter toast with a lavish hand. 'What else you doing today?'

Jane ran the sentence, 'Acting as a pickpocket' through her mind, and grinned inside. 'Oh! Just getting my hair done and having a coffee with Dorothy.'

'She's nice Dorothy. Bit out of our class though, Mum. Mind she doesn't make you spend too much.' Fraser paused, he too was careful not to upset the boat after past storms. 'I can lend you a bit if you want.'

Jane laid a gentle hand on his arm for a second. 'Thanks, love. But I've budgeted.'

'You're a wonder, Mum.' Fraser grinned and popped the final mouthful of toast in. He washed it down with the tea and stood up. 'York, here I come.'

'Don't forget to look out your washing, and look at the great door of the cathedral.'

He said, 'OK.' to the first part of the sentence and, 'I will if I get a chance. But I think I'm going to be a bit busy.' to the second, as he exited the kitchen door.

Jane watched him go and poured herself another cup, draining the pot. She swallowed the guilt along with the slightly stewed tea. It had been fun at first, but she was coming to the conclusion that it was time they stopped. That wallet last night had made her uncomfortable and she had seen Dorothy wasn't happy about it either.

HUGH AND HARRIET WERE eating breakfast too. It was a more leisurely meal, if just as early. Suki had been returned to her mistress, and Harry had only managed to lock herself out, thereby getting her reluctant guest out of bed by ringing the bell, burn the toast when she got in, and knock a chair over on the way to the table. For her it was a negligible list of accidents.

Hugh had watched her, keeping his distance as she moved around the room as if it were a pin machine and she was the ball. He breathed a sigh of relief when she finally sat down.

'Harry.' She didn't even look at him; she'd been sitting holding a slice of uneaten toast for the last five minutes. He tried again slightly louder. 'Harry.'

This time he got a response as she dropped the toast and knocked over her mug. She hastily pushed back the seat and went into the kitchen for a cloth. Hugh watched the relentless crawl of the puddle of coffee towards the edge of the table for a few seconds before damming the flow with words and actions. He put the newspaper in the way.

He stood and went into the kitchen to find Harry holding the cloth, leaning against the sink and gazing down the plug hole, muttering, 'I wonder why they didn't use fresh water.'

'Harry.' He took the cloth from her hands and set it on the draining board before taking hold of both hands and crowding her against the draining board. He didn't want her creating more chaos. 'Harry. I have to go home, I'm much better today. Can I do anything for you? You seem a bit pre-occupied.'

Harriet smiled at him, her blue eyes finally focusing on his face. She twitched her hands, but he held firm. 'No, I'm good. I was thinking.'

'I noticed. I'm grateful for the loan of your bed and your care last night.' He watched the red crawling up her cheeks with faint astonishment now what had he said.

'There's no need to be sarcastic.'

'Eh!' All at sea he looked at the now angry blue eyes.

'I know I'm not very good at caring for people, but I do care.' Harriet scowled.

Hugh shook his head. 'I know you do, that's why I'm thanking you.'

'Oh!' Harriet looked at him and wriggled her hands some more. 'I thought…' she frowned; her eyes had drifted away and back to the sink. 'I wonder if it's something illegal.'

Hugh scowled, then shook the hands before releasing one and capturing her face, holding it gently between finger and thumb so that she was forced to look at him. 'Harry, I don't know what's on your mind, but pay attention for just a few seconds until I get out of your hair.'

'Sorry.'

'Right.' He frowned at her, assessing how much of her attention he had. 'I am grateful that you took me in last night, I probably would have been a lot less comfortable and a lot more worried if I'd woken up on my own. I'm going to go home now. I shall put my address and phone number on the board next to your telephone, should you want to talk to me again. I should like to talk to you, you're a nice person.' He took a breath but continued to gently hold her face, afraid if he let go she would drift away again. 'Clear?'

'Yes, Hugh.' Harriet gave him a nice smile. 'I've enjoyed your company too.'

Hugh let go and tapped her on her nose with a long forefinger. 'Take care of yourself, Harry.' He turned and went out of the kitchen, leaving her leaning against the sink.

He picked his jacket up and pinned the sheet of paper on the board next to the front door, smiling as he looked at the post-it notes already there. Most written in red ink and capital letters. 'HAVE YOU GOT YOUR KEYS?' 'DID YOU TURN OFF THE GAS?' HAVE YOU GOT YOUR MOBILE?' 'MAKE SURE YOU KNOW WHERE YOU PARK THE CAR!!!' 'Three exclamation marks and underlined, wonder how many times she's forgotten.' He went out into the bright early summer morning and walked along the street.

He was half way home before Harriet realised he'd gone. 'But he's supposed to be looked after for seventy-two hours. Bother!' she spoke to thin air as she hurried to the door and looked along the street then stepped back inside, shaking her head. 'Oh bo...' She looked at the notice board, spotted the address and phone number, and smiled before going to get her briefcase and light denim jacket.

HELEN MCKENZIE WAS SITTING rather primly at her desk. She was due to go on duty at the café at ten, but had come in to work to sort out some of the paperwork with her partner, Michael, beforehand. The primness was occasioned by the catcalls and whistles that had been directed her way from her so called friends, who ought to know better.

Michael was just as bad. 'Wow! That's a nice skirt you're almost wearing.'

'This is sexual harassment and I've got leggings under it.'

Michael nodded, ignoring her imputations about harassment. 'And they leave very little to the imagination.'

'I don't want to know anything about your imagination, Michael.' She shook her head, making her big hoop earrings bounce near her shoulders. 'Disgusting!'

Michael grinned at her and pulled out a chair on the opposite side of the desk. 'So how do you want to play it today, boss? I wish we could practice a little entrapment.' His face lost the grin. 'I'm tired of coffee. I'm tired of thieves who spoil people's holidays, and I'm tired of people flouting the law as if picking pockets didn't count. It's dirty and petty and makes life miserable for law abiding folk.'

Helen nodded agreement, she waited for him to focus on the work, but they all needed to spew feelings at times. She watched him tuck the feelings away again.

'Do you think it would be classed as entrapment if we created a diversion like yesterday and saw who moved?' He offered a wry look over the desk.

'Probably.' She offered a wry look of her own. 'But we can be alert to those moves.'

'Yeah. Come on, Delilah, I'll give you a lift to work.'

'Gee, thanks.'

They left the police station in Michael's car. He dropped her off near the town centre and went to find himself a parking place. Helen sashayed along the street through the Saturday shoppers and swung in through the door of the café, noting the very early customers.

She went through front of the premises sighing to herself, not just at another day of serving coffee, but at the exposed bags, wallets, jackets and mobiles ripe to be snatched, that she had walked by on her way into the back and the small changing room.

She understood the principle of using a briefcase or jacket to keep a table free of intruders; it was a very English habit. She even understood the significance of using a mobile to give the impression of being in contact with others and thereby not available to roving males. But it did make for easy pickings when they were busy texting instead of watching their possessions.

As she stowed her own bag in a locker and turned the key she thought about the things that had been stolen. She stood still for a minute, looking blankly at the closed door. 'Hang on. Have we missed something here?' She spoke softly to herself and then pulled her own mobile out from her pocket, pressing speed dial.

'Michael.'

Her partner spoke through a seeming riot. 'Yeah.'

'Where the hell are you?'

'Marketplace. What's up?'

'Just a thought. Have any mobiles been nicked?'

'Hang on.' Michael, on his way out the market doors, moved down a back alley and leaned against a wall opposite an upmarket clothes shop. 'That's better. Mobiles? No, I don't think so. Wallets, card cases.'

'In fact only men.'

Michael nodded at his reflection in a shop window. 'Now you come to mention it...Yeah.'

'I wonder if that's significant?'

'Don't know, Helen, but I'll think about it. I'm about two minutes away.'

'See you soon then.' Helen flicked the machine shut, tucked it away and went out to begin serving coffee to the thirsty population. She'd hardly got through the swing door to the front area when all hell seemingly broke loose around her.

FRASER WAS TRAVELLING DOWN the motorway. He'd been a bit surprised when Mr Ratcliff had elected to travel in the front seat of the Daimler. He'd also been a bit nervous. But Henry Ratcliff had chatted gently to him and Fraser gradually relaxed.

He would have been astonished at how much personal information he was imparting to the elderly man beside him. As they pulled in to Te-Bay Henry said. 'I'll go and sit down, Fraser. I'd like a cup of Earl Grey and a piece of shortbread. I'll be in the back area.'

Fraser watched him make his slow way through the crowded room leaning on an ebony cane; and then joined the queue at the counter for the requested tea. He took the tray of things and made his own way towards his boss who was using a mobile phone which he put back in his pocket as Fraser approached.

'Thank you. Now, if you would get a copy of the Times and then take the car and make sure we are full. I don't want to have to find a petrol station on the way back. I'll be about twenty minutes here.'

Fraser nodded. He went back through the crowd and into the farm section, buying a paper and also getting himself a Styrofoam cup of coffee. He carried it carefully away to the car and moved off to the garage. He filled up and then drank the coffee, heading to the loo as well, before going in search of his boss.

Having seen Ratcliff safely stowed, in the back this time, he set off down the motorway again. Henry Ratcliff picked up his paper and scanned the headlines, but in truth he had very little interest in the current crop of fraud, scandal and illicit sex. He presently laid it back down and closed his eyes. Not so much to sleep, as to think about what he'd learnt that morning both from his chauffeur and his phone call.

The boy was fatherless, lived with his mother, who he seemed fond of, and had a girlfriend who he seemed to have little respect for. He had passed his 'A' levels but found nothing in the job market that he enjoyed doing. He had ambitions towards university. And he wanted, but hadn't dared ask, to look at the library. The face twitched and a faint smile came and went. Henry Ratcliff nodded to himself, if the boy kept going he should get his wish. In a quiet way Ratcliff liked to see those about him satisfied, it made them better workers for him.

Ratcliff's mouth turned up a bit, he imagined the sedate speed they were travelling at present might not be a preferred option without Fraser's boss in the back. Fraser did like the Daimler. He'd waxed enthusiastic about its comfort and performance.

Ratcliff opened one eye and looked at the back of his chauffeur's head before closing the eye again. Yes. The scamp looked as though he'd enjoy a bit of speed. Ratcliff liked to flesh out the private eye's reports of his employees. He'd taken to Fraser when he'd attended the interview and he felt his judgement was justified. He dozed after that as Fraser made his way first along the A65 and then on to the A59 heading towards Harrogate and an early lunch.

Fraser was enjoying himself too. The car was a dream to drive. The hidden power of the engine a decided bonus. He glanced in the mirror a couple of times but his boss appeared to have gone to sleep. He hummed a modern tune quietly to himself, while he thought about this job. Yes, he'd been bloody lucky to get it. Now if only he could get a look at the books in the library he would be well set. He didn't want to steal them just read them. He envied Hugh Kegan the right to look, but hadn't quite screwed his courage up to ask for himself yet.

5

WHEN HUGH ARRIVED AT his home address Harry was waiting. She was sitting in the driving seat with a notepad on her lap and an absorbed expression on her very pretty face as she read through what she had been writing.

Hugh could have gone into the house without her noticing but he felt that the action would be rather mean. Anyway he was curious as to what had brought her out of her reverie long enough to get her across the town in a car. As he approached he found himself wondering if she was actually safe on the roads and then shook his head. 'Don't be nasty, Hugh.' He spoke under his breath and went around to the driver's side, tapping gently on the half open window. The total lack of response caused him to rap a bit harder.

'Harry!'

'Oh! Hello, Hugh.'

As if, he thought, she wondered why he was there. 'Harry, did I leave something behind.'

She looked at him in an abstracted manner for a second or two. 'Oh, no. But you aren't supposed to go.'

She put a hand on the car door handle and Hugh almost skipped out of her way, placing his briefcase in front of his groin. He stood back as she extricated herself and laid her paperwork down on the driver's seat.

'I'm not supposed to go where?'

'No. You have to be watched for seventy-two hours the papers said, so I thought I'd better come and watch you. I brought my work with me.'

'Harry, I feel fine. You don't have to nanny me.'

Harry shook her head, her curls bouncing about. 'I'm responsible for you being ill. I should watch you.'

Harry shrugged. 'You'd better come in. But be warned, I'm not going to bed.'

'Well, I should think not! I'm not that kind of girl.'

'I didn't mean...' He caught her grin this time, just in time. 'Come on, you can put the kettle on while I find a change of clothes.' He walked across the pavement and put the key in the lock, before turning to her. 'Keep your mind in the present, Harry, please. I haven't paid off the mortgage yet.'

'Cheek.' He heard the faint mutter as he went indoors, dumping his briefcase on a telephone table behind the door.

Harry followed him in and he heard the catch snick down as he went along the corridor, by-passing the stairs. He'd suddenly thought about the state of his kitchen sink. He opened the kitchen door and looked across the expanse of tiling. Raised an eyebrow at his own tidiness and stepped into the room, turning as he did so. 'Kettle, teapot, mugs. I'll just be a few minutes.' He indicated with a hand before walking around Harry and giving her a smile as he headed towards the stairs.

Harry, left in charge of miles of stainless steel and Formica, took time to get her bearings. As she had said, if she was concentrating on something she could function perfectly well. She set the kettle to boiling and found mugs, milk and sugar. As she waited for the water to boil she went over to the window and looked out on a garden more nearly resembling a hayfield ripe for scything, than a lawn.

She had two mugs of tea on the table and was investigating the shelf of books on top of the freezer when Hugh returned, smelling of soap and with damp hair. 'A shave seemed like a good idea while I was up there.' He nodded at the ceiling.

'Mmm.' She smiled at him, sniffing gently at his aftershave. 'You have some very strange recipe books.'

'Eclectic is the word you're looking for, my mother buys them in the hopes that I will cook and prepare proper meals for myself.' He grinned. 'It doesn't work. Not when I can persuade girlfriends and herself to cook for me.'

'How very chauvinist of you.'

Hugh shook his head. 'Nope, not chauvinist, just lazy.' He went and sat at the table. Then leaped up again so that, Harry moved back and slopped tea slightly.

'What.'

'Mother.' Hugh looked guilt stricken and Harry wondered if he was one of those men who referred everything back to mother.

'Mother?'

'I should have visited last night. She'll be worried, where the hell's my mobile.' He walked briskly out of the room and returned with the small silver square. 'Yeah, three texts. I'll just reassure her.' He sat and bent his head to the task, muttering as his fingers stabbed the keys. 'There, 'got

caught up with work, sorry, see you next week sometime'.'
His looked across at Harry and pressed send. 'That should hold her.'

'Now what papers were you talking about, Harry?'
He watched her seat herself opposite him.

'The papers I was given at the hospital. They said you should be kept under observation for forty-eight to seventy-two hours.'

'I really do feel fine, bit of a headache where the stitches are but otherwise, OK.'

'What about the weird dreams?'

Hugh shrugged and sipped tea. 'What about them? Dreams are just that, I can't do anything about them.'

'But you said you could remember them. Is it somewhere you've been?'

'No, I don't think so. I haven't even got a passport, so I've certainly not been to Cyprus. I'm pretty certain that was where I was dreaming of, that's part of the setting for my novel.'

'So why dream about it?'

Hugh shrugged again, relaxing on the kitchen chair. 'I'm a teacher, but I'm trying to write a book about the Knights Hospitalers. It was probably just a mish-mash of things I'd been researching and the day's events.'

Harry nodded. 'OK.' She set her mug back down. 'So what are you going to do today?'

'I had nothing planned, except perhaps to sort out my notes from yesterday.' He smiled wickedly at her. 'If you really feel you must stay you can organise lunch in a bit!'

'Not me. I forget to feed myself.' Harry grinned back.

'Touché. Come on then, bring your mug and we'll go into the sitting room and work on our paperwork until it's time to eat. Then maybe find somewhere that sells food, because I doubt there's much in my fridge.'

'There isn't. Have you ever wondered why they have a 'sell by' date on sour cream?' Harry followed him along to the front door, speaking as she went past him and intending to go out and fetch her bag of notes from the car. Hugh picked up the briefcase, giving her a very odd glance as she disappeared outside. Then he went into the front room.

Harry returned, closing the door after her, and entered a comfortably furnished room with a generous expanse of dining table covered in paperwork. Holding a small notebook in his hand Hugh looked across the room at her. 'Is this yours by any chance? It certainly isn't mine.'

Harry looked at the plastic covered blue notepad, shook her head and said, 'Nothing to do with me.'

'Odd.'

He flipped it open and scanned the first page. 'Doesn't make a lot of sense. It's all numbers.' He tossed it lightly over the table and Harry picked it up and opened it for herself.

'Columns of numbers. Nope means nothing to me either.' She laid it down and looked at him. 'I picked up your brief case in the café; I don't think anyone else had a chance to knock anything inside it. So where could it have dropped in?'

'Work I suppose.' He leaned back and smiled. 'I'll take it with me on Tuesday and see if it belongs to anyone there.' He nodded at the pile of papers Harry was setting down on the table. 'So what are gribbles?'

'I didn't think you'd been paying that much attention.'

'I'd have to be half dead not to pay attention to a pretty girl like you!' He smirked, then spoiled it by allowing a genuine grin to sneak onto his face.

'Oh yeah!' Harry offered her own version of a leer before reciting. 'A gribble can be any of 56 species of marine isopod from the family Limnoriidae.'

'And now I know.' He laughed at her.

'And now you know.'

He pushed aside the pile of papers in front of him. 'Tell me about your isopods?'

'I bet you say that to all you girlfriends.' Harry grinned.

DOROTHY SKEAT WAS ON her way into the café that the police currently had under surveillance. She was rudely pushed out of the doorway as two young people, dressed in black, entered behind her. She tutted, and began to get out from under their rush, when one of the two swung around and grabbed her by the throat holding her with a knife pressed to her ribs.

She stood still in the grip, taking on board the aroma of cheap deodorant, and even cheaper perfume. A voice spoke in her ear. It was either a very young man or a girl. 'Keep still or I swear I'll stick you.' Dorothy became even more statue-like, the sweat popping out on her forehead the only visible movement.

She watched the drama unfold before her. The other person who had entered was shouting at the waitress who had just emerged from the back premises.

'Open the till.' He was pointing at the young woman. 'You lot...' He, and Dorothy was sure that one was a he, gestured with another knife at the gawping customers. 'You lot, empty your pockets onto the table, or else.' His voice was rising with a mixture of fear and excitement.

The waitress was moving very slowly towards the counter. She looked directly at Dorothy, then at the nearby table where the usual salt and pepper pots and bowl of sugar packets were arranged in the middle. Dorothy pretended to sag, she made her voice weak and trembling. 'I'm going to faint.'

'Oh, for God's sake!' The young girl shoved her towards the table. Dorothy grabbed the pepper pot and threw its contents over her shoulder.

The waitress pounced on the young man as he turned to look at his compatriot's shriek of anger and astonishment, and a young man came through the door and grabbed the woman. Both parties were wrestled to the ground.

The young woman lay and sneezed, pawing at her face and risking blinding herself with the knife she still clutched. Michael let go as it became obvious she wasn't going to be a danger to anyone but herself.

'Michael, cuffs?' A pair of police restraints sailed through the air, were caught, and the man was left sobbing on the ground his hands firmly manacled at his back. The man called Michael was on his mobile talking urgently.

Dorothy subsided onto a seat, breathing out deeply and then looking down her person for signs of damage. Everyone started talking as if their tongues had been released from bridles. She looked at the young girl, who, between pepper and emotion was weeping copiously, and sighed softly. The girl sagged and leaned back against the table leg as the man called Michael laid a heavy hand on her. He looked at Dorothy. 'You alright, ma'am?'

'I've been better.'

He turned back to the girl. 'Name?'

'Julie. Julie Robson.' Her voice came through a barrage of sniffles.

'I'm arresting you, for attempted theft and holding to ransom. Do you understand?' He began to recite the Miranda, the girl spoke over his recitation.

'I only wanted a fix, he said we could get a fix, there was always lots of money here. I only want a fix.' She looked first at Michael and then at Dorothy in a pathetic way and wiped her hand under her nose repeating 'All I wanted was a fix. I wasn't gonna hurt nobody, honest.'

Michael shook his head repeating. 'Do you understand?' Then looked out of the shop doorway. A white wagon was pulling up on the pavement with a squeal of brakes, and blue uniforms where descending like leaves in the autumn.

'OK, Helen?'

Helen was busy turning her prisoner over and sitting him upright. Reading him his rights and generally acting like the tough policewoman she was. Michael offered a wry smile to Dorothy, and then hauled his prisoner upright and led her out the door as other police swarmed in.

Dorothy was shivering slightly now, partly from shock to the recent events but also because she realised they'd been picking pockets in full view of a couple of coppers.

She looked up to find the waitress called Helen standing in front of her. 'Do you need a doctor, Mrs...?'

'Skeat, Dorothy Skeat. No, love, I'm fine. I think I want to go home though.'

'I just wanted you to pretend to faint or something. Ask to sit down, maybe. You were brilliant.' Helen offered a brilliant smile of her own.

Dorothy gave a lopsided smile. 'I didn't know you were a police officer.'

'We're undercover, but I guess we've blown it.' She looked around at the customers being interviewed by the long arm of the law. 'Do you feel able to come back to the station and give a statement?'

Dorothy nodded, what choice did she have?

'I'll get you a lift.'

Which was how Jane came to see her friend being helped into a squad car. Jane turned smartly about and went back down the street. She stopped several shops away and tried to make some sense of the comings and goings. She rubbed her nose to prevent herself from bursting into tears. She was scared, not just for herself but for Dorothy too. What did they do to pickpockets these days? And what would Fraser say?

FRASER WASN'T THINKING ABOUT his mother. He was enjoying his day out. He arrived at the old watering place of Harrogate at just before twelve in the morning. He had parked outside an exclusive hotel and escorted his employer up the two steps and through the revolving door before handing him over to a *maître de.*

Fraser's instructions were to park the car and get himself a meal and return in an hour and a half. He walked out of the hotel and looked at the big shiny Daimler and glanced about the high street. Yellow was the predominant colour in the gutters. He looked at the doorman, resplendent in enough gold braid to satisfy an admiral, and said, 'Where's the best parking, please?'

If the man was an admiral, it was a row boat in Hyde Park he commanded. 'Cross the road and round the back, mate.' A broad cockney accent assailed his ears.

Fraser gave him a nice smile with his thanks; it won him the further comment that, 'There's a café in the next street what did a good cuppa too'.

'Thanks again.' Fraser got behind the wheel, swung the big car across the junction and went to park it. He climbed out, got a ticket from the machine, and then locked up before strolling off to find the café.

It did indeed do a good cuppa; it also did a nice bacon butty. He settled down to enjoy his meal and study the map he'd thoughtfully provided himself with that morning. He had no idea why he was taking his boss to York but he wasn't going to be found wanting when it came to navigating around that old city. When he thought about it he had no idea what his boss did. He just knew that the man was loaded and he'd like to enjoy some of that money himself. For now though he'd content himself with a trip to the Railway Museum.

THE ONLY THING THAT had been loaded about Hugh and Harry was the plate of chips in front of each of them. They had talked for an hour over one cup of tea each and then several coffees. Now having decided they must eat they had visited the local chippy and brought it back to Hugh's house.

Each was enjoying the other's company, much to the surprise of both. However, Hugh was sagging slightly. His headache, which had bunked off for a pint and crisps, was back refreshed and was now shouting for attention at the bar of his mind.

He winced as Harry set the plates into the sink. She turned around and spoke before she'd taken in the expression on his face. 'What do the Chinese call their good plates?' She registered the wince and saw him closing his eyes in pain.

'Eh!' Hugh scowled.

'Doesn't matter. I think its time you took another pill, Hugh.'

'Unfortunately so do I. I think it's the pills that are giving me the funny dreams.'

He pulled the strip of tablets from the back pocket of his jeans and popped the foil off two of them before taking the glass of water she'd just filled for him.

Downing water and tablets he grinned a bit feebly. 'Are you staying?'

'Oh, Yes. I shall work in the front room.'

'I will be alright, Harry.'

She nodded. But it was obvious she wasn't going anywhere.

Hugh shrugged, offered another smile and went off upstairs, there he had an accident - he fell into bed and snuggled down.

Three hours later Harry thought she heard him calling her. She pushed back her chair and went soft footed upstairs to find him still tucked into bed but dreaming again. She leaned against the doorjamb while she studied him a bit anxiously.

He was mumbling and moving about the bed, but didn't seem in imminent danger of throwing himself out of it. Bearing in mind the last time she'd gone to his rescue she stayed by the door.

She sniffed the atmosphere and breathed in an aroma of 'Brut' and fresh linen. The place seen through the dusk of drawn curtains was free of dirty washing and dust, which she considered remarkable enough, but its very spartanness was somehow rather daunting. The only untidy feature was a small pile of books resting on the floor at the side of the bed.

She brought her gaze back to Hugh as he gave a final mutter and sat bolt upright in the manner of an elderly spinster insulted by a cad, before opening his eyes and looking blankly at her.

'Hello, Hugh.'

He continued to gaze at her blankly for several more seconds. Long enough for her to become slightly worried before his lips moved in a slight smile. 'Harry you are a sight for sore eyes. I was dreaming again.'

'So I gathered. I didn't want to end up under the bed again and you didn't seem inclined to toss yourself out, so I stayed over here.' Harry came further into the room. 'How's the head now?'

'Not too bad, would you pull the curtains back for me and then maybe I'll be able to assess the damage a bit better.'

Harry moved over and eased open one side, watching his face as the sunshine of early evening slid over it. 'OK?'

Hugh nodded. He hitched himself up in the bed and leaned back against the headboard. 'I was dreaming about my alter ego again. He has far better adventures than I ever do.'

Harry came and perched on the bottom of the bed, waiting for him to continue.

'I sort of know where I was too.'

'Back in Cyprus?'

'No. As a matter of fact I was somewhere on the Solway here. I think I might have been there, or maybe I've just seen a picture.' He offered a slightly strained smile. 'Hugo and this Theobald chap where tramping across the Cumbrian countryside. Very strange but helpful, if I can remember it all.' He paused for thought, looking at the way the light caught at his companion's hair. 'I think I'll get the car from the garage and go there tomorrow.'

Harry shook her head. 'You aren't supposed to drive.'

'I'm fine.'

'Look, I've got to do some research on the ground about here this week, how about I drive you there.'

'That sound's very like nannying to me.'

Harry smiled. 'Humour me? Anyway I could use a second opinion.'

'What I know about engineering you could put on a postage stamp, Harry.'

'Oh, it's not the engineering, it's the gribbles.'

'I know even less about ship's worms.'

'You could keep me from hurting myself. Besides I have a report to write to the Receiver of Wreck. I could use a bit of help.'

'On the experience of the last twenty-four hours, Harry, I doubt it; and shouldn't that be wrecks in the plural?' He shook his head.

'No. Wreck singular, covering all aspects of flotsam, jetsam, derelict, lagan and royal fish. And it's a she.'

Hugh raised an eyebrow. 'I have no idea what you just said. No wait!' He rubbed a hand over his tousled hair and smoothed down his moustache. 'Royal fish are whales aren't they?'

'And dolphins porpoises and sturgeon.' Harry grinned at him. Then said, 'Please, Hugh. I feel responsible for you.'

Hugh sighed. 'Go away, Harry. I want to get up.

When I come down we'll talk about it.'

Harry took the hint as he twitched the covers on his bed. She went down and into the kitchen and put the kettle on before going through and shovelling most of her notes into her large tote bag. She was busy thinking about her host, so that she inadvertently shoved several of his notes, and the blue notepad, in the bag too.

The kitchen resembled a London fog when she returned, and she hastily put the lid on the kettle so that it stopped boiling. A few minutes later Hugh found her standing looking at two mugs and holding a carton of milk which was slowly dripping into the sink.

'Had it gone off?'

Harry turned absent-mindedly so that the milk dripped onto his tiled floor and said, 'Eh!'

Hugh came forward hastily and took the carton out of her hands. Harry looked down at her feet and the puddle of milk spreading slowly towards her trainers. 'Whoops!'

'Had the milk gone off?'

Harry looked at the container which Hugh was sniffing a bit dubiously. 'I don't think so, why?'

'Well, you were pouring it away.'

'Oh! No, I was thinking. I was wondering how they got non-stick Teflon to stick to the pan.'

Hugh said, 'Mmm,' and gently moved her to the side while he dealt with the mess. He moved her to the table and pushed her into a chair as she seemed to have gone off into some cataleptic trance. Finally he pushed a mug of fresh tea in front of her and spoke, 'Harry.' He grabbed the mug in time to save it being knocked off the table as Harry swung her eyes and the rest of her head and a hand in his direction.

'Harry. Give me your attention.' When he was sure he had it he continued. 'I think you should go home, Harry. You've obviously got things on your mind.'

Harry, roused from her stupor, shook her head at him. 'Oh no, I couldn't do that. What if something happened to you?'

Hugh, resisting the temptation to tell her, again, that she had, smiled. 'Tell me what you're thinking about then. Maybe if you talk it will stop you drifting.'

'No, it's alright. I often think about odd things. Tell me where you were dreaming about.'

Hugh nodded, he'd noticed one or two of those odd things already, he sighed, shuffled on the seat, turned his mug about and took a sip, and then realised she really was still focused upon him and waiting for him to talk. 'I'm writing about the Hospitalers, as I told you. I was here in Carlisle at the Leper hospital in the dream.'

'I didn't even know we had one.'

'We don't anymore. It was burnt down in the thirteenth century.'

'So where was it?'

'Near St Nicholas Bridge.'

Harry grinned. 'Can we go there? Now?' He could see she was genuinely eager, he thought she looked rather like a spaniel that was waiting for the office to fetch the kill. He kept the reflection to himself fearing, rightly, that she wouldn't take it as a compliment.

'I suppose so. But there's not much to see.'

'But you can tell me what there was and I can tell you about the bridge structure.'

Hugh grinned in his turn. She was enthusiastic in a way his pupils never were, it was infectious and massaged his ego beautifully.

6

FRASER HAD ENJOYED HIS day in York. He had dropped his boss at one of the more exclusive hotels, parked the car, and, following instructions, had gone off to see the sights. Now he was driving home with the sunlight bouncing off the bonnet and Henry Ratcliff next to him in the front seat. Mr Ratcliff had climbed in with a deep sigh and closed his eyes. Fraser glanced across a time or two but believed the man to be asleep so had driven, perhaps more carefully than usual, out of the city and wended his way along a few quiet back roads heading towards the motorway. He was somewhat surprised then to find himself being addressed.

'So what have you done with your day, Fraser?'

Fraser gave a quick look from the road in front of them and met the piercing blue eyes of his boss. 'I went to the Railway Museum, sir.'

'Ah yes, tell me about it? It's quite a few years since I visited there.'

Ratcliff was treated, in the next few minutes, to a welter of data about double and single gauges, funnels and tanks, PSI and brass work. Fraser had apparently absorbed a vast amount of information and was eager to share. Ratcliff was happy to encourage him. He decided that there was a lot of good in this young man.

What he himself had being doing, was not revealed to Fraser, and it wasn't until Fraser was putting away the car that evening that he realised that he still knew nothing of his boss's business. Fraser, busy checking oil levels and getting out bucket and cloth to clean the bodywork, pondered.

The man had been remarkable pleasant for much of the journey until, that is, his mobile rang. The conversation had consisted of several terse no's and one final yes from Mr Ratcliff. After that he had requested Fraser to concentrate on his driving in no uncertain terms.

James had been hovering in the hall when they had returned and had swept his master into the sitting room and turned at the door to tell Fraser to see to the car and do a proper job of it this time.

Fraser, washing the wheels with a small brush, pulled a face at himself, reflected in the shiny paintwork next to his head. He didn't think it was anything he had done to upset the boss. He shrugged and gave another brush of the already clean wheel. He would have been pleasantly surprised to hear Ratcliff's comments to James, though perhaps not so pleased with the reply.

'He's a kind young man, James.'

'Maybe, sir, but idle like all youth.'

'He did as I asked.'

James, by virtue of long standing employment, shook his head as he said, 'I should think you let him away with things, sir. A half holiday at your expense in York is not to be sniffed at.' Here James did sniff.

'Don't be stodgy, James. He drove me there safely as requested, and did as I asked.'

'Mmm!' James didn't like his position being usurped. 'You're worn to a thread, sir.'

'It's my choice, James.' Henry Ratcliff sniffed in his turn. 'Now I need you to ring up Joe Jenkins for me.'

'But...'

Ratcliff looked at James down his hawk-like nose. 'But...'

'Nothing, sir.'

It was Henry's turn to practice consonants; 'Mmm.' there was a certain interrogative accent to the sound.

'I'll fetch your supper, sir. And then phone Joe.'

'No. Joe first, I want to see him tonight.'

James nodded and backed out of the room. He thought he knew where Joe was and it wasn't in this country. Joe had told him on parting that morning that he was going to Holland on the late evening ferry.

He went into the wide and spacious kitchen and looked out of the window at Fraser assiduously cleaning the Daimler. He set the kettle to boil and tried Joe on his mobile. He stood, watching absently as he waited.

'What do you want James? I'm about to board.'

'The old man wants you.'

'Well he'll have to want; I've got people to meet.'

'What'll I tell him?'

'That I'm out of the country, he's not my only client.'

'He isn't going to like that.'

'Can't be helped. I gotta go.' The line went dead,

much to James frustration.

HUGH WAS FEELING FRUSTRATED, it was the frustration of a man who knows he drew money out of the cash machine but can't for the life of him remember what he's spent it on. Nevertheless there isn't money in his pockets. He was in Harry's car. She appeared to be an excellent driver. His fears in that respect totally allayed.

She pulled up in a service centre near the old St Nicholas Bridge and turned in her seat as she flicked off the seat belt. 'Is your head bothering you again, Hugh?'

He shook said head and a small wince raced across his face doing the four minute mile. 'The stitches are pulling and it's sore. But in all honesty I can't claim much sympathy now, Harry.'

'So what's troubling you?'

'It's these blasted dreams.' He sighed. 'If they were real I could write a brilliant book.'

'Why has the book got to be real? I like my history filtered through fiction.'

'Yes, well, but, I'm supposed to be an historian.' Hugh shrugged.

The shrug was echoed. 'So be an historian with your dusty tomes, but I'd still rather get my history in a story, imagine a world without hypothetical situations?' She grinned. 'I'd rather have my pills in jam.'

'Yeuk!'

'Come on, oh worthy one, show me the site of this leper colony. Why did they have one anyway?'

Hugh followed her out of the car and waited while she locked up and put her keys in an inside pocket. She was in figure hugging jeans and a light blouse today and while the charms of yesterday's clothing still set off frissons of delight in the back of his mind, this ensemble was doing just as much for his libido. He sternly repressed the feelings. She was quite an innocent in her own way, and in her own way she could be devastating.

They began to stroll down the street and, leaning on the bridge parapet, he talked history in its dustiest form.

'You know about the crusades?'

'Which one? There were about a dozen weren't there?'

Hugh nodded. 'Not quite a dozen but certainly successive waves of them. The idea was to regain the Holy Land for the Europeans and kick out the infidel. Various popes, and at one time there were two at the same time, both infallible,' he lifted an eyebrow and grinned at her, 'promised forgiveness of sins and a swift passage through the pearly gates if they defended the Land of Christ.'

'Yeah, I heard.' It was said a bit cynically.

Hugh cocked his head on one side. 'And what you heard you didn't believe?'

'Don't see how a man could do that...'

'No, well let's leave that one to the theologians for now. Its part of my problem but...anyway the crusaders came back from the Holy Land having left a present of TB and syphilis and bringing back leprosy and worms. Not your kind of worms…at least I don't think so?'

Harry smiled. 'Don't know where my worms originated. Once we started to sail the sea in our little wooden boats we brought it from all corners of the globe back to sunny England. I assume you mean the intestinal kind?'

'Yeah, most of the people of medieval times were riddled with worms of one kind or another. Tape worm, was a biggy.'

'Literally?'

Hugh gave a snort of laughter. 'Probably, but I meant widespread, because they didn't always cure or cook the pork well enough.' He nodded at the river running sluggishly between the banks. 'Back came the crusaders with their bugs and germs and ailments. Most of which had no known cure and the good friars provided a hospital to care for them.'

'What kind of care, if they hadn't got a cure?'

Hugh swung round, leaning his elbows against the stonework, and watched the traffic rushing by in clouds of dust and exhaust. 'Mostly worse than the diseases. But for leprosy, prayer because it was considered a curse for sins committed.'

'Hmm.' Harry also turned and watched the traffic. 'So what has this got to do with your dreams?'

'Apparently Theo has leprosy and is being taken to the colony here in Carlisle.' Hugh shrugged.

'So write about him, Hugh. Make it personal; give it the human interest touch.'

'But he didn't exist.'

Harry watched the droopy moustache on her companion as it twitched above his lips, then lifted her eyes to the puzzled blue ones above. 'Think about this, if you try to fail and succeed what have you done?' She grinned as he opened his mouth to reply and then shut it again. 'Now as a change from me trying to follow you, you can listen to me.' She grinned. 'We had to check out every bridge in Cumberland after the flood the other year. Stanchions, buttresses, metal fatigue. They haven't finished yet. Or rather they've done the survey now comes the repair work.'

'Which brings us to gribbles I suppose.'

'We...ll sort of.' By mutual consent they began to walk back to the car. 'Do we need to get anything for supper before we go back?'

A quick trip to the supermarket later, they were pulling up in front of Hugh's door. He was wondering if this young woman actually found him attractive or if her motives were purely altruistic. She was wondering if she'd packed the right notes for her research and thinking she was lucky that the man she was currently looking after didn't think like the Americans who seemed to have a culture based on suing for every minor accident.

7

Sunday

DOROTHY WAS TELLING JANE they were lucky. She was talking to a very distraught Jane. 'Calm down, Jane. Everything will be OK.'

'Oh! Dorothy, I've had a dreadful night worrying about you. I didn't dare ring or call in case they were watching the house. I didn't think you would tell them my name, not for one minute. But I thought they might know you had a partner.' Jane used a tissue to blow her nose vigorously and took a sip of the scalding hot tea that Dorothy had just poured her.

They were sitting in Jane's kitchen and it was barely eight-thirty on Sunday morning. It was promising to be a beautiful day. The sun was streaming through the windows along with the scent of early roses. Dorothy poured herself a cup of tea, planted her elbows on the table, and picked up the cup, looking over the top of the rim as she watched her friend. 'I told you, it's OK. And no, I wouldn't have told them about you, love. I got you into this. We have to stop now though. I don't know which gave me the bigger shock. That young girl coming into the café and sticking a knife into my side, or the waitress saying she was a copper.'

Fraser, coming down the stairs, paused with his foot

poised to step onto the hall carpet as he heard their visitor speaking through the partially opened door. His left eyebrow rose and his lips gave a silent whistle. What had his mother be doing? What he wondered had they 'got into'? He shook his head. He'd told his mum Dorothy Skeat wasn't in their class. It seemed she was in a different class altogether. He waited for more revelations but it seemed that was all he was destined to hear for now, as his mother said, 'Hush, Fraser will be down in a minute.'

He retreated to the bottom of the stair and deliberately stood on the squeaky bit on the corner before clattering across the floor and shoving the door open. 'Morning, Mum.' He feigned surprise. 'Hello, Mrs Skeat. You two plotting something special being here so early?'

Jane smiled and shook her head, but they talked about the weather until Fraser had gone away to meet his girl.

Nevertheless, after Fraser phoned his girl and went out, they made a fresh pot and went over their activities, reassuring themselves that they hadn't left any clues as to their crimes.

'Look, Jane, we've never touched bonds or cards or anything like that. We've only ever taken the cash. We haven't kept any of the wallets. We've been lucky. I say we stop now. While we're safe. Agreed?'

'Yes, Dorothy.' Jane had made a real effort to pull herself together so that Fraser might not realise there was anything wrong. She thought she'd done a good job of it.

'Come on, buck up. Let's go for a walk down the park and then you can come back to my place for lunch. Fraser won't be back, not from what he was saying on the phone to his girl.'

Jane looked doubtful for a moment, and then she nodded. 'I'll get my coat. The weatherman said rain later.'

Dorothy watched her leave the room and gathered up the mugs, putting them into the sink and filling them with cold water. She turned round as Jane came back in and offered a smile. 'It will be alright, Jane. We've had fun, but it had to end sometime, and to be honest I'm relieved that our hand has been forced a bit.'

Jane offered her own version of a half smile. 'Me too. I'm glad we sent that ring back. It's the first time I've felt really guilty about it.'

'Yeah!'

The two women turned and left the kitchen. Once in Dorothy's car Jane seemed to relax a bit more. They had been travelling for a few minutes before either spoke and then it was Jane on a slightly different subject. 'You know I never thanked you properly for coming to my rescue that day. We…we aren't the same and I'm sure you wouldn't normally move in my circles.'

Dorothy glanced across, taking her eyes briefly from the Sunday traffic crawling along in front of her, then she went back to her driving. She began to speak as the car edged forward. 'You did me a favour, Jane. I was so lonely.' She took a breath before continuing. 'After Giles died I thought I could do what I wanted, a vista of days of freedom. But it was just boring. I hadn't had a friend since I got married. I almost didn't know how to make friends. So you did me as big a favour. My circle, as you call them, well they no more wanted a single widow on their hands than I wanted to be a gooseberry at their do's.' Dorothy glanced across again at her silent passenger.

Jane shook her head. 'I've never had a close friend. I've always been too busy and too poor to socialise, single mothers don't tend to go to do's. It's nice to have someone to do things with. But…'

'But nothing, we're pals now, Jane.' Her face crinkled into a smile to the detriment of her make up but nothing else. 'Let's just enjoy each others company.'

Hammond's Park, at the south end of Carlisle's sprawling suburbs, was nearly empty that Sunday morning. The two women strolled along the well tended paths, Jane talking about the shrubs with a knowledge that Dorothy found surprising. She concealed her astonishment. Realising, that for all her words earlier, she was inclined to sell her friend short when it came to education.

She eventually said, 'I wish I knew as much.' It was a gentle probe into a past that had been kept shrouded up to now.

Jane looked up at the kind face next to her, read the genuine interest and care and replied, 'I was training to be a gardener. I loved it but I got pregnant, and it was just too hard to pay for courses, besides I couldn't afford the childcare as a student.'

'What about your parents?'

'They were more than ashamed; they didn't want to know either of us, their loss.' There was just a hint of bitterness.

'The father?'

Jane shook her head. 'He had a good job. He was a bit higher class than me. I didn't tell him. I just faded out of the picture.'

Dorothy stopped walking and looked at her friend. 'Didn't he wonder, question you, try to find you?' She shook her head. 'Sorry, Jane. None of my business, but he might have wanted to be a Dad.' She grimaced. 'Giles wanted children. But it just didn't happen.'

Jane laid a gentle hand on Dorothy's hand. 'It ain't all it's cracked up to be at times.'

'I'd have liked the chance.'

'I did try to find his Dad, just after Fraser was born, but he'd changed jobs so I went away again. I love Fraser. He's a good lad. I loved his dad too. But...' She sighed and they started walking again. 'I was never sure if he loved me or just wanted the sex, Dot.'

Dorothy nodded. 'It was just the sex with Giles, and someone to run his house; socially it was the right thing to do, according to my parents.' She looked at Jane, deadpan. 'Nothing wrong with sex, Jane, but it has a high price tag sometimes.' They exchanged a grin and then Dorothy said. 'Lunch, friend, and then we can plan what we're going to do with our free time this fine Sunday.'

HUGH WOKE UP AND looked at the ceiling. He followed the small crack along to the light shade and frowned as he recalled the previous day. He was no clearer as to his guest's motive today than he had been on Friday. She was a pleasant companion who seemed genuinely to care about what she'd done to him. As far as he could tell that was all. He sighed. It was probably just as well, there was nearly twelve years difference.

He heaved his body from the bed and, after a quick glance at his watch, went to have a shower. Harry was already downstairs when he arrived freshly shaved and dressed. She was gazing at the table while the kettle boiled its head off.

Hugh crossed the floor and turned it off before looking into the coffee pot, 'Where's the coffee?'

Harry didn't even look up but did answer, 'Columbia.'

Hugh sighed, then spotted the packet on the side. He made the experiment of mixing grounds and water before he turned around to look at his guest; she was still lost in thought. He set breakfast in train and waited for her to land from whichever planet she was currently circling.

Breakfast was a leisurely meal as Hugh talked about his work. Harry enjoyed his conversation, but he was rather fixated on the given subject.

'There's not a lot of written evidence by the hoi-polloi, plenty written by the monks and the Templars, and of course by the masons who built the cathedrals. But each of those groups had their own axes to grind.' Hugh was doodling on a piece of scrap paper as he sat at the kitchen table and talked over yet another cup of coffee.

'Well, yes, I've read that Bede painted the Vikings as vicious killers and rapists and the Romans as bringing civilisation to the savage British. I'm not quite sure what his 'axe' was?'

'He was promoting the Roman Catholic Church, he didn't want the Celtic church to be right, because then his church would be seen as bullies.'

'OK, and the Vikings?'

'Oh, that was because he thought the British were a load of sinners who needed to change their ways, the Vikings were just God's instrument.'

Harry nodded. 'So what's this book actually about? I know you said it was a medieval history. What are you looking for in these special manuscripts you've got access to?'

'They give charters by the Edwards, they tell me when things were built,' he grinned, 'or burnt down. Nearly two thirds of Carlisle was burnt down by a disgruntled young man in 1292.'

'If a pig loses its voice is it disgruntled.' She smiled impishly and continued, 'I wouldn't have thought you could burn that much.'

'That's because you see the modern city. The Medieval one was built mainly of wood.' Hugh held up a hand. 'What is it with the imponderables?'

'If you can't get the guys to like you at school, get 'em laughing with you instead of at you.'

'Oh!' Hugh nodded. 'You're a beautiful young woman now, not a school girl.'

'Maybe. But...'

'No maybe about it.' Hugh smiled at the frowning face.

'So this Ratcliff guy, he's got a library of old manuscripts that he's let you look at.' Harry changed the subject, and for now Hugh let her, but he intended to get back to the subject. This young woman had too much going for her for him to let her pull herself down this way, whether she was interested in him or not.

'Yeah.'

'How long have you been looking at them?'

'About two months.' Harry nodded. 'How much more research have you got to do?'

'I don't know. I've only been at it for four years.'

'Four years!' She frankly gapped at him. 'Isn't it time you started to write something.'

Hugh shook his head. 'I keep finding new stuff.'

'You always will, Hugh. You'll be writing it in your dotage at this rate.'

'You wouldn't start an engineering job without properly surveying the area.'

'True, but once I've surveyed, I make a start using the architect's plans. If it needs changing I change it. It becomes a work in progress; you're not even into the foundations yet!'

Hugh grinned and nodded. 'I know, it's my biggest failing. My ex-wife used to get just as annoyed as you.'

'Ex-wife?' Hugh nodded again. 'She went back to London in exasperation at the way I forever put things off.' He looked across his mug top. 'She's got a nice fella down there now. We're still good friends, we just can't live together.'

Harry smiled. 'She has my sympathy.' She set her mug down. 'Finished? Yeah. Let's go and look at some more areas you're researching. It's too lovely a day to stay inside.' They stood and Harry put the mugs in the sink before they both headed out the door.

They drove away. Harry concentrating on her driving to the exclusion of her passenger, so that Hugh eventually said softly. 'Should I have told you about the ex earlier?'

Harry glanced over and gave a smile. 'Eh!' Processed his comment and then shook her blonde locks. 'No, of course not, Hugh. I was thinking about Boring Piddocks.'

Hugh refused to be sidetracked by the abstruse and obscure. 'But it does make a difference, doesn't it?'

Harry shook her head again. 'You're a nice guy, Hugh, but...'

Hugh gave a soft sigh. 'There's usually a 'but'.' He gave a chuckle of laughter. 'It would never work anyway. You drift off, and I procrastinate.'

'Yeah. The male ego gets very upset when I drift off.'

'There's a man out there for you somewhere.'

'But do I want him?' Harry pulled up near the Cathedral precincts and prepared to listen attentively to a disquisition about foundations.

'Why have you brought us here, Harry?'

'Because you are using it in your studies. If you talk about it to me, maybe you will be able to get enough incentives to start writing about it. And...just maybe, you might sort out these dreams of yours.' She smiled at him over the car roof as he stood on the pavement waiting for her.

An irrefutable argument that left Hugh opening and shutting his mouth like a stranded salmon.

JAMES DOVE WAS ALSO mimicking a particularly fine cod on its last gasp as his employer put an unanswerable question to him. 'So where is Joe then?'

As if, thought James, I should know. He said as much.

'Find out then, don't just stand there. I know you have his mobile number. Has he gone out on that boat the pair of you keep at Silloth?'

James took a second to wonder how his boss knew about a boat the pair of them had kept quiet about, before he shook his head. 'He said he was going to Holland. I spoke to him last night.'

'Then I imagine we will have to await his return, James.' Henry Ratcliff swallowed impatience with his Sunday afternoon tea. 'I am going to end any connection with Joe Jenkins and I suggest you do the same. I had several disturbing phone calls yesterday. One from the police. They will be with us bright and early in the morning, James, and I wish to say truthfully that he is not in my employ. You will wish to claim a lack of connection also.' It was a command. Ratcliff watched his factotum swallow.

'If you don't, you will not be in my employ either. Do I make myself clear?' The very softness of the tone caused a further ball of bile to be swallowed by James before he nodded.

Ratcliff raised an eyebrow. 'I object to the police questioning my movements. They will be here tomorrow and I wish to know what he has been doing before I become sullied by his business. You, James, had better have your story straight too.'

The bombshell dropped into the silence between the two men, James did a bit more silent mouthing.

'Don't stand there like a stuffed fish. Go and get me my tea and send for Fraser.'

'It's Sunday.' James was having a bit of trouble keeping up with events.

'So what.'

'Day off.'

'Ring him. I want that young man here in the next half-hour. Now go and find my tea and see that the toast is hot.' And Henry Ratcliff very deliberately turned and looked out of the dining room window at his garden, dismissing his factotum.

James stood for a second longer before turning smartly on his heel and leaving the room. He went over to the phone in the hall and picked up the phone there, punching in Fraser's home number and hoping like hell the young man was around.

THE POLICE WERE LISTENING to the sound of humming as they peered down at the mortal remains. The humming was occasioned by the bees' busily gathering nectar from some overhanging gorse above a deep ditch with about three inches of sluggish water trickling along the bottom. The body was resting face down in the bottom. The ditch was approximately three miles from the sea, it wasn't, however, one of the ditches of Holland, but rural Cumberland.

Detective Inspector Sandy Bell put his head on one

side and, looking like an elderly robin, eyed the corpse. 'What do you reckon, Bob?'

Detective Robert McInnis was also eyeing the corpse, though his look had more of the raven about it, sleek and ready for the corpse to speak to him. 'I don't think he was going for a quick dip in the stream.'

'No, me neither.' Sandy motioned the forensics team forward. He looked at the medical examiner who was climbing out of the ditch.

'Dead how long?' Bob offered an elegant hand and hauled the older man up the few feet to the bank on which they stood.

'I should say ten, maybe twelve, hours. He's in full rigor.'

'Cause?' Sandy wrinkled his nose at the smell of decay as the corpse was turned and the rotting vegetation was disturbed.

'Hard to tell. Drowning perhaps, there are contusions but they could be the result of falling. I need to get him back to give you cause, and until then it's just suspicious. He might have just fallen in and knocked himself out.' His expression said he very much doubted it, but he was a doctor not a detective. He shrugged, watching with the detectives as the body was swung up the bank and placed into a black zip-up body-bag.

Bob nodded at the officer patiently waiting, as both detectives moved over and looked at the face. 'Can't say I recognise him. You, Sandy?'

'Nay.' He looked at the Doctor. 'Not been moved, Jonesy?'

'No. Blood's settled and undisturbed, pronounced lividity in the face.'

Sandy nodded. He donned purple gloves and carefully began a search of the pockets of the rough corduroy trousers worn by the corpse. 'Empty.' He pulled a face, before flipping back the donkey jacket and searching the inside pocket of the heavy material. He shrugged and looked at the waiting men. He drew the zip closed over the face and said, 'Right take him away and do your thing.' He turned, walking towards the young teenager standing at a good distance from the scene holding a small wire haired fox terrier on a lead. A constable was standing guard, either to stop her running away or to offer support. They would find out if they had a bold one or a shrinking violet in a minute. Bob McInnis fell into step beside Sandy.

The young woman watched their approach with a mix of fear and excitement. The two tall men, one oozing authority to go with his grizzled hair, the other with just a hint of grey at the temples but handsome as they come, approached as if out for a morning stroll. It was a deceptive look. Both were keenly summing up the surroundings and the youngster they were approaching.

They stopped in front of her and Sandy gave a quick jerk of the head to indicate the constable keeping her company should move out of earshot. The small dog sniffed at Bob's wellingtons before jumping up at his legs. 'Jock!' She smiled an apology as she pulled on the lead. 'He's only a pup yet. Sorry.'

Bob bent and patted the small animal and then smiled back. 'He can probably smell my dog.' He looked at Bell, waiting for the older man to start the questions but Sandy gave a small shake, so Bob carried on. 'You found the body, Miss...?'

'Laurel, Laurel Rains. Yes, well no, well Jock did really. We walk along here every morning; I can let him have a run off the lead. I thought he'd found a rat. He was barking, so I called him to come away, but I didn't have much hope of him obeying. I came over to fetch him, and saw the body.'

McInnis continued to pat the dog as she looked away for a minute. She was either gathering her thoughts or stopping herself throwing up. By the swallowing he observed in her throat it was the later. He knew how she felt.

'Did you touch him?'

A shake of the head to go with the, 'No.' He watched her gulp again. 'I pulled Jock off, he was sniffing and growling and then he tried to...to lick him. I could see he was dead. His face was right in the water.'

McInnis, carefully separating pronouns, gave her a gentle smile. 'That's very clear. So you didn't recognise him or his clothes?'

'Nooo.' The word was accompanied by an emphatic shake of the head.

'And then?'

'I used my mobile, dialled 999. They said to stay put and they'd send an officer. I rang my mam to say I would be a bit late back, she isn't very happy about it. And I came over here. I didn't want to have to...'

'That's fine. I think you ought to go home now. This officer will take you and explain to your mother.'

'She gets mad at me when I miss meals. Says I'm being antisocial. I'm not really. I just like a bit of peace.'

Bob nodded again and looked at the constable. 'Inform the young lady's mother that we will be calling in the very near future, probably this afternoon, Constable. Make sure she understands that Laurel has been very helpful.'

'Sir.'

Bob watched the man stride away with the teenager almost skipping to keep up, and gave a wry grin.

'Now why did I get to do it? You're the one with the teenagers.'

Sandy offered his own grin. 'She only had eyes for you, lad.'

'I protest. I'm a happily married man, Sandy Bell.'

'Aye, lad, I ken that. But sometimes you have to play to your strengths. She would have seen me as an authority figure.'

'Mmm.' Bob didn't sound convinced. But he turned away and the pair strolled back to their crime scene. Halting once again on the stream bank they watched one of the team taking samples of water. Another was directing a group to begin a fingertip search of the stream bed. A third was speaking to a cluster of constables holding something that resembled wind breaks, they didn't look as though they were going for a rest on the beach, all their faces were grim.

'If he isn't a local, Sandy, how did he get here?'

'Dunno, but he was dressed for night not day, wouldn't you say?'

'Yes. It might be summer but the nights are still cool and that donkey jacket looked warm enough.'

Sandy looked around at the field they'd crossed to

reach the rough path along the side of the stream bank. There was a fence and stile which they'd both crossed to get here, and at the other end of the path a metal gate hanging half off its hinges, held in place by binder twine. 'I think we'll head back for now, Bob. Until we know who yon corpse was we can't do much but wait for the clues to come rolling in.'

'We should be so lucky.'

8

Monday

Detective Sergeant Helen Mackenzie hated paperwork. Especially on a Monday morning. She was scowling at the accumulation on her desk with a ferocity previously reserved for the state of her husband's laundry.

'How come it's all on my side of the desk?'

'You're the senior partner.' Michael smirked as he swung his big frame into the chair behind his own desk and faced Helen.

'And you remember this now because...?'

'Because we've been out in the field and we've got a lot of paperwork to deal with.'

'Thanks a bunch.' She pushed half the files across the desk onto her partner's pristine section.

'Well if you will go catching crooks you must expect to have to deal with the fallout.'

Helen sighed gustily and scowled at him. 'Pick up your pen, my lad. We might as well do this; our cover is well and truly blown at the café.'

'And how.' Michael started to sort files in order of importance and date. Shuffling some onto the floor, and others into his in-tray, as he spoke. 'So what did you make of the upstanding Mrs Skeat on Saturday?' He paused with a file in both hands, scanning the titles as he absently talked.

'I thought she was a fool given her age, but I applaud her actions because it made my life easier.' Helen spoke just as absently as she picked up an envelope that had been forwarded through internal mail. 'Good grief!'

'What's up?' Michael turned his full attention on Helen as she uttered the exclamation and waved a jiffy bag at him.

'Haven't they x-rayed?'

'Yes. Pink slip to clear it.' Helen scrabbled in a drawer and pulled out a pair of disposable blue gloves, before opening the flap and pulling out a wallet from the bag. She set it down on top of the jiffy bag. Then, very carefully, as if indeed it might have been an unexploded bomb, she flipped it open with her biro and began to survey the contents thus revealed.

Michael stretched out a long arm and picked up the clearance notice in his own gloved hands. He began to read under his breath. 'Delivered to the central station on…hmm that would mean it was posted overnight Friday…checked for explosives, drugs, DNA and bacterial agents, cleared… dusted and printed, so why have we got it, Helen?'

'Because we are, or rather were, dealing with the pickpockets and the boys in the back think it's probably connected to our case.' She was unfolding a small screw of tissue, she let a gold ring drop onto the bag and looked at the pieces of paper she'd also found. 'Find the list of people who reported their property stolen, Michael.'

He began reading, his finger moving down the list in alphabetical order 'Brown, Dodgson, Ericson ...' He stopped as his partner gave a small sigh and shook her head. He turned over a couple of pages and said, 'It's all alphabetical.'

'Damn.' She look at the ceiling for a moment, looked back at the piece of paper she held and then scrabbled in the open draw of her desk, hauling out a handful of old pink slips some leaky pens and a rusty stapler. These she dumped on the desk and then fought the gap to find a dog-eared telephone directory.

'Got ya.' She licked a finger and began to go through the pages before settling on one and running a pink-tipped fingernail down the column.

'Grab your coat; we're back on the trail.' Helen gave a huge grin and, picking up her own jacket and bag, left the paperwork for another day as she tucked the ring, wallet, and assorted paper into the envelope and the envelope into the clear evidence bag and strode out, away from the workstation. Her bemused partner shrugged and grabbed his coat as instructed. She would tell him what was going on in due course. He hoped.

Dorothy Skeat should have been shaking in her boots; she might have been if she'd known about the fuss her missive had caused at the Police Station before it got to Helen and Michael. She would have been even more perturbed at what they did next.

Dorothy, however was busily dusting her lounge. She had been quite sincere when she had told Jane she had never had a friend before. They had discussed their actions several times while they had strolled and dined the previous day. They had come to the conclusion that they were damn lucky they had got away with it for so long.

Dorothy had been left reasonably well off when her husband had died. She had no need to steal, to pay her way. She knew Jane had been struggling before they had started; now she was trying to think of a way to help her friend financially without hurting her pride.

She had got as far as Hoovering the upper landing when she had what she considered a brainwave. She pressed a foot to the pedal and set it upright, then stood looking out of the landing window at the back lawn. After five minutes of frowning thought she abandoned the machine and went downstairs to the front room, picking up her landline as she entered. She stabbed at the numbers, and then stood tapping a finger impatiently against the receiver.

'Jane, are you busy this morning?' She listened to the reply and then nodded her head a couple of times. 'OK, come and have lunch. About two? Great!' Dorothy jiggled the receiver and punched in another number, smiling to herself. Yeah, it just might work. After that phone call she went back to her hovering, humming under her breath.

'I COULD DO WITH a bit of free time.' Helen looked at her partner as he spoke and shook her head at him. 'Well it's alright for you, you're married, how am I supposed to get lucky and meet the girl of my dreams when you keep my nose to the grindstone?'

They were travelling in his car to the address of a gentleman who Helen believed was the owner of the wallet and ring.

'Money in the wallet.' It was a speculative comment from Michael.

'No.'

'So why send it back?'

'Thief with a conscience.'

'Ain't no such animal.' Michael was watching the lights and pulled away with more vigour than the manoeuvre warranted as they changed.

Helen glanced across. 'No. But there is the colour grey.'

Michael sniffed and began to whistle through his teeth. Helen cocked her head on one side so that the dangling earrings brushed her shoulder as she tried to figure out the tune. It was one he was fond of, one day she'd get around to asking him what it was. He stopped as they pulled up at the address. 'Right, boss, here we are.'

'Yeah, so I see.' Helen didn't move. 'You know we haven't followed through on that theory.'

'Which one?'

'That it was only men that were the target.'

'No...o.'

'I think we'll just check when we get back. You're right, there ain't no such thing as a thief with a conscience.'

They exited the car and walked up the well kept path to knock on the door of a late Victorian house. The bay windows twitched and a pixie face poked out before disappearing again, and they could hear a dog bark once. The door opened to reveal a very ugly mutt and a very plain man in a neat pinstripe suit.

THAT SAME MONDAY MORNING the door to the Ratcliff household had been opened to Fraser by a sickly looking James Dove. 'Thank God you've got here.'

Fraser nodded but didn't speak. He followed Dove into the kitchen and accepted the mug of tea thrust at him, before sitting down at the kitchen table.

'What did the old man say to you last night?'

Fraser took a sip before answering, trying to decide how he should answer, James Dove was grey-complexioned today with bloodless lips. And he'd never invited any conversation beyond work before. Fraser frowned as he answered, trying to see what was at the back of the question. 'He wanted to know if I'd had any dealings with drugs.'

'Have you?'

'Smoked a few joints at school. Nothing more, and nothing since I left school.' He uttered an amused grunt. 'Lost my supplier, he got done, three hundred hours community service. That was a big enough warning for me.'

'What did Ratcliff have to say to that?'

'Said he was pleased I was capable of telling the truth.' Fraser shrugged. 'I guessed I'd been checked out before I got this job. Classy place like this, they weren't gonna let me run tame without a bit of checking up.'

'What else did he want to know?'

Fraser shrugged and sipped again. 'Asked if I had any ambitions to take over your job. I told him no. I like driving and mending, I don't want to clean silver and open doors.'

'I do more than that!'

'Yeah, I know, keep your hair on; I don't want your job. I got some ambitions though, I'm gonna go to uni' some day when I've saved up enough. I don't want to get saddled with a loan bigger than a mortgage.' He watched the middle-aged shoulders sag slightly.

'OK.' James picked up his own mug and took a healthy swig of the brew, before setting it down again and looking straight at Fraser. 'I don't know what's in the wind. All I know is that the police are due to visit this morning and he wants us to be careful what we say.'

'Said the same to me last night. I ain't broken no laws.' Fraser finished the contents of the mug and stood up. 'I'll go and make a start on that window frame upstairs.'

James Dove nodded and watched him go out. He hadn't allowed himself to become aware of the worm of jealousy that lurked in his soul, until last night. Now, however, he was having to acknowledge it and it was eating away at his conscience, because Fraser Wilson had never done anything to deserve it.

DETECTIVE INSPECTOR NILS JAKOB WAS without conscience where drug dealers were concerned and he thought he might just have found some behind the stately doors of James Ratcliff's house. James Dove let them in with his nose in the air. 'Gentlemen, your identity cards?'

They raised an eyebrow apiece, but produced identification. There was a squad car at the gate and a uniform sitting at the wheel but...

'Thank you. I will just let Mr Ratcliff know that you are here.'

'As if he doesn't know.' Nils Jakob was a charming man to his four ex-wives, but his charm never extended to drug pushers. Those he hated with a fierceness only equaled by his grandparents for the Nazi régime.

He had picked up a few hints that the man he'd come to see might be involved in the trade and he didn't care how much money or social standing anyone had if they dealt in drugs. The hall was certainly opulent enough for a drug dealer. Black and white marble and what looked like a genuine Monet on the wall. He glanced at his Detective Sergeant and gave a grin. 'Close your mouth, you're embarrassing me.'

James Dove came back out and indicated with a wave of the hand the doorway to the sitting room. 'Gentlemen.'

Jakob strode forward with all the confidence his partner lacked. 'Mr Ratcliff.' He held out a hand to the hawk-nosed man seated near the window. A parrot on a perch, at least he hoped it was a live parrot, it would be cruel to do that to a dead creature, lifted its head from the peanut it was dismembering and put it's head on one side to better view the approaching constabulary.

Ratcliff shook the proffered hand and said. 'Detective Inspector. I'm afraid this is one of my 'bad' days so you will excuse me if I won't stand. Take a seat and tell me how I can help you.'

Jakob nodded and sat down. His Sergeant, a man built on strong and silent lines, leaned casually against the door. He didn't know if he believed the line about 'bad' days, and he wasn't taking any chances.

Jakob weighed up the man before him and decided that shock tactics and a total lack of BS might get more results than social niceties. 'Your name has been mentioned in connection with drug trafficking.'

Ratcliff raised an eyebrow. 'I do not traffic in drugs. Such drugs as you will find in this house are either over the counter medications or those prescribed by my doctor for a heart problem. I cannot, of course, speak for my butler or cook. Though I doubt either has the time or inclination for such business.'

'We understand that an employee of yours, Joseph Jenkins is...'

Ratcliff held up a hand. 'Joe is not an employee. I have, on occasion, accepted various items which he has brought back into this country. They have come with full provenance and import certificates.'

'He's bringing you things, you're using him in that capacity, and paying him, doesn't that make him an employee?' Jakob smiled grimly.

'No. He offers, I accept. I do not commission him. He is a salesman.'

Jakob snorted. 'Sophistism, Mr Ratcliff.'

'Semantics, Inspector.' James Ratcliff waited for the next volley.

'Whatever,' Jakob scowled. 'We believe that while acquiring things,' he sniffed, 'for you, he has been importing drugs.'

'Also for me, Inspector?'

'As to that, sir...?'

'As I said you are welcome to search the premises. Bring on your dogs. My security will assist you in any way you wish.' Ratcliff pushed a small round knob on the wall and Fraser appeared in the door, almost knocking the sergeant over with his entrance. 'Fraser, these gentlemen may go where they wish. If they wish access to the manuscript room ensure that they wear gloves.' He turned and spoke to the parrot. 'Would you like another peanut, Polly?'

Jakob frowned. He sat still. 'I hadn't quite finished, sir.'

'I, however, have finished with you. I am tired. Go away.' He continued to look at the parrot, offering a closed fist with a peanut shell in it.

Jakob stood up, stepping closer to the old man and his parrot. 'Very well, sir. We will take up your kind offer.' Sarcasm, dripped like water on a stone. It rolled over Ratcliff and dissipated into the silence.

Polly dropped the shell and sidled up her perch to the Police Inspector. She stepped daintily onto his hand and looked at him expectantly. Both men gazed at her in astonishment. 'Er!'

'You had better give her a peanut, Inspector. She rarely honours such as you.' Ratcliff offered a shell to the quietly fuming Inspector. Jakob accepted the small treat and offered it while surreptitiously trying to slide the bird back onto her perch. 'Polly likes you, how very interesting.' Ratcliff offered a wrist and the bird exchanged one hand for the other.

Jakob nodded and turned to see his subordinate and the young man who'd been introduced as Fraser, with identical grins. 'We'll send for that team, arrange it, Smaith.'

'Sir.' Sergeant Smaith moved, taking out his mobile and calling up the team they had stationed a block away.

Fraser stepped back. He was nervous, but Henry James Ratcliff had been quite clear last night when he had called Fraser in. The interview still reverberated in his head. He stood back now and watched as the two policemen stepped out into the hall and stood waiting for their men.

9

HUGH, WAITING FOR HARRY to gather up the shopping bags, looked across the space to the driving seat. 'It would seem I'm getting as bad as you. Maybe it's catching.' He nodded to his front door which stood ajar. 'Monday mornings, ah, well,'

He grinned as he got out of the car and strolled across the pavement to the sound of a muttered 'Cheek.' He approached his house with a grin on his lips; it was his last smile that day.

Pushing open the woodwork he discovered that the place had been trashed. Harry walked into him and stood in the doorway, gasping, before she dropped a plastic shopping bag and broke half a dozen eggs.

'What the…?'

'Just what I was thinking.' Hugh pulled his mobile out and punched in 999, before stepping away from the doorway and towing Harry back into her car. He spoke into the small machine as he pushed her unresisting body into the passenger seat. 'My house appears to have been broken into. The hall is a mess. I haven't gone any further. Yes, Yes, I'll keep out until the unit arrives.' He looked at Harry. 'OK, kiddo.' Harry just shook her head and stared at the partially opened doorway with her mouth in a large 'O' of horror.

The police when they arrived were very efficient.

They donned white suits before they entered and then came back out to take Hugh inside. It was worse the further into the house he went. The kitchen cupboards had been ransacked, cornflakes and sugar tipped into a heap on the worktop among teabags and biscuits. In the bedroom the mattress had been lifted bodily from the frame and set half on the floor so that the sheets trailed half-way to the door. His books and notes where all over the floor of the sitting room, some of them with pages torn out.

'It's difficult, but can you tell us if anything is missing?'

Hugh shook his head as he looked around the sitting room. He scanned the shelves where his CD's had formerly lived. They sat in a forlorn pile on the floor, not one in its proper case. The player was skewed but still there, as was the rest of his pricey stereo equipment.

'It doesn't look as if anything has been taken, Sergeant. It just looks as though someone has taken an unreasonable dislike to me.' Hugh began to sit, and then jerked from the seat as a young constable moved him swiftly away.

'Printing, sir.'

'Sorry.'

'So tell me who dislikes you.'

Hugh smiled a bit wryly. 'I actually thought I was quite a likeable sort. Maybe one of my pupils is pissed off at getting a 'c' instead of an 'a'.'

'I understand the young lady you were with knocked you out on Friday?'

'Harry?' Hugh shook his head and glanced around

before lowering his voice a bit, even though she was in another room being questioned separately. 'Harry is just a nice girl with a genius for creating chaos in an absent-minded manner.'

'So it was an accident on Friday?'

'Yes. Look how do you know about that anyway?'

'The incident was noted by a couple of plain clothes, and since your name was fresh in the system...' The sergeant suddenly grinned, his whole face lighting up for a few seconds. 'But to be honest, she's busy implicating herself.'

'Oh! Right. Talk about 'Big Brother is Watching', but this isn't 1984, nor are we on TV, Sarge.'

'No, sir. So aside from some rebellious youths, is there anyone who has a grudge? Anyone at all?'

The questioning had gone on far longer than Hugh's head wanted it too. They'd taken the keys from him and talked about 'processing the scene'. He'd eventually left them to it and gone back to Harry's house again. She looked a bit shell shocked.

As he sat down she glanced at him. 'I think it's my fault!'

Hugh nodded cautiously. 'It might be. What are you talking about, Harry?'

'Your house. People breaking in. It's my fault.'

Hugh put his head on one side, looking her over. 'What on earth are you talking about?'

Harry looked a bit startled for a minute. 'I've been thinking, since the police started asking questions, and I think it might be my fault.'

'Yes, you said that before. Now tell me why?'

'It's the Boring Piddock. I knew it wasn't right. They should have used fresh water.'

Hugh grabbed his slipping patience. 'Are these Piddock boring because of their lifestyle, do they need to drink lots of water, and what has that got to do with the state of my front room?'

''Eh!'

'Look, Harry, let's start again. My house was trashed sometime this morning. Nothing was taken. It could be a pupil with a grudge, or someone anxious to get their hands on the brilliant book I'm not currently writing, because I appear to be living in a mystery instead. How can any of that be you fault?'

'Because I'm investigating an outbreak of a type of ship worm called a Boring Piddock.' She stopped and grinned. 'Boring as in drilling holes. And the problem in this instance could have been prevented, but I think someone wanted to collect the insurance. Engineers don't just build stuff; they make sure it stays up by putting in safeguards.'

'Right. Now I'm with you. So where are these Piddocks?'

'America; I've just got back from there.'

'Do you seriously expect me to believe you've been pursued over the Atlantic by American hoods?' Hugh was more doubting than Thomas.

'I don't know.' Harry remained calm. 'But you were alright until I appeared on the scene.'

'Too right.' But Hugh said it under his breath,

forgetting his desire to be involved in an adventure, then spoke more loudly. 'If it was you, why not ransack your house, not mine.'

'Because I wasn't at my house. I was at your house until we went shopping this morning.'

'This is true, Harry. But I still find it hard to believe anyone takes that much notice of you or me.'

'It's all my fault. If only I didn't drift off I might notice more.'

'COULD HE HAVE DRIFTED down with the tide?' Bob McInnis was back at the crime scene. It was now a murder investigation. The preliminary examination had shown that the proverbially blunt instrument had been applied with some force to, not just the obvious head wound, but apparently several other parts of the body too.

A uniformed officer was standing with him in the field, both wearing green wellingtons and shirt sleeves. Bob managed to look elegant even so. 'Tidal, isn't it? You've got crowfoot, a bit of scurvy-grass and even some early sea-lavender over there.' Bob pointed at the far bank where a small patch of leafless stems showed budding pinkish-purple flowers. 'And there's that.' He nodded at the sluggish stream which seemed to be slightly higher up the bank this afternoon.

'Well, not to say tidal, not this far inland, but certainly we get a bit of brackish water mixed in with the fresh.'

'So the scene of the crime isn't necessarily this crime

scene?'

'No, sir. Could have come up stream a bit, but not much at this time of year. Winter and a good storm and it'll rise three, four feet, but not now.'

'So are we looking...?'

'Yes, sir. Got men working their way back to the coast. It's about a mile and a half over the fields to a small estuary. Empties into Moricambe Bay.'

Bob nodded, bringing a mental picture of the area up from the study of the map he'd made that morning. 'OK, let me know how you get on.' He turned to Sandy, a silent bystander. 'Where to now, Sandy?'

Detective Inspector Sandy Bell, also resplendent in green wellingtons and shirt-sleeves, nodded dismissal of the senior constable and then looked at Bob. 'I know sea-lavender, I was going to get a bit for my Sarah, she likes it for flower decoration, but how ye ken that other stuff...' Sandy offered a wry grin to match Bob's. Bob shrugged.

Sandy looked about again as he continued speaking. 'We have a name, from his prints, but let's see if the name means anything to anyone around here. He obviously didn't get here in any form of transport that we can see, so either he drifted or it was shank's pony, or someone brought him, and they must have left some trace, Bob.'

They began to pace along the side of the stream bed, heading downstream towards the estuary seen in the far distance, stepping around willow bushes and avoiding the muddy patches on the rough pathway left by the weekend showers. Both men were checking the ground for anything that might help. The police team was by now searching the other bank.

'There isn't a path over there, Bob.'

'No, I know, but if he didn't get in the water this side, and this field, he might have gone in over there.'

Sandy nodded, stopping as he came to the stile and watching as Bob climbed over. 'It was mostly dry last week. Aside for those few wet patches from Saturday and last night there isn't much trace to go on.'

Bob nodded as he waited for the older man to climb over in his turn. He looked at the stile as Sandy stepped away. 'You're right, not much of anything on this.' He nodded at the stile and they continued their search of the bank as they walked through another field with flourishing patches of both cow parsley and cow pats towards a wooden gate.

'We know who he is. Joe Jenkins. Jakob has been on his trail for a few months now. Nothing he can prove, just a policeman's nose. He has form from way back for dealing, but only Class C.'

'I wish we had an address or place of work.' Bob scowled at the gate they were rapidly approaching.

'So do I, Bob, but we take what we get with murder.'

HELEN MCKENZIE WAS ALSO WILLING to take what she could get. 'Mr Chappell?' She fended off the ugly mutt for the third time.

Adrian Chappell said, 'Sorry.' for the third time as he pulled the beast away again. It appeared to be a mixture of greyhound and deer hound with the worst of each breed's physical features.

'We have received a wallet through the post and would like to know if you can identify it for us.' She pulled the wallet in its sealed bag from her briefcase and held it out for his examination, but continued speaking. 'There were several items inside it.' She waited for him to speak and watched the blush spread over his cheekbones.

'Sir?'

'Er! Yes, it looks like mine.'

'Do you know what was in it?'

'A ring, a certificate, a photo and a condom. Plus forty pounds in notes.' The blush became a tidal wave of red.

'Oh!' Helen glanced at Michael, his face gave nothing away.

'As to the condom and money, er, no, but a ring, certificate and photo certainly. There was a packet of stamps too.

'Stamps?' Adrian shook his head. 'Maybe, I don't remember?'

'No, sir.' She watched his shoulders hunch as if he was guarding himself against a blow. The photograph was the reason I connected the wallet to you, sir. I remember the case from a couple of years ago. Your wife was killed taking your daughter to school one morning. Hit and run. The case is still open. You didn't report the wallet stolen?' It was a tentative question.

'No.' He shook his head, and his overlong brown hair flopped into his eyes only to be thrust back in a careless and habitual gesture.

Michael took up the conversation. 'What we would like you to do is tell us every person you can remember as being in 'The Café' it's the one opposite the Cathedral.' He waited for a nod. 'The day we believe your wallet went missing.'

'I might have just dropped it, I'm very careless.' Adrian frowned. 'I was in The Café on Friday but... I don't think I did, but I might have lost it there. I don't want to get someone into trouble. They have returned the wallet.'

'Minus the money.'

'Money they might have needed.' The man seemed determined to give the thieves a get out of jail free card, it was obvious to the dimmest that he didn't want them there.

Michael grabbed his temper before it escaped under the door of patience. 'Can you tell us anything about the people who were there when you were, sir?'

Adrian sat looking at them, a scowl making his face even more plain; they were interrupted by a pre-teen, with floppy hair and glasses perched on the end of her nose. 'Dad, I've made the toast and I've put the beans in the saucepan.' She looked at the couple sitting on the chairs in the sitting room. 'I can make more toast.'

Helen smiled nicely at her. 'No, but thank you for offering. Your dad lost his wallet and we think we might have found it. We're police officers.'

'Coo. That's great, init, Dad?'

Adrian smiled at his daughter, it transformed his face. 'Yes, love, great. I won't be long. Can you set the table? I just have to talk a minute or two longer before I get back to work.' The hint had all the subtlety of a chainsaw.

'OK, Dad.' She whisked out of the room.

The police looked from the child to the man and thought they had the source of his unease when he said, 'She still gets upset. The police were in and out trying to track down the person who hit her mum, and questioning her about it.'

'Ah right, sir?' Helen nodded as he looked at the closed door. The child didn't seem that distressed, but you couldn't always tell with children, and he was her father.

'I don't really...' He gazed at her for a second or two, then nodded as if coming to a decision. 'There was a group of kids, teenagers, they all look alike to me, jeans, t-shirts, spiky hair, four of them I think. There was a fat man at the next table, he smelt of sweat and had a bald head. But so many do now.' He looked at Michael's thatch of hair with approval. 'There was a young mum with a baby in a pushchair. A couple of middle aged women gossiping, and you.' He suddenly looked back at Michael. 'You were in there too, sitting reading a paper.'

'Yeah, I was trying to catch the thief. Sorry.'

Adrian shrugged. 'At least you were trying.'

'Now,' Helen hitched forward on the seat slightly, 'Who walked past you.'

Adrian gave another smile as he looked at Michael. 'You did.' He nodded at the other man. 'The young woman with the pushchair, in fact it jammed for a minute on the chair as she walked by but...'

'Anyone else?'

He shook his head. 'I wasn't paying that much attention. I go there several times a week, it's near to my work.'

Helen smiled nicely at him. 'You've been really helpful, sir.'

'Can I have my wallet?'

Helen shook her head a bit regretfully. 'Sorry. Evidence. You can probably collect it in a couple of weeks.'

'Oh! Alright.' He sighed and stood up as the police made their own way to the door.

'We'll be in touch, sir.' She strode down the path. 'Let's get back to the office. I've got a hunch I want to explore.

10

VARIOUS MEMBERS OF THE police were now set on a converging course. Jakob had been informed, on his return from a fruitless search of Ratcliff's house that Joe Jenkins body had turned up minus Joe Jenkins spirit. He had a satisfied smile on his face as he waited for Detective Inspector Bell to return to his office. He had no sympathy at all for drug pushers and one less on the streets was, for him, an occasion for rejoicing.

Sandy and Bob coming into the office to find him waiting, raised their eyebrows and looked at each other.

'Nils, what can we do for you?' Sandy said he always felt itchy when in Jakob's presence. But that didn't stop him from agreeing that the man had a remarkable track record when it came to his own speciality.

'I hear you've got Jenkins.'

'Well, Dr Jones has certainly got the corpse of yon man.' The soft Scots accent was a gentle warning; Sandy didn't take murder, not even the murder of a felon, lightly. He didn't care for quite so much jubilation at death. However, he nodded at a chair and sat down himself. 'I was coming to pick your brains. We could do with a bit of background.'

He waited until they were grouped around the desk and Bob McInnis had pulled forward a notepad, before he looked enquiringly at Jakob.

'He was slime.'

'Aye, but I still have to find the man who killed him.'

Jakob scowled. 'Latest rumour I had was that he was running with a group from the Isle of Man. He'd got himself a little fishing skiff and used it to bring stuff in. We've been trying to catch him for the last month. I've been out to see one of his employers...' He scowled even more fiercely for a second or two, 'this morning, but the guy was clean. I've got my eye on him though. Bloody parrot.'

'Eh!' Bob lifted his head from the copperplate notes he was making and looked with astonishment at Nils. 'Parrot?'

Nils shook his head. 'Doesn't matter. Anyway, we're watching the port of Silloth, where he keeps his boat. Or rather the boat he and his partner had shares in. If I can prove it was bought with drug money, I'll see he doesn't keep it for long.'

'Silloth? We found him near Brownrigg. It's not exactly a long way from one to t'other. Think ye...' Sandy gazed off into space for a minute. 'Mmm, were you lot watching him last night?'

'He'd got a ferry booked to Holland over at Newcastle, Saturday evening. I had a man ready to track him when he boarded. He never got that far. I've only got so many men.'

'OK. OK.' Sandy waved a hand before relapsing into thought. Bob watched him as he twitched his tie down to half-mast and rubbed his nose.

Nils Jakob was watching him too. He was caught in the trap that said he didn't want the murderer arrested but he didn't want to see crime go unpunished either.

'So have you got a current address, records haven't, and who is this employer?'

Jakob smiled grimly, dictating the address to Bob before telling them about his interview that morning with Ratcliff. 'He got right up my nose. This death will give me another reason to go back and talk to him and his butler. James Dove is in for a shock when I tell him his boat is forfeit.' Bob was reminded of Jakob's Geordie background every time the man said 'bo..at'. It was one of the few words that gave his origins away.

'If you don't mind...' It might have been politely phrased but Jakob knew there wasn't any question of him arguing, not with a senior detective like Bell. 'I think we'll go and interview the gentleman next. I would appreciate it if you could do the background; track his movements over the last week or so.' He looked across the desk. 'I'll get my coat, if you've got nothing more to tell us for now.' Sandy stood up, scraping back his chair and Bob hurriedly put away the notebook, this time exchanging the glance with Jakob. Something had rung a chime with DI Bell.

THE DOORBELL GAVE A musical chime and Jane looked at Dorothy, her neatly shaped brows drawing together. Dorothy carefully laid down the knife and fork that she had just picked up and smiled at Jane. 'Relax. Whoever it is I'll get rid of them. Don't let your meal get cold.'

Jane watched her friend leave the kitchen with anxious eyes. Fraser had told her all about his interview with his boss the previous evening. Instead of reassuring her it had just left her even more worried. If Fraser had been investigated, did that mean they had investigated Dorothy and herself? Did someone know what they had been doing? She had come round to Dorothy's house for a late lunch and a discussion of this new development.

She looked at their meal and picked up the oven gloves preparatory to putting the baked potatoes back in the oven. Dorothy walked back in, she spoke across the room to Jane, who stood holding the dish in the gloves. 'Jane, thanks. This is Detective Sergeant Michael Jorkvil. He was at the café on Saturday when...'

Jane nodded and fear crawled across her face, disturbing the pleasant planes and making her look much older than her forty-five years.

'It's alright, Jane.' She turned to Michael. 'Jane was very upset when I told her about it. We go there regularly, don't we, love? We were just wondering if we could face using the place again.'

Jane, becoming aware that her hands were beginning to burn, hastily put the dish down on top of the stove and turned back to the two others, the brief respite had allowed her to get her face, if nothing else, under control. 'Yes, it was horrible what happened to Dorothy. But it's not fair to do them out of business through no fault of their own though, is it?' She looked at Michael Jorkvil and moved towards the table and her seat again.

Michael, assailed by the smell of home cooking and warmth, looked from one woman to the other and became conscious of his stomach rumbling quietly. It seemed a long time since breakfast. He felt the saliva pool in his mouth and swallowed hastily. He was going to keep this interview short for his appetite's sake. 'I'm sorry to interrupt your lunch, ladies.'

'Would you like a cup of tea, Sergeant?'

'Er, no thanks.' Michael smiled at both, he wasn't so taken up by his internal organ's behaviour that he was oblivious to the atmosphere and he was slightly puzzled, he sensed, but couldn't quite figure out, what was wrong. 'I only need a quick word with you Mrs Skeat. My partner explained to you that we were looking for pickpockets.' He watched the colour drain from Jane's face.

'Are you alright, Mrs...?'

'Miss Wilson. Yes, fine, Sergeant, it's just the heat of the kitchen.'

Michael watched her sitting slowly down and glanced quickly across the room at Dorothy. She was watching her friend with a curious expression on her face part fear, part anxiety. He shrugged mentally as she swung her head and fixed her eyes on him saying, 'So, how might we help the police this time.'

'We're trying to establish who normally frequents the café, and if you have noticed anyone who has started using it in the last week or two. We are going back over those who have reported things missing in the hope that they can give us descriptions of customers.' He grinned, hoping to dispel anxiety; some people with nothing on their consciences could become nervous when confronted by a policeman. 'We rather blew our cover on Saturday, so we have to tackle things a bit differently now.'

Michael watched her go around the table and lay a

gentle hand on Jane's shoulder before she answered him. 'Do sit down, Sergeant.' She glanced at Jane, and pulled out a chair next to her, sitting herself. 'I don't know, we don't take much notice of people, do we, Jane?'

Jane looked at Michael, some colour coming back into her cheeks. 'Not really. We just have a coffee there sometimes, I work three mornings a week and Dorothy and I use it as a meeting point.' Her voice was almost, but not quite a whisper.

'It's a good place to start or stop.' Dorothy gave him a nice smile. 'I like window shopping, and then having a seat while I wait for Jane. I need to rest my feet.'

Michael found his lips curving up in reply. 'So you can't pinpoint anyone new.'

'There was that extraordinary young woman last Friday. And I don't think the man she knocked over has been coming all that long. But they aren't my idea of pickpockets, Sergeant.' The smile broadened

Michael nodded at Dorothy before he grinned too. 'No, nor ours.'

'Anyone else?'

Dorothy exchanged a glance with Jane before she answered. 'No. As I said we use it more as a jumping off point. I suppose we ought to take more notice, but we're generally talking about Eastenders or Coronation Street. We're both fans, aren't we Jane.'

Jane nodded, looking at Michael.

'Well, thank you for your time anyway.' Michael stood up and nodded at both women.

'I'll see you out, Detective. Put the meal in the microwave for a minute, Jane.'

She came back a minute latter to find Jane still sitting at the table.

'Come on, love, pull yourself together. He's gone.'

'Oh! Dorothy...'

'Yes, I know. But so long as we keep our heads we'll be safe, Jane. Now let's heat up the lunch, and then I suggest we relax in the sitting room.'

Jane pushed her meal around her plate while Dorothy watched her and ate her own. There wasn't much she could do to help, she was worried on her own account, but she was determined on one thing, Jane wasn't going to suffer for her stupidity in starting this silly game. If the police came accusing her she'd make sure Jane wasn't included in the accusations.

Dorothy's three piece suite was white leather with red velvet cushions. They sat with the tea tray on a coffee table, a discrete affair of glass and wood, conveniently placed in front of them, in the quiet sitting room. Only two pictures hung on the walls. One a peaceful scene of a watermill, the other a woodland idyll.

'OK, love?'

'Yes, Dorothy, I'm OK now.' Jane grimaced and then smiled at her friend. 'I'm being silly, I know. But you don't know what happened last night.'

'So you'd better tell me, Jane.' Dorothy leaned forward, putting milk into two china cups before adding the tea. She handed over a cup and sat back expectantly.

'Fraser had to go into work last night. He doesn't normally work Sundays except by special arrangement.' Jane took a sip of scalding tea and looked over the brim. 'His boss wanted to know if he'd been doing drugs or anything.'

'Had he?'

'No, not since school. He's a good lad, Dorothy, we might have had our problems when he was a teenager but he's good to me, pays his rent and never asks for a loan. He even offered to give me more.'

'So what's the problem?'

Jane sipped more tea. 'He said his boss was expecting a visit from the police and wanted his employees to have clean sheets. Then...' Jane sipped again. 'Then his boss said as how he'd already checked Fraser out, he just wanted to be sure Fraser was telling the truth, so that he knew he could trust him like.'

'And...'

'Well, Fraser told him he'd done the drugs and that he hadn't been in bother and his boss agreed that that's what his PI had said. Only...well, I was worried that the PI might have been checking up on us too, Dorothy.' There was the hint of a wail in Jane's voice, like a siren beginning to be wound up.

'I don't think we need worry about it, Jane.' Dorothy offered in a soothing voice that was like a damper applied to a bell. 'Unless we have to.' Dorothy nodded to her over her own cup. She set the cup down and picked up a plate of biscuits, offering them and said casually as she set them down. 'I was thinking about what you were telling me yesterday.'

'Which bit?'

'About Fraser. How did you come to name him that, was it his father's name?'

'Oh, no. I read it in a romance and liked it.'

'He's got your surname…'

'I thought…if his dad doesn't know about him, it's not right using his surname, so I used mine.'

Dorothy nodded and bit into her own custard cream. 'Where were you living then? I got the impression it wasn't Carlisle, didn't you say your parents had chucked you out?'

Dorothy shook her head. 'I had him here, but I moved across town, away from where mum and dad lived. They were ashamed of me and, anyway, I didn't want to meet his dad accidental and me big as a house.'

Dorothy picked up her cup. 'So you're a Carlisle girl. I wonder why we didn't know each other at school.'

'I bet you went to Margaret Creighton. Me, I was just secondary school fodder. Which was just as well, I could walk to school, we didn't have much in the bank for bus fares.

'Mmm, but 'A' stream for all that.' She watched the blush edging its way over Jane's cheeks. 'Don't you sell yourself short, my girl. Tell me some more about this course you started. I've got a plant in the back garden, just coming into flower; I wish you would see if you could name it.'

THE FLOWER OF MANHOOD that had been Joe Jenkins was spread-eagled across the dissecting table. Dr Ryan Jones carefully removed part of the liver and dropped it into a glass dish before speaking into the mouthpiece recording his findings. 'Some cirrhosis and biliary stones present.' He moved the remainder of the liver aside and began to examine the veins leading to it. He was just dissecting out the stomach when his phone rang.

He looked at his assistant. 'Lift and get the contents, Tom. I'll get that.'

He wiped his hands on a towel and walked over to the phone hanging on the wall, pushing the speaker button and watching the competent way Tom was pouring a greeny mixture into a glass vial.

'Yes?'

'Jonesy?'

'Who else? This is the morgue!'

'Bob, here.'

'Yes, Bob, I did recognise your voice, but if you want a report it will have to wait.'

'I realise you won't have finished, Jonesy. I just had a query.'

'What?'

'Can you check if he drowned in the sea or in fresh water?'

'Who says he drowned? I didn't.'

'Ah!' Bob McInnis on the other end of the line pulled a horrible face at Sandy and Sandy shook his head sadly at him. 'Sorry. Jonesy, it was just that...'

'I'll let you know when I know, go away, Bob.' He

flicked the switch and walked back across the room. 'Impatience.' He shook his grey head. 'Water from the lungs sent off Tom?'

'Yeah.'

'Good, get the stomach contents away too.' He picked up his scalpel and made a neat incision into the tissue holding the spleen in place. 'I wonder why Bob wanted to know so urgently.' He grinned at his assistant, who gave a snort of laughter as he left the room with his murky vessel.

JAMES DOVE WAS SWEATING slightly under the piercing look of his boss's eyes. Lunch had been late because the police had swept through the premises like a gale in the autumn, disturbing everything and setting things down in new places. James had followed after, clucking like a hen, putting things back where they belonged.

As Jakob had said there was nothing to be found, and he had looked, upstairs, down stairs, and in my lady's chamber. The lady in question being Ratcliff's cook who was, 'sure she never did, and if they came again she was going', after which, emulating the police, she too had swept out, back to her cooking pots which she had rattled like a one man band. It had taken James a good half hour to calm her down and get lunch on track.

Ratcliff was again sitting in his lounge next to the window and he'd requested the presence of his major domo without loss of time.

James Dove had presented himself. He was inwardly shaking. The only thing that gave him away however was a tendency to wipe his hands occasionally on his pin-stripped trouser legs.

'I trust the police were satisfied and will not be returning, James?'

'I couldn't say, sir.'

Henry Ratcliff raised an eyebrow and sighed noisily. 'Let us sincerely hope not anyway. Have you set the rooms to rights?'

James nodded.

'Good. Send young Fraser in to me, I have one or two commissions for him.

'I could...'

'I am aware that you could go. However I want you here, James.' He turned to look out of the window, his back signifying dismissal.

The Daimler stood quietly inside the garage, like a passive pit-pony brought into the light; it was as filthy as one of those beasts brought up into the light too. Now, after a late lunch, Fraser had retreated in the hope that he would be ignored by everyone for a while. He intended to clean the spark plugs and check the oil. He thought it had been a little slow starting on Saturday. As far as he was aware he was the only one that drove it, but now he was standing shaking his head and muttering under his breath. There was yellow/orange mud under the chassis and around the mudguards. He was sure it was clean yesterday, he'd popped his nose in when he came last night to check on the petrol gauge.

He'd arrived early this morning; James had been hovering, ready to show the coppers around. Fraser mentally shook his head. He hadn't heard the car go out. Mr Ratcliff had been in the study when he'd arrived. James, now, he'd been in the kitchen, hadn't he, when he wasn't following folk around, so who had taken the car out? It must have been before he arrived, and he'd been here on the dot of eight 'o clock.

Fraser didn't know whether to say anything. Maybe Mr Ratcliff had taken it somewhere. But why employ Fraser if he was going to drive himself? His musings were interrupted by James coming out into the yard and shouting his name.

'Fraser. Where are you?'

Fraser poked his head around the door and looked cautiously at James.

'Yeah?'

'The boss wants to see you now.'

'What for?'

'How should I know? Move yourself.'

Fraser shrugged, wiping his hands on a piece of rag and disentangling a thread from his fingers as he walked over to the kitchen door. 'I'll just wash me hands first.'

James stood back, watching him suspiciously as Fraser ran water over his hands and picked up the soap. 'Get a move on, he's in a foul mood.' He lifted his head like a hunting dog scenting prey as the doorbell rang in the kitchen. 'What now?' He hurried out of the room, leaving the door swinging, so that Fraser heard him say clearly. 'We don't want double glazing and I've been saved.'

A soft Scottish voice answered him, echoing down the corridor. 'I'm happy for you on both counts, however we are the police.'

'Your lot came earlier.'

'And now we're here again, we wish to speak to Mr Ratcliff.' Fraser set the towel back on the rack and moved through the door himself as James said. 'I'll let him know you're here, stay.'

Fraser looked at the two tall men, their faces in shadow as they stood in the doorway with the light at their backs. He watched them exchange a look and heard a quiet 'woof' from one of them before they stepped into the hall. He swallowed the grin as he came forward, nodding to them. 'He's a bit rattled like. He doesn't mean anything. If you come into this room for a minute. The boss is a bit frail sometimes.'

Sandy looked at the young man. 'Thank you, we'll wait here if it's all the same. What might your name be?'

'I'm Fraser, Fraser Wilson. I'm the handyman cum driver.'

'And how long have you worked for Mr Ratcliff?'

''bout five months.'

Bob nodded. 'Like it?'

'Any job's good in this climate, but it's a decent job and the car's a dream to drive.' Enthusiasm peeked out and as quickly retreated in the face of the authority standing in the hall.

'Like Mr Ratcliff?'

For the first time Fraser looked cautious. 'He's OK.' He glanced at the closed door. 'Got a mind of his own.'

'And you drive him about?'

'He's got a dickey ticker, he doesn't drive.'

'Who else drives his car?'

'Just me.' He glanced at the door again. 'I'm not sure I should be talking to you.'

'We're just making conversation, lad.' Sandy turned as the door swung open and James came back out.

'Mr Ratcliff will see you now. Fraser you're to go to the bank for the Boss. He's got a parcel and an envelope for you.'

Fraser nodded and went into the room in front of Sandy and Bob.

'Fraser.' Ratcliff ignored his visitors and handed him a jiffy bag and thick cream envelope. 'For the manager; into her hand, Fraser.' He nodded, picking up a second envelope. 'Hand delivered to that address, and then go to M and S and get some more peanuts for Polly.'

'Right, sir.' Fraser nodded at his boss, glanced at Sandy and Bob and left the room.

Sandy Bell had been examining Henry Ratcliff with the eye of a policeman. Now, having come to certain conclusions which weren't exactly complimentary to the civilian, he opened his mouth, but was forestalled.

'James tells me you are yet more policemen. I gave at the office, gentlemen.' He offered a smile that just curved his lips and left his eyes cold.

'Further information has come to our attention, sir.'

'I can't imagine what. I presume this is more to do with Joe Jenkins?'

'Why should it be, sir?'

'It was this morning; that thick Geordie seemed to think I had something to do with Joe's trade. I don't.'

'That's probably as well, sir. Joe Jenkins is dead.' Sandy watched in vain for some show of emotion, while filing the description of Jakob for later examination.

'That of course is regrettable, but has nothing to do with me.'

Bob hadn't spoken, he was taking in the comfortable airy room, the expensive pictures on the wall, the kind of carpet pygmies might be hiding in, and the dense curtaining. He looked at James Ratcliff, seated in a high backed chair next to the fireside. He sniffed gently and tracked the source to the area around Polly, sitting on her perch next to a large, oak, knee-hole desk. She was regarding him, her head on one side and a claw raised to her mouth.

He glanced at Sandy still standing in the middle of the carpeting. He advanced towards both Polly on her stand and her master's desk. Sandy was checking out the scene too, he might like a bit of distraction.

'Hello.' Bob spoke to the parrot as people commonly address small children and the village idiot, confirming Ratcliff in the suspicion that Sandy was the one to watch. 'Who's a pretty bird then?'

'Polly dislikes being patronised, Inspector Bell.' Ratcliff looked at the senior man.

'Oh, he's harmless.' Sandy's lips twitched. 'Now, sir. What was your connection to Jenkins?'

'I've already told the police. I used the man occasionally for commissions.'

'You employed him?'

'He occasionally obtained things from abroad and brought them to me. If I wanted to buy I would, if not, I didn't.' Ratcliff spoke in arrogant and condescending tones.

Sandy offered a half smile. 'And just what was he offering you, sir?'

'Not drugs.'

Sandy raised an eyebrow and took a couple of steps further into the room. Then he just stood there.

Ratcliff reassessed him. Maybe not quite village idiot status after all, possibly town clown. 'Nothing illegal, Inspector.'

Sandy just stood waiting, the eyebrow cocked like a question mark above his brown eye. It was obvious to the meanest intellect that he wasn't leaving until he got some sort of answer.

'If you must know,' The Inspector's head tilted a little more, and Ratcliff sighed gustily, 'I import acacia and myrrh from certain Arab factions. Other factions aren't always happy about it.'

'And this was all the business you had with Jenkins.'

'Yes. If his goods weren't up to the right quality I didn't buy.'

Sandy nodded, glancing at Bob who was still standing next to the parrot. He was gently stroking her head with the back of his forefinger apparently absorbed in the task. Sandy wasn't fooled. 'I presume you can show me import licences?'

'I can. But I really don't see why I should.' The hawk-like nose twitched as if Ratcliff had caught the smell of something nasty in his drains.

'Because this is a murder investigation. And you have been dealing with the victim. I can get warrants, sir.' He paused. 'I also need you to account for your movements over the weekend.'

Now it was Ratcliff's eyebrow that winged up. 'Murder!' it was said in the tones of one remarking on the weather. 'I seldom go out. I am not always a well man. However, Saturday I was in York. Fraser, the young man I spoke to, can verify that. I retired early. I am seldom up beyond nine at night.'

'And yesterday?'

'Only outside for a breath of fresh air in the garden. I had another early night, the trip had been more fatiguing than I realised. Isn't that right, Polly?'

Polly continued to make small squeaks of enjoyment under the ministrations of Bob's finger and ignored her master's voice.

Sandy nodded again, sometimes people told you things if you didn't ask too many questions.

'I neither disliked nor liked Joe Jenkins; he was useful. My dealings with him were strictly legal. I had no reason to murder him, even if I'd had the physical strength, which I haven't.'

'What makes you think strength was required, sir.'

The question dropped into a pool of silence, even Polly had ceased to make a noise.

'I assumed, since it was murder and the man was fit

and healthy, that he hadn't died without a struggle, Inspector.' The sentence was uttered as smoothly as cream, very sour cream.

'Yes, sir.' Sandy nodded, frowning slightly as he looked at the visage opposite, whatever he read there caused him to say, after a pause, 'I think that will be all for now, I wish to interview your staff?'

'If you must.' Ratcliff stretched out a hand, sighing heavily as he pressed the small bell at the side of the mantelpiece. James Dove appeared in the doorway. It was apparent to everyone that he'd been just outside the door. No-one remarked on the speed of his arrival, however. 'These gentlemen wish to interview you, James. I expect you to be honest with them.' He looked at Bob as he spoke. 'I assume you will be bringing a warrant for my papers, Inspector McInnis?'

Bob McInnis sniffed gently and, after a final stroke, followed Sandy outside, almost getting his heels trapped by James as he shut the door behind them.

'If you'd like to step in here, Inspectors.' James led the way into a dining room; the long mahogany table stretched out in front of them and matched an equally long sideboard laden with silver chaffing dishes.

Bob could almost smell the fear coming off the man. They moved so that they formed a vee and effectively blocked the exit to the room.

'I'm Detective Inspector Bell this is DI McInnis. Your name, sir?'

'James Dove.'

'And how long have you worked for Mr Ratcliff?'

'Fifteen years nearly.'

'In what capacity?'

James looked at Bob; the serious face offered him a faint smile.

'Head cook and bottle washer. I did do the driving for the last couple of years but Fraser came a few months ago, he's good with the car. It's getting on, like us, but he can handle it.' Bob watched the man relaxing this wasn't the line of questioning he'd been expecting.

'Now, we just need you to corroborate Mr Ratcliff's statement. Can you confirm his movements over the weekend for us?'

James looked from one face to the other. 'What did he say he was doing?'

'You tell us what he was doing and we'll know if it's right.' Bob kept his face still.

'Oh, oh yeah, I see, well, er.' James gazed off into the distance. 'Saturday he left about nine. Fraser drove him to York. I don't know what he did there. They got back at about seven, seven thirtyish. He had supper and went to bed. Sunday...'

'Just a minute, do you sleep in?'

James nodded. 'I sleep over the garage.'

'Anyone else?'

'No.'

'Sunday...?'

'Sunday he got up really late. He was shattered. I told him he'd done too much on Saturday. He pottered about, had a late lunch and went back to bed for a couple of hours. Sunday evening he…'James stopped.

'Sunday evening he what…?'

'Oh, you lot had phoned to say you were coming this morning and he wanted to let me know about it. That's all.'

'Thank you.' Bob offered a smile the equal of any Henry Ratcliff could produce. 'And now if you could tell us about your movements.'

'Why do you need to know? I ain't done anything wrong.'

'And we haven't accused you of anything, sir. We are investigating a murder?'

'Murder?' What? Who? I don't understand?'

'A Mr Joseph Jenkins, I understand you have part…' Bob watched James Dove pale to skimmed milk, and a small vein start to beat rapidly in his left temple, 'ownership in a fishing vessel with him.' He completed the sentence as he watched a hand reach out and claw at the back of a dining room chair.

'Joe. Dead! But…I thought that policeman this morning was talking about drugs.' James' knuckles were turning white as they gripped the chair and small beads of sweat were beginning to form on his forehead.

'Inspector Jakob is investigating a separate issue, sir. At the time he visited he was unaware that Jenkins had been killed. Now, sir…your movements over the weekend?'

'But I didn't kill Joe, why would I?'

'You have got a half share in a boat.'

'Yes. But...I mean, no, well yes, but...I've been buying it off Joe over the last couple of years, it's more eighty/twenty now.'

Like a tongue at a nagging tooth, Bob kept poking to see what reaction he would get. 'And therefore you benefit by his death; so what were you doing over the weekend? Sir.' The reaction was all and more than he could have hoped for. James Dove sighed quietly as he slithered rather gracefully to the floor.

'Whoops!' Sandy offered softly, as he went forward and checked James out. It was only a momentary faint. James was already shaking his head and trying to get up. 'I should stay where you are for a minute, Mr Dove. Would you like me to phone for a doctor?'

James Dove shook his head. 'No. I'll be alright.' Sandy helped him up and onto a chair and glanced at Bob as he went over to the sideboard and brought back a small snifter of brandy.

'Perhaps you'd better sip this and go and lie down for a spell, sir.'

James sipped, pulled a face, coughed and nodded, before looking at their concerned faces. 'I haven't been out this weekend. I had a kip Saturday morning after the boss left, and then I pottered about the house. Sunday I cooked lunch, Mrs M doesn't come Sundays. I watched a game on the box in the afternoon. Honestly, I wouldn't murder Joe.'

'Very well, sir. We'll need to get this verified but for now...'

'Yeah, if you don't mind, I feel a bit queer.' He stood up shakily, his features waxen and twitching, and tottered away, leaving them marooned in the chilly dining room.

Sandy and Bob, left in the quiet house, exchanged looks. 'What did you see on the desk, Bob?'

'I'll show you later, Sandy.'

'Aye.'

'I think I'll go and have a word with Jonesy, try to pin down cause and time.'

'Aye. OK, I'll finish up here.' Sandy nodded, they were both thinking about the previous half hour and would discuss their findings back at the station without anyone overhearing them.

11

'WHAT ARE WE DOING here, Dorothy?' The two women were walking along a quiet backstreet in Upperby. 'I thought you wanted to show me a hat shop you'd found.'

'I do. I think I've found the perfect hat for my niece's wedding and I'd appreciate your input, Jane.'

'But...'

'All in good time. I was going to do this as a surprise but in view of this mornings revelations I don't think it's such a good idea.

Jane shivered despite the sunshine. 'I'm not sure I want any more surprises, Dorothy.'

'No that's what I thought.' Dorothy's lips curved into a smile as she tucked her hand through her friend's arm. 'Come on, love.' She swung them towards a discrete doorway past a brass plaque which Jane didn't get a chance to read. They were confronted by an elegant set of stairs with a curving pine banister and the smell of lavender. The door clicked shut behind them.

'Dorothy?'

'Hush. I want to give you something. You don't have to have it but...' She began to climb the stairs and Jane was steered inexorably towards a solid door on the landing.

She glanced at her friend and began to ascend. The door at the top was solid pine. It stood ajar; the two women walked through and looked across the room at a leather desk, with a nondescript man in a beautiful suit seated behind it.

'Dorothy. How lovely to see you.' He came around the desk and took both Dorothy's hands, leaning in to peck her on both cheeks. 'And this is Miss Wilson?'

Jane nodded, totally confused.

'Have a seat. I'm Dorothy's 'soon to be nephew'. My name is Paul Temple.' At her faint smile his lips twitched. 'Yes. Like the private detective from the thirties. I thought since I couldn't live the name down I'd join the ranks. Dorothy tells me you've lost track of your son's father. I understand you'd like to find him?'

Jane looked at Dorothy. 'Eh!' Dorothy was sitting down, and Jane found herself being offered a chair in front of the desk. She sat, and then looked up at Paul as he walked around the desk and sat down himself. 'But…'

'I'm sorry, Jane. I rather took things into my own hands.' Dorothy turned in her chair and looked at her friend. 'You sounded as if you still cared for him. I was going to get Paul to try and track him down for you. Then I thought you could decide if you wanted to take it any further. But with you worrying about, Fraser being investigated and maybe us…' She cast a quick look at the silent man, 'I thought I'd better not. But Paul here is willing to look if you want him to.'

'I…I…I just don't know, Dorothy.' Jane looked at Dorothy's face, and then at her own work roughened hands clasped in her lap. She bit her lip and the other two watched her as she thought about the proposition.

Paul, with a great deal of sympathy in his blue eyes, glanced from one woman to the other and waited a minute longer. 'We don't have to do anything. What little information, Aunt Dorothy has given me can be shredded.'

Jane lifted her head as he spoke and offered a half smile. 'No, I think I'd like to know, I think I'd like to be able to tell Fraser where his dad is, he might want contact. I don't know if I do, but he might. It's a long time ago. He might be married now and I don't want to upset anyone if he hasn't mentioned me. And he doesn't know about Fraser. So I might not tell even so, but I think I would like to know.'

'WHAT I WOULD LIKE to know is…' Michael paused in his frantic tapping of the keyboard and looked over the top of the screen at Helen as he apparently became transfixed by something in the far distance and failed to complete the sentence.

Helen waited for a second, then waved a hand in front of his face, saying, 'What you want to know is…'

Michael emerged from the reverie as one surfacing from a deep sleep. 'Eh!'

'You said, what you want to know…now tell me or shut up, I've lost track of what I wanted to write now.' They were seated at their desks in the fading evening light. They were trying to type up various interviews, and file, in triplicate, for the benefit of a computer in the basement, the activity of their day.

Michael gave her a rueful grin. 'Sorry, Helen, I told you about my interview with Mrs Skeat.'

'Yeah.'

'It wasn't her though, it was her friend, she acted odd.'

'People do when they find themselves in the presence of coppers.'

'Yeah I know. But she was shit scared.'

'Guilty conscience. She's probably fiddling her taxes.'

Michael shrugged. 'Something wasn't right. Mrs Skeat was blocking her for me.'

Helen looked at him as he scowled at the screen for a minute. His instincts were good. If he'd spotted something off, then there probably was something off.

'Do you want us to re-interview?'

'Nah. Not at the moment.' He shrugged again, smiled a bit ruefully, and attacked his machine with renewed ferocity.

'Sir.' He looked up ten minutes later to find himself alone at the desk, and with a constable standing exuding Lynx and sweat in equal proportions.

'Yeah.'

'You remember that woman at the café, the ditzy one, the one who trod on your foot?'

Michael nodded cautiously. He had been vocal about the damage to his foot, now look where it had landed him, his foot was apparently right in the icky brown stuff it seemed.

'She's downstairs asking to speak to someone in authority.'

Michael raised an eyebrow. 'Why me? Oh Lord!'

The constable, obviously taking this as addressed to him, said, 'You're the senior man in at the moment, sir.'

'Have you checked? Please tell me you haven't checked and then go and do it.'

'I've checked. It's nearly seven, most of the day shift have clocked off, sir.'

'OK. I'm coming. Where?'

'Room three.'

Michael sighed, pushing back his chair with a scrape of metal that set both their teeth even more on edge. 'Lead me to her.'

He pinned a suitable smile on his face as he went into room three and looked at the 'ditzy blonde'.

'Miss Branwell. How can I help you?' He indicated a chair at the table and went to sit down, pulling out a notepad. 'I'm Detective Sergeant Jorkvil.'

'How lovely you know my name, are you Polish or Czech or something?'

'Neither. My Grandfather was a Pole in the RAF during the war. I was born here.'

'Oh. They did wonderful work didn't they?' Harry smiled at him. 'Was he based here or over in Galloway?'

Michael opened and shut his mouth. 'Er! Here. Now, Miss, how can I help?'

'I'm sorry.' She offered a nice smile. 'You see, I remember you from the café. You struck me as being nice then, you had such a nice smile and I stood on your foot. I've wanted to say sorry but I didn't know who you were.'

'That's fine, Miss. Your problem...?'

'Oh yes. Well, it's the gribbles and paddocks. I think someone is trying an insurance scam, but Hugh disagrees. I thought maybe you could just check it out, because I can't think of any reason for anyone to trash his house otherwise.'

'I have no idea what you're talking about, Miss.'

'Oh!' Michael watched the blush begin its slow journey from her cheeks to the tips of her ears, before she said, 'Damn!' softly and looked at him. 'Can I start again?'

He nodded.

'I'm a civil engineer, specialising in marine environments.'

Michael settled down to listen and take notes. After one or two questions that threw her so completely off track she ended up not just on a branch line, but a different railway altogether, he decided to let her tell it her own way. Eventually she hit the buffer of silence in the room and offered him a tentative smile.

Michael nodded and offered a smile of his own before saying, 'To summarise. You caused an accident last Friday and have been keeping an eye on Dr Kegan over the weekend because he was suffering from mild concussion. In order to care for your reluctant patient you have been staying at his house. This morning you both went out to do a bit of shopping and when you got back you discovered that his house had been burgled.'

'Hugh thinks its school kids, or just a general break in. But I think it had the hallmarks of someone searching for something.'

He watched the smile and said, 'Since Dr Kegan doesn't think he has anything worth stealing and since his notes are about ancient history, and you have some notes that implicate a firm in possible fraud, in the here and now, you conclude it was your work they were after, even though you were staying at his house.'

'Yes.' Harry sighed with relief. 'You do believe me?'

'I can understand how you arrived at your conclusions. I will certainly see that the fraud division is informed and they'll send out a man to have another chat and have a look at your notes. As to Dr Kegan, what does he feel about all this?'

'Oh, Hugh is being pig-headed. He can't see what all the fuss is about. He's a nice man, but he does put things off. I wish you'd come and have a word with him.'

Michael shot back the cuff of his blue shirt and glanced at his watch. 'I'm off duty an hour ago. OK, I'll come and let Dr Kegan know what is planned and have a word with him myself.'

'I'm going to Hugh's house to help him clean up the mess. If you want to follow me you could speak to him tonight.' There was the irresistible pleading of a small girl lurking in Harry's eyes. Michael caved.

'Come on then.' He began to think longingly of his supper, but found his mind distracted from stomach regions to those slightly lower down as he followed her figure out of the room and his eyes rested on the shapely legs displayed for his delectation.

THE LEGS ON DISPLAY for Bob McInnis were not the kind that would inspire such thoughts. They had the texture and colour of candle wax that had been dropped on a hairdresser's floor. They were devoid of clothing and life and Bob was looking at them in preference to the opened stomach that Dr Ryan Jones was bending over.

'I did say I wasn't finished, Bob.' Jones lifted a vein between a pair of tweezers and peered at it over the top of his glasses, sniffed and said, 'Hm!' and allowed the evidently offending, or offensive, vein to slide back into the cavity.

'I was hoping you might give me, if not cause of death, at least what kind of weapon to search for.'

'Which would imply I knew cause of death!' Jonesy's lips turned up lightening his face for an instant before he became serious again.

Bob snorted. 'Yeah, Sorry, Ryan. We're floundering a bit. SOCO have brought back a ton of old bikes, shopping trolleys, boots and bottles from that stream. You wouldn't believe how much junk was in there. If nothing else it'll flow beautifully next winter, but none of it is helping us. We don't know if it's a dump site or the primary even.'

'Well, he was breathing when he went into the water.' Jones nodded at a dish on the side containing a large lump of pink/white organic material that had once been a lung, surround by lots of froth like a small atoll in a sea of krill. 'I still can't tell you if it was ditch water or sea water yet. I'll have the result of the diatoms back in another hour and then I can answer that one. He's got multiple contusions of the upper body from something hitting him on the left side. Bruised to hell.' Jones shook his grey hair and looked back at the open cadaver. 'Someone didn't like your man very much.

His front teeth are newly chipped, and fingers have been crushed too, otherwise I'd say he might have fallen overboard and hit something underwater.

'OK.' Bob smiled, his brown eyes crinkling at the corners. 'That's a start.'

Jones shook his grey head of hair again. 'Wait for the results, Bob.'

Bob nodded. 'I'll be in the office until you ring through.' He left the autopsy room with a quiet whoosh of chilly air, which he mimicked as he left the building. He didn't like visiting the mortuary but it was part of the job, viewing corpses.

HUGH WAS EMULATING A corpse. But thankfully only emulating one. He had been sitting in Harry's front room working on his notes, trying to fill in the gaps and copy out the parts destroyed by the burglar. When the doorbell rang, he thought it was Harry. 'Forgotten your ke...' He said as he walked along her hall and began to open the door. There had been a flash of dark green and a hairy face and then the world went black.

Harry, arriving home with Michael Jorkvil, pushed against her door, and came up against the solid body of Hugh. She squeaked. It had overtones of mouse sighting owl. Michael looked at her, then gently set her aside and eased the door open to find her erstwhile lodger out cold on the floor.

He knelt and looked at the large purple bruise flowering around a long, narrow, weeping cut on Hugh's head. He put a finger to his lips and whispered, 'Stay.' before

151

moving off towards the open door of her sitting room.

Harry, emerging from her stupor, started to follow and heard a thud, she speeded up. A stranger shot through the inner door. She tried to get out of his way, caught his foot with hers and tripped the pair of them over, sitting down on his chest. 'Oh, no! I'm sorry.'

Michael was right on the stranger's heels. He grabbed a flailing arm and twisted expertly. 'You have the right to court disaster by moving, you have the right to remain silent...' he continued to caution the silent, by virtue of being completely winded, man. Before putting a pair of restraints on him.

'You can stand up now, Miss Branwell.' He looked at Harry frantically trying to stand in the confined space and eased her upwards with one hand, as she stood on the unprotected knee of the suspected thief, who yelped. She teetered upwards and delivered a slap as she flailed to a standing position.

'Keep her away, she's a menace.'

'Not half as much as you are. Who are you?'

'Fred Blogs.'

'Ah! I've heard of your family.' Michael smiled cynically.' Big in the burglary business, is what I've heard.'

'Fred Blogs' shrugged and leaned against the doorjamb.

'Would you fish in my inside jacket pocket, Miss Branwell, and pull out the phone you'll find there.' He waited for her to tentatively grope him, while he kept his eyes fixed on his prisoner. A very tiny part of his mind said, 'wow nice', as her hand worked down the side of his chest wall. He refused to listen to it and spoke out loud, 'Now find speed dial and phone my partner, Helen McKenzie, then put it on speaker.'

Harry might be clumsy sometimes, but she could follow instructions, and she was no technophobe.

'Helen. I've got a prisoner, can you come to…' He looked at Harry who obediently recited her address before he took over the conversation again. 'Bring a team, if you can get one.'

'Five minutes. I'll try to send a local to help 'til I get there.' He heard the phone click and then, in the spirit of helpfulness, Harry turned the phone and took a photo of the would be thief.

'Now it doesn't matter if you try to escape; we can find you again.'

Michael groaned under his breath. The thief swore loudly.

Another groan came from one of the participants in the recent drama. 'Oh, poor Hugh, I'd forgotten about him. I'll get an ambulance.' Harry punched in 999 and arranged an ambulance to call at her address in the immediate future, then went to his side and looked at Hugh as he squinted blearily at the hand he was currently using to feel his head.

'Who? What? Oh God, not again.'

'It wasn't me this time.' Harry protested as she helped him to move and rest his back against the wall. 'I've sent for an ambulance for you, Hugh. I came back and found you like this.'

Hugh, trying to look at her through half closed eyes and think at the same time, closed the eyes. This was no time to discover if he could multi-task. He'd leave it to women.

Two of these specimens of humanity appeared in his future within a few minutes. They knelt at his head and feet, but not to worship him. They began to check out his body. It should have been the stuff of dreams; to have nubile females handling him. It was more the stuff of nightmares. They would prod. It wasn't just his head that ached. His body had, yet again, come into contact with a floor and wished to register a complaint, in triplicate.

He brain gave up the unequal struggle between pain and ache and faded out.

'We'll take him in, love. Get the doctors to look him over. I think he might have broken something.' One of the nubile lovelies smiled across at Harry.

She nodded. 'I'll come and see how he's getting on later.'

'I should leave it until the morning now. They'll likely ward him. He doesn't look so flash.'

'Thank you.' Harry watched Hugh tenderly lifted onto a stretcher and carted away, before turning to Michael. She bit her lip. 'I seem fated to injure poor Hugh.'

Michael had been observing the examination closely enough to form an opinion of the relationship the couple appeared to have, but not so closely his prisoner could disappear over the horizon. Now he smiled and opened his mouth to make a comment, only to be forestalled by Detective Sergeant Helen McKenzie walking through the door with a couple of uniforms in tow.

'Here's another fine mess you've got us into.' She grinned at Michael and then turned and jerked her head at the uniforms, who moved purposefully towards 'Fred Blogs' and took an arm each. 'Cautioned?'

'Yeah.'

'Take him to the nick and let him cool his heels until we get there.' She watched him frogmarched out before turning to Michael again, 'My husband is less than pleased with you. We were just sitting down to supper.'

12

Supper in the Ratcliff household was a fraught affair. The cook had rattled her pans in the manner of a trainee drummer preparing for her first big gig. The meat had been more cremated than burnt and the veg had turned to water with fright at the extended period they'd been required to remain over heat. It was best to draw a veil over the spotted dick. Or better still a shroud.

Henry Ratcliff sighed and pushed himself away from the table. Good cooks were so hard to find and Mrs MacGillivray had practically gone into hiding today. She was, generally, a good cook, but the events of the day had seriously disturbed an equilibrium more centred than a gyroscope in normal circumstances.

James coughed as he set the chair back under the table and began to pile plates and cutlery onto a tray. 'She was distressed by the police interview, sir.

'I hear you were as well, James.' The piercing eyes looked down the hawk nose and watched his major domo as James stopped stacking and scowled fiercely at an inoffensive pea that had strayed onto the tablecloth. 'No, it wasn't, Fraser. It was that Scots copper he stuck his head around the door before he left and told me you were unwell and unavailable for an hour or two.' Ratcliff raised an eyebrow and waited. He gave the impression he could wait for eternity, or until an answer was forthcoming, whichever was the longer.

'I've been overdoing it a bit lately, sir.'

'Perhaps you need to stop night fishing. I thought you had more sense, James.'

'It wasn't that, sir. It was Joe. I...I...'

'Yes, unfortunate. But I feel that in the circumstances, it is one way of cutting an undesirable connection. Unless of course you...'

'God, no, sir. I couldn't, I wouldn't...'

'No...o.' Ratcliff cocked his head onto the side and examined James. 'I wouldn't have thought so. But people can be full of surprises, James.'

'No, sir.' James shook his head violently and dropped, with a clatter, the fork he'd just picked up. He looked in horrified fascination at his boss. 'How could you think I could...?'

'I have found that a good many people are capable of a good many things when they are sufficiently pressured, James. It's one of the reasons I am as wealthy as I am.' Ratcliff moved slowly towards his chair near the fireplace. Tonight a small log fire burned in the hearth, despite the summer evening. 'I will take a small brandy and soda.'

James nodded and picked up the tray. 'I'll bring it through in a moment, sir.'

'Take your time, James.' Ratcliff arranged himself in his chair and pulled forward a small table upon which rested a pair of black framed glasses and a slim volume of Horace's odes.

THE CONSTABLE HAD BEEN wrong. Both Sandy Bell and Bob McInnis were in the police station. However, it was understandable that he hadn't found them for both were on the flat roof which had been set aside as a sort of garden in the sky, at the new, and environmentally friendly, police station. It had a fine crop of petunias and a noisy bee hive in one corner. Neither man was into apiary nor, at the moment, floral offerings; they were gazing off to the distant view of the Northern hills of Cumbria as they talked quietly about the case.

'So what did you see on yon desk then?'

Bob grinned, his superior, and close friend, wasn't renown for his patience, he was amazed Sandy had waited this long to find out. He pulled his notebook out and flicked it open. 'I couldn't make it all out, Sandy. And I'm no Leonardo da Vinci, so I'm not good at reversed writing, but, Ratcliff had used a fountain pen to write with and the last couple of lines on the blotting paper on his desk were still damp.'

Sandy's expression said a good deal. He was of the opinion that his colleague had gone round twice when they were handing out the brains. He bent a sapient eye upon the copperplate being offered for his inspection, reflecting that his partner might not be a Leonardo but he could give Vergece a run for his money, but all he said was, 'Do tell?'

'I take it it's the letter to his bank manager, 'the bearer to place the package in my safe deposit and transfer the sum'. I think it said £5000, but it could have been 50,000.' Bob looked up from the paper and watched the silent whistle form on Sandy's lips. 'I couldn't swear to it in court, Sandy. It was reversed and only partial. I'm guessing at some words.

'That's a hell of a big sum of money, either way, Bob. I wonder who it was going to…'

'Couldn't read it, Sandy. It was too blurred, that bit had soaked in.'

'Shame. I wonder what the going rate for a hired killer is these days, Bob.'

'He could just have been paying his taxes.'

'Well, yeah he could have…' Sandy sniffed again. 'But if I earned enough to pay that much in taxes I wouldn't be stood on this roof, I'd be enjoying life. And another thing.' He wagged a stumpy finger under Bob's elegant nose. 'What was in the package?'

'Your guess is as good as mine; you saw the size of it. A4 padded envelope, couldn't hold a gun. Wasn't big enough for a cosh. Might just have been private papers. Anyway we can't get a peek without 'due cause' and we haven't got that.'

'No.' Sandy shook his grizzled curls and rasped a hand over his chin. 'Who else have we got?'

'So far. Jenkins's associates on the Isle of Man. The butler,' he stopped and grinned, 'but of course the butler always does it, in the library with a blunt instrument.'

Sandy offered a grin of his own. 'Mighty fine actor that butler, if it was him.'

Bob nodded, serious for a moment. 'I'd faint if I'd killed someone and the coppers got onto me that quick.' He shook his own sleek head and rubbed a finger under his nose. 'Associates, on the Isle of Man and in Holland, buyers including our Mr Ratcliff. There's this Professor that is studying his manuscripts, but he hasn't been near the place since Friday. We'll interview him tomorrow.' He was ticking off on his fingers. 'Jakob left a list on the desk. Some fine sterling characters they are, and I don't mean they're little stars or martlets either.'

Sandy looked askance at his partner. 'What are you blethering about, Bob?'

Bob offered a singularly sweet smile. 'Sorry, Sandy. Etymology of the word sterling. Norman, it was supposed to be because the coin had a star on it, Edward 1, because it had four birds, starlings or martlets.'

Sandy grunted and waited for Bob to continue.

'We haven't got anyone else yet, but all the scum haven't crawled out of the woodwork yet.'

'Jonesy come up with a cause yet?'

Bob nodded his head. 'Mixture of diatoms, which means,' he grinned at Sandy's exaggerated sigh, 'Could have drowned at sea or in the stream, the water was brackish.'

'Huh, fat lot of help that is and how come you know what flowers indicate brackish water anyway?'

Bob cast him a look, more fly fishing than seine net in appearance, he hadn't realised that Sandy had noted that bit of the conversation. 'Bird watching. However,' Bob held up a hand to stem the flow of comment about whether the birds were feathered or not. 'Jonesy phoned to say the body injuries show the classic triple that indicates pedestrian hit by car.'

'Which means the poor sod was first hit, then dumped.' Sandy sighed. 'Tell me again why I'm a murder cop.'

Bob shook his head. 'So the bad guys don't win.'

Sandy ignored this sally. Bob waited quietly, looking out at the scene as he waited for Sandy to finish thinking about the information. 'Anything more we can do tonight?'

'Waiting on forensics.'

'I'm going home, and if you've any sense so will you.'

JANE WILSON'S HOME WAS once again playing host to her friend. 'I could have got my own tea, Dot.' Jane sat at the kitchen table again and watched as Dorothy put the kettle on and got out mugs and plates and then set a cake tin on the table.

'Yes, I know you could but I wanted to be sure you understood what I'd done, and what you'd committed yourself to, that's why I came back with you.' Dorothy brought the teapot over to the table and set it down, before fetching the milk jug from the fridge and settling on the chair opposite.

'I do understand, Dot. This young man of yours is going to see if he can track down Fraser's father, discreetly, and then he'll let me know where he is and what he's doing.'

'And he won't do anymore unless you tell him to. OK?'

'OK.' Jane smiled. 'Now can we forget about that for now and talk about...' She hesitated before saying, 'The pick-pocketing.'

Dorothy nodded, pouring tea into thick mugs and pushing one over the table. 'We've covered our tracks, no-one has connected us to it, and we aren't going to do it again.

We've got the perfect excuse for not going to that cafe again, especially after Saturday.'

Jane nodded. 'I agree, but I still think we should go there. I just have a feeling that...'

Dorothy waited, her head on one side as she looked at her friend over the mug of tea.

'I have a feeling we are meant to go there. Oh! That sounds so silly, but I think we're supposed to be there for someone.'

She looked at her friend, who was eyeing her a bit strangely. 'You haven't gone and got religion have you?'

Jane giggled. 'No, don't be daft. All the same,' she sobered, 'I think we are meant to do some things.'

'OK, and as far as it goes, I agree with you.' Dorothy smiled across the table. 'But we keep ourselves safe first, Jane.'

The door opened with a small creak and both women looked over with guilty expressions as Fraser came in. 'Hi, Mum, Mrs Skeat.' He offered equal smiles to each lady and moved to the cupboard to get himself a mug. 'I could murder a cup of tea, and, talking about murder, guess what?' He waited for a reaction from his audience; both women looked up at him with a mixture of fear and trepidation on their faces.

'Your boss is OK isn't he?'

'Yeah! It's one of the men who used to bring him things. The coppers have been round twice today asking questions.'

'But it's nothing to do with you, Fraser.'

'No, Mum. But I work for him see, and they have to question the whole household about it.' He pulled out a chair, and gently pulled the cake tin over. 'Coo, gingerbread, got any cream, Mum.'

'Fridge.' Jane watched as he stood up again and came back with a can of spray cream and a knife. 'So what questions did they ask you?'

'This Detective Inspector Bell, he asked how long I'd been working there and if anyone else drove the car, and...' Fraser cut cake with a lavish hand, put it on a plate and sprayed cream with an equal fervour before looking back at his expectant audience. 'What else I did. Then he asked about the boss and how well he could get around and about James and Mrs MacGillivray and what she did. I think they were trying to...' He sniffed, took a bite of cake and spoke thickly around it, 'establish alibis.'

'And have you got one.' Dorothy spoke as she pushed him a square of kitchen towel as a hint not to lick his fingers.

'I dunno, he asked for lots of times.' Fraser ignored the kitchen roll as he watched his mother's face, which had gone waxy white. 'All Friday and Saturday and Sunday. Now, I was out with Sue Friday night. Saturday I took Mr Ratcliff to York but I wasn't with him all the time. I know where I left him and where I picked him up and such, but what he did in between...?' Fraser shrugged and ate more cake before continuing. 'I went to the Railway Museum, I've got the entry ticket and I've got a receipt for me lunch, 'cos he said I could claim it back. That's got a time and date on it. But I didn't do much yesterday.'

'You were only just up, when we went out and then

you went off to see Sue.'

'Didn't stay there. I mooched about a bit, went off for a game of footy with Phil, but he'd gone out. Had a burger, came back and watched a bit of TV, I've not exactly got an alibi.'

'Oh! Fraser, do you really think you need one?'

'Nah, Mum. It's only they were asking us all. It's quite exciting really.' He finished his cake and washed it down with tea before standing up. 'I suppose they'll be interviewing the Prof next. He's due in tomorra morning. I'm going for a shower, Mum.' He nodded at Dorothy. 'Mrs Skeat.' And disappeared out the door. They heard him clattering up the stairs and the door thump open in the bathroom.

'Oh dear, you don't think they'll investigate us too? Do you?'

'No, love.' Dorothy reached out and stilled the restless hands which were now stirring Jane's tea into a small whirlpool.

'How do you fancy going to the pictures?'

'I don't think...'

'The trouble is you're thinking too much, Jane. It will be OK. Trust me. Now come on, let's go and look what's on TV if you don't fancy going out. Allow yourself to be distracted. Please.' Dorothy pulled a long face. 'I feel guilty enough having got you into this in the first place.'

Jane stood up, taking her mug over to the sink before turning back to face her friend. 'I'm responsible for my own actions, Dorothy. We're in it together.' She shook her permed head. 'But, OK, we'll watch TV and then you'll stay to supper and distract me. If Fraser is having a shower it means he's going out with Sue. There'll just be the two of us.'

13

Tuesday

THE SUN WAS JUST tingeing the clouds to a pretty shade of pink on Tuesday morning, they moved in stately fashion across the sky in a massed flotilla, Detective Inspector McInnis thought of the Spanish Armada's doomed invasion of England as he pulled on a clean shirt and glanced out of the window. Detective Inspector Bell thought of his bed and the delight of staying under the rumpled duvet for a few minutes longer as his wife called him from downstairs to come and get his breakfast

Jane Wilson shivered slightly under her duvet, bent her knees and curled her toes up a bit to find a warmer spot and Dorothy, padding about her kitchen in a soft dressing gown, getting her breakfast, inexplicably thought about mounds of scrambled egg as she looked out at the skyscape.

Hugh Kegan was thinking about palfrey's and ladies in hats like upturned ice cream cones but then he couldn't see outside, and Harry was thinking about a certain detective of possible Polish extraction and wondering if maybe her mother might not have got one or two things right after all, as she wandered about her bedroom getting dressed.

James Dove wasn't thinking of much at all. He was walking towards a room situated on the ground floor and not far from the kitchen. He was carrying towards Henry Ratcliff's bedroom a tray on which resided a china cup and saucer and a small coffee pot, a plate with a buttered croissant and a small bottle of medicine.

Henry James Ratcliff wasn't thinking of anything either, but then he was dead.

James gave a gentle tap on the door and pushed it open with a shoulder. The room was semi-dark, the curtains blowing in the slight breeze from the open window. He could see Ratcliff propped up against the pillows. He advanced, setting the tray on the little side table and speaking as he turned away. 'Will I draw the curtains back, sir?' Without waiting for a reply he moved over and flicked them part way, tutting as he saw that the casement window was wide. He leant out and pulled it closed, turning back to speak to Ratcliff.

'Sir.' He hurried over as the early light shone on his master's face. 'Oh God!' He felt the cold hand and shuddered slightly before averting his eyes from the open and somehow reproachful ones, of Henry Ratcliff.

He left the room, pulling the door behind him at what amounted to a run, went to phone the doctor from the phone in the study. After an impatient wait where he tapped his foot against the floor and was passed from the night service line he finally spoke to a Doctor. 'No, Doctor. It's rather sudden. I think his heart must have given up. He's been under a strain the last few days, and he wasn't strong.' He listened to the voice on the end of the phone for a minute, nodding his head. 'Yes, yes. I understand, but why? He's tucked up in bed.' James nodded some more. 'Very well, I'll wait then. No, I won't disturb him.'

He set the receiver back with a shaking hand and wiped his forehead with the back of his hand. He was turning to go to the kitchen when the doorbell rang. Muttering under his breath he went and opened the door. Fraser was standing there. 'Morning, James, How's...'

'Oh, thank God you've come. He's dead.'

'Eh! Who? Here don't...' Fraser caught the older man around the waist as he seemed to go weak at the knees. He half walked, half carried, him across to a hard chair set against the wall and pushed him into it, before placing a firm hand on the back of his head and waiting.

'Let me up.' James spoke in a calm voice a half minute later. 'Sorry.'

Fraser released the pressure and stood back, watching critically as the older man straightened up on the chair. 'Sorry. It's Mr Ratcliff he's dead. I went to take him his cuppa and he was stone cold in bed.'

'It'll be his heart.' Fraser offered a wry grimace. 'Have you phoned the doc?'

'Yeah. He said I wasn't to disturb anything.'

'OK. Come on. Let's go and get you a strong cup of tea.'

James nodded, beginning to walk towards the back of the house. 'I went in as usual and spoke like normal and drew back the curtain, and there he was sitting up in the bed - just staring. I pulled the curtains back and shut the window and turned and he was just staring at me.' He gave a shudder as he repeated himself.

Fraser nodded. 'Is Mrs MacGillivray in yet, or the Prof?'

'No. She'll leave, I know she will. She said the copper being here yesterday was the last straw. I had to talk fast to get her to stay.'

'We'll all be leaving. No boss, no job.'

James sat down heavily on a kitchen chair and sighed. 'Oh God, I hadn't thought about that. What'll I do?'

Fraser looked at James with a certain amount of sympathy. He was young enough to find other work; James wasn't a youngster any longer. Jobs were hard enough to find for the fit and able-bodied. He shook his head as he went to fill and switch on the kettle. 'What did the doc say?'

'That because Mr Ratcliff hadn't been seen for a while it would maybe mean a PM. So I said OK. And that we weren't to touch him because that helped determine time of death and things.'

Fraser ran a hand over his hair, pushing it back, and looked at the other man as he sat slumped on the chair. 'I'll make us a cuppa while we wait then.'

'I couldn't touch anything.'

Fraser nodded, but nevertheless went on with his preparations; he put a mug of hot sweet tea in front of James. 'I need something, and I think you do too.'

He moved to sit down, but his bottom hadn't reached the seat before the front door bell went again. 'I'll get it. Drink your tea.' He headed out and along the corridor, opening the door to McInnis and Bell. 'Hello. I don't think it's a police matter, it's his heart.'

'Pardon?' Bob swapped a quick glance with Sandy before both advanced purposefully, preventing Fraser from shutting the door with them on the wrong side of it. 'We've come to see Mr Ratcliff?'

'Well, yeah. But it ain't suspicious.'

'What isn't?'

'His death.'

Sandy swapped another look with Bob. 'We seemed to have missed a bit of the script, lad. When did Mr Ratcliff die?'

'James found him this morning, in his bed. Looks like his heart gave out.'

'Doctor sent for?'

Fraser looked from one very stern face to the other.

'Well, yeah. James rang straight away. Doc's on his way.'

'I think we'd like to see Mr Ratcliff anyway.'

Fraser shrugged. 'If that's what takes your fancy. I haven't been in the room yet.' He turned and led the way to the back bedroom. He pushed the door ajar slightly but didn't go in. 'There you go gents. Enjoy.' He turned and went back to the kitchen, suppressing a shudder. He wouldn't want their jobs.

Sandy and Bob stood just at the entrance of the bedroom door looking at the scene.

'What do you think, Sandy? It's very convenient, this death.'

'Aye.' Sandy nodded and ran a hand over his ear in the manner of a rabbit cleaning. Indeed he had the alert look of someone on the lookout for danger. 'It could have been his heart. He told us himself he was having a bad day.'

'I'll go and have a word with James Dove.'

'Aye, I'll wait for the doc. See what he has to say.'

Bob made his way along the corridor and pushed against a door behind which came the murmur of voices. James and Fraser looked up as Bob put his head around the door and then pushed it fully open and came in.

He nodded at Fraser, then said, 'Mr Dove, Fraser tells me you found Mr Ratcliff this morning.' He waited for the nod, before continuing. 'Given the circumstances, we will need to look at this death a little bit more carefully.' Both men nodded again.

'I was just saying you seemed to think it was a bit suspicious like.'

Bob looked at Fraser and offered a half smile, then looked at James Dove. 'I'm sorry to distress you further. You said yesterday that you've been with Mr Ratcliff for a good few years. This must have come as a shock to you.'

'It was his heart. All the fuss yesterday with you lot coming and going, and rushing about at the weekend. I told him he was overdoing it.' James sat nursing the mug of tea and look angrily at Bob.

'We have to do our job, sir.'

'Yeah, well look what your job has done now.'

Bob mentally shrugged and became more formal. 'Yes, sir, just so. Now I want you to tell me exactly how you came to find Mr Ratcliff this morning.'

James opened his mouth and then closed it as Bob spoke again. 'This is an official enquiry, sir.'

James Dove visibly swallowed and then nodded. 'OK.

171

I'm sorry, Inspector, I'm a bit upset.' He started to relate the events of the early morning while Bob stood listening.

'The window was open you say. Was that normal?'

'Sometimes. Not often. He used to say he got air hungry.' James wrinkled his nose. 'I dunna what he meant quite. But when he had a bad pain and he was troubled with his breathing, he would want the window open, said it helped him to breathe.'

'And last night was one of those times?'

'To tell you the truth, no. I thought he was just put out with all the questions and such. He was tired. But not like he gets when his heart's playing up.'

'Did he open the window himself?'

James started to speak, then put his head on one side looking at, and almost through, Bob. 'Now you mention it, no. Generally he let me do things like that. I suppose he must have though.'

'Thank you, sir.' Bob McInnis nodded at the silent Fraser and James Dove and left the room again just as the door bell rang. Fraser followed on his heels. 'That'll be Mrs MacGillivray forgotten her key again. Proper put out she'll be.'

Bob looked over his shoulder. 'Not half as put out as Mr Ratcliff.'

'Too right.' Fraser opened the door to a tall thin man and Mrs MacGillivray. 'Ah! James is in the kitchen, Mrs MacGillivray. I'll just take the doc to see Mr Ratcliff.' He swung around and winked at Bob before stepping aside to allow her to get past him.

The doctor's name was Ethan Isherwood. He looked questioningly at Fraser, then Bob, but waited until Mrs MacGillivray had swished past and gone down the corridor. 'Police. I recognise you, Inspector. I've seen you at court.'

'Separate enquiry, Doctor. However we would like to check things out before the scene is disturbed too much.'

'Fine. Do you want me to pronounce?'

'Yes. That would be helpful.'

Both men walked down the corridor, following Fraser. He stopped and stood aside at the door. 'Gents.' He watched them go in and walked away.

HELEN MCKENZIE WAS WALKING down long dull corridors this fine summer morning. The clouds were burning off as the sun rose higher in the sky and she'd paid homage to early summer with a short sleeved dress that showed her rather nice figure off for the entertainment of passing males, and the envy of most women.

If asked she'd have declared her bust too big and her legs too short but few men had any fault to find. Certainly Hugh, seeing her standing next to his bed as he opened his eyes, had nothing to complain about.

'I'm Detective Sergeant McKenzie and my Partner is Detective Constable Jorkvil, Professor Kegan. How are you this morning?'

Hugh hitched up the bed a bit and wished he'd shaved when they gave him the chance. 'I'm fine.'

Helen just waited, looking at him.

'Well, OK, not fine exactly, but I'll survive.'

'Are you well enough to answer a few questions?'

Hugh nodded and wriggled up a bit more. He looked at Michael Jorkvil who had just arrived at the end of the bed. 'Er.' He frowned. 'Am I in trouble?'

'No. Not at all.' Helen pulled a plastic chair around and sat down, crossing her despised legs, and sending the blood pressure up in the gent in the bed opposite. 'However you have been attacked in what amounts to a home invasion, which is a serious offence. Are you prepared to prefer charges?'

'Yes.' Hugh nodded to emphasise the degree of annoyance he felt, and waited for his cranial Atlas to settle back on to his cranial Axis with what felt like a dangerous wobble.

'Very sensible. However he does have friends who will not be happy.' Helen noted the wince with sympathy but continued talking.

'I should imagine so. But that's no reason to allow myself to be intimidated.'

'Hmm!' Helen exchanged a look with Michael still standing at the end of the bed. 'Good. Now can you give us a statement? That way we can continue to hold him while we ask a few more questions.'

Michael started taking shorthand notes as Hugh started to speak. After a quick glance, Hugh ignored him and continued. 'I hurt my head last Friday and...' Before he could complete the sentence, Helen held up a hand.

'We know about the incident with Ms Branwell. I understand she stayed with you overnight to ensure you were alright.'

'She stayed with me all weekend. Her heart's in the right place and we got on like a house on fire.' His lips twitched/ 'Ever been in a burning building. People run around like headless chickens as they try to help each other. It's a scary experience.'

Helen noted the twinkle and offered a small grin. 'We did see her in action at the café on Friday.'

'Yeah. So,' Hugh took a breath, 'Friday I stayed with her. To be honest I passed out with concussion and medication. Saturday I went home and she stayed at my house. Sunday we went for a run in the car. Yesterday morning we went out to do a little shopping. She wanted to make sure my cupboard and fridge were stocked before she went home.' He grinned briefly. 'When we got back the house had been trashed. There's no other word for it.' He sighed. 'So, very generously, she told me I could go and stay with her again while the police processed the scene.

'Yesterday evening she nipped out on some private business. I'm not sure what, and I thought she'd forgotten her key. I heard someone at the door and went to open it. Some guy barged in and caught me a crack around the head and the next I know, Harry is peering at me while I'm lying on the floor. I don't remember much else except that she said she didn't do it.' Hugh leaned back and watched the detective constable's hands working their way down the page until Michael stopped and looked at him.

'Yes, we've spoken to the team who were called to your house. They said you didn't think anything was stolen.'

Hugh shrugged. 'I couldn't see anything missing. I intended to have a better look today, after I'd been to work.'

'I thought you were on sabbatical. Writing a book.' Michael looked up from his busy scribbling and fired the question at him.

'I was, I am. I'm doing a bit of research in one of the private libraries in the town.'

'Ah! Do they allow you to take the books home?'

'Not a chance.' Hugh smiled, his lip moving upwards in the semblance of a smile. 'It's mainly manuscripts, and they have to be preserved at the right temperature. I'm not even allowed to take them out of the room, never mind the house.'

'So it isn't those books that the thief might have been after at your house?'

Hugh shook his head.

'And you don't have large sums of money, paintings, stamps, anything small, portable, and worth stealing?'

'Nope. I'm a divorcee. When have we men got much left after the divorce?' He gave a half sniff and then said, 'No, that's not fair. My wife was generous in her demands and we're still on speaking terms.'

'So you don't think she might be behind it?'

'Good God! No. Eleanor wouldn't wish me ill. She just can't cope with me.'

'We'd like her address, nevertheless.' Helen spoke firmly. 'People have been known to harbour resentment that their spouses have no knowledge about.'

Hugh raised an eyebrow but supplied the address down in London. 'She really wouldn't wish me harm, Inspector.'

Helen nodded again. 'So you've nothing worth stealing. You're on good terms with your ex. How about the research; does it have any value.' She frowned. 'Would anyone else want the same knowledge?'

Hugh gave a soft chuckle. 'Hardly. It's not a political thing or an expose, just an historical treatise.'

'OK.' Helen sat silent looking at him. 'To be honest we're floundering a bit. 'Fred Blogs' or, to give him his proper name, Peter Oldershaw, is known as a second story man who works to order. He doesn't generally do opportunistic work, so we think you were target specific.

We'll go over the reports from forensics and see if there are any clues lurking there. Thank you for being so patient with us, Professor.'

'My pleasure.' He offered her a smile and leaned back against the pillow.

Michael Jorkvil spoke from the end of the bed. 'Ms Branwell came to see me last night; she seems to think it's something to do with her work as an engineer.' He watched the older man's face, checking for signs of jealousy and finding none.

Hugh grinned; it lit up his face for an instant. 'That'll be the gribbles and piddocks. I told her she wasn't being pursued across the Atlantic, but she wouldn't believe me.'

'No, I find it hard to believe too, but we'll look into it anyway because frankly, Professor, we're not finding anything in your background to account for the break-ins, and we have to start somewhere.' Michael nodded and turned to follow his partner.

14

HE RANG TO SAY the background checks are coming along nicely, Jane.' Dorothy and Jane were sitting in their usual seats. Both had steaming mugs of latte in front of them and plates with a cream doughnut apiece. 'He thinks he might be able to give you an address by the end of the week if not sooner.'

'And he won't do anymore unless I tell him?'

'No. I promise.'

Jane smiled across the table. 'OK.' Her shoulders sagged slightly. 'What are your plans for the day, then?'

'I thought you might like to come and help me get a pair of shoes and a handbag for this wedding. I appreciate your input, Jane.'

Jane looked at her friend and saw that the comment was genuine. 'That sounds like fun.' She looked around the café and lowered her voice a bit. 'Do you think they're still trying to catch the pick-pockets?'

'I should think so. Good luck to them.' Dorothy picked up her doughnut and took a small bite. 'Mmm nice.' She swallowed. 'We've retired.'

Adrian Chappell looked across the café and noted the two women; he thought about the police interview and tried to think if he'd mentioned them to the Detective. He thought their faces were familiar.

He turned back and smiled at his daughter as she swung her legs against the chair and munched a bag of crisps. 'First day of the school holidays, Maggie. What do you want to do? Anything special this summer?'

'Can we go to the sea-side one day?'

'I should think that can be managed. Anything else?'

Margaret Chappell grinned at her father. 'And maybe have a picnic.' He hated them and wasn't keen on the seaside either and she knew it. She giggled at the face he pulled. 'Or not.'

'Maybe, we'll see. Drink up, I've got to get into work. Got your pencils and your book? I've booked you some extra drawing lessons now you're on holiday. And you said you wanted swimming lessons too.'

'Thanks, Dad.' Maggie sighed, but quietly. It was no fun spending her holidays in the back room of the chemist's shop where her dad worked. It had been lots better before her mum died, less money for things but more people time. She knew her dad worried enough about it without saying anything. 'Can I check the stock? I won't open any bottles, I promise. Just do the packets and tick things off like I did at Easter.'

Adrian looked at her, smiling eagerly at him. 'Alright, but you mustn't touch anything that's not pre-packaged, promise?'

'I promise.'

'I PROMISE.' HARRIET BRANWELL was making promises too. She

looked at Hugh sitting in the bed. He'd managed to have a shave, and in consequence was feeling much better. 'I'll go to the address and tell them you can't come today, probably not this week.' She smiled nicely at him. 'I'll give your Mr Ratcliff this note,' she tapped a paper against her hand, and then put her head on one side, looking at him critically. 'How does the head feel?'

'A hairline fracture is a bit painful but it doesn't seem to have affected my brain. The police are concerned about the attack though, so take care, Harry. Try to stay in the here and now.'

Harry grinned. 'I'll stay in the here and now, if you'll stop procrastinating.'

'Away with you.' Hugh smiled at her as she stood up. 'I'll plot the first chapter while I'm in here. After all what else can I do with my time?'

Harry gave a chuckle, dropped a kiss on his brow and left the ward. She walked down the corridor, stuffing the note inside her overlarge bag. Outside the sun shone down and she shrugged out of her light denim jacket and threw it into the back of the car, before getting in and heading to Henry Ratcliff's house.

She didn't seriously think that she was in any danger but she had to admit, poor Hugh was in the wars. She moved up a gear and shot across an intersection, then neatly swung down a side street and pointed the car southwards towards the far end of the town.

She parked neatly on the gravel sweep in front of the old Edwardian house along the London Road. She got out of the car and looked around her as she locked the door and gave a silent, and unlady-like, whistle. The place was crawling with white vans and squad cars.

Before she had gone two steps a large, and somewhat hirsute, policeman was blocking her path. 'I'm sorry, miss. What's your business here?' He laid a hand on her arm, preventing her from moving any further. He spoke in friendly tones, but looking at the man she was quite pleased he wasn't an enemy.

'I've come to see Mr Ratcliff.'

'And what is your business with Mr Ratcliff?'

Harry looked at him; he obviously wasn't going to let her see anyone without an explanation. She smiled nicely. 'It's OK; I only have to deliver a note from Professor Kegan.' She shrugged off the restraining hand and began to hunt through the small suitcase-sized bag slung on her shoulder.

A fresh voice spoke. It had overtones of Cumbrian and undertones of education. 'Officer?'

Her companion swung around as she looked up from her task. The suit clad man talking to her uniformed friend was handsome in an understated way, a way enhanced by the expensive suiting he was wearing; he was looking between them, waiting for an explanation.

'Hello, I've come to see Mr Ratcliff.'

Bob McInnis looked her over and offered a half smile. 'Perhaps you'd like to come inside for a minute and have a word.' He nodded at the constable and gestured with his hand for her to step through the front door.

Harry walked into the hall and stopped. 'Oh lovely, is it a real Monet?'

Bob looked first at her and then at the pastel

drawing. 'If it is, he nicked it from the Tate.'

'Oh shame. It's a good copy though.'

'Yes. Now, Miss…'

'Miss Branwell.'

'Miss Branwell, if you'd come into this room and tell me your business… I'm a police officer.' Bob pulled out his warrant card and held it out for inspection.

Harry looked it over and then looked at the stern face watching her. 'Is this to do with Hugh getting attacked then?'

Bob shook his head. 'First tell me why you're here.' He waved to a seat and waited for her to go over and sit down, before sitting himself, as he did so hitching his beautifully pressed trousers in what was obviously a habitual gesture.

'Professor Kegan is doing some research into the medieval period, around the beginning of the fourteenth century. He's been using Mr Ratcliff's private collection for research.' Harry looked at Bob as he watched her with intelligent brown eyes.

'And he asked you to come today and bring a note.'

'Like from the teacher.' Harry grinned at him. She got a flash of teeth and a small chuckle for her pains.

'And why can't he come to school today?'

'Because someone broke into my house and hit him with the door and now he's in hospital with a hairline fracture of the skull.' She watched his lips form the words fracture and the wince.

'He was attacked, you said. This was the attack. Why did the person break into your house?'

'Well, I think it was gribbles; but Hugh, Professor Kegan, thinks it's just opportunism.'

'I heard they were causing huge amounts of damage to underwater wrecks. I understand even the Titanic is at risk. The Americans are doing a lot of research to prevent destruction of their marine archaeology. But why that should lead to...'

'You know about gribbles?' Harry interrupted him with a comment and a stare. Her flabber had never been so gasted.

'I know a little about gribbles, Miss Branwell.'

'How? I mean mostly I have to explain what they are, never mind what they do.'

Bob offered her the first genuine grin. 'I have friends in both the archaeological world, and an officer who is a member of the Nomadic society over in Belfast.'

'What fun!' He surprised another grin from her.

His grin was switched off and Bob became official again, 'Anyway, the Professor was attacked, in your house. When?'

'Last night.'

'Was he visiting?' For the first time Bob McInnis showed a tinge of red in his cheeks.

'No, his house had been broken into. I knocked him over on Friday and gave him a concussion and I was looking after him.'

Bob shook his head as if to shake out a troubling noise in his ear. 'Miss Branwell, er, could we try again. I'm…' He stopped as an older man came in. 'Ah, this is Inspector Bell.'

Sandy nodded at her, and looked at Bob with a raised eyebrow.

'Miss Branwell has come to deliver a note from Professor Kegan. He will not be visiting today.'

Inspector Bell held out a hand. 'May I see it, Miss.'

Harry rummaged through her bag again while the two men watched with faint smiles on their faces. She muttered to herself. 'That's not it, oh, where have you got to? What…?' She pulled out a small book and looked frowningly at it before dropping it back into her bag again and scrabbling about a bit more. 'Ah, got ya.' And then held out the note, saying, 'He's in hospital. Why are you here?'

The two policemen exchanged looks. Bob received a tiny nod. 'Mr Ratcliff has died suddenly and as a matter of routine we are looking into the circumstances.'

'Pull the other one.' Harry looked from one man to the other. 'A couple of plain clothes men for an unattended death.'

'Aye.'

Harry sniffed. 'Don't tell then, it'll be in the paper quick enough. I saw one of the Press lurking outside when I came in.'

'Damn. Bob, would you…?'

'Yeah, I'll see to it.' Bob nodded at her and left the room.

'Now, Miss. If you'll just wait while I look at your note, we needn't detain you any longer than necessary.'

'Oh, but I'd like to be detained.' She watched the faint glimmer of a twinkle appear and disappear. 'Oh well.' She stood watching while he read the brief missive and then saw him fold it up and put it in his inside pocket.

'Thank you for your help, Miss Branwell. If you could just tell me which ward the Professor is on.'

Harry supplied the information and then sighed as he ushered her outside. 'I shouldn't talk to the press, Miss.'

'No. I won't. Not that I know anything, yet.' She offered him another smile and got into her car, driving off as Bob returned through the gate.

'Ghouls.'

'Aye, lad.'

IN THE KITCHEN OF the late Henry Ratcliff's house, James Dove and Fraser were sitting at the table looking gloomily at more tea. They had the demeanour, if not the habits, of ghouls themselves. Mrs MacGillivray, upon being told that her employer was dead, had not, as James feared, thrown such a wobbly that she'd fallen over. She had nodded, gripped the sink for a minute, and then turned and filled the kettle before switching it back on and remarking that they'd all do better for a cup of tea.

Now Mrs MacGillivray sat with her eyes closed, holding her cup in large, work reddened, hands which in turn rested on a large stomach. She had yet to take off her hat and coat. The two men looked at each other and then at their silent companion as they heard the approach of official feet. She, however, remained, and looked from a certain angle, as apparently enigmatic as the sphinx.

Fraser got a quick nod from James and stood up as Bob came into a room redolent of sweet tea, coffee and the click of a radiator. 'Ah.' He glanced from one man to the other, unsure which would give him the answers he needed.

'How can we help, Inspector?' Fraser stepped forward and came over to the door.

'If you could just clarify one or two things, sir.'

Fraser nodded and went past Bob and out into the corridor. Bob, perforce, following if he wanted any answers.

'They're a bit upset like, Inspector. What can I tell you?'

'Well, first, where's the parrot?'

Fraser gave him the kind of look used by Englishmen in foreign countries. It said, 'Why can't you speak a language I can understand'. 'Parrot?'

'Yeah. Yesterday there was a parrot here. Polly. Looked as if it was being plucked feather by feather for the Sunday joint. Nice thing.'

'I don't know. On her perch I suppose. What's that got to do with...'

Bob shook his sleek head. 'I've looked in all the downstairs rooms. No Polly. I wondered if she had a special sleeping place.'

'Sleeps in the boss's room. He talks, talked, to her at night if he couldn't get to sleep.'

Bob nodded. 'She isn't there now.' He followed as Fraser went to the open door of the bedroom and looked in at the busy men in their all-in-one white suits. He glared at the empty perch. 'Have they…'

'Yes, they've taken Mr Ratcliff.'

Fraser wheeled about and went down the corridor to the study, opening the door and fixing his eyes on the empty perch there with a look of disgust.

'No parrot.' Bob spoke quietly.

'No. Where the hell has she got to?'

'That was my question.' Bob spoke patiently. 'Mr Dove said the window was open, would she have flown off.'

'Couldn't. She had a broken wing.' Fraser spoke while still frowning absently at the empty perch. He turned and looked at Bob. 'That's bloody queer.'

Bob continued to watch and wait.

'I'll ask James.' He turned to go.

'No, don't do that, sir. I'll ask him in a moment. Perhaps you could answer a few more questions for me.'

'OK. What?' It was obvious to Bob that he was still thinking about the parrot, but he turned back and looked at Bob.

'Have you the key to the library and the bottom drawer of his desk, and can you tell me what they contain?'

'Mr Ratcliff kept the keys.' He scowled. 'They will be on his key ring. The library's papers. Old ones. Parchment and such. Some of them are on sticks all rolled up. Some really old books. I was going to ask if I could look at them when I'd been here a bit longer.' He sighed. 'I don't know what's in his desk.'

'Do you know how he made his money?'

'Haven't got a clue. He was seriously loaded. I know that. Well, this day and age you don't keep 'staff' do you?'

Bob shook his head. 'No.'

'Well, he'd got James and Mrs MacGillivray and me. I'm a recent addition, I told you yesterday. But I get a good wage. Not the basic rate. And all my meals while I'm here. And I'm just a glorified odd job man. I don't know where I'm gonna get such a good job again. And I was saving to go to uni too.'

Bob nodded again, there wasn't much help he could offer, but here was someone who definitely didn't benefit from the death of his employer.

'Alright, thank you.'

Fraser gave a nod. 'I'll see if she's upstairs.' He turned around and went over to the wide staircase, mounting two steps at a time.

Bob watched him disappear around the bend in the staircase and then walked off to the study they had been using. 'Sandy.' He spoke as he went through the door. Sandy Bell looked up from the letter he was re-reading.

'Found it?'

'Nope.'

'Odd. What do you think, flew off? Nicked? Those birds are worth a fair bit on the black market.'

'It couldn't fly. And nobody in their right mind would want that moth-eaten specimen.'

Sandy gave a soft chuckle. 'No, you're right there, lad.' He frowned, tapping the letter against his hand. He went over to a hard chair and sat down at a small desk. Bob came further into the room. 'Do you think it's a murder, Bob?'

'I just don't know. We have to treat it as suspicious, Sandy.'

'Oh, Aye. But murder? I dunno, Bob.'

'Go through the motions, which is what we're doing, and wait for the forensics and results of the PM.' Bob offered a small smile. 'In the meantime should I waste anymore time on the parrot? Do you think it's pertinent?'

'It's a loose end. I mislike them, Bob.'

'Alright. I'll set a couple of uniforms on to ask around the neighbourhood. It couldn't fly but it could hop, so it might have got out the open window.' He gave a slight shrug. 'I'd like to know why that window was open. It wasn't that warm overnight, even if it is nearly July.'

Sandy nodded. 'Key to the book room?'

'Dove has it. I'll get it in a minute.' He looked at Sandy, 'If this is a double we need a few more men?'

'Aye, I'm going back to the station to talk to the Super. Which one do you want?'

'I'll take the possible. You can go out in the field, literally!' He offered a sly grin as Sandy scowled. 'You did offer a choice.' This time he laughed at Sandy's expression. Sandy gave a bark of laughter himself and stood up.

'Right. I'll see you, about fiveish, back at the office? It'll take that long to sort out the basic scene of crime, stuff.'

Bob nodded and watched him head out the door. He

glanced around the room and then walked out himself to see how the team was getting on in the bedroom.

15

Sandy got into his car and set off up the London road. He swept past his turning, however, and continued north towards the Cumberland Infirmary. He might have given the case to Bob McInnis, but he had a letter in his pocket that might repay investigation. It was probably just a loose end to snip he argued with himself, and it would save Bob a bit of time.

He found Hugh Kegan lying back in the bed with his eyes closed. He nodded quiet thanks to the nurse who'd shown him the way, and pulled up a chair. He settled down to wait. Five minutes later Hugh opened a sleepy eye and looked at him. One eyebrow gave a slight twitch and he rolled his head slightly on the pillow before opening the second eye.

'My name is Detective Inspector Bell.' Sandy's slight Scots accent wafted over him like a gentle breeze.

'Heavens. I knew home invasions were serious, but I didn't think I warranted a Senior Detective as well.'

'I haven't come about the home invasion, sir. I understand you are currently using the library of Mr Ratcliff?'

'Well, yes. Is he complaining? I assure you, tempted though I am to take away some of those papers I haven't given in to temptation, honestly.'

'No, sir. I'm afraid Mr Ratcliff is dead.'

'What? Blimey! I knew his heart was a bit…' Hugh waggled his hand. 'But I didn't think it was that bad.'

'So you wouldn't have expected him to die?'

Hugh rolled his head gently on the pillow in negation. He'd learnt his lesson, nodding was for donkeys.

'Can I ask the nature of the work you were doing?'

Hugh frowned. 'Research. I'm preparing the background for a book about the crusades. He's got some interesting rolls from the period. Information I've not come across anywhere else.'

'Valuable.'

Hugh frowned. 'Priceless. In fact…'

'Sir?'

Hugh frowned a bit more. 'I wondered where he'd obtained it. But you don't look a gift horse, and he was allowing me to study the stuff free, gratis and for nothing. I wasn't going to pick holes.'

'What bothered you?'

'I can't quite put my finger on it. It was…'He waggled the hand again. 'It was just I'd never read some of the stuff before, not even a foot note in another book.' Then he grinned. 'But some of it was to do with the Knights Templar. Awful close that group, highly secretive.'

'Was Mr Ratcliff a Mason?'

'Don't think so. But how do you tell? They don't go around with one trouser leg permanently rolled up do they?'

Sandy shook his head. 'No, I shouldn't think they do, sir. Do you know Mr Ratcliff's source of income?'

'Haven't a clue.'

Sandy hitched on the chair and pulled the note out that Hugh had sent with Harry. 'This note you sent. You say you'll return the little book when you're discharged from hospital. I thought you hadn't taken any books?' A hint, a mere whiff of suspicion coloured the words.

Hugh shook his head. 'There was a notebook in among my papers, I found it Saturday. It wasn't Harry's or mine. I concluded that it belonged to Mr Ratcliff. As far as I know it's still among the papers and I wanted to return it.'

'Oh right, sir. Do you mind if I collect it. Mr Ratcliff's death is officially classified as suspicious at the moment. Anything pertinent over the last few days might help to clear it up quickly.'

Hugh shrugged. 'Harry's still got my keys. She can take you or let you have them. The place is still a tip though.'

Sandy nodded and pushed back his chair, saying. 'Thank you verra much, sir. You've been helpful.'

The doors had given a soft whoosh of colder air as they closed behind Sandy Bell, before Hugh wondered how he would find Harry.

BOB MCINNIS MEANWHILE WAS organising his team before settling down to look at the paperwork on the desk of the recently departed gentleman. Yesterday he'd have given a fair sum for a quick look over it. Today he looked over it with a niggling feeling of guilt, because he didn't wish any man dead.

He picked up a leather tooled book face down on the desk and looked at the revealed pages, raising an eyebrow at the words he read softly to himself, '*Fugerit invida aetas: carpe diem, quam minimum credula postero.* Envious time has passed pluck the day, putting as little trust in tomorrow.' Well, he couldn't fault Horace's sentiments and they had certainly been borne out by the events of today. He closed the book and laid it gently down at the side of the desk before reaching for the handle of the top drawer.

He pulled it open and found a bunch of keys and such paraphernalia as can be found in most desks. He noted that the evil paperclip elf, normally found in his work draw had been at work here also and had strung about fifty together in one corner. A packet of elastic bands was regurgitating its contents into a small pot filled with bent staples and a handful of bent roofing nails. Several fountain pens with badly pitted nibs jostled each other at the front of the drawer.

McInnis picked out one of the pens and examined the point critically, as an aficionado of calligraphy he had his own collection of ink pens. These had been badly maltreated at some time, which he considered shameful as they weren't cheap or easy to obtain. He set it down with a sigh and moved on.

The next drawer had bills neatly held together with bulldog clips. Bob fanned them out BT, electric, gas; evidently Mr Ratcliff didn't care for the prevailing green wave that recommended electronic billing. Bob wasn't that keen on it himself. It involved using technology. He operated a 'you leave me alone and I'll leave you alone policy' with his computer at work.

He looked at the cheque and paying-in book, the few

stubs that had been filled in seemed to relate to household affairs. None of the sums exactly large. He pushed back the chair and leaned down, trying to pull the bottom drawer open without success.

He pulled out the bunch of keys and tried each one. Before sniffing and tossing the bunch onto the top. 'Damn.'

Sitting back he looked around the room. Yesterday it had been slightly too warm for comfort and had a slight aroma compounded of polish, parrot and peanut and an indefinable something that still hung around like a tortured miasma. Today the polish still lingered and this close he could smell the perch of the parrot, but not the parrot herself. That odd smell was still around too. 'I wonder where you've got to, Polly.'

A constable poked his head around the door. 'Did you want something, sir?'

Bob looked over the expanse of carpet at the beetling eyebrows, blue chin and hint of white suit. 'No, I was talking to myself, Josh.'

The head disappeared.

Bob pulled a pen out of his inside pocket and picked up an A4 pad that was lying on the top of the desk. 'I need to prioritise.' He spoke softly to himself.

'A. What would A. be? Is it murder, I suppose? B. If it is, who gains?

C. Was he involved in Sandy's murder case? Did he know something about it? Instigate it? Benefit from it? D. Where's the damn parrot? E. Alibi's for the staff. No. The parrot shouldn't be that relevant.' He paused and looked across the room out of the window at the quiet garden. 'Only, in my bones, I know it is.' He sniffed. 'Now suspicious or just convenient, I need to find out what he was up to, because I'm sure he was up to something. Nobody has that much cash to spare, legally.'

He stood up and walked across the room, going along the corridor to the bedroom. 'How we doing?' He stood outside the door, making sure he wasn't contaminating the scene.

'The bedside cabinets are dusted, sir. Nothing on the bottles.' A blond man nodded at two sealed bags containing a couple of sprays and a bottle of tablets.

'Do you mean nothing that shouldn't have been there or wiped clean, Mark?'

'Clean.'

'Ah, interesting. Anything else?'

'Judging by the, er…guano…on the carpet. The parrot was a bit nervous.' Mark grinned, and pointed with his chin at the floor near the bedside.

Bob spoke. 'Safe to come in?' He got a nod and went over and looked, careful to touch nothing. 'Hmm!' Get a sample or two of that, Mark.' Mark nodded, stepping two paces across to his big black case and abstracting a small corked bottle. He stooped and wrinkled his nose as he twirled a cotton bud into the mess on the carpet and stowed the specimen. He signed and dated as Bob watched, then Bob stood with his back to the window and looked again at the room. 'It doesn't look disturbed, Mark.'

Mark nodded agreement, even though every level surface was now liberally sprinkled with white powder as if there had been several exploding tins of talc around.

'Any keys about?'

'Nope.'

Bob nodded, and with the same caution he had entered, he left the room and went into the kitchen. James Dove and Mrs MacGillivray still sat at the table.

'I would like a word with each of you. If you'd come along to the study, Mrs MacGillivray.' He spoke pleasantly, but it was clear that he expected to be obeyed. He turned on his heel and went out.

Mrs MacGillivray stood up. 'Alright, James?'

'Yes. Don't fuss.'

She shrugged and caused a Brownian motion of scent to waft across the table towards him. James grimaced, but said nothing as she walked out of the room.

She made her way to the study to find Bob standing at the desk and a constable just inside the door.

'Mrs MacGillivray isn't it? Have a seat.'

'Edith.' She sat and the chair creaked slightly. Bob moved behind the desk but didn't sit down.

'Just a few questions, Mrs MacGillivray. How long have you worked for Mr Ratcliff?'

'Fifteen years. James and I were took on at the same time.'

Bob noted the comment but followed his own line of questions for now. 'Did you get on with Mr Ratcliff?'

'I kept out of his study and he kept out of my kitchen. No fancy stuff, just good plain food, and we got on fine.'

'Did he seem ill or worse, over the weekend?'

'No. He was his usual grumpy self.' She sniffed. 'He was supposed to stick to a diet, but he never did. He liked that Earl Grey tea, but I could never make it right for him. Joe used to bring him a special mix; he liked that for his breakfast.'

'That would be Joseph Jenkins?'

'Yes.'

'Have you got any more of the special mix?'

'Got some in the kitchen in the special tin, Joe brought a new lot on Friday when he came. I like a good cup of proper tea myself, and so does James. I'll fetch it for you if...' She started to rise and Bob waved her back down.

'No, you can show me later. Now this is just routine; but can you tell me where you were last night?'

'Why? 'Ere what you getting at?'

'I'M NOT QUITE SURE what you're getting at, Constable?' Sandy smiled pleasantly at the young woman in front of him.

The young woman was obviously nervous, she glanced at her older male colleague, Sergeant Gareth ap Rhys, but there was no help there. His expression said, 'your idea, your problem'.

'Can I show you on the map, sir?'

She waited for the nod from Sandy before producing, with the air of a magician, a map in square clear plastic from her brief case. It was obviously personal property. There were red felt-tip lines and squiggles of blue ink at the sides of it. 'I'm part of the Cycle Club at Silloth, sir. This is the National Cycle Track.' She warmed to her theme as she realised she had Sandy's full attention. She ran a finger along the track, 'This is where we found the body, and over here the track goes right beside the River Waver

'I don't think he was carried in on a bike, lass.'

'No, but you don't understand, the bikers use our track, big Harley's sometimes, but mostly trail bikes. We campaign against it; they do thousand's of pounds of damage to the trail. But you have to catch 'em in the act.'

'I still...'

'No. But listen;' She waved Sandy to silence as she got into her theory, and Gareth winced. Sandy ignored the breach of protocol. 'There was a bike run Sunday, we were all grumbling because one of the big bikes had churned up the track. I didn't think anymore of it, but just supposing he was killed upstream not down. We've all been looking down towards the sea 'cos it was assumed he'd maybe come up with the tide, what if he was going down as it ebbed.'

Sandy put his head on one side, looking first at and then through her.

'Si...'

'Whist.' He brought the young constable back into focus, looked across at the senior man. 'Have we looked upstream, Gareth?'

'Not far yet, just the immediate surroundings. Constable Stanton only proposed the theory when she was assigned this morning.'

'Set some men on pronto. And find me a tide-table.'

'Chief.' He turned away, jerking his head for the woman to follow.

'No. You stay here, lass. I'm no good at tide-tables for a start, and even worse at reading tracks. I want you to show me some of this damage.'

'Sir.' She looked excited and terrified at the same time.

Sandy nodded and stood waiting for the tide-table while he looked about the field and stream area where the body of Joe Jenkins had been found. His companion opened her mouth twice and closed it again, finally settling into parade rest and looking about herself.

'What were you going to say?' Sandy spoke and drew her attention back to himself.

'Sir, what, sir?'

'Just now when you opened you mouth.'

'My boyfriend isn't a member of the force, sir, but he's got lots more experience biking, he knows the trails really well around here. I was thinking he might know different roads that get you onto the track that aren't marked on the map.'

Sandy raised an eyebrow. 'Working?'

'Fisherman, sir. Tides full, he'll be out, maybe till Thursday if the fishing's good.'

Sandy nodded again. 'See how things go, I might like a word with him.'

He took the tide-tables from the constable who appeared at his elbow. The small book was well thumbed and folded open at the month of June. A highlighter had been used to mark the high tides for Sunday and Monday. 'Thanks.'

'Now, Lass. We haven't got a time of death yet so when, in your opinion, would the body go out? And how far up this stream does the tide stop tiding.' He grinned.

Constable Stanton flourished the map. 'You see these little things like grass, sir, at the side of the stream, roughly where they stop, it stops being tidal. The cycle track runs alongside it here, where these dots are, so if he went in about here, he might get washed back a bit towards the coast from here.' She pointed with a rose tipped fingernail.

Sandy nodded. 'And this is the area we've looked in, beyond Brownrigg towards the coast. Aye, I see what you're getting at.' He looked at the patiently waiting senior man. 'Get that set up, up to this area just beyond where the track turns away. We're looking for...' He glanced at Constable Stanton.

'Deep ruts. I'll show you, sir.'

'No, show him.' Sandy pointed a finger at ap Rhys. 'But before you go... tides?'

'If we assume he was going out, sir, change the time of death by maybe six hours, sir.'

'Thank you, Constable Stanton. Your ideas will be noted.' Sandy gave her a gentle smile and won a grin back. He watched her stride across the field with an extra bounce in her step and turned back to the scene, seeing how men were being re-deployed to the new area while he thought about the new information and how it slotted into what he already knew.

It was true that they didn't have a time of death but he wasn't sure that six hours was going to make all that difference. They could re-canvass the area for those who might have been out and about between the new times, but until they had a suspect there was no chance of checking an alibi, and so far they had no suspect.

What the hell was the man doing here? Sandy was almost sure it was a secondary site. And now they had a possible means of transport for getting the body over two fields and into the river. That meant someone who knew the area.

Now that could mean locals, dog walking, ramblers, a motorcyclist or biker and he would have to check out the Silloth club, and a nice fiddly job that would be. His lips pulled into a grimace as he looked across to the busy young female constable. Did PC Stanton realise she was giving him a reason to check out all her mates, including her boy friend? Being a copper was no fun when it came to relationships.

Sandy had speculated that Jenkins had been at his boat for some reason, and he already had a team checking out the moorings around the area to see if the man had been seen over the weekend. Jakob was scouting around for known drug dealers and importers in the area. Their word couldn't be trusted that far, but if it was just a case of confirming someone else's alibi they might oblige with a little inducement.

Sandy nodded to himself and strode over to the senior man. He waited patiently while further instructions were issued, then spoke. 'Make sure her input is noted, Gareth. Hard enough for women to get on as it is.'

'Yes, Chief.'

'Got enough men?'

'Yes.'

'Good. Tell me if you need more, this might be a double murder yet.' He smiled grimly at the suddenly startled look, and began to fill Sergeant Gareth ap Rhys in on the death of Henry James Ratcliff.

BOB WAS ALSO TALKING about the death of Ratcliff. He was making better progress with Fraser Wilson than he had with Mrs MacGillivray. Fraser sat on a chair next to the fire while Bob leaned against the mantelpiece as he asked his questions.

'Mr Wilson...'

'Call me Fraser for God sake! Mr makes me feel ancient.' Fraser grinned.

Bob smiled back, but the smile didn't reach his eyes. 'Fraser, your employer, Mr Ratcliff, how long have you worked for him?' He held up a hand. 'I know we talked yesterday, but that was informal. This is now very formal. We suspect Mr Ratcliff might have been murdered.'

Bob watched the chest rise and heard the intake of air through the young man's nostrils. Fraser jerked forward in the chair as if he would have risen. Bob had intended to shock, he'd wanted a reaction and he'd got one, he didn't think that this man was his murderer though, not unless he was an incredibly cool customer.

'Christ.'

Bob winced. He was a good Catholic and didn't like to hear his Lord's name taken in vain.

'But…but he had a dicky heart and he was in his bed.'

'True. But there are more ways of killing than a bullet or knife.'

Fraser shook his head, took another gulp of air and then eased back in the seat again. 'OK, OK. Murder, so…you what… need my fingerprints and an alibi and…' He looked at Bob. 'I don't know what else they ask for on the TV, my mum would know.' He scowled. To Bob's eyes he looked as though he'd have liked his mum there to hold his hand despite his years.

Bob offered another grim smile. 'We will be asking for your fingerprints, but at the moment that will just be for elimination purposes. As to an alibi.' He set his head on one side. 'Tell me what you've been doing lately.'

Fraser ran a finger under his nose and frowned. 'Er, how far back do you want, I was here, Friday. Just doing a bit of jobbing, got the car ready for Mr R's trip. We went to York, Saturday. I went to the museum. He was nice, nicer than he's been anyway, I thought I might ask if I could go in the library, coming home, only he got a phone call and went all…' Fraser groped for a word 'All snarky.' He offered.

'Er! Yesterday I was here; I came to work as usual. Your lot were here. Sunday night Mr R told us the drugs squad were coming; he called me in special to say they were coming Monday morning and we had to co-operate.' He suddenly offered a grin. 'They should be a good alibi. I buggered off to the yard halfway through the morning to tinker with the car only…' He stopped and looked at Bob. 'I don't know if it's relevant…' He spoke slowly as he looked up at Bob's leaning figure. 'And it ain't nothin' to do with me alibi, but someone had taken the car out. It was all mucky round the tyres.

'I cleaned the car Saturday after we got back from York. Pristine it was, you ask James, he checks I've done me work proper.' He screwed up his face. 'It's just his way, he don't really mean anything by it. Anyway, yesterday, be about half one, 'cos dinner was way late. I'm hiding out a bit, away from all the fuss, and I go out to the shed and the car was mucky. I dunno who drove it, 'cos Mr R doesn't, and James was busy with you lot all morning.'

Bob nodded. 'OK, So was it dusty, muddy, just the tyres or the chassis too. Was the engine warm?'

Fraser opened his mouth, then paused in thought before saying, 'Engine was cold. It was mainly the tyres, more dirt than mud or dust. Bonnet was a bit scratched, like it had gone on a rough road and the hedges had brushed it a bit.'

Bob nodded again. 'Which side?'

'Passenger. And the bumper, now I come to think of it.'

'Good. That's very helpful. Now,' he offered another small smile, 'what else did you do yesterday?'

Fraser rubbed under his nose with his left forefinger again and frowned. 'Went home at the usual time. Caught the five-fifteen bus, drops me off at the end of the road. Mrs Skeat and Mum were in the kitchen drinking tea. I told 'em about the other Inspector and how we had to say what we'd done over the weekend. Mum wasn't happy she's been...' He stopped and looked at Bob. 'Never mind about mum, I went and had a shower and went to meet Sue, she's my girl. We went to the pictures.' He stopped again and stood up, pulling a battered card case out of his pocket.

Bob watched as a confetti of receipts followed the card-case and dropped onto the carpet. Fraser bent and scooped them up, shuffling them and straightening while he peered at each one. 'Gotcha. That's the receipt for the pictures and that's for the pub after.' He waved two flimsy bits of paper at Bob. 'I took her back home and we er, well we...' He blushed slightly under Bob's fascinated gaze.

'Anyway,' he said after a moment, 'I got in about half twelve, Mum was abed, and I went straight up. I can't prove it, but I was in bed until seven this morning and then I was rushing about until I got here.'

'Thank you. And when you got here?'

'James said Mr R was dead and he'd phoned the doc and we weren't to touch anything.' He gave a slight shudder. 'I wasn't gonna touch him. And James was near to fainting, so I took him into the kitchen and made a cuppa, and then you came and I thought you already knew about him when I let you in.'

'So, have you been in Mr Ratcliff's bedroom at any time?'

'Went in there in February, window catch had busted, I fixed it, went out and got a new one and put it on. I remember the date 'cos it was Valentine's Day and I snuck off and got Sue some flowers while I was out.' He frowned in thought. 'Don't think I've been in there since. Haven't needed to.'

'That's very helpful.' Bob nodded. 'How did the catch become broken?'

Fraser shook his head. 'Just think it had rusted, like I

said, and one of them had opened it too rough, snapped off the handle where the lock goes. I had to fix another one this week same problem.'

Bob nodded again. 'Thank you again, Fraser, perhaps you can ask Mr Dove to come in. I'd rather you didn't share this interview with anyone else.'

'OK. But I don't think James did it, he's a softy under all that primness.'

'Nevertheless.'

Fraser nodded and headed out of the study door. Bob moved over to the desk and seated himself behind it. He was busy making notes in his beautiful copperplate handwriting when James Dove came into the room. Bob stood up. 'Come and sit down Mr Dove. This must have been a terrible shock to you. I'm sorry for your loss.' Bob spoke formally as he looked the Major Domo over.

James Dove was wasn't exactly good looking to start with and shock and grief had done nothing to improve his looks. He pulled out another chair next to the desk and sat down. 'I don't understand why you have to ask us questions. Mr Ratcliff really wouldn't like all these people tramping about the rooms. He didn't like the police much.' He looked up from his seat and the contemplation of his hands and offered Bob a hint of a smile. 'He always said you were meddlers.'

'We are. We poke and pry until we know everything about everyone and then when we're sure of our facts we go away.'

'Yeah.' James' lips twitched in a parody of a grin. 'Leaving chaos in your wake.'

'Possibly. Now, Mr Dove, because of the enquires yesterday and the sudden death of Mr Ratcliff overnight we have to poke and pry a bit more. First could you verify something? I understand Mr Ratcliff informed you that the police would be coming here on Monday morning?'

'Yeah, told us Sunday evening Inspector Jakob was coming. Had me phone Fraser at home, wanted him to come in and speak to him personal about it.'

'Thank you, that's helpful. Now, I need you to tell me about your activities for the last twenty-four hours. I understand you live in. So start by telling me when you last saw your boss alive.'

James nodded. Bob could see him working out the import of the question as well as the answer. 'You think someone done him in don't you?'

Bob McInnis gave a fractional nod of the head. 'We have to consider that idea.'

James gave another nod. 'I locked up about nine, nine-thirty. He was tired. He was having a bit of a go at me; he didn't mean anything by it. I had served his dinner and I was clearing away, and he was just having a little poke.' James shook his head. 'He knew I had a boat with Joe, he sort of hinted that it was very convenient for me, Joe dying. I don't think he meant it serious-like. But he liked to poke himself.' James' cheek twitched slightly. 'Then he went and sat down and asked for a brandy and got his book. I knew he was tired then, because he normally would have gone on a bit longer.'

'What time would that be?'

'About eightish, I brought the brandy and then I

went and loaded the dishwasher and took Polly into his bedroom. He came through about nine-fifteen as I was turning down the bed and setting his medicine out on the bedside table along with his spray. He told me to lock up and he wouldn't want me until this morning.' James shrugged. 'That's how he was.'

'Did you open the window in the bedroom?'

'No.' James shook his head. 'I only opened it if he asked, it weren't a normal thing.'

'So were you surprised to see it open this morning?'

James gave another small shrug. 'Sometimes he did it himself. I thought he'd been hot, or had a bit of an attack.'

'And you didn't touch the body?'

'No, I told you before.'

'Yes, sir. Now after he went to bed what did you do?'

'Me. I went to my own room. He's got a bell he can ring if he wants me in the night.' James looked up again with an almost pleading look. 'I mean he could. Only he didn't. So it must have been a sharp attack, mustn't it?'

Bob saw the guilt, but he wasn't sure it was guilt of murder. 'We don't know how he died yet, sir.' He watched the frown.

'So it might not be my fault.'

'Fault?'

'I was a bit short with him. I wondered if he didn't like to ring and it got worse before he could get me to come. But you think something killed him...or someone?' James shook his head. 'I wouldn't, we got along. We argued and he used to annoy me, but we got on. What do I gain? I'm 46 years old and all I know is butlering. I won't get a job easy after this.'

'No, I don't think it's your fault, Mr Dove. But his death is very convenient for several people. Now, can you tell me how he made his money?'

James raised an eyebrow. 'I dunno much. He had people come with papers. Some of them he kept at the bank. I think he played the stock exchange. He always made sure the household accounts were in order, and he wasn't close with his cash. If I said we needed something he'd order it or tell me to, he didn't check. I could have diddled him but why would I? I had to live here, he'd soon know if I was pulling a fast one.'

'Why would you indeed.' But Bob kept the thought to himself. 'Do you think I could look at your room and this bell?'

James stood up. 'You're going to anyway so it's nice of you to ask.' His cheek twitched again. 'Come on, it's out the back and over the garage.'

16

HARRY WAS JUST BACKING her car out of her garage when Detective Michael Jorkvil drew up that afternoon. She managed to slap the brakes on in time, just. She climbed out and came to meet him. 'OK. It was probably my fault. I was thinking of fresh water.'

Michael raised an eyebrow and looked at the two cars, bumper to bumper in the driveway. 'That's what bumpers are for, to bump against, but you didn't so it's alright.'

Harry smiled at him. 'That's nice of you. Are you sure? I thought I felt a jolt.'

'No it's fine.' He looked her over, even without the evidence of her sitting in a car he would have known she was going out. He admired the trim figure presented to him and did experience a little jolt of his own. But it had nothing to do with cars. 'Can you spare five minutes.'

'Yeah, I was just going round the coast to look at a stream.' She lifted her hand, looked helplessly at it, and then said 'Ah!' and went back to the driver's door, opening it and pulling out the keys; she grinned across the roof at him and walked towards him without shutting the door.

Michael raised both eyebrows, took the key from her unresisting hand, walked back and shut and locked the car door and came back to her. Harry was still standing with a blank look on her face.

'I'm not sure this is such a good idea.' He murmured the words as he edged her towards her front door. Harry returned from whichever planet she'd gone to visit as he competently opened her front door again and ushered her inside.

'Sorry. I was thinking. You look quite Slavic in a good light. I wonder what other things you've got in your ancestry.'

'I'm a mongrel, like the rest of the British.' Michael found her preoccupation with his origins strange, but he had other things on his mind.

He waited for a moment to see if she would invite him further into the house but she'd gone off again, so he took the initiative and led the way into her sitting room. 'Miss Branwell, I had an idea about a case, I was wondering if you could help.'

'Do call me Harry.'

'You are the most unlikely looking Harry I've ever come across, why on earth…?'

'Work, if they think it's another man they're writing to, their attitude is so…o different.'

'What happens when they finally meet you?'

Harry grinned. 'I blind 'em with science, and if that doesn't work I play the helpless little woman card, thereby confirming all their prejudices, but getting my own way anyway.'

'Hmm!' He looked at the grin, enjoyed the look on her face for a minute and then mentally shrugged; he needed to concentrate on police work for a few minutes and put aside his personal feelings. 'When we first met...'

'I stood on you; it is nice of you not to hold it against me.'

Michael, reflecting that he'd like to hold her against him any day, felt his lips curve upwards, but dragged his mind from that particular gutter long enough to finish the sentence. 'As I said, when we first met, you were at a café in the town. I and my partner were on surveillance there, trying to catch a group of pickpockets. We believe that your 'accident', he offered a smile, 'with Professor Kegan, was a distraction which gave them an opportunity to pick a few more pockets. I was wondering what else you might have noticed then. People and what they were doing?' He watched the absent look steal back onto her face and nodded to himself.

Harry moved over to a dining-room chair and settled on it, still frowning. 'I was worrying about my current obsession with the gribbles, part of my mind was on that and part on Suki.'

'Suki?'

'Next door neighbour's dog. I'd taken her to the vet, so I wasn't really there.' She gave a faint grin. 'I remember, there was a woman with a new hairdo, it looked like candy floss, all stiff, and there were three boys about eighteen or so.' She looked at the rather nice suit and silk shirt in front of her. 'I do hate this habit of wearing their pants at half mast and showing off their boxers.' She wrinkled a nice nose in disgust.

'Who else?' She stared at the pearl tie pin displayed in front of her nose. 'There was a gaggle of girls, a bald guy, a couple of older women, and a really ugly man. But he gave a woman with a pram a nice smile.' She frowned a bit more. 'No can't think of anyone else. They were just drinking coffee, and talking to each other or playing with their mobiles.' She looked at Michael's face. 'Sorry.'

Michael Jorkvil nodded, 'That's fine; it confirms our other witnesses. We can narrow it down a bit more and see where that gets us.'

Harry nodded. 'Are you still on duty?' She glanced at her watch.

''Fraid so, until six. I'll let you go look at you stream.'

Harry nodded again. 'I need to talk to a couple of fishermen.'

'I'll let you get on.' Michael moved back and watched her stand up and wriggle the legs of her tight jeans down. 'You take care.'

She walked with him to the door and watched him get into his car and drive off, before she turned and locked her front door and got into her car. She backed out with care and applied her mind to the task of navigating the roads that lead towards Silloth.

THE ROAD TO SILLOTH was unexpectedly congested, or so Harry thought as she wended her way towards Abbey Town. Others thought it was congested too. Detective Inspector Bell for one was muttering about afternoon drivers under his breath. Sergeant Gareth ap Rhys shook his black head of hair but continued to manoeuvre the four-wheel drive with masterly patience as he, all unknowing, overtook Harriet Branwell.

'I can hear you thinking, Gareth.'

'And what might I be thinking, Chief.'

'That I'm an impatient bugger.'

'Not me.' Gareth assumed an air of false virtue. 'I was brought up a good Methodist, we don't swear.' He glanced across and grinned at the fuming detective next to him. 'Besides, it's me that's got a date with your daughter tonight. I'll be the one to catch it if we're back too late.'

'Nay. My Clare is too well trained to make a fuss.' Sandy sighed and then shrugged, changing the subject. 'I'm sure this isn't the kill site even if they do think they've found the place he went into yon river.'

'I agree with you, chief, but...'

'Aye. It might be the place he drowned, but it wasn't the place the murder took place, Gareth.'

Gareth nodded. 'It's technically the murder site.'

'Technicalities.' Sandy was feeling grumpy. He didn't care for outdoor murders, even in summer. He didn't like murder at all, but muddy fields held even less attraction when he had to visit them on foot.

Gareth spun the wheel and took the Land Rover onto a dusty trackway with grass growing up the middle. They jolted along for a minute or two before Sandy said, 'This is a road?' With a quirk of the eyebrow.

'It is indeed a road, badly in need of repair and attention, but nevertheless...' Gareth slowed to a stop and pulled on the brake. He glanced across at his passenger, then nodded at the gate seen through the windscreen about ten yards ahead. 'It's shank's pony from here, Chief.'

Both men climbed out and slammed doors. Sandy sniffed air redolent of manure and scowled before tracking the smell to a friendly Friesian peering at him over the hedge at the side of the roadway. He looked down and noted the deep ruts in front of the gate.

'Forensics have taken casts and will get back to us. We've eliminated the tractor and trailer belonging to the farmer. There are several trail bikes and a big monster, Yamaha or Harley. Can't be sure which yet. There's also a wide wheelbase vehicle which the farmer says doesn't belong to him.' Gareth nodded at the sign on the ground and watched his boss quartering the ground with his eyes.

'OK.' Sandy Bell looked across, and a faint smile crossed his face so that Gareth wasn't sure he'd even seen it. 'Let's go and see what else you've found since this morning.'

17

'WE'VE GOT AN INFORMER in the ranks.'

'He's got to be found.'

The room was quiet. The only sound the hum of a computer, the flick of a fluorescent light whose life expectancy could now be measured against a mayfly's and the thoughts of the two men sitting drinking tea from two large white mugs. The silence had been going on for five minutes. Now Sandy Bell broke it with all the finesse of a pile driver hitting plate glass. 'How dare a copper be bent in my nick?'

'Or any other.' Bob murmured the words and waited for Sandy to get over the initial anger. He'd known how Sandy would react; that's why he'd demanded tea before they took it to the Super upstairs.

'You're positive?' Sandy said the words, but he knew that Bob wouldn't make a mistake with something as serious as this.

Bob nodded. 'Both Fraser Wilson and James Dove said that Mr Ratcliff had called them in and spoken to them Sunday evening. He informed both that there would be a visit from the drugs squad on Monday morning and that they were to be co-operative. He even named Jakob.'

'Bloody hell!'

Bob winced as he watched Sandy straighten his tie and push back his chair with a scrape against the wooden flooring. He too stood, twitching his jacket into place and shooting his cuffs down, running a hand over his hair to smooth it out. He followed his partner, and friend, upstairs to the Superintendent's office.

A brief moment later and a quick rap, and they went into the quiet office. It smelt slightly of perfume and roses.

Bob eyed the small bouquets of red flowers on the desk and filed the query for future investigation, now definitely wasn't the time to ask about them.

'Ma'am, we have a serious problem.'

An inclination of the head and the Super sat back in her chair, removing her reading glasses the better to listen to the report. 'Bob.'

'Ma'am.' Bob began to detail the course of the enquiry so far. 'Inspector Jakob was chasing down a drugs link, and visited the home of Mr Ratcliff yesterday. We had been called to a suspicious death out at Brownrigg. Our death, a Joseph Jenkins, turned out to be one of the people that Jakob's was investigating. We decided to see if there was a connection and went for a preliminary enquiry yesterday afternoon. Further to that we went back there this morning; where we discovered that Mr Ratcliff had also died under, possibly, suspicious circumstances.'

'Is this going to involve lots of money and the drugs and customs office?' The Super smiled at them but the smile faded, it should have won at least a glimmer, but the faces of Sandy and Bob had apparently become frozen.

'Probably, Ma'am. However the problem is that Mr

Ratcliff not only knew that there was going to be a raid, but the name of the officer leading it. He also knew our names when we arrived yesterday. We only decided to visit over the lunch hour. He was prepared for us too. Knew our names and why we were there.'

Sandy glanced at Bob. Bugger, he'd missed that bit yesterday. Annoyance with himself only fuelled an already volatile temper. 'We've got an informer. If we can't trust our own men who can we trust?' He almost spat the words.

'Very true, Inspector Bell.' She raised a well shaped eyebrow as Bob frowned at Sandy. 'Who is aware of your findings?'

'We came straight to you, Ma'am.' Bob spoke in soothing tones, as he transferred his attention back to his superior.

'Very well. I will organise an internal investigation. I will deal with it. You appear to have two murders to cope with. I take it you trust Sergeant ap Rhys?'

Sandy looked scandalised. 'Gareth? Of course I do!'

'Then I suggest you take him into your confidence and work from there.'

'Yes, Ma'am.' Sandy nodded.

'I will find him, or her, Inspector Bell. This is my nick too.' A glimpse of her well bottled temper poked through the refined accents, and Bob gave an involuntary and miniscule shudder.

'Thank you, Ma'am.' The pair turned and headed back to their own office, before they got there, however, Sandy veered off and went up the stairs two at a time. Bob, puzzled but willing, followed his partner and emerged out on the roof top.

'I think for a while I'll be bringing you up to date here, or home, Bob.'

'Yeah.'

'WHEN CAN I GO home?' Hugh move restlessly on the bed and lay looking at the nurse. She had a Swedish accent and a strong personality; it almost had a life of its own. She didn't look as though she would allow more than shallow breathing under the bed covers, and regarded all patients as something that made her ward look untidy.

'Not today, Professor. You must wait for the doctors to pronounce.'

Hugh shook his head. He'd heard that phrase before; it usually meant the body was dead. Maybe he was. Perhaps this was a punishment for procrastination, forced to lie idle when he wanted to get on with something. Like that poor chap from the book '1984', Winston Smith, in room 101. The nurse pulled the covers even tighter and smiled at him. At least he hoped it was a smile.

He relaxed slightly as she marched away, and then he looked at the clock. Nearly seven in the evening, and half the visiting time over. As much as he hated to admit it, he was hoping that Harry would come and visit him. He was so fed-up of his own thoughts. He therefore warmly welcomed Michael Jorkvil as he strolled onto the ward five minutes later.

'Hello Professor. How are you feeling now?'

'Much better. They won't give me a day for discharge, but at least I'm only seeing one of you now.' He offered a smile.

Michael pulled up an institutional green plastic chair and sat at the side of the bed. 'We've been in contact with your ex down in London. She seemed genuinely upset that you'd been hurt and she has a cast iron alibi. A new prospective husband and a visit to an ante-natal class.'

'Yeah! That's great!' Hugh grinned, then paused before saying, 'Should you be telling me that?'

'She asked me to pass on the message and says if you checked your e-mail you would have known about it three weeks ago.'

'Whoops!' Hugh exchanged a smile with Michael. 'Still, that's me all over and she knows what I'm like. So, what can I do for you now?'

'I know you don't know if anything is missing yet. I wondered if you'd had any other ideas about this break-in, however.'

Hugh shook his head regretfully. 'Nope. I'm still in the dark about it. I sent a note to Mr Ratcliff, the man whose library I'm using, to tell him I'm stuck in hospital. But I understand he died today.' Hugh looked sad. 'He was a funny old guy, but he had some great papers he was letting me look at.'

Michael sat still for a minute and Hugh wondered what he was thinking. Finally he spoke. 'This would be Mr Henry James Ratcliff?'

'Yeah, that's the man.'

'How did you come to hear of his death?'

'A Detective Inspector Bell came by to ask a few questions. He seemed to think the attack on me might be related.

Michael nodded. 'I haven't caught up with current gossip in the station. My partner and I have been out of the office all day; I'll have a word with DI Bell. See if he thinks it ties in.'

Hugh waited, watching the man. 'Have you spoken to Harry?'

'Harriet nearly ran me down a couple of hours ago. And, yes, I've had a word with her. However, I was asking about the spate of pickpockets which I and my partner are currently investigating. You and she provided a wonderful diversion last Friday, I was wondering if she had noticed anything.'

'Harry!' Hugh gave a choke of laughter. 'She usually has her head in the clouds, or the ocean rather. I doubt she would notice someone dancing stark naked.'

'Actually she was surprisingly accurate in her recall of the people present.' Michael smiled. 'Once I managed to drag her mind away from her precious gribbles. She was going to look at them I think.'

'Oh, yeah. She told me about that. I went with her for a preliminary recce, somewhere down near Abbey Town it is.'

'When was that?'

Hugh frowned. 'Sunday, I think.'

Michael pursed his lips. Frowned and then said, 'I'm getting distracted.'

'Harry does that to you.'

'Yeah.' Michael grinned. 'So. This café near the cathedral. Can you remember who was there when Harriet knocked you over on Friday?'

Hugh frowned. 'Not really. Some woman who screeched like a parrot. Three teens. I only remember them because their MP3 player was so loud I could hear it without the earphones.' He shrugged. 'A woman and baby, I had to walk round her push-chair.' He shrugged again. 'Sorry. I'd barely arrived before I left, if you follow.'

Michael smiled. 'Don't worry, it was just a hunch. I'm asking around.' He pushed back the chair and stood up. 'If you have any more thoughts you can always ring me.' He laid down his card, on the overhead bed table, with a slight click of the cardboard, and nodded at Hugh.

'I don't think it's likely, somehow.'

'We'll be in touch about your attack.'

'OK.' Hugh watched him leave the ward and settled back against the pillows, reflecting on the fact that his head was aching again and maybe, just maybe, the doctors might be wise to keep him in for a bit longer.

'HOW MUCH LONGER WILL they be there?'

'I don't know Mrs MacGillivray.' James sighed and lowered his hind quarters onto the hard kitchen chair. 'They seemed to have moved out of the bedroom, but there's a strip of yellow tape over the doorway and a big policeman guarding it.

'Well, can I go home? I've put a casserole in the oven for you.'

James shook his head. 'I'm not hungry.'

'You still have to eat, James.'

James just looked at her and then through her. The housekeeper gave a sigh of her own before turning to switch the kettle on yet again. She was staring sightlessly out of the kitchen window when Sandy and Bob walked in.

They looked at the two silent people and exchanged a glance before Bob cleared his throat. 'We have released your rooms, Mr Dove.' He looked across at the housekeeper now standing leaning against the sink with her arms crossed over her formidable bust. He swung his eyes back to James.

'The rooms that have been taped are to be left for now. A constable will be left on duty overnight. I'm sorry but they will be changing shift. Depending on the results of the Post Mortem we will be able to free up the house. Do you know who Mr Ratcliff's solicitor might be?'

James stood up and came over, saying, 'I'll find the letter unless...' He looked from one officer to the other. 'It's in his bedroom.'

'Right, sir, lead the way.' Sandy was left standing in the kitchen looking at the housekeeper. Her eyes were red in a face pasty with grief and tiredness.

'Can I go home?' She walked over and lowered herself into the chair James had been occupying. 'I don't know what I'm supposed to do. Do I come back tomorrow? What'll James do? He's feckless in a kitchen.' She looked for help from the Sandy Bell.

'You can certainly go home. But as to whether you

come back tomorrow I can't help you there.' He came over and sat down at the table next to her. 'I should keep coming in for a few days anyway. I should imagine the estate will pay your wages.' He offered a half smile. 'Tell me about your boss.'

'What do you want to know?'

Sandy wrinkled his nose. What did he want to know? 'What kind of a boss was he?'

'He was particular. He had a special diet, for his heart I think. Special tea.'

'Yes, we've got that.'

Mrs MacGillivray shrugged. 'It's just tea. I wasn't allowed in all the rooms. I couldn't clean in the book room. James cleaned and hoovered in there. He was generous with housekeeping money. He liked nice food. But he was private. I get a good wage. Or I did.'

'Did he have people to dine? Relatives?'

'Don't think he had any. He hasn't had anyone in for a meal for months; Christmas would be the last time. An American man. He stayed two nights.'

'Name?'

She looked up from contemplation of her rather large and red hands. 'Mr Ratcliff called him Charlie.'

'Anyone else?'

'Local man; I don't know his name. He came for half an hour sometimes, once he played chess.'

'How do you know he was a local?'

Edith MacGillivray sniffed. 'He came on foot and left

his dog outside.'

Sandy looked up as Bob came back in with James. He noted Bob's nod and then returned to the middle-aged face next to him. 'What did you think of the parrot?'

'Polly.' A smile strayed over her face and quickly left. 'Daft bird. Leaving her seed on the floor. He loved that bird. About the only thing he showed any real affection for.'

'Has she been found yet?'

A negative shake came from the two retainers.

'Alright. Thank you. Bob?'

'Mr Dove gave me the will. Small safe, designed to looked like a dictionary on the bookshelf. The team had dusted but not opened.'

Sandy nodded. 'We will be back tomorrow. I should get an early night. Where's the young man Fraser?'

'He's gone to fetch some fresh bread and milk. The copper on the door said it would be alright.' James looked at the two men with worry writ large on his stove-in face.

Sandy nodded again. 'Fine. Tell him he can go home as well.'

FRASER, WHEN HE GOT the message, went home with more haste than grace. He banged the front door and went into the kitchen calling his mum's name.

Jane looked up from the crossword she was working on at the kitchen table. 'What's up, love?'

'Boss is dead.' Fraser pulled out a chair with a scrape of wood on lino and almost fell into the seat. 'They think he's bin murdered, mum. It was horrible.' He settled down to tell her all the not so gory details. 'They asked all sorts of questions, mum. Where I'd been, and who with, and could I prove it. Only you can't if you don't know you have to, can you?'

Jane patted his hand. 'So how was he killed?'

'I dunno.'

'But you said he was murdered. How could they tell?'

Fraser rubbed his nose. 'I dunno that either. It wasn't as if he'd got a knife stuck in him or a gun smoking on the carpet.' He frowned. 'I dunno, Mum. Now you come to ask. But they seemed sort of sure.'

Jane shook her head. 'I suppose this means you've lost your job again, love.'

Fraser sighed. 'Yeah. I liked it too. I was gonna ask if I could look at his library. I hadn't quite got the nerve up.' He offered a lop-sided smile. 'James said I should keep turning up until the solicitors had contacted him or the police. He says we've still got to keep the house going if they want to sell it.'

'He sounds a very sensible man. What's he going to do?'

'I don't know, but he's out of work too now. And it'll be a lot harder for him than me. He won't have a home either.'

Jane nodded, biting her lip while she thought. 'You tell him he can have the back bedroom if he's stuck. Just until he's sorted.'

Fraser looked at his mother in surprise.

'Well, he's been good to you, Fraser, and I hate to see anyone stuck.' She offered a quick smile. 'And the rent for lodgings wouldn't hurt us.'

'OK, I'll let him know. I'm going up for a shower.'

'Are you out tonight?'

'Nah. I'm gonna have t' watch the pennies now.' Fraser gave her a half smile and went clattering upstairs.

Jane sat on at the kitchen table, frowning in thought and biting some more on her maltreated lip. Her first reaction was to ring Dot and tell her what was happening, but she didn't want to worry Dot unnecessarily. There was no reason the police would need to talk to them. That's what Dot had said yesterday, and a night's sleep had her agreeing. Nevertheless she was worried for Fraser. He really did want to go to college without a huge debt at the end of it. He was determined to save, but jobs were so hard to find. The temptation to pick a few more pockets was strong. Fraser would have been horrified at the thoughts his mother was indulging in.

SANDY AND BOB WERE sitting on hard chairs in Sandy's back garden. It was still a nice evening, though the dusk was drawing the shadows in blurred outlines on the grass. Their respective children were asleep and Bob's wife was in the kitchen drying up dishes as Sandy's wife washed them. Both women were in view of the two men.

Sandy smiled at his Sarah as she pushed back her nut brown hair with a sudsy wrist and said something that had Jenny laughing, then he turned his head and looked at Bob, also watching the women.

'Bob?'

'Yeah. I was just enjoying the moment, Sandy.'

'Aye. But…' He sighed.

'Aye.' Bob wrinkled his nose. 'The case, before we start worrying about who's crooked in the nick.'

Bob pulled out his notebook and began to bring Sandy up to date. 'Edith MacGillivray she's got a solid alibi and no reason to wish Ratcliff dead. For that matter none of them have, they'll all be out of jobs.'

'Unless he's left them a pile in the will.' Sandy shook his head as Bob sniffed.

'Unlikely. This special tea I was hearing about. It's just a high end green tea. I suspect it hasn't paid import duty, but that's all it is, tea.'

'I like a nice cuppa myself, Bob.'

'I don't think you'd like this stuff, tastes like mouldy grass.'

'You never went and tasted…' Sandy looked horrified.

'Nah. One of Jenny's colleagues is for ever touting the benefits of green tea, antioxidants and stuff. No, I don't think the cook is guilty of anything except maybe bad cooking. We'll know better when we get the PM back. Fraser, the handyman. He's bright enough, bit ambitious, wants to go to uni. He didn't understand some of the questions and if he's committed a crime he doesn't know how to set up an alibi for toffee.'

'Which brings us to James Dove.'

'Which brings us to Dove. He's been up to something, Bob.'

'Yes. I don't know what yet but...' Bob glanced up for his notes. 'He sleeps above the garage. Fraser reckons the car was out Sunday night. Dove never mentioned it. Now he's a bit Mutt and Jeff, and I don't think he is. He wasn't there, or he took that car out himself.'

'What kind of car?'

'Nice old Daimler. No steering lock. You could push it out onto the street and start it that way, or jump it with a couple of wires. It purrs, Sandy, lovely beast.'

'So, which do you incline to, Bob?' Sandy ignored the glint in Bob's eye. He liked nice cars, but he wasn't keen on old ones.

Bob grinned, accepting the partial change of subject. 'I don't think he was there. He's eaten up with guilt that his boss might have rung for him and he wasn't there to answer in the hour of need.'

'So you don't think it was a murder?'

'I ain't speculating until after Jonesy gets back to us.'

'Where do you think he was?'

'Now there, Sandy, you have me.' Bob shook his sleek head. 'He could have been off murdering Jenkins.'

'Aye.' Sandy wrinkled his nose. 'He could have been dealing drugs.'

'Yeah, if they knew Jakob was visiting next day he might have been doing a little house cleaning. Do we think he's capable, Sandy?'

'I think any man is capable if he thinks he might be locked up for a crime, Bob.'

Bob grunted and sat back on the hard seat. Sandy sat back too and looked up at the fading blue sky. He kept his eyes on a cloud as he began to detail his own activities.

'We're pretty sure now that Jenkins was dumped in the river and the tide took him out to where we found him, not brought him in. Forensics are checking tyre prints and tracks. He was a nasty piece of work, Bob. He'd gone up market a bit in the drugs world. The crowd he was running with were dealing with class A and B. Jakob's right to be sore about it. He was moving in on the gang, and now he's lost a player and the whole lot have gone to ground. Jakob thinks Jenkins was using his fishing skip to bring the stuff into the country via Silloth.'

'It's not the first place you think of for a drugs racket, Sandy.'

'No. which is why Jakob thinks he was using it.'

'So do you think it was a deal gone sour?'

'It's what it's shaping up like. And God help us if that is the case, Bob. Because half of them have holed up over on Man and the rest have disappeared into the undergrowth. I can't find any connection, save that he visited your man, that would tie Ratcliff into the drugs trade.'

Bob grimaced, still watching the clouds. 'So do we pull James Dove in and see if he had a finger in the pie, or do we leave him and see who makes contact?'

Sandy glanced over at Bob. 'I'll let you know when I've thought about that.'

'Which brings us to our informer. Because whatever we decide we have to make sure Dove doesn't get to know about it beforehand.'

Sandy nodded. 'Gareth was put out.'

'Put out! When I saw him he was ready to spit bricks, and I just hope we catch him before Gareth does, or he'll be mincemeat.' Bob smiled, whoever it was would be mincemeat if Sandy Bell caught them first too. 'Jonesy's preliminary was interesting on Jenkins. He says knocked over then dumped. His liver was mincemeat too; he wouldn't have survived even if someone had found him, Sandy.'

Sandy grimaced. 'Aye not a nice way to go, Bob.' He watched a blackbird shouting on his ridge tile for a moment, before saying, 'It's going to be hard to co-ordinate without letting the men know what we're planning, but I think we can do it this way.'

Bob nodded as Sandy talked on in the gathering dusk.

18

HARRY WAS PEERING INTO the gathering dusk too. She could see the incipient signs of damage on the small stanchion, and cocked her head on one side while she listened to an older man in need of a shave talking about flood waters. 'Yes, I agree, a good solid tree trunk and the whole lot will go. We don't want a repeat of Cockermouth. I'll write up the report and get the council on to it as a matter of priority.' She offered him a smile and got one in return.

'Did you hear, young missy, as how they found a body, found it up the stream they did. He would have knocked out the bridge and no mistake.'

Harry took her attention from the muddy stream and looked at a pair of bright green eyes in a face that hadn't seen a razor in days, possibly because no razor yet invented could have got between the creases. 'What?'

'They did find a body I heard, yesterday it was, some poor soul fell in the ditch and drownded.'

'Oh! How terrible.' Harry stepped away from the bank slightly.

'Aye, you'm be careful missy. One body is plenty. I'll walk you to your car, young thing like you, out alone.'

Harry looked at the elderly specimen in front of her. He looked as if a good puff of wind would blow him over. She accepted the arm gallantly offered, nevertheless.

Michael Jorkvil was waiting by the side of the road. He was leaning against his car and apparently watching the passing scenery.

'Hello, Harry.'

'Good grief, how on earth did you find me, Detective Jorkvil?'

'We have our ways.'

Harry nodded at the ancient gent hanging onto her arm. 'Jock and I were just checking out the bridge.'

'I thought you and Hugh did that on Sunday.'

Harry cast him a curious look. 'We did.'

'Do you know him?' It was a sibilant whisper.

Harry turned and looked at the old face. 'Yes. He's a policeman.'

'That's OK then.' Jock peered at Michael Jorkvil, giving him another long look. 'I thought I knew you, but now I get closer I sees you ain't him.' He turned to Harry. 'In you gets, Missy, night's drawing in now.' He held her door and watched her climb in and fasten her seat belt. 'Tain't no time to be jawing in the countryside.'

'I'll follow you, Harry. OK? I want another word.'

Harry nodded and started her engine. Michael got back in his car and started it, swinging the car around in the narrow lane and offering Jock a brief hand wave as he passed the old man walking towards his car.

Harry was half conscious of the escort behind her, but she was more intrigued to know how he'd found her in the first place. She pulled up at her house and saw Michael parking neatly on the street. He got out, slamming the door and coming around and up her driveway.

'How did you find me then?'

Michael grinned. 'I told you we have our ways.'

'Hmm!' She stood looking at him.

Michael scratched at his chin, looking down at her. 'Actually I was heading out to our murder scene and saw your car parked up. I came back after I'd dropped off something my oppo asked me to deliver, and you were still parked, so I stopped.'

Harry remained leaning against her car. 'Murder! Jock seemed to think it was an accident. Drowning?'

Michael shook his head. 'Murder.'

'Nasty.'

'Not my case. I was just an errand boy this evening.'

Harry opened her mouth to make another comment, looked at the face in front of her and decided that she'd change the subject. 'How did you know I'd been there Sunday?'

'Hugh told me.'

'Hugh?'

'Yeah. We're trying to catch a ring of pickpockets centred on the café where you met him; I was hoping he might have seen something. Now do you think I can come in? I'm off duty now.'

Harry offered a grin. 'We...ll Jock seemed to think I'd be safe enough with you.' She raised an eyebrow and got a faint grin in return.

Michael shook his head. 'Don't be too trusting, Harry.'

Harry cocked her head on one side and observed that the grin didn't go to his eyes. She went faintly pink at the rebuke.

THE SETTING SUN HAD a tinge of red about it. James Dove was sitting in the cabin area of the small boat that he and Joe Jenkins had owned together. He didn't know what to do with himself.

He had tidied the house and wandered about, but the police were still very much a presence in the building. Big burly men who made him feel acutely uncomfortable.

Eventually he'd asked if it was alright if he took his car to go and get the groceries and the officer on duty had shrugged and said he could see no reason why not.

Now the car was sitting in a car park five minutes walk away, on the outskirts of Silloth.

He sipped hot tea from the tin mug in his hand and felt the gentle sway of the boat as it moved to the tide. He gazed out at the open sea and wondered if he could live on a boat all the time. He had a good bit put away. Living in, and with all his meals provided had meant he could save, for that at least he was thankful. But there wasn't enough to buy a house and, anyway, he didn't want to retire and sit in misery.

He looked up as the boat gave an extra wobble and the tea slopped over onto his fingers. He shook his maltreated members as he looked up.

Gareth was standing on the gang plank, looking at him. 'May I come aboard, sir?'

James Dove looked at the uniform and the six foot of black haired giant and wondered how he could prevent it! He gave a nod, standing up and setting aside his mug. 'Of course, Sergeant. How can I help?'

'I understand this boat belonged to Mr Jenkins.' Gareth took two strides and was in the cockpit with James.

'We shared it, but it mainly belongs to me.' James shook his head. 'I suppose it all belongs to me now.'

'I need to search the boat, sir.'

'Search... What like customs?'

'Yes, sir.'

James Dove offered and expansive hand. 'Feel free, Officer.' He stood back and indicated the small space.

Gareth offered him a half smile and turned to nod to a couple of men and a woman standing waiting on the pier, one of whom had a dog on a leash. They advanced and nodded at James Dove. 'If you'd mind stepping ashore for a minute, sir.' It might have been a request, but it was going to be obeyed.

Gareth followed him down the gangway, cursing quietly under his breath. It had taken them half the afternoon to get the customs people and locate the mooring. Dove being on board meant that anything incriminating was probably already over the side. There was nothing he could do about it however, he smiled grimly and moved next to Dove dwarfing his smaller figure.

Both men appeared to watch the black and tan dog going up the gangplank wagging its tail, nose to the ground.

'I'm told a German shepherd has up to 220 million olfactory nerves.' Gareth was watching Dove now.

'Have they.' Nothing but interest showed on Dove's lined face as he turned to look at the sergeant. 'I always wanted a dog, but living in I couldn't, and the boss didn't like any animal save a daft parrot.'

'Have you been here long, sir?'

'Just arrived. My tea's still hot.' James looked at his neglected mug with a faint sigh as it sat next to the helm.

'How often do you take her out, she looks a nice neat boat?'

'Once or twice a week.'

'Catch much?'

'Bit of lobster, bit of mackerel. Caught a salmon once, but that was a rarity.' Dove looked at the boat. 'She's a bit of a handful on my own. I crewed mainly.'

'And when do you go out?'

'Depends on the tide. Joe liked night fishing.'

'Oh, did he now.' But Gareth kept the thought to himself and wondered if the man before him felt safe, or was just innocent. 'Living in, it must have been difficult to get away at night.' He watched the colour rise in the cheeks and Dove looking fixedly at the men on board as they lifted up creels and ropes.

'I'm never going to forgive myself for that. Not being there when the boss died. I was supposed to answer his bell if he felt ill, and I wasn't there.'

Gareth waited with monumental patience to see if anymore unconsidered trifles would fall from the guileless lips. But James Dove just shook his head and continued to look at the men.

Gareth nodded to them as one poked into the fuel space and another leaned precariously over the side and checked inside the fenders and old tyres decorating the side of the boat. 'Do you have a buyer for your fish?'

'Never caught enough for there to be a need.'

'It's a good fishing ground twixt the three kingdoms.'

James Dove nodded. 'We didn't get that far out. Stayed between here and Man mostly.'

'And thank you for that.' Thought Gareth, storing up the crumbs of information. He smiled as the dog handler looked up and gave him a faint shake of the head before all three of the customs officials came back down the gangway. 'Thank you for your co-operation, sir. We appreciate it.'

'No bother, Officer.' James Dove nodded at the four personnel. 'Can I go back on board?'

'Yes, that's fine.'

James walked up and went to retrieve his mug, flinging the contents into the sluggish swell and going under the canopy to make himself another brew as the officials walked away.

'Well?' Gareth strode ahead with the man and dog.

'Masie didn't react. If there have been drugs there, they're long since gone.'

'Damn.'

The custom's man shrugged. 'You win some, you lose some. Sorry we couldn't get here earlier.'

'Couldn't be helped.' Gareth offered a hand as the man slammed the tailgate and Masie looked at them through the wire mesh. He watched the van drive away and turned to his own car. He had some news anyway for DI Bell. Chances are they already knew, but he'd pass on his gleanings.

'TWO DAYS AND WE'RE still no further forward with this blasted murder.'

'Give us a chance, Sandy.'

'If we didn't have to work in this hole in corner fashion we could get going. I'm second guessing myself and eyeing the men. It's not good for working relationships, Bob.'

It had been a frustrating day so far, information was beginning to dribble in from forensics, statements were piling up like a snow drift on their desks and both men were finding it difficult. Sandy had swapped the teams around out at the stream site, so that he was working with completely different men; though Gareth was still in charge. He had put them into small groups who didn't know each other and were unlikely to gossip so freely when it came to tracking down witnesses. He had yet other small teams following up leads of sightings in the Silloth area and the Newcastle police were doing their bit at the ferry terminals.

'If Jenkins had been going to board a ferry, then he changed his mind for some reason on Saturday. We need to know why and where he went instead.' Sandy spoke his thoughts aloud.

The trouble was that neither man knew just where to point the finger. 'If it was our insider, then he'd have told him he was being watched.'

'Logical.' Sandy sniffed and scratched at his wiry hair. 'It has to be someone who was either part of Jakob's team, to inform him Saturday, or in the office on Monday.'

'And Jakob has worked with that team for two years now. He trusts them with his life.'

'Aye, he has to, with drug dealers.' Sandy shrugged into his jacket and walked over to the door of the large room. 'See now, Bob, from here I can see five sets of desks in this open plan area. The uniforms come and go but they don't linger, so I think it's a detective.'

Bob nodded reluctantly, he'd come to the same conclusion. 'I don't like it.'

'No more do I then, lad.' Sandy swept the empty room again with his eyes until they swung back to Bob. 'Roof I think.'

'Yeah.' Bob picked up his own jacket and shovelled the notes on his desk into the drawer, turning the lock. He sighed as he watched Sandy walk over to his own desk and do the same thing. 'I hate this.'

'Aye.' Neither man spoke until they had left the room and climbed up onto the roof top, and were once again standing amid the flower beds.

They turned, resting their elbows on the lowish wall and their backs to the distant hills, looking at the door through which they'd come. 'The Super has the roster for Monday and where everyone was supposed to be, but it was lunchtime, men coming back for their butties or stopping off with reports on their way to the canteen. We've narrowed it down to half a dozen.'

'Aye, lad.'

'Do you think it's been going on long, Sandy?'

Sandy gave a slight shrug, then shook his head. 'Don't think so. More things would have gone sour. I don't understand why, Bob?'

'Money. Isn't it always money?' Bob almost growled the words. It was obvious to Sandy that he was really angry under his calm.

Sandy looked at the nice suiting next to him. 'Some would say you don't know what it is to be short, Bob.'

'I...' Bob swallowed. 'You know I haven't always had the cash, Sandy. And what I did have, I earned.'

Sandy waved a placatory hand. 'I know, lad. You've suffered for yours, what little you'll touch.'

'It belongs to Caitlin, my daughter can enjoy it.'

'It belongs to all of you; your Beth wouldn't have wanted you to go without when it was sitting there.'

'I don't. Beth died and her money was left to me, but my daughter comes first. If I don't spend it, it's because I don't need stuff.'

'You don't have to defend yourself to me, Bob.' Sandy offered a wry smile, 'Actually what I was thinking, before you sidetracked me, was who else has been dressing a bit flash lately.'

The tinge of red in Bob's cheeks slowly subsided as

he thought about that. 'Ah! I need to have a think about that one.'

'Well, while you think about it, I'll tell you what Gareth had to report.'

Bob leaned back against the low wall and enjoyed the late sun on his back as he looked at his partner. 'I thought you said you were no further forward.'

'I'm not, but you might be, my lad. These cases are connected.'

Bob nodded. 'Even I don't believe in that much coincidence, Sandy.'

'No, me neither.' Sandy sniffed. 'Anyway. I set Gareth to finding Jenkins' boat out at Silloth and trying to find if it was involved in the drug trade or not. Unfortunately he got there too late. James Dove was already on board.' Sandy flashed a grin. 'And I suffered the wrath of my daughter, she had a date with him.'

Bob frowned. 'Well, the investigation couldn't have waited. But...she does have my sympathy.'

'Wasn't the lad's fault, by the time he'd located it and got the customs people on board, Dove was drinking tea in the galley.' Sandy grinned at Bob, a quick flash of his slightly crooked incisor, before his face went serious again. 'Dove claimed he'd only been there a few minutes. The port authorities agree he hadn't been there long but no-one in authority was watching him. However, there's always someone idling at the seashore, Bob.'

'And.'

'Couple having an ice-cream and gawping at the boats while having an evening stroll. They saw him arrive. He didn't jettison anything. They were watching particular 'cos they thought he might put to sea and they wanted to take a photo. It's a neat little boat according to Gareth.'

Bob raised an eyebrow.

'Seems Gareth's been out on the water a few times with Officer Pretty out from Maryport. It works to our advantage, Bob. He says the main fishing ground for Jenkins and Dove was between the Solway and the Isle of Man. Dove crewed because the boat's a bit big for one man. That they did night fishing by Jenkins choice and...' He put up a hand to forestall the utterance trembling on Bob's lips. 'And, that he wasn't there to answer when his master took ill and died on Monday night.'

'Well I'll be damned!'

'Gareth didn't think Dove had joined up the dots enough to realise we would be talking to each other about both deaths.'

'No. Dove told me he thought his master hadn't been able to call him. He seems to think its natural causes, Sandy.' Bob grinned, then frowned. 'Wait a minute, do you think he could have been there on the Sunday night too. Do we think he arranged to meet Joe Jenkins and killed him?'

'I dunno, lad. But he's lied to you once or twice now.'

'Yeah, I want a word with Mr James Dove.'

Sandy looked at the stern face, but he felt no pity for Dove. They were dealing with murder, only a guilty man or a fool lied in those circumstances.

HUGH FELT A FOOL. He sat out at the side of his bed in an institutional leather chair and looked at the young woman coming down the ward. She offered him a lovely smile and waved a paper bag, nearly catching the pole of a neighbouring patient's drip. He realised, while she offered apologies and charmed the elderly man, that he loved her. 'Oh God! What a stupid thing to do.' He spoke under his breath and summoned up a smile for her.

'Hi, Hugh.' She looked him over somewhat critically. 'Nurse said you were a lot better. I must say you don't look it.'

'Gee, thanks!' He grinned, but it didn't get to his eyes.

'I brought you a doughnut. I thought,' she grinned, 'everyone brings flowers or fruit but what you really want is something tasty.' She deposited the paper bag on the top of the locker and sat her jeans clad bottom on his bed, wriggling back so that she could examine him more closely. 'Would you rather I went away again, Hugh. Have you got a headache?'

'No and yes.' He smiled at her. 'You look very bright.' He admired the light green cashmere jumper and floaty scarf about the slender neck.

'I've been out to Brownrigg to look at my stanchions, written my report and done my good deed for the day.'

'I don't think one doughnut was much of a good deed.' He moved quickly, putting a protective hand over the bag before she could take it away. 'It is much appreciated though.'

'Cheek!' She grinned at him. 'No, my good deed was to give that notebook we found to Detective Jorkvil to pass on. I was quite clever to remember it, don't you think?'

Hugh scowled. 'How did you come to meet Detective Jorkvil?'

'He came to ask me out for a drink, but I said I'd got to see you before visiting was over.'

Hugh swallowed his comments before they could escape. The little green god gave a whimper as he was clouted back into submission. 'It's appreciated.' He looked at her as she became momentarily distracted by the activity of a nurse who'd just stepped onto the ward and halted next to a bed on the far side of the room.

'Do you think I would make a good nurse, Hugh?'

The unbidden and unvoiced 'God forbid and God help the patients' was swallowed. Hugh took a hand that was waving about in an absent manner indicating the busy nursing fraternity, and endangering his body. 'I think you make a brilliant engineer.'

'How tactful of you, love.' Harry gave a chortle of laughter and she turned a pair of bright blue eyes on him. 'What you mean is, they would have their stay extended if I got anywhere near them.'

Hugh opened and shut his mouth a time or two and then offered a small chuckle of his own. 'Perhaps, you're best suited in the job you're in, Harry.' He smiled as she touched him lightly on the shoulder and then said. 'Have you had anymore thoughts about your gribbles?'

'I'm sure there's a bit of deliberate neglect happening in America. Gribble and piddock activity can be halted by fresh water. They live in a saline solution. You only have to shift the boat up stream. This particular boat could have been, and wasn't, moved. I've sent the authorities a nice long e-mail detailing my findings and asking if anyone is missing or travelling to the UK.'

Hugh looked at her suddenly serious face. 'An excellent engineer. Take care, Harry.'

'I thought you didn't believe me.'

'Whether I believe you or not doesn't matter, Harry. I got clonked on the head and there has to be a reason.'

Harry nodded.

'You don't pay attention to what is going on around you, Harry. You get involved and don't notice things.' Hugh risked patting her leg.

'I will be careful, Hugh.' She smiled at him. 'I promise. Now is there anything I can bring in. I rang your Mum by the way, she seems like a nice woman, if somewhat surprised to hear a female voice.'

She raised a nice eyebrow at his quiet, 'Oh bugger.'

He looked at the surprised and slightly worried blue eyes watching him. 'Shouldn't I have…?'

'No. That's fine. I should have called her, I just never thought of it. I'm pretty much a crusty bachelor now.'

'And you talk about me forgetting things.'

'Ah! But I've got a fractured skull.' Hugh lifted his nose in pretended virtue.

'Yeah, sez you. It's only hairline.' Harry wriggled forward on the bed and stood up, smoothing the jeans legs down and straightening up. 'Eat your doughnut. I'll be back tomorrow.'

Hugh took one of the hands moving in front of his face. Standing up he gave her a hug. 'Thank you, Harry. Take care.'

Harry looked somewhat surprised by the fervent manner of the simple words. 'OK, Hugh.' She dropped a kiss on his cheek and walked away, turning at the door to offer him a wave before she disappeared.

Hugh sat down slowly and put a hand on his cheek where the thistledown kiss had landed. 'Oh bugger.' He said it again and much more quietly, and then closed his eyes.

19

Wednesday

WEDNESDAY MORNING WAS CLOUDY. Both Sandy and Bob felt that the issue of betrayal was clouding their brains to the detriment of the investigation. They stood in front of the Super's desk while she talked from her side about the negligible progress she had made.

'I approve of the measures so far taken, Inspector Bell. I also sympathise with your frustration at the slow progress. However,' she laid her glasses on the clean blotting paper and straightened a pile of typewritten sheets at the side with one hand while pushing her black hair behind her ear. 'You have made progress. Other less difficult cases have taken longer.'

She suddenly offered one of her rare smiles. 'Stop beating yourself up, Sandy.' She looked from him to Bob McInnis. 'Now…' she became formal again. 'Have you sufficient men?'

'Yes, ma'am.' Bob answered for both of them. 'Depending on the PM report, which Dr Jones has promised for this morning, we might be able to scale down the investigation at Mr Ratcliff's house today. I should like to keep a couple of men on the search for the parrot?'

'Ah yes, the parrot. Why?'

Bob offered a faint shrug. 'It just niggles, ma'am. A hunch, a smell!'

'Yes, you've had those before, Inspector, and it always pays off. So yes, keep searching for your parrot.' She smiled charmingly at them both.

'Thank you, ma'am.' Bob and Sandy gave her a sketchy salute and left the room.

'Parrot?' Sandy raised a scandalised eyebrow as they walked down the corridor, and by mutual consent headed up the stairs to the roof-top. 'We shall be fit if we have to keep coming up here, Bob.'

Bob only grunted as he pushed open the door to the outside and gave a slight shiver as the early morning mist began to settle on his hair. Sandy, following, put his shoulders back and walked across to the low parapet. He looked around the area, noted the deserted aspect of the place and grinned wryly. 'And it's not my idea of the ideal place to get a cuppa.'

Bob gave a small snort and leaned his body against the wall too, having done his own survey of the area. 'How do you want to divvy up the work today, Sandy?'

'Let's give Jonesy a ring and see what he says.' He suited action to word, pulling out his mobile and pressing speed dial and waiting. Bob watched him as he listened intently to the Medical Examiner. Sandy's face darkened the longer he held the phone.

'Let me guess, murder?' Bob spoke as Sandy flipped the small instrument shut. How?'

'Enough digitalis to kill a horse. He was taking digitalis to keep his heart at a regular strength, but he only required something like 0.5mcg. Jonesy spoke to forensics; they confirm the dose in the pills was huge.'

'Didn't he have a spray? Wasn't that to relieve the pain?'

'Yes, but the spray was water and nitro a weakened mix. It should contained pure nitro-glycerine, it didn't.

'Like the explosive?'

'Aye.'

Bob shook his head and then said. 'Checking the chemists?'

'Done. Reputable, and anyway those come in sealed sprays.' Sandy shook his head.

Bob stood frowning. 'Was...?'

'Aye. Was...?' He cocked his head on one side waiting.

'Was it a new bottle?'

'The man had had it a couple of months. But... there was a proper bottle of the stuff on the side as well.'

'Odd.' Bob paused, thinking about the medication when he'd last seen it in evidence bags. 'Couldn't it just have been an accumulation in his system? Dove told me he set out Ratcliff's meds at night.'

'Could. No fingerprints though, Bob. And it wasn't just the excess Digitoxin, it was the fact that he had some drug called Thiazine in his blood stream. It's a diuretic, it helps you lose water so your heart doesn't have to work so hard, but you shouldn't mix it without careful supervision, and the doctor said he didn't prescribe it.'

'No, that isn't right.' Bob spoke slowly as he thought through the sequence of events. 'There were two sprays and one bottle, not two. So, someone's been playing ducks and drakes with his medication for months, Sandy. He was slowly being poisoned, we can't assume that this death was just convenient anymore.'

'No, lad. It was planned, and no-one would have investigated it if it hadn't happened just when Jenkins body turned up.'

'Don't you have to have blood tests and things?'

Sandy gave a shrug. 'Dunno.' He watched Bob frowning over the information. He held his peace as that man decided what he wanted to do. 'Fraser Wilson has been in Ratcliff's employ for only a few months?'

'Aye?'

'He runs the errands now.'

'Aye?'

'Do we think he's capable of murder? He was very calm yesterday when he was telling us about the death.'

Sandy put his head on one side again. Then shook it. 'Nay then, I think yon lad was calm because he hadn't actually looked, if ye ken.'

Bob nodded. He did understand, a mental understanding rather than a physical encounter meant that Fraser might not have realised the full horror of death in the way that Dove had, and had reacted. 'But does he fetch the meds?'

'We hadn't got as far as asking that one yesterday.'

'OK. I'm going to have a word with Jonesy on my

own account, Sandy, then I'm going back to the house to re-question everyone.'

Sandy nodded. 'I shall be here at my desk this morning; I've got a mountain of interviews and witness statements to wade through. I'll talk to you at lunch time, Bob.'

They both started to walk towards the stair door when it was thrust open by Gareth. 'Chief, Bob.' He gave each a nod. 'Thought I'd find you here.'

'Do you want us both?'

'Just you, Chief.'

Bob offered a wry smile. 'I'll be off.' He disappeared through the door, leaving the other two standing in the dull air.

WHAT'S GOING ON MICHAEL? Helen McKenzie spoke quietly as she looked at her partner and pulled out her chair with a scrape of metal on wood.

'I dunno.'

Helen sat down with a graceful flick of her skirt under her bottom and hitched her seat forward. She looked about the nearly empty squad room, then lowered her voice a bit more. 'Something's in the wind. Maybe it's an audit. I remember the last time they did an audit. All the paperwork!' She scowled at the desk and the usual muddle of casework; open, pending and closed. The cursor of her computer blinked at her from a half filled in form.

Michael Jorkvil shook his head. 'I wasn't here for

that. Or if I was I don't remember it.'

'Believe me, you'd remember.'

She shook her head. 'Let get this lot up to date and then you can tell me what progress you've made.'

Michael looked at his own overflowing in-tray with the expression of a man asked to load the washing machine. 'What, all of it?'

'Believe me if it's an audit this will just be the tip of the iceberg.' Helen nodded at her own desk and pulled the first pile of files towards her.

They had been busy for a good hour and a half before she lifted her head and said. 'I need coffee, Michael. Time for a break; you can update me on our pickpockets.'

'Some break.' Michael's lips pursed a bit wryly, but he stood up and came around the desk. 'OK, boss. What do you want to know?'

'How did the interviews go?'

They began to make their way down to the canteen as they talked.

'I spoke to the pair of old biddies.'

'Don't be disrespectful, Michael. You'll be old one day, and one of those 'old biddies' helped us out on Saturday.'

'Sorry, and you're right.' He gave a half smile. 'They weren't very observant; they did confirm most of the other witness statements. Not many coming and going at that hour, the only person leaving was the young girl, Lesley, with her child. I think we can cross her off the list. Even though she did make contact with Adrian Chappell. That leaves a fairly short list. Hell, we were there, Helen.'

'Yes, I know, that's why I'm so mad.' Helen, arriving at the machine, inserted a coin and waited for it to dispense a cup of hot, but indeterminate, liquid.

'I'M SO MAD WITH myself, for even thinking this way, Dot.'

Dorothy nodded and sipped some coffee. They were once again in the café near the cathedral. The place smelt of hot toast and the coffee they were both drinking. The two women had met up after Jane had finished work for the morning.

'It's odd; it was all a giggle when we first started. But now...well I wonder why we did it.'

'I did it because I was angry for being ignored, Jane. You did it because I persuaded you that it was just a bit of fun. But you're right; it's all turned a bit sour on us.' She looked over at the counter to where another young woman served coffee with far more efficiency and genuine pleasure in her voice than Helen McKenzie had ever achieved. 'I wonder if she's another copper.' She gently tipped her coiffured head towards the waitress as she spoke quietly.

Jane wrinkled her nose, speaking equally quietly. 'I don't know, but I ain't taking any chances. I'm living life as if there's a camera in here.' She gave a look around. 'There might be for all we know.'

'Yes, dear. You're quite right.' Dot nodded and sipped coffee. She glanced around. There were a few people she recognised by sight. The young woman with the pushchair was sitting in a corner, discretely breastfeeding her child. She caught Dot looking and offered a faintly defiant look. Dot gave her a smile and a nod and watched her relax slightly. She saw Jane was looking too and said. 'It's nice to see that.'

'Yeah. There aren't many places were you can be comfortable.' She too looked at the other clientele. 'There are one or two others I know the faces of, Dot, but any of them could be coppers.'

Dot glanced about. 'That ugly guy is in again; his child is very well behaved.'

Jane nodded and emptied her cup. 'Don't worry, Dot. I'm not going to be tempted. I shall have to find another job though, one that pays a bit more than the cleaning. I should have done that instead of…well you know.'

'Yes, I know. But…'She hesitated, 'Don't do anything yet, Jane, I might be able to find you something.' She looked over the table at her friend who was gathering up her handbag. 'Promise?'

Jane stood up as did Dot, she looked at the other woman, took a breath and let it out slowly. 'OK, but don't take too long, Dot, with Fraser losing his job I'm going to need the cash.' She held up a hand. 'And don't you dare offer; I didn't tell you about Fraser for that.'

'I know you didn't, but we're friends.'

'We won't be if…'

'Alright, Jane. Just give me a chance to ask around. Alright?'

'Alright.' Jane offered a half smile and Dot linked arms with her as they walked away from the table and out into the dull day.

BOB MCINNIS WAS SITTING down behind a table. Doctor Ryan Jones sat on the other side of the table, looking with serious grey eyes at the younger man. He pushed a hand through his thick grey hair and sighed rather heavily. 'What can I do for you, Bob?'

Bob eased back on his chair. 'I can come back, Ryan,'

'No, you're fine. It's not you.' He grimaced. 'I don't like to think of anyone in the medical profession who might have engineered a death though.'

'Positive about that.'

'Oh yes.'

'Wouldn't it be picked up by blood tests and things?'

'Yes, if the man had bothered to go for them.' Jones sniffed, then ran a forefinger under his nose. 'You can't blame the doctors, Bob. They're not mind readers, if a patient doesn't go and tell his doctor of any side effects or illnesses the doctor isn't going to chase him up. He's got enough on his plate with those that do present at the door of the surgery.'

'So when did he last see his Doctor?'

'Eleven months ago. He was due for his annual MOT next month. He had high blood pressure, angina, and mild diabetes. His prostate was a bit iffy too. The doctor was aware of all of those things but...the man didn't turn up and it ain't our job to run after patients, we have enough treating those we do see.

'Would the doctor have picked up something then?'

'Oh yeah, blood tests would have shown he was not in a good state. He should have been going for the tests every three months, but he was apparently squeamish and kept putting them off. He slipped through the cracks, yes, but he did have a responsibility for his own health as well, Bob.'

Bob eased back in his chair and frowned in thought. Ryan Jones watched him absorbing information. Finally Bob sighed. 'So whoever did this must have known a bit about the man and a bit about the drugs?'

'He would certainly have to have a working knowledge of the commonly prescribed meds. A trawl through the doctor's computer would perhaps give him an inkling of the man, Bob. We like to think the notes are secure, but any decent hacker could get into some of them, not all doctors are computer savvy enough to have firewalls and safety nets to prevent the public from prying.'

'He was into speciality teas and a few faddy foods.'

'If you're sick, and you can afford it, you'll look at a few alternative routes to health.' Ryan Jonesy settled back in his chair and it squeaked slightly. 'Tea has flavonoids, amino acids, vitamins, and caffeine, recent research shows beneficial effects on blood pressure and heart disease. He had those in abundance. Green tea is the best for those.' The grey eyes twinkled as he looked at Bob over his glasses. 'And knowing you, you'll know more about tea than I would ever want to before the day is out.'

Bob grinned, shook his head but said. 'But if he ordered things over the net…?'

'Yeah that would be another way in. I haven't got all the blood work back yet, Bob.'

Bob nodded and frowned again. 'I've looked at the immediate suspects; none of them struck me as falling into either category, Ryan.'

'Can't help you there, Bob. I'm a doctor not a detective.'

'So you keep telling me.' Bob offered a wry smile and stood up. 'Thanks, Ryan. I'll go and talk to the butler. But I don't think he did it in the parlour with a medicine cup.'

Ryan Jones gave a bark of laughter, despite the seriousness of the situation. 'No, Bob, not unless he's a secret hacker with a chemistry degree too.'

Bob smiled himself and left Ryan Jones to pull a pile of forms forward and get a pen from his pocket.

Bob got his car and drove off to the town house of the late Mr Ratcliff. He felt as though he was taking part in a third-grade thirties movie written by an inferior Agatha Christie look-alike, and he wasn't shining in the part.

HUGH WASN'T SHINING EITHER, he was not a patient, patient, and the discovery he'd made the night before of his feelings for Harriet made him even more impatient with himself. He sat out at the side of the bed and stared out at the patch of dull afternoon sky he could see through the window cut into the opposite wall.

He had been for a CAT scan and an MRI that morning and awaited the results. Part of him wanted to leave the hospital and disappear from general circulation until he'd got a handle on his emotions. He'd spent a considerable part of the night arguing with himself, but the results were rather inconclusive. Now he leaned over and pulled a pencil and note pad off the locker and onto his knee.

He looked around a bit surreptitiously, then drew a line down the centre of the page and headed it pro's and cons. He put his head on one side and then started in the 'con's column. 'Twelve years older. Been married. Procrastinator. I'm set in my ways. She's a klutz.' He looked up, and a wry grin settled on his face as he thought about Harry.

He stared off into space for a few minutes then sniffed and looked down. 'OK.' He spoke softly. 'Pro's.' He bent his head and wrote. 'I love her, I want her, I want to protect her from herself, and she's gorgeous.' He shook his head as he looked up from the paper. 'I wonder what she wants.' He pulled the paper from the pad and screwed it up, dropping it onto the bed table amid a welter of other screwed and balled pieces of paper and going off into a mini reverie, staring blankly into space.

The object of his thoughts wandered onto the ward while he was daydreaming. Harry came over, ruining for the elderly man opposite Hugh the effect of his blood pressure medication, by the length of her skirt. She bent over, dropping a small bunch of sweet peas on the over-bed table, amid the papers, and shuffling the books together that Hugh had been studying.

'Hi.' She smiled at him as Hugh looked up in surprise. 'Are you finally getting to grips with your book?'

'Hi, yourself.' Hugh couldn't help himself, he had been feeling a bit down and there she was smiling at him. He beamed back at her.

Harry grinned at him. 'So what have you been doing

with yourself today?'

'I've been having my blood taken and then they put me in this tin can and threw stones at the outside of it and then they poked me a bit. A man's peered into my eyes and ears. A woman has come and asked me if I know who I am and who the prime minister is and when I was born and if I can remember what I had for breakfast.' Hugh shook his head as he mildly grumbled. 'I'm fed up, Harriet. I want to go home.'

'I'm sure they'll let you go as soon as they can. Then you are to stay with me, Hugh. I feel responsible for you. First I knock you out, and then someone else does in my house.' She smiled gently at him. 'You are staying and I don't want any arguments.'

Hugh who had been opening and shutting his mouth as she shook a neatly trimmed finger at him, now shook his head. 'None of this was your fault, Harriet.'

'I should quit while you're ahead, Hugh. I'm determined. Now. Tell me about the stone rattling machine. How does it work? Do you know?' she settled on the bedside and looked expectantly at him.

Hugh dragged his eyes and mind from the length of leg on display and tried to explain the MRI machine. They had been talking for about twenty minutes when Sandy Bell turned up.

He brought his body, in its rumpled suit, to a halt in front of the couple and smiled at them both.

'Dr Kegan, Miss Branwell. How are you today, sir?'

Hugh gave a slight shake of his head. 'I'm a bit fed up of being in hospital, but I'm definitely feeling better,

Inspector.'

'Hello, Inspector Bell. Have you solved your suspicious death yet?'

Sandy looked over the young woman half smiling at him, he was sorry he was going to have to wipe the smile away. 'I'm afraid it's a murder investigation now, Miss.'

Hugh looked from one to the other then said, 'What on earth have you been up to now, Harry?'

'Not me, him. Your rich sponsor, Mr Ratcliff. He's dead.'

'Well I know that, but that's not murder. That was a heart attack, wasn't it?'

'I'm afraid not, sir.'

'Oh! Bummer.' Hugh looked at the face watching him so carefully. He gave a slight shrug. 'Well at least I've got an alibi, thanks to you, Harry; I've been in this hospital bed or yours for...' He reddened. 'That isn't how it sounds, Inspector. I...'

'It's OK, Hugh.' Harry looked at Sandy. 'Hugh has been injured, I was looking after him. We weren't sharing a bed.'

'It's none of my business if you had been, Miss Branwell. However, the murder isn't quite as simple as that.' He looked at Hugh again. 'Can you tell me when you first came into contact with Mr Ratcliff, sir?'

Hugh, his colour leaching to leave him white about the lips and cheeks, nodded. 'It would be Easter. I took time out from the beginning of the Easter break and that's when I took up the letter of introduction that one of the other lecturers had given me.'

'Why didn't you leave it until the end of the school year, sir?'

Hugh offered a half smile and glanced at Harry before saying, 'Shingles.'

'Ah! Painful.'

'Yeah. Some brat came to college with chicken pox and before I could sneeze, I was itching all around my waist; I didn't get to the doc in time and suffered the full blown effects. It's left me a bit run down, so I quit while I was ahead.'

'Oh, love, and there was me adding to your troubles.' Harry laid a gentle hand on Hugh's shoulder.

Sandy looked from one to the other and pursed his lips at the look that passed between them, so that was how the wind blew. But if this man had only come into contact at Easter it seemed unlikely he would murder the man. Unless...Sandy paused in his reflections. Unless he wanted to get nearer to finish the job.

He was interrupted in these musings by Harry, who stood up abruptly. 'Hugh hasn't murdered anyone, Inspector; truly, he's been with me nearly all the time since last Friday.' She shook her curls vigorously and turned to look at Hugh before saying, 'Look at him, he hasn't got the right temperament for one thing. He'd put it off so long the victim would die of old age before he got around to it.' She offered a half smile to Hugh, her eyes twinkling for just a moment before she sobered again. 'I won't believe you, not this man.'

Hugh looked at the profile presented to him. 'Well it's nice of you to champion me, Harry, but you haven't known me that long.' He felt slightly chagrined at her assessment. 'Not that I did kill the man, Inspector.' He looked at Sandy silently watching the by-play.

'No, sir, I don't think you did either, but nevertheless the man is dead and I need to interview you, if you are fit enough?' There was the hint of a question.

Hugh nodded.

'I'll come back later, Hugh.'

'No.' Hugh spoke abruptly. 'Stay, if the Inspector doesn't mind.' He patted the bed and Harry slowly sat down again at Sandy's nod. 'So, Inspector, what do you want to know?'

Sandy stepped to the next bed and removed one of the plastic chairs from the side of it, bringing it over and sitting down. He pulled out his notepad and glasses and settled himself while the couple watched him.

'Tell me who gave you the introduction, what you were studying and how long you had been going to the house?'

Hugh started to talk and Sandy took notes. Harry kept quiet, watching the inter-play of emotions and expressions on Hugh's face. She blushed slightly when he got to the events of the previous Friday. 'Poor Harry here was daydreaming and knocked me over. I got dragged off to hospital and, apparently, a couple of your detectives got a chance to catch a pickpocket, only they didn't.' He grinned. 'DC Jorkvil came to see me about it.'

Sandy nodded encouragingly.

'I saw him too, Inspector. I gave him that little book we picked up by mistake, Hugh.' She swung her head and looked at Hugh, before looking at Sandy. 'He said he would pass it on for me.'

'Ah! Right, Miss. I haven't spoken to him yet.' Sandy paused, the pencil resting on the page while he thought. 'I think that's all I need to know for now, sir.' He smiled at Hugh. 'You've been very helpful. I may have to come back to you, but I don't think so.' He put his glasses away and stood up, stowing his notepad at the same time. 'Thank you again.'

Hugh watched him leaving the ward as Harriet watched Hugh. She had learnt a lot about this man in the past half hour, and she was wondering why he'd allowed her to know so much about him suddenly. She began to smooth out the papers on the tabletop piling them neatly, and absently shuffling them together. Hugh was still busy watching the Inspector leave as she caught sight of her own name on one sheet.

She read, because curiosity overcame her. Hugh turned at the small gasp and noticed that his companion had turned a painful red.

He looked at the paper in her hand, he looked at her face, and then he met the blue eyes looking at him.

'I'm sorry.' Both spoke at once.

Harry blushed even more. 'I didn't mean to pry, Hugh. I was...' She indicated the neat pile of papers.

'It's alright. It was stupid of me to leave it in full view.' He took the hand waving the papers about in front of his face and endangering his eyesight and captured her attention. 'Forget it, OK?'

'But I'm not sure I want to!'

'Oh!' Hugh looked a bit nonplussed. 'Harriet...'

'Let's see how things go, Hugh. I was offered a date tonight with that nice Detective Jorkvil, but I wanted to be here. I'm not sure I should be here but... I am... and doesn't that tell you something?'

'Er. Maybe... but I'm not sure what yet.' Hugh grinned at her. 'Ok, we'll see how things go.' He didn't let go of her hand, and she didn't ask for it back for the rest of the visit.

20

Bob MEANWHILE WAS VISITING the late departed Mr Ratcliff's house. The door was opened by a pale-faced and unshaven Dove, who nodded at him and then held the door wide.

'Ah! Mr Dove, just the man I wanted to see.'

To James Dove it sounded like the voice of doom. 'Inspector?'

'Might we go into the sitting room?' Dove looked at the stern face looking at him, and nodded, leading the way into the expensive room.

Bob McInnis moved over behind the desk and sat down, indicating with a well kept hand the chair opposite. 'Now, Mr Dove, I'd like some answers and I'd prefer it if you didn't offer me anymore lies.' He watched the mouth in the creased face open and gave a gentle shake of his head.

'You weren't in your bed on Sunday night. Just where did you go in that rather nice Daimler out there?'

'I didn't, I...?'

Bob cocked his head on one side waiting.

'I never touched the Daimler.' Dove looked down, wiping his hands down his trousers before looking up again at Bob. 'I went out, but not in the boss's car. Alright? God forgive me, I should have been there for him and I went out.

He said I should sort things out with Joe and cut the connection. That Inspector Jakob was coming to search the house and he wanted the place clean.'

'So you crept out to see Joe Jenkins. Did you have a fight when he didn't want to break up the partnership?' It was spoken softly, but James Dove felt the shiver all the way down his spine. He lowered his eyes and addressed his knees. 'I rang him; he was supposed to have gone to Holland, but he said he'd meet me out at the boat. Only he never turned up.' He looked up at Bob. 'You have to believe me.'

'Well, no, I don't, you have consistently lied to me. I see no reason why I shouldn't arrest you for the murder here and now.'

'Oh God, I didn't kill Joe. We didn't have a partnership. We had a boat, I went out as crew. I know he was doing drugs, but I had nothing to do with that.'

'You didn't think it was you're civic duty to report him?'

James shook his head. 'I never even thought about that. It was hash. I know he got a bit for the boss, but it wasn't big stuff.'

'Dealing in hash is a criminal offence. It invariably leads to hard drugs.'

James was shaking his head again. 'No. The boss said it calmed him; he never took anything else that I knew of. Just the odd spliff when he was upset.'

Bob leaned forward, resting his arms on the desk and linking his hands together. 'Mr Dove, you are in serious trouble, so far you have committed perjury, and attempted to pervert the course of justice. I suggest you tell me all you know, unless you want to find yourself inside a jail for the rest of the week.'

James Dove, nodded, breathing deeply through his nose.

'You went out Sunday evening. What time was that? And how did you get to Silloth if you didn't take the Daimler.'

'It was about ten thirty. The boss was settled. I could hear him snoring a bit.' He looked up at Bob. 'I'd given him an extra big brandy, more brandy than soda. He niver said anything, just knocked it back. I went out in my mini. I keep it parked in the courtyard at night, in front of the garage gates. I niver thought to look in the garage; you saw, my entrance goes up the outside stairs to the old loft. Far as I knew the Daimler was still in the garage. I drove out and off to Silloth. Joe said he'd meet me at the boat at eleven thirty. That's what we used to do sometimes. I'd go and crew and do a bit of fishing and be back in time for the boss's breakfast. I didn't think he knew about it.' James sighed and returned his eyes to his clammy hands, wiping them on his trousers again.

'He did know though, didn't he?'

James nodded. 'He told me last Sunday he'd always known.'

'So what next?' Bob raised an eyebrow.

James Dove shrugged. 'I went on board. I waited. It was getting on for midnight and he still hadn't turned up. I made a brew and tided the boat and went and sat on the deck. But he never turned up. Honest to God.' He looked at Bob again. 'I never saw him, and I couldn't raise him on his phone. So I drove home again. I got in about two. I was mad with him, a wasted night when I could have been sleepin', and the boss needed me and I wasn't there. I'll never forgive myself for that.'

'Did you notice if the Daimler was there that time?'

Dove gave a slight shrug of the shoulders. 'I was knackered. I just parked the car inside the gates and came in to bed.'

'Where do you keep the keys?'

'I leave them in the car. It's in the yard, ain't it?'

Bob put his head on one side. 'I meant the keys of the Daimler.'

'Oh.' Dove rubbed at his neck. 'They hang on a hook in the garage, in a little glass box thing.'

Bob nodded, watching the man opposite as he licked his lips and rubbed a finger under his nose. 'So tell me about these drugs. How did Jenkins get them?'

'I dunno.'

'Yes you do, Dove. You were partners on that boat for nearly nine years, men working together that long know a lot about each others business.'

'I...I...'Dove licked his lips again.

'You?'

'I don't know about all of it.' He gulped. 'I'm gonna be out of a job. I need the boat, I've put a lot of savings into it.'

'That isn't my problem. I'm trying to find out who murdered your master and your partner.'

'Oh God. He was never murdered. He just had a

dicky heart, I should have been there.'

'He was murdered, and at the moment I am quite happy to lay the blame at your door, you gave him his medication.'

'I wouldn't do that.' The sweat popped out on his forehead and Bob watched impassively as a small bead ran down the grey face and snagged on a whisker at chin level. Dove raised eyes now filled with tears of self-pity. 'What am I gonna do?'

'Tell me what you've done, and I might be able to help.' Bob McInnis unclasped his hands and leaned back slightly in the chair.

Dove licked his lips and looked suddenly small on the opposite side of the desk. 'What do you want to know?'

'First, Drugs?'

'A boat. I niver saw it, honest to God. We had a pre-arranged point and time. Joe made the contact; I just put out my pots and a line and kept watch. The boat would come up and Joe would throw down the cash in a packet and haul in the bundle and I'd put it among the fish 'til we got into port. I niver touched it, I just acted as crew. Joe took it away with him.'

'Co-ordinates always the same?' Bob watched the nod. 'If you co-operate, allow us to use your boat, I might be able to talk to the public prosecutor.' He shook his head at the eager look. 'Don't hope for too much. You are as much involved as Jenkins was, and Inspector Jakob is not a happy man.

'Now, Medication. You put it out for Mr Ratcliff?'

'Yeah.'

'What?'

'Well, what the chemist sent?'

'Describe it?'

Dove looked at the handsome face and the serious brown eyes, waiting; the man was obviously going to keep on waiting until he got the right answer. 'I don't understand?'

Bob sighed. 'Describe the medication he received from the chemist.'

Dove scratched at his unshaven chin, shrugged and said, 'Little spray thing, made of glass, red stuff inside,' He checked to see if that was what Bob wanted and got a nod so he shrugged again slightly and continued. 'Little blue pills in a brown plastic bottle with one of those childproof caps on. Silver strip with triangle shaped pink pills that you pop out.'

'And that's what you gave him on Monday night.'

'Yeah, honest to God. I set them out on his table like always.'

'And did you remove any of them Tuesday morning when you found him?'

'No, no. I swear. I felt him all cold and I went and phoned the doc and he said leave everything exactly as it was so I shut the door and Fraser came and I went into the kitchen with him, and then you came.'

'I want to know every man, woman and child that has had access to this house for the last year. If you didn't alter the medication, I want to know who did. Understand.'

'I understand.' It was a muttered whisper. James Dove thought he glimpsed compassion for a minute on the face opposite and sighed.

'Now, has the parrot turned up?' The question came from left field and the major domo looked astonished.

'No.' He stared at Bob in silence, his mouth slightly open.

'OK. Go and ask Fraser to come here, please.' Bob nodded dismissal.

'You won't tell...'

Bob McInnis shook his head gently. 'Fetch Fraser.' He watched Dove leave the room and picked up the phone, asking to be put through to Jakob. He had just finished speaking to that Inspector when Fraser Wilson entered.

'Sorry, Inspector, I was in the attic. James didn't know where I was.'

'Attic?'

'We've got one of those dormer windows in the roof at the back. It was leaking like, the boss asked me to have a look last weekend, check it was shut properly. But what with one thing and another,' he shrugged, 'I thought I'd have a look at it since I'm doing nout else.'

Bob waited as Fraser shrugged again. 'Couldn't find the leak, there's a patch the size of a dinner plate on the boards though. I was up there, so James couldn't find me.' He repeated.

Bob indicated the chair James Dove had vacated. 'Tell me about this leak.'

'You want to know about the leak?' Fraser looked scandalised.

'Yes.' Bob spoke patiently. 'Better still take me to see it.' He stood up.

Fraser raised an eyebrow, shrugged, and then frowned and stood up again. 'OK. If that's what you want. It's just a leaky window.' He led the way out of the room and up the stairs to the first landing. They went through a door of good walnut and up a second flight of uncarpeted stairs to what at one time would have been the servant's quarters. A large attic bedroom opened out before them, filled with lumber from a past, and slower, age.

Bob saw the puddle straight away, it was right next to the window. He stepped over the floor with the care of a cat, not sure if the floorboards would bear his twelve stone. Fraser had no such inhibitions, wading through inch thick dust to thrust the window open, leaving a rising tide of dust motes in the air. 'You see, she fits snug as you like.' Bob came up to him and looked out onto a flat roof with the top of an iron fire escape poking shyly over the top. He looked back into the room at the floor and the tracks he could see, among the detritus of years.

He eased past Fraser and onto the roof and cautiously approached the edge. Fraser stayed where he was. 'It's safe enough, only I don't like heights like. So I'll stay put if it's all the same with you.'

Bob nodded, taking careful note of the cast iron. 'I'll go down this way.' He carefully swung his body over and found he was enclosed for the first flight in a sort of circular iron cage terminating in a flat platform at bedroom level. The next flight was open; he walked down and found himself in the shrubbery. He looked around and noted the nearby windows. Stepping over, he looked through the nearest and saw Ratcliff's bedroom. 'Mmm, very interesting.' He spoke softly to himself.

He walked around to the front and rang the

doorbell. Fraser opened the door with a grin and spoke slightly breathlessly. 'Inspector.'

Bob gave a faint smile. 'So who knows about the outside stairs?'

Fraser shrugged. 'We all do I suppose.'

'And how did Mr Ratcliff know about the leak?'

'Eh?'

The two men made their way back to the study, and Bob shut the door as Fraser went over to the desk and sat down again. Bob resumed his own seat before speaking. 'Everyone has told me Mr Ratcliff was ill. He presumably didn't go up there and find the leak. How did he know about it?'

Fraser frowned. 'I dunno.'

'Would Mr Dove have told him?'

'James didn't know about it, that's why he couldn't find me. He was shouting my name, and wanted to know what the hell I was doing up there.'

Bob pushed his hand through his hair, then said. 'Now, I'd like you to tell me about the packet and letter you took to the bank on Monday when we first visited. Who was it addressed to?'

'The parcel was for the manager. For a safe deposit Mr Ratcliff's got...had.' Fraser frowned, 'I suppose he's still got it.'

'Do you know what was in it?'

'Grey stuff.' Fraser shrugged again.

Bob raised an eyebrow.

'Look, I dunno what it was. He's asked me to take some of it to the bank before, mostly he kept it in the safe here, but sometimes I had to take some to the bank, it was just grey stuff like putty, it smelt sorta odd, like sickly perfume - but I dunno what it was and I wanted my job, so I asked no questions. He didn't smoke it or inject it or sell it to anyone. I don't think it was a drug, or I wouldn't have touched it.'

Bob, who had his own ideas about the mysterious substance, nodded encouragingly. 'Was that the only thing you took to the safe deposit?'

'Sometimes it was pieces of parchment or a book.'

'Hmm. And the letter?'

'A PO box. Smith.'

'Can you remember the address?'

Fraser nodded. He picked up a pen from the desk and Bob pushed his notebook over at a clean page, watching as the younger man wrote down the short address. 'Thank you. You've been very helpful. I don't suppose you've heard anymore of the parrot?'

Fraser shook his head and brushed his hair back. 'Nope, not a cheep.' He grinned.

Saying 'thank you' again, Bob dismissed him and sat at the desk, pondering the information he'd just received.

IT WAS HEADING TOWARDS another nice summer evening when Bob returned to the police station and walked into the general office. Sandy was sitting at his desk, two fingering his way across the keyboard and sipping occasionally from a large blue pottery mug. Without looking up he remarked, 'Funny lunch time this is.'

'Eh!'

'Said you'd be back at lunchtime.' Sandy now looked across the room as Bob took off his jacket and swung a chair round so that it faced Sandy across the desk. 'I've been here, slaving away, waiting for you…'

'Damn. I'm sorry, Sandy.' He caught the twinkle and smiled tiredly. 'Yeah, but I'm still sorry, I could have phoned. I got engrossed in following clues and forgot all about our meeting.'

'Doesn't matter, lad. I wasn't here myself. I left a message for you. Let's hope we've both made progress. Do you want to get a cuppa?'

'Nah. I'll do until I get home.'

'Debrief here or there?'

'There.'

'Give me five minutes to finish this and I'll come with you; Sarah borrowed the car.'

'Fine.' Bob nodded and leaned back in his chair, closing his eyes and sighing.

Sandy glanced at him and then returned to his typing. He came to a triumphant stop and sighed himself, picked up his mug and drained the dregs, and watched as the serious brown eyes of Bob McInnis opened and looked at him. 'Finished?'

'Aye, lad.'

Both men stood and put their jackets on. Sandy shovelled the paperwork into his desk drawer and turned the key. He switched off the computer and grinned grimly 'I've changed the password twice today.' Then he gave a wicked chuckle. 'I hope I can remember what I used last.'

Both men left the office and stepped into the warmth of a summer evening, the birds coughed in the evening rush hour traffic and a plane roared overhead. 'Peaceful ain't it?' Sandy grinned as he fastened his seatbelt and settled back in his car seat.

'It will be just as peaceful at home. Caitlin's really whiny at the moment and your Beth isn't a lot better.' Both men grinned this time as they thought about their very young offspring.

'We could...'

'Yeah!' Bob spun the wheel and headed towards the Blackwell Bridge and thence to the Upperby cemetery. They remained quiet as Bob drove the short distance and pulled up near the gates, parking neatly so that they could both get out and walk into the quiet area.

'Ahh!' Both spoke together and breathed out as they strolled along the asphalt path between the newly cut grassed areas.

Instinctively Bob made for the area where his first wife was buried, and sat on a nearby bench. Sandy lowered his bulk next to his partner and both sat quietly with their eyes closed. 'I still miss her you know, Sandy.'

'Of course you do, lad.'

'I was thinking about the money, what you said about Beth wanting me to use it.' Bob swung his head and looked at the older man. 'Money greases the wheels; I don't have to worry too much about paying the bills. The insurance on Beth paid the mortgage, so there's just day to day stuff. I've got a job I love,' he grinned, 'mostly.'

Sandy nodded, waiting for Bob to arrive at the point.

'I can understand someone being desperate enough to betray for money if they needed cash. But officers, we aren't paid a fantastic wage, but mostly we can manage a good lifestyle if not an extravagant one. So why would someone need money that much?'

'You're being too generous, Bob. Good old fashioned greed might be enough.'

'Yeah, I know, but I want it to be something else,' he offered a half smile, 'gambling or behind with the mortgage, or even a drug habit. Something, some trouble that some poor sod has got themselves into, even blackmail. I can understand that a bit, but greed for greed's sake. I can't quite get my head around that.'

Sandy offered a half smile of his own revealing the slightly crooked eye tooth and an unexpected sympathy. 'I do understand, Bob, and to a certain extent I want the same thing.' He shrugged. 'But, I don't think so, lad, this has the smell of greed to me.' He shrugged again. 'And it's putting the lives of other officers at risk so I can't condone it, whatever the reasons.'

'No, I should know better.'

'I'm older and more cynical, less tolerant and less forgiving, Bob.'

'So,' Bob nodded, 'what has your cynical soul uncovered today?'

'That the majority of the population sleep heavily and wouldn't react if a bomb went off under their beds. The witness reports have everyone going to bed early because, 'they had work in the morning', or because, 'the baby didn't disturb them', or because, 'it's a proper lovers-lane, down there, officer, and can't you do something about it?'

'No witnesses then?'

'Oh! A couple heard a car on the top road about eleven but thought it might be the neighbour getting back late. It's the closest we've come to a time anyway. I tell you, Bob, the population is so unobservant it drives me potty.' Sandy shook his head in apparent despondency, then grinned slyly.

'Ah ha! Not all of them?' Bob wagged a finger.

'No. Dog walkers, bless their lonely hearts, and a despised courting couple. Said dog walker, saw a Daimler at eleven twenty going over the crossroads next to Brownrigg. Noted it because it was 'the old class', driver, male, middle-aged, grey haired.'

'And the couple?'

'Same description, they were 'enjoying the amenities of the back seat', Sandy smiled and his eyes twinkled. 'But the man noted the car passing because he thought it was the cops coming to see what he was up to. Apparently his girlfriend isn't too quiet about her enjoyment and the landlady had complained.' Sandy gave a chuckle as Bob wrinkled his nose up.

'Dove?'

'He's still in the picture, Bob, but he ain't grey-haired.'

'Effect of lighting?'

Sandy shrugged. 'The dog-walker and the lover have agreed to come into the station and look at the books. Work with an artist. I'm not holding my breath though.'

'We need to find the primary...'

'Aye, I've been going through traffic reports until my eyes are ready to drop out. I think I might have a report of a 'hit and pick him up'.'

'Eh!'

'Found a report in the area of Ratcliff's house, old lady making a cup of cocoa and looking out her window while the milk boiled. She says she thought she saw a man knocked down; but the driver got out of his 'posh car' and helped the other man in, and drove off. Her eyesight isn't exactly twenty-twenty, and she says it was at the end of the street. It's a wee cul-de-sac about five minutes walk away from Ratcliff's address and she lives at the bottom of it, a good three hundred yards from the junction.'

'Time?'

'Not accurate, but 'about half ten'.'

'You could get to Brownrigg with time to spare.'

'Aye, I think we've got the primary, but whether it was a covered up accident I dinna ken, Bob.' Sandy ran a forefinger under his nose and leaned back. 'What you got?'

'Oh, nothing as good as you.' His eyes twinkled at the grin from the older man. 'I went back to interview, as you know. Dove is a mess; he's up to his neck in the drug running, albeit by default. He knew what Jenkins was up to alright, but decided that because he wasn't actively doing anything it was none of his business.'

Oh! Aye!'

'Aye.' Bob nodded. 'He's agreed to co-operate and Jakob is setting up a sting, the PPS will do their best to keep him out of prison. If he keeps helping.' Bob leaned back and looked up at the dusky sky. 'But my best lead is a dormer window. I think I know how the drugs were being changed about and delivered.'

'Do tell.'

Bob moved, slewing round slightly on the seat. 'Yesterday we found the body, got in SOCO and very properly set them to gathering evidence in the bedroom of the deceased and all points north. Or rather all downstairs.' He grinned a bit wryly. 'Everyone told us the old man couldn't get about much, so I concentrated on the bedroom, and his sitting room. It was still only a suspicion and a tenuous suspicion at that.'

'Get on, stop defending yourself, lad. No-one has accused you of misconduct.' Sandy moved to watch his young companion's face.

Bob smiled slightly. 'OK, dad.' Watched the sly grin appear on Sandy's face and then continued marking the points off on his fingers. 'One, Dove sets out the meds last thing. He described them to me, one nearly used bottle of TNT and a new unopened one,' he offered a faint grin to replace the smile before going on, 'one bottle of blue tablets, they'd be the digitalis, one strip of triangular tablets in a strip. That's would be the thiazine which the doctor hadn't prescribed. OK?'

Sandy nodded. 'So Dove is setting them on the

cabinet every night.'

'Yes. But when Mark was collecting there was only one spray and one bottle of digitalis at the right strength.'

'Swapped?'

'Swapped. I thought maybe someone had come through the open window but they all said Ratcliff didn't open the window. Then Fraser started talking about how Ratcliff told him to fix a leak in the attic.'

'And you wanted to know how a sick man knew about it?'

'Huh! Don't spoil my fun when I'm showing how brilliant I am.' Bob mock scowled.

Sandy grinned again. 'Go on genius, what did you find in the attic?'

'A damp patch from an open, not leaky, window and a fire-escape that led directly to his downstairs bedroom.'

'So it's looking more like an outside job, Bob.'

Bob shook his sleek locks and brushed them back in a habitual gesture. 'I'm not ruling anyone out just yet; but I don't think Dove has the know how to manufacture a false trail, and Fraser Wilson has no motive at all.'

'The cook?' Sandy raised an eyebrow.

'She couldn't get through that dormer window and down those fire stairs; it would be like pushing a melon down a straw. And why go to all that trouble when you work there?' He stopped speaking and grinned at Sandy's chuckle. 'However, she did tell me about a visitor, came on a bike to play chess once a month. No name but a local who left his dog outside.'

'Hmm! We're getting on, lad.'

'Well, we're eliminating at least.'

'That's half the job, Bob.'

'I asked Mark to put a rush on processing the Daimler. He said you'd already asked.'

Sandy nodded. 'I wondered if there were any traces of Jenkins in the car.'

Bob nodded back. 'Same here, I was just speculating, I didn't want to miss anything. Like where Ratcliff's mobile has gone?'

'Ah! Not with the effects?'

'Nope.'

'So you think we've got someone coming in, swapping the drugs and taking the mobile.'

'Yeah. And maybe doing for the parrot. I can't find hide nor hair of it and it didn't fly away or climb out that bedroom window. But it did leave a couple of feathers on the front seat. Mark hadn't finished, but he did pass on that titbit.'

'Well its plain then, the parrot did for him and drove away knocking down Jenkins on the way.' Sandy grinned as he stood up. 'Time to go, lad, Sarah will be worrying.'

Bob nodded. 'OK, I won't be a minute.'

'I'll see you at the car.' Sandy strolled off up the path and Bob walked over and plucked a bunch of wilting carnations from the brass vase on the grave he'd been unconsciously looking at for the last twenty minutes.

'I'll bring Caitlin and Jenny at the weekend, love, and

some fresh flowers.' He smiled as he looked down, and then sighed slightly as he turned away going to drop the flowers in a compost heap as he too made his way towards the gate and the patiently waiting Sandy Bell.

'OK, lad.'

Bob nodded and they drove home in the gathering dusk, satisfied they were making progress on their murders at least.

JENKINS'S MURDERER, OF HIMSELF, was such more by accident than design. Granted he hadn't intended to knock anyone down, but having realised who his victim was, he was quite happy to make sure that Jenkins was dead.

He just wished he could find out a bit more about the progress of the coppers. The gossips in the area were free with their speculation but that's all it was, speculation, and unlike Bob McInnis' there wasn't a lot of information behind it.

He lay in solitary splendour in the big queen bed and stared at the ceiling. Killing the old man, yes; killing Jenkins, that had been a fluke, not that he regretted it. He turned over in the bed and looked at the wardrobe, product of MFI and not standing up to the strain of being improperly put together, and then filled to overflowing with clothes.

He focused on the bedside clock, two-ten. He must get some sleep he had work in the morning and a host of other things to do, maybe if he made a warm drink? He crawled out of bed and pulled on a dressing gown and slippers over stripped pyjamas, pushing his greying hair off his brow and walking softly down the stairs so that he didn't disturb the other occupants of the house.

The trouble was, he thought, as he set the electric kettle to boil, that he hadn't expected the old man's death to be recognised as a murder. He wanted him dead, but he didn't want anyone to realise that he'd been killed. It was his own fault. Killing Jenkins had made them suspicious; if only he could have got to the man in time to swap the drugs back around earlier, and prevent him dying quite so quick. If only, now there was a phrase; his life seemed to have been made up of 'if only's'.

He poured water into the tea-pot and sighed. The dog in the basket next to the back door open an eye and looked at him, but didn't stir. He poured tea into a mug, added a dollop of milk, and then as stealthily as he'd come down returned to his bedroom, to sip tea and then try to sleep.

21

Thursday

IT WAS A BRILLIANT MORNING, a harbinger of coming events; at least Bob McInnis hoped so. He was certainly lodging a request with the Almighty for a break in their current case. He said as much to Sandy Bell as they climbed into the car and drove away from their respective homes.

'We are making progress, Bob. I'll grant its slow, foreby, something has to break soon.'

'I know, Sandy, but the longer it goes on, and the more information that comes in, the muddier I feel the waters are getting. And...' he sighed and changed up a gear, 'we still don't know who's telling who what.'

'Aye, lad. I ken what ye mean. I hate this hole in the corner work my own self.'

Bob cast him a glance. 'Bethy kept you up last night.' It was a statement.

Sandy glanced across. 'And you ken this because?'

'You've gone broad on me.'

Sandy hunched a shoulder. 'It's the croup, we've spoken to the doctor, he says stick her in a steamy room and it'll clear of its own self, but in the meantime we all lose sleep, Bob.'

'I hope the murderer is losing sleep too. You become careless when you're tired.'

'Is that a hint?'

'Good grief, no, Sandy.' Bob gave an astonished glance away from the road for a second or two. 'But be careful, man, for all that.' He returned his attention back to the traffic.

Sandy lifted a shoulder. 'Sorry.'

'Don't be. But if you need to get a bit of kip you've got the key to the house, get your head down for a hour. Jenny is taking Caitlin to jungle gym this morning, so the place will be empty.'

'Thanks, but, well, no thanks. I'll be alright. I'll stay in the office and co-ordinate from there though, if that'll make you any happier.' Sandy sniffed, he sounded just like an indignant Scotty dog on the scent of a peppermint.

Bob gave a chuckle. 'Well, I have to look after the old folk.'

He received a poke in the ribs as he pulled up outside the police station, and the pair went inside with smiles on their faces.

The big internal room that they shared with nine other inspectors of various ranks was seething like a kicked-in ants nest. Sandy and Bob stood at the door and watched in astonishment as men and women struggled under piles of white A4, the resemblance to the ants nest heightened by their frantic activities, as if each worker was rescuing a precious egg.

'What the hell...'

'I think this might be a diversionary tactic, Sandy.' Bob spoke softly out of the side of his mouth as he watched the activity.

Gareth, his arms loaded with files, veered away from the desk he was heading towards and came towards them instead. 'Message from the Superintendent, Chief. Could you go up there as soon as you get in?'

'Both of us?'

Gareth nodded. 'Sirs.'

Bob and Sandy swivelled on their feet and headed out and up the stairs. Neither man spoke. Bob gave a perfunctory knock and went in shoulder to shoulder with Sandy.

'Ah, Inspectors.' She sat behind a desk crowded with files and forms which formed a barrier against the oncoming tide of paperwork. 'Do you realise how much paperwork you've managed to create?' A faint smile crossed her face and was echoed by Sandy.

'I take it yon stramash downstairs is your doing, ma'am.'

'Er, yes,' the smile grew as she looked at Sandy. 'I'm hoping to scare up a rabbit.'

'Oh, I think you might do that, ma'am.' Bob also smiled.

'Now,' she brushed aside the teeming activity downstairs for the comparative activity of her two officers. 'Update please.'

Sandy and Bob left the office some twenty minutes

later, having informed their superior of the current state of their cases. They headed back down to the office with some reluctance, Bob peeling off to fetch some much needed liquid refreshment. However, things appeared to have settled down slightly when Sandy arrived at the doorway. He waded through the mass of humanity, and was just about to sit at his desk when he spied Michael Jorkvil among the throng.

'Hi, Michael.' Sandy scratched at a badly shaved chin with one hand and beckoned the detective constable with the other.

Jorkvil came over. 'Sir?'

'You've got some evidence of mine.'

'Sir?' Michael looked astonished. 'I have?'

'Aye, a wee book. A young lass by the name of Harry passed it on to you.'

'Oh, of course. It's on my desk.' He glanced across at the mountain he had accumulated that morning with a certain amount of horror on his face and hesitated.

'Well fetch it then, before it becomes totally submerged, laddie.'

Michael looked from the senior detective to his desk and back and teetered on his heels. 'Do you want it now, sir?'

'No, next Christmas! Of course I want it now.' Sandy sighed with seeming exasperation. But he watched keenly as the younger man went over and began to shift files from one side of the desk to the other. He kept his eyes on him, even when Bob returned with tea in large mugs and spoke to him.

'Whist.'

Bob subsided, looking where Sandy was watching.

'Rabbit?' He spoke quietly for Sandy's ears only.

'Aye, possibly. He dresses a bit flash.'

Jorkvil came over with the small coloured book between his first two fingers as if handling a smelly nappy. 'Sorry, sir. I didn't get a chance to see you yesterday and hand it over.'

'Thanks.' Sandy nipped it out of his hands and handed it to Bob with a quiet nod. Bob retreated to his own desk and sat down. He hunched his shoulders against the noise, and opened the book at the first page.

The next time he looked up it was because it had gone curiously quiet. He and Sandy were the only men left in the room. His tea was stone cold, with a scum like an oil slick floating on the surface, and Sandy was standing next to him.

'Well, what is it?'

'Why do you think I should know?' He took the new mug of tea Sandy offered and watched as Sandy pulled up a chair next to him. 'Thanks.' He took a sip and sighed.

Sandy just smiled quietly.

'OK. I think Ratcliff must have been a member of the DSA.'

'Which is?'

'The Duzenal Society of America.'

'And now I ken all!' Sandy grinned and sipped his own tea.

'They work from either base twelve or base sixty rather than a decimal base. It's easier for fractions, and ratio's division is simpler too.' Bob glanced at Sandy, read the genuine interest, and sipped more tea. 'Numbers are fascinating, Sandy, why do we use the decimal system for some things and sexagesimal for others. Your watch is sexagesimal, seconds and minutes. We owe the Babylonians for that, but they got it from the Sumerians.'

Sandy eyed Bob over the top of his mug, waiting to see where all this was heading.

'Anyway,' Bob reigned in his enthusiasm slightly, only to digress again before he was halfway through his explanation, 'I think Ratcliff was using the system to keep a tally of his dealings. Bought and sold. I haven't worked it all out because I'm not used to the system, but I believe he was dealing in stocks and bonds.' Bob smiled a bit wryly. 'Did you know that the only time that the stock market has brought down a parliament was in 1834? They burnt all the obsolete tally sticks held by stock men in the furnaces under the Houses of Parliament and it set fire to whole building.'

Sandy merely raised an eyebrow.

'Yes, well, er!' Bob's cheek bones went a trifle pink. 'So, he was dealing and I'm not sure there wasn't some insider trading going on. If he lost this little gem he'd want it back.'

'Do you think he paid someone to retrieve it from Dr Keegan?'

'Quite possibly. It's certainly one explanation, and a better one than gribbles.'

'Gribbles. No, don't tell me, I can only take so much information at one time, Bob.'

Bob grinned, but continued speculating. 'Dr Keegan couldn't give a reason for being attacked. According to Miss

Branwell, who I spoke to on Tuesday, persons unknown were searching for her notes and pictures about a fraud connected to marine damage.'

'But you don't think it's that, now. Or you never did?'

'I was always a bit sceptical, now, while I think the fraud squad in America can check it out, I don't think there are any gangsters in Cumberland after the fair Harry.'

'No, I'm with you there, Bob. So, what do we do now?'

'I'll pass this to fraud; get them to give it a proper going over. I think it explains the source of his money, Sandy, and it might give us a motive. We can leave it to them to search out the connections though. We've got enough suspects, if not much motive of our own to deal with.'

'Agreed.'

Bob glanced around, the room was still empty, but he lowered his voice nevertheless, 'On the subject of rabbits...'

'Aye. This audit will hit us as well, lad, it would look odd if we didn't do it too. It's a bugger, but I've set a couple of young constables onto sorting out our cases. I'm busy with a murder or two and that takes priority.'

'Thank God for that, we might avoid it yet.'

'Don't bank on it, Bob.' Sandy grinned, a quick glint of teeth, before he said, 'And talking of banks, I've got the warrant through for Ratcliff's safe deposit if you want to take that this afternoon.'

Bob shot back a cuff and looked at the thin silver dial on his wrist. 'Good grief, doesn't time go fast when you're having fun. I'll nip out and get a butty on my way, Sandy.'

'Aye. I'll finish up the witness reports and get to the other stuff, see you back here about four for a confab.'

'Fine.' Bob pushed the book across the table and Sandy picked it up, he wasn't letting that bit of evidence out of his sight just yet. Bob stood up, straightening his jacket and fishing in his pocket for his keys.

JANE WAS LOOKING FOR her keys in her bag with one hand, and trying to hold a thick envelope with the other.

'Give them here, Jane.' Dot took the keys and opened the front door. They had been to lunch and Dot had handed over an envelope from her soon-to-be nephew. 'I'll put the kettle on, Jane, if you want to open it.'

'No, I'll...I'll wait until we're both sitting down.' She smiled a bit tremulously at Dot and laid the envelope on the side in the kitchen and sat down, still in her coat, at the kitchen table. 'My stomach's all a flutter, Dot.'

'You don't have to do anything about the information, Jane. You don't even have to open the envelope.' Dot turned and filled the kettle, flicking down the switch and getting the teapot off the shelf. Jane watched the neat movements as her friend moved about her kitchen finding the tea things.

Neither spoke until they had steaming mugs in front of them. Jane kept looking at the envelope, turning it over in her hands.

'For heaven sake, Jane, the suspense is killing me. Do

one thing or the other.'

Jane nodded, sticking a finger under the flap and pulling out several sheets of typed paper. She carefully smoothed them out on the table and began to read.

Dot watched her, her head on one side.

'So...'

'He was married, he's a widow and he's got a child. He lives near you, Dot.' Jane passed the papers over the table and nodded as Dot looked at her. 'Read it. I still don't know what to do. But Fraser has a sibling. I just don't know if I should tell him.'

Dot smiled. 'OK. Don't worry; you don't have to do anything if you don't want to.'

'It's not just me though, is it? It's Fraser and this young child too.'

'Drink your tea.' Dot watched as Jane gulped tea and swallowed tears. 'I wish I'd never meddled. I'm sorry, Jane.'

'No, you were right; Fraser needs to know and there's this other child too.'

'What do I need to know, mum.' Fraser stood in the doorway. 'What child?'

Jane swung round in the hard wooden chair and looked at her son as he stood in the doorway of the kitchen. He was clad in jeans and a t-shirt in keeping with the warmer weather, but his face had all the aspects of an approaching thunder storm.

'I wasn't deliberately listening, mum. I've just come in. James said to come home, there wasn't anything I could do for now.' He advanced into the room and pulled up a chair next to his mother and ignoring Dot, who was sitting like a statue on the opposite side of the table. He took hold of his mother's cold hands and looked at the tear drenched eyes. 'Come on, mum. You've been acting funny-like for days. What have you been up to?'

'It's my fault. I encouraged your mum to do something she hadn't thought of doing, and now I wish I hadn't.'

Fraser ignored Dot's comment. He gentle squeezed the hands. 'Mum?'

'You've never asked about your father, Fraser.'

'Weren't any of my business. You've always looked after me good enough. If you didn't want to have anything to do with him, then we wouldn't.'

'You never even asked when you were little.'

'Lots in the same boat, mum. Lots of kids only had the one parent. I always thought I was lucky. Some of me school mates spent every other weekend packing bags and moving from one house to another. At least I had only one bedroom to clean, and no-body telling lies about the other parent. No rows either.' He scowled. 'Believe me, mum, the tales some of me mates told, I mostly didn't want a dad.'

'You never said.'

'You never asked. I thought you were happy, mum.'

'I was, I am. Only...only I thought maybe you should know who your dad was.' Jane looked down at their linked hands.

'Only if you want me too.'

'I don't know what I want anymore.' His mother

wailed the words and started to cry.

Dot spoke into the silence. 'I'm going home. You two need to talk without an audience. I'm sorry, Jane. I didn't mean to cause harm. I apologise to you too, Fraser, I've obviously disturbed something that should have been left alone.' She stood up on the words.

Fraser looked at her; it wasn't an altogether pleasant look. 'Bit late for that now.' He looked at his mother. 'But maybe it is time to clear the air, if there's another child involved.' He raised an eyebrow and waited as the silence drew out. His mother sniffed and Dot passed over a nice flowery hanky. She dropped a hand on Jane's shoulder and gave a gentle squeeze. 'Call me, if you can both forgive me.'

Fraser ignored her, and Dot smiled grimly and left the quiet house.

Jane cried messily for a minute or two and then got a hold on her emotions. 'I'm sorry, Fraser.'

'Don't be. You've done what you thought right, and I haven't turned out too bad.' He offered a faint grin. 'Come on, mum, finish it.'

Jane pushed the neglected letter across the table and picked up the hanky, blowing her nose and wiping her eyes. 'Dot and I were talking, she was asking about you and your Dad. She wasn't being nosy, Fraser. She was interested, she cares about me, we're friends. I've never had a close friend.' Jane took a breath and gave a shrug. 'She asked did I know where your dad was, and then she said she could help me find him if I wanted to.'

'Are you that lonely, mum?'

'No.' Jane shook her head. 'I'm happy, really I am;

only I got to thinking how you might want a man around. The way you talked about James and Mr Ratcliff these last few months, you obviously enjoyed their male talk and I thought... well I thought I wasn't being fair keeping you from your dad.'

'James is alright, mum. But I got plenty of mates.' Fraser smiled. 'It's alright, mum. Honest.'

'Read the letter, Fraser. I'll make us a fresh pot and you can decide what you want to do.'

'OK.' He watched her stand up and busy herself. Then settled to reading the closely written report supplied by Paul Temple.

'What do you want to do, Fraser?' Jane sat down, bringing with her two fresh mugs of tea.

'The question is what do you want to do, mum? Why didn't you stay with him when you were pregnant, was he married then?'

Jane shook her head. 'No, we were both young and stupid. I don't regret having you, love, not for one minute, but he was half way through uni'. He didn't want a family. I never told him about you. It was a summer romance the year I was eighteen. Your Gran and Granddad are a bit...' Jane waved a hand. 'They didn't want an unmarried daughter, and I didn't want all the rows. So I left and got on with it.'

'Well, it's their loss ain't it, mum?' Fraser nodded at her and picked up his mug. 'We've managed fine together. I dunno if I want to meet up or not, I'll have to think about it.'

'He, your dad, he doesn't know I've been investigating. He might not want to know either.' Jane's lips pulled down. 'I can ring, there's a phone number, but I'll leave it alone if that's what you want.'

Fraser nodded. 'Leave it for now, mum.' He pushed his chair back and pulled his mobile from his back pocket. 'Here, phone Mrs Skeat. Your friend will be worried about you.'

'You're a nice lad.' Jane took the phone.

'I was brung up to be nice. But I'm going upstairs 'cos I'm still a bit angry with her for upsetting you, mum. And,' he shuffled back and stood up, 'I want to have a think. I don't know how I feel about having a baby sister or brother around. That would be kinda nice, maybe. I did want a brother when I was little.' He gave a half laugh and dropped a kiss on his mother's head before he left the room.

BOB WAS IN A GLASS booth; he wouldn't have described it as a room. It had a table, with ubiquitous computer terminal, two matching metal chairs and a very clean pad of blotting paper. The place smelt of air freshener, dust and carpet.

He'd been issued into this room five minutes ago with the promise that 'someone would be with you straight away'. He leaned back, allowing his mind to free wheel with the known facts of the case. He had just come to the conclusion that he needed to look into the background of his various suspects again.

It was obvious that Dove had something to hide, but whether it was just the smuggling and a grey attitude to the law, or if he was complicit in his master's murder, Bob wasn't sure. The cook he dismissed out of hand, Fraser... here Bob mentally paused and brought the young man into focus. The fresh and cheery face didn't fit his idea of a murderer. There were no nasty depths to the boy. Bob shook his head and went back to considering Dove. He was scowling at the blank wall opposite when the manager came in.

Bob hastily pushed back his chair as the youngish woman turned to shut the door behind her. 'I'm terribly sorry, Inspector McInnis, I had no intention of leaving you to cool your heels in this unattractive little room.'

'That's alright Ms Cartwright; it gave me a small amount of thinking time, rather than filling in the paperwork.' He sat down again, as she too sat behind the desk, and gently inhaled the scent of Charlie. One of the few perfumes he recognised. His first wife had worn it sometimes.

Ms Cartwright offered a charming smile. 'Now, how can I help you? I gather from Ruby that you aren't wishing to take out a mortgage.'

'I'm investigating a murder, one of your clients; I have a warrant to look into his safe deposit box. I would also like access to his accounts.' Bob carefully laid the warrant paper down on the table in front of her.

'Ah! I've never seen one of these before. I'm sure it's perfectly in order, but I'll just read it.' She nodded and offered another smile.

'You don't seem very surprised?' Bob's eyebrow winged up.

She gently shook her head, making her long silver earrings sway against her neck. 'Gossip is rife in any small community and Mr Ratcliff had a lot of money invested in this bank.'

'Ah!' Bob sat back slightly and waited for her to read the warrant.

She laid the papers down after a minute or two. 'I'll get the keys for you and arrange for a full statement to be printed out. How far back do you want it to go?'

Bob scratched his head and grinned. 'I'm not used to so much happy compliance. I was expecting to have to bargain a bit.'

'Well you can bribe me with a drink after work if you want!' She grinned.

Bob shook his head, gently tapping his right forefinger against a gold band on his left hand.

'Oh, what a shame! She's a lucky woman.'

Bob's eyebrow winged up again and Ms Cartwright frankly laughed at him. 'Forgive me, Inspector. I'm divorced and just getting back into the swing of dating. Don't be offended, it's so difficult to know when to push and when to hold back when you've been out of the game for so long.'

Bob nodded, but he didn't smile again. She stood up. 'I really won't be a moment, I'll fetch the keys.'

A minute later, the young girl, Ruby, arrived; her black corn-rows gleamed in the overhead lights as she came into the room. Bob stood as she entered and spoke to him. 'Ms Cartwright says I'm to show you the deposit box, sir. If you'd come this way.' She turned around as she spoke and Bob followed her out, admiring the bright fuchsia pink summer dress. He waited while she keyed in a number to a back room with a chair and table its only furnishings. She indicated the chair. 'I won't be a moment.'

She disappeared and returned with a box approximately fifteen inches square and about six deep. 'There you go. Just knock on the door when you've finished.'

Bob nodded and waited for her to leave before inserting the key in the lock. A strong smell hit him the moment he lifted the lid. It was a smell he'd encountered before in Ratcliff's sitting room and bedroom. Bob lifted out the small manila envelope he'd last seen in Fraser's hand as he took it out of Ratcliff's study. It was nestling among the other contents. He thumbed open the flap and peeked in. 'Hmm! Yes, I'm almost certain I know what you are.'

He laid the packet down on the table and looked at the other contents. There were several books with tooled leather covers, a couple of rolled manuscripts and a quantity of stocks and bonds. At the bottom wrapped in tissue were two solid gold bars about the same size as a pair of Mars Bars. 'Good grief!' Bob hefted them, and then gently replaced them in the box and removed the remaining item, a small pot of liquid. He gently swished it from side to side, even more gently removed the cork and gave a tentative sniff. 'Phew.'

Opening his brief case Bob put the re-corked bottle, the books and manuscripts with the packet in his briefcase and locked the box again before knocking on the door. Ruby opened it and smiled at him. 'Ms Cartwright says these are for you too.' She handed him a folder and nodded.

Bob handed back the key. 'Thank you very much. I've removed certain items in accordance with the warrant.' He held out a paper. 'This is the receipt, please give it to the manageress for me.'

He strode across the grey carpeting of the outer area of the bank and out to the back car park. Sliding behind the wheel he drew a deep breath. Then he pulled out his mobile and keyed in his wife's number. 'Hi, darling.'

Jenny, on the end of the phone, watched her step-daughter jumping up and down in a tub of bright coloured, and soft, balls, of various sizes, and smiled. 'Hi yourself.'

'I love you.'

Jenny turned her head to one side while she continued to watch the child. 'I love you too, Bob. Is anything the matter?'

'No. I just needed to hear your voice.'

'OK.' Jenny smiled down the phone. Bob was a very private man. 'I take it you're alone.'

'I'm outside the bank, in my car.'

'Are we running aground?'

'Police business, Pet, not our bank.'

'Oh!' She watched critically as Caitlin scrambled out of the pit of balls and flung herself into an equally large pit of soft toys. She wished she could see Bob's face. 'Caitlin is having a splendid time throwing things about and generally using up a bit of energy. I'm taking her to see Granddad Fielding this afternoon.'

'Good. She needs wearing out, but don't let her wear you out too, Pet. I need you too.'

'Well that's nice to know, Bob, and right back at you.'

'I gotta go, Jenny. I'll see you tonight. I love you.' Bob clicked shut the phone and breathed out deeply. Then he started the car and headed back to the Police Station, stopping to make a couple of purchases on the way.

MICHAEL JORKVIL WAS ALSO buying things. He had even had them gift wrapped at the same time. Something Bob hadn't thought about. Now Michael had turned up at Harry's door as she was preparing her kitchen for the planned weekend activities.

The melamine side was covered in clean empty jam jars. Sugar and a bottle of pectin sat on the shelf and the sink was full of sudsy water. She tutted mildly as the bell rang, turning away and heading in the direction of the front door.

'Hi!' Harry stood with a dishcloth in one hand and a saucepan in the other looking at Jorkvil as he stood on the doorstep. 'More investigations?'

'No.' Michael offered a smile. 'I was hoping to persuade you to go out for a drink tonight.' He proffered a box wrapped in bright pink, rose-patterned, paper.

'Oh!' Harry looked from the brown eyes watching her and back to the parcel, and then tried to open the door further with a saucepan filled hand. It was a heavy pan such as one might use for jam making, as indeed she intended to do that weekend. Pan, door and cloth became entangled and Michael wasn't quite quick enough to back out of the way. The pan landed with a resounding clang on the step, having bounced off his leather clad shoe.

Harry winced at the look of agony passing rapidly over his face and then said, 'Sorry, sorry, oh dear, not again.' As Michael Jorkvil hopped on one foot, shaking life back into partially recovered, but still bruised, toes.

'You know if you don't like me, you only have to say.' He smiled. 'You don't have to keep hitting me. I'll go away quietly.'

Harry bit her lip, she didn't return the smile. 'I do like you; you're a very nice man.' She mangled her lip a bit more.

'I can hear the 'but'...'

She proffered a smile, trying to soften the blow a bit. 'I'm not into dating just now and I think if I was...'

'It would be Dr Kegan?'

She gave another half smile. 'Maybe, jury's still out.'

'Any chance I can subvert the course of justice?'

She shook her head, her blonde curls falling over her face; she pushed them back with the cloth covered hand and shrugged while she looked at him.

'OK, I can take a hint. But I don't like chocolates, so please will you have them anyway?'

'I don't...'

Michael picked up the saucepan and gently laid the packet inside before handing it back. 'Here you go. No damage done.' His look said to the saucepan or my heart, at least that's what Harry thought he meant. He gave a brief wave and turned away, going back down the path and getting in his car.

Harry watched him drive away and turned back to go to the kitchen. She nodded to herself, muttering 'London buses.' Before putting the pan complete with chocolates, somewhat absently down on the kitchen stove, and going upstairs to get changed for a visit to her earstwhile lodger and possible lover.

Michael Jorkvil meanwhile was shrugging and trying to decide what to do with his afternoon off. While he had been trying, his brain had automatically kicked in; he found he was taking the turn-off for the police station. He looked at the familiar landmarks and continued up the ring road. The new building loomed up and he decided, since his subconscious wanted him there, then that was where he would be.

As he swung through the doors he half grinned, Helen would be in for a nice surprise tomorrow if he cleared his desk. He wended his way up to the squad room and looked across at his desk. Helen was nowhere to be seen, but she had said something about taking the afternoon off if her husband was free. A glance, however, showed that the desks were piled high with paperwork. He almost turned around and fled. However, the place was quiet, he figured he might get some uninterrupted work done and shrugged, walking over and taking off his jacket.

He was slightly mystified at the emptiness of the room, but settled down to some serious auditing of his cases. He had been working for nearly half an hour when Sandy returned, bringing with him two mugs of tea and a small stack of gingernut biscuits. Michael looked up and nodded, looked back at his desk, and then spoke a bit hesitantly across the room.

'Inspector Bell.'

'Yes, lad.'

'Have you been in the office all afternoon?'

'Aye most of it.' Sandy offered a faint smile. 'I just nipped out for supplies.' He indicated his mug.

'It's just; I've got a bit of a problem. I wonder if you could help?'

Sandy raised a ginger eyebrow, set the mugs down

on his desk, and strolled across the room to the younger man's desk.

'It's these notes, Inspector. I know I left them tidy, and now some are missing. Do you know if my partner took any away, she said we might be audited and I was to get everything up to date.' He turned a worried face to Sandy. 'Only I've never done an audit before, and I'm a bit rattled if I'm honest.'

Sandy nodded. 'Blasted things. We all have to do 'em sometime, lad. Which cases were they? Maybe they've got shifted. Folks were walking around with files all morning.'

'No, they were on the desk this morning. I shifted them to get that little book for you. They were about a hit and run two years ago. Helen, Sergeant McKenzie, was looking at them because we think the husband had his pockets picked.'

'Eh!'

Bob came into the room as Sandy stood scratching his head and looking at the detective constable with a totally confused look on his own face. 'Problem?'

'Start again, lad.'

Michael Jorkvil took a deep breath. 'We've been trying to catch some pick-pockets. We've been doing a bit of undercover work in a local café. Saturday our cover was blown.' He waved away the 'how', he could see forming in the air around the other two like a small cumulonimbus of puzzlement. 'Monday we received a cleared packet. Wallet and some contents possibly taken by the pickpockets. There was a picture inside and Helen recognised it from a hit and run she'd worked a couple of years ago when she was in traffic, so we went to see the guy. She pulled the files Tuesday. They were on the desk as a cold case. I saw them this morning and now I can't find them.'

'Maybe Sergeant McKenzie took them?'

'She isn't in today. We've both got the afternoon off.'

'So why are you here, lad? Fine day like this.'

Michael looked from one slightly suspicious face to the other and blushed under their fascinated gaze. 'My... er, I asked someone for a date, Harry turned me down.'

'Oh!' The 'oh' said so many things, and the eyebrows of both men said a lot more as they looked at him.

'No...o, I'm straight. Harry's a girl.'

'Ah!' This time both men nodded sagely and smiled, indeed Bob frankly grinned. 'Blonde bombshell? Sounds like a latter-day Monroe?'

Michael nodded rapidly.

'She's sweet on the Doctor if I don't miss my bet, Bob.' Sandy grinned in his turn as he looked at Bob.

'Yeah, I got that impression this afternoon.' Michael shrugged as he spoke.

Bob nodded. 'Interesting, but it still doesn't find your missing files, Mike.'

Sandy looked at Bob. Both were thinking the same thing. Sandy spoke, 'We'll have a scout on the other desks, lad. You go and get yourself a cuppa. It's probably just got mixed in with someone else's stuff. When you come back you can maybe tell us why you think a pick-pocket would return the goods?' Sandy smiled kindly at Michael. 'Away with you, lad.'

Michael sighed with the relief of a burden shared and stood up. Both senior men waited until he'd left the room for the far reaches of the canteen before they spoke. 'Need to know the source of the cash, but I don't think he's the 'rabbit', Bob.'

'No. We'll have a scout round, but it's interesting, Sandy. A file going missing. The day after the audit is started.'

'Aye.'

When Michael returned they'd checked most of the other desks, without noticeable success. 'Nope. Don't worry, man. It won't be far away.' Bob settled his weight half on the edge of Michael's desk, sipping his own tepid tea as Michael sat down.

'So why did the Sarge think it was something the pickpocket had returned?'

Michael shrugged. 'She recognised the photo, like I said. She said, even if it was just a find someone had returned anonymously, we should take it back and check it out.'

'But she seemed to think it had been returned by pickpockets?'

'Yeah.' Michael put his head on one side. 'It's odd now you come to ask.' His lips moved into a nice smile. 'I suppose that's why she's a Sarge and I'm just a constable.'

'Maybe.' Bob sipped more tea. 'So you took it back and...?'

'Oh, the guy was pleasant enough. He couldn't say if it had been stolen or if he'd just dropped it. But he had lost it at the café. So it probably was nicked.'

'So...?'

Michael shrugged. 'We told him it was an ongoing case and he could have it back after it had cleared evidence.

'What was he called?'

Michael frowned. 'Adrian er...' He snapped his fingers. 'Adrian Chappell. Lives over the south end of the city. His wife was killed in a hit and run when taking their daughter to school.' He went painfully red as he looked at Bob and recalled certain scuttlebutt about the man in front of him.

Bob shook his head gently but all he said was, 'Nice girl, Harry.'

Michael grabbed the change of subject like a lifeline. 'Yeah. Shame I met her after Dr Kegan, still no broken heart here.' He grinned at Bob and patted his chest, then glanced across at Sandy methodically dunking biscuits while he turned the pages of a report. 'I thought he'd be madder at me, I forgot to give him that evidence this morning.'

'Oh, Sandy's alright so long as you feed his addiction.'

'Eh? Addictions are dangerous if you're a copper, that's what my old man used to say, he served over the border in Dumfries. He reckons I'm addicted, but it fills the coffers nicely.'

Bob raised a mobile eyebrow and half smiled. 'Sandy's addiction is Gingernuts, what's yours?'

Michael leaned back slightly and drank some more of his coffee. 'Well, don't spread it around; I don't want anyone to think I'm a geek, but I design computer games. I've sold a few. You can get hooked, it is addictive, but I think I've got it balanced.'

Bob nodded. 'You've sunk yourself now, Mike. I hate computers. I know where I'll be coming to sort out my problems.' He smiled, and at a 'hi' from Sandy gave a friendly nod. 'Back to work. Don't worry about the files, I'm sure they'll turn up.'

22

ADRIAN CHAPPELL LOOKED AT his daughter and smiled. She was munching her way through a bag of crisps in an absent manner while she read her book. The small independent chemist was quiet at this time of afternoon and he'd popped into the back room to see what she was doing.

He spoke to her down-bent head. 'Don't get grease on it, love.'

'S'OK, dad. I'm being careful.' She looked up with a smile of her own.

'What you reading?'

'Doctor Doolittle.'

'Have you got to the push-me-pull-you yet?'

She shook her head. 'I won't spoil it for you.' He grinned. 'I wondered if you'd do me a little job. But you have to promise to be very careful.'

She looked up eagerly, jumping down from the high stool she'd been occupying. 'I'll be very careful, I promise.'

'OK. Here's a fiver. I want you to go to the little bakery in the Lanes and buy a loaf and two cakes for tea.'

'What kind?'

'Buy what you fancy, love. I want an Eccles cake.

Now mind, you haven't got to cross the road, stay on the footpath, and don't talk to strangers. Promise?'

'Promise.' She grabbed her light jacket and carefully put the money in a little leather purse around her neck, before stretching up for a kiss and skipping out of the shop.

Adrian watched her from the door for a moment before he spoke into the shadows. 'She'll only be ten minutes, so you'd better be quick.'

BOB WAS ALSO EXCHANGING information rapidly and quietly. 'I've got the bank statements, Sandy.'

'Aye, so I see.' Sandy nodded at the file resting on the desk; he too kept his voice down even though, for the present, they had the squad room to themselves. 'What else you got?'

'Stocks, bonds, he had a couple of gold bars. About so big.' Bob measured the size with his hands. 'Some books and manuscripts. I thought we could pass them under the nose of Dr Kegan. See what he thinks they are. And then there are these.' Bob poked his finger at the plastic bag of grey powdery lumps which he'd extracted from its manila envelope, and the small bottle of liquid.

'Fairly stinks, Bob. You'd better get it to forensics. Any ideas.'

'I'm almost certain it's ambergris.'

'Come again.'

Bob looked at Sandy's empty mug and grinned a trifle evilly. '*It is strange that fine ladies and gentlemen should regale themselves with the essence of the inglorious bowels of a sick whale'*. Or something like that, Sandy. I'm probably misquoting Melville, but he devoted a whole chapter to ambergris in Moby Dick.'

'Did he now?' Sandy waited for more, with Bob there was always more.

'Ambergris is the faecal matter or vomit of sperm whales. It's mostly illegal these days, not many countries allow import or export because to get it you sometimes have to kill the whale.' He shook his head gently. 'It used to be used in the perfume trade, now they use synthetics to fix perfume. It is also reputed to be good for headaches, epilepsy and one or two other ailments. I would speculate that our Mr Ratcliff was importing it for that purpose. I smelt it Monday in the sitting room, and in the bedroom on Tuesday.'

'Did you now? All I could smell was parrot.' Sandy wrinkled his nose fastidiously. 'And how come Mark didn't pick it up Tuesday?' He frowned as he spoke. 'You'd think forensics would pick up that smell.'

'Oh! He did pick it up, literally.' Bob grinned quickly, and then sobered again, 'But when it's, how can I put it, matured a bit, it smells like isopropanol. That's hand sanitiser to you and me; he probably thought someone had just cleaned their hands before going on to the next clue.'

'OK,' Sandy nodded, 'but how do you take it? Like that?' It was his turn to poke the bag. 'Surely not.'

'I dunno, but I don't think so. Maybe as small pills. I would think it would be rolled or powdered or something. And I'm speculating again but...' He grinned at his partner's snort of amusement. 'I think the same person who was doctoring his meds was making this stuff edible for him, if you know what I mean.'

Sandy nodded. 'Do we think Jenkins was supplying it? The man had been with something that weekend, Dove admitted that. Ratcliff admitted Jenkins supplied him with various substances from foreign parts. Jenkins had been in Italy the week before; Jakob has sent us a memo about that somewhere.' Sandy put his glasses on his nose and shuffled the papers on his desk.

'Hah! Italy's one of the legal exporters. But we don't allow it in. I asked at that little place where you can buy personalised scent.' Bob grinned ferociously. 'It's coming together, Sandy.'

'Aye.' Sandy nodded his head. Then sat back and frowned into the near distance, twirling the metal arm of his glasses and pulling his tie down to the default position that denoted he was seeing something everyone else should have spotted too. Bob sat back; he was waiting to see what Sandy wanted to do next. Michael Jorkvil came into the room and looked at the pair of them.

'Er. Shall I go away?'

'No, man. I've got a little job for you, if you'd like to help.'

'I'D LIKE YOUR HELP, Dot.'

'Are you sure, Jane? I've made enough of a mess already.'

'All the more reason to help.' Jane gave a rather lopsided smile. She had sat thinking for a good half hour after her son had made his way upstairs, before she had phoned Dot.

Now they sat with yet more mugs of tea around her kitchen table. She looked at her son. 'I think I need to meet up with Fraser's father, first on my own. If he doesn't want anything to do with either of us then that's the end of it. But, if he does, then we'll arrange another time and place where you can meet him, Fraser.' She rubbed the back of her hand over her forehead and smiled at him. 'I've heard some funny things about siblings meeting and falling in love. If it's a girl, I want you to know what she looks like, even if your father doesn't want any contact with us. We live in the same town it's important.'

'Yeah. Alright, mum.' Fraser nodded at her and then looked across the table at Dorothy Skeat. 'I was angry, I don't want to see mum hurt, but she's right, keeping it quiet could lead to worse things in the future, so thank you. You've been a good friend and, having me, well she hasn't had too many of them. Leastways not ones who haven't pitied her or looked down on her, and they ain't proper friends' By the end of the speech he was red in the face and buried his face in his mug as soon as he stopped speaking, refusing to make eye contact with either woman.

Jane looked at Fraser, she hadn't realised how much he'd picked up of the scorn and snobbery that she'd suffered over the years.

'So, what do you want me to do, Jane?' Dot drew her attention away from a youth who didn't need to be looked at just at that moment.

'I want you to come with me.' Jane looked directly at her.

'But…'

Jane waved her to be quiet. 'I thought if we met on neutral ground it would be best, maybe that café in town. I don't want you to sit with me, just be there; because whichever way it goes I'm going to be a mess afterwards.' She smiled a bit mistily. 'I'm a proper watering pot, Dot, and I'm going to want someone there to get me out of there, if you follow.'

Dot nodded. 'Alright, love, if you set it up I'll sit in a corner and wait to pick up the pieces.' Her mouth made a moue of regret. 'After all I caused the pieces, its only right I should stick them together again.'

JAMES DOVE WAS WISHING he had someone to pick up the pieces of his life. However, he seemed singularly bereft of friends at that moment. Inspector Jakob had put him through a very fraught hour that morning, and he knew that the consequences of turning Queen's evidence were not guaranteed to be pretty if the drug pushers discovered it was him.

Now the police had appeared on the doorstep yet again, in the shape of Inspector's Bell and McInnis this time. He tried to bluster it out. 'Gentlemen. How can I help you now?'

'Just a few more questions, Mr Dove.'

'You'd better come in. Not that I can stop you.'

Sandy spoke. 'No, sir, you can't. This is still a crime scene.' He shouldered his way past, followed by Bob McInnis. 'I think we'd like to talk to you in the sitting room first, sir.'

James Dove followed them as they nodded at the constable on duty in the hall taking note of all who came and went. They headed into the sitting room and shut the door as Dove moved into the centre of the room.

'Now, Mr Dove, I'd like you to tell us about the other pills.'

'What other pill? That Inspector this morning kept asking about the drugs. I tell you I had nothing to do with it, I just crewed for Joe.'

Bob nodded. 'I'm sure Inspector Jakob was satisfied with your answers. We, however, want to know about the non-prescription drugs that Mr Ratcliff took.'

'Oh those!' Dove gave a little nod. 'He got them off the net mostly, always trying to find a cure.' Bob watched as he physically relaxed.

'And the ones he didn't get off the net. The ones you removed before the doctor came?'

'I...I...'

'Yes. We know. You spilled something, where is it? And just why did you take it?'

Dove was as grey as his eponymous name might suggest. He walked over to a hard chair and lowered himself, before looking at the two stern men in front of him. 'Joe brought it last weekend. I swear I don't know what it was. The boss got it every so often; he sent it to the chemist. I thought it was just one of these quack things like rhino horn or something. But I thought if you knew about it you might find out about me and Joe and the boat.' He scowled. 'You found out about that anyway.'

'Where is it?'

'I dunno. The fresh stuff came last Friday. I think he must have sent it off to the chemist, because the new pills were on the side when I found him. So I hid them.'

'Right.' Sandy nodded. 'Go and get the bottle, and I suggest you stop impeding the course of justice, you're in enough hot water already.' He looked at Bob. 'Desk?'

'Yeah.' Bob walked over and unlocked the bottom drawer. 'I looked but I didn't see, Sandy, I put it down to the usual desk clutter, he even told us he'd got it and I didn't make the connection.' He pulled on an evidence glove and took out the contents. Gathering a small bottle of Gum Arabic and a handful of metal nibs suitable for dip pens. He put them in an evidence bag saying, 'I bet you used these at school, Sandy.'

'Aye, I'd always got an ink stain on my forefinger,' he grinned a bit lopsidedly, showing his eye tooth, 'and my face and usually my hanky. Biro's were my salvation, lad.'

'I like an ink pen myself. You can write something elegant with an ink pen.'

'Hmm!' Sandy, whose handwriting was small, spidery and illegible, scowled. 'I'll be in the bedroom, Bob.'

Bob came into the bedroom a few minutes later, holding a small brown bottle in a large evidence bag. 'I got him to put it in, Sandy. Thought we might lift a few prints, but if the rest of the stuff is anything to go by it'll be wiped clean'

'Aye, like as not.' Sandy didn't look as his partner; he appeared to be focused on the bedside cabinet. Bob, after a glance of his own, kept silent as he looked in the same direction.

'I can see how you've come to you're conclusions,

Bob. But I'd like to look in the attic and see yon staircase my own self.'

Bob nodded and led the way out and up the stairs. Neither man felt the need to talk until they had walked through the scene again. Standing outside the downstairs bedroom at the bottom of metal staircase, Sandy nodded. 'Aye. I think you've got the right of it, but how do we prove it?'

Bob glanced at his watch. 'Mark is due with a SOCO team in the next few minutes.'

Sandy nodded again.

'Loccard's principles, Sandy. It's all we can ever go on. He left something and he took something. We'll find it. This was a nasty little murder, there's no passion or anger. It's just slow poisoning and patience.'

'Aye.' Sandy sighed. 'We still need a motive, and we still haven't got a suspect. But...I agree with you, yon man inside is too spineless and too fearful to have done it.'

The two men walked around the house to the front door and nodded again at the constable on duty as they went back in to await forensics.

Mark Forester, when he arrived, offered both men a cheery grin. 'What did I miss?' He shook his golden curls at them and sighed gustily.

Bob shook his own sleek locks back. 'You didn't. It wasn't an area you were asked to process, but now...well, let me take you on a little tour and I'll explain our theory.'

The three men walked along to the downstairs bedroom yet again. 'We did in here, not a hint of a smudge on the surfaces.' Mark indicated with a sweep of his hand the dust covered furniture in front of them.

'I want you to look at the window again.'

Mark raised an eyebrow. 'OK, you're the boss, Bob, but it's too narrow to admit someone.'

'Agreed. I wondered if someone could have opened it and leaned in from outside to talk.'

'Ah!' Mark went over and cast an experienced eye over the frame. He gave a muted bellow. 'Johnson, outside window, dust, footprints, fibres, anything.' He spoke as a small dumpy man in glasses appeared at the doorway. Mark nodded to the empty space as Johnson disappeared, and then looked at Sandy and Bob again. 'And...?'

'Upstairs, attic floor, iron staircase.'

'Bill!' Bill appeared, heavy silver case in hand, and Mark lifted his chin in the direction of the upper storey. 'Attic and all points downwards.'

'Yo.' The voice echoed downwards.

'And me?'

'What did forensics find from the parrot droppings?' Bob grinned as Mark wrinkled his face up.

'You were right, Bob. Ambergris.' Mark shrugged. 'There were some parrot droppings too, that bird must have been fed exclusively on the best seed going.'

'And the little bottle.'

'Give a man a chance...' Mark grinned. 'Oak apple gall. Have you tried the diet coke and mentos eruption? Works much better with acacia gum, reduces the surface tension.'

'Eh.' Sandy looked at the two men grinning like school boys at each other.

'I'll explain later, Sandy. Sufficed to say, our Mr Ratcliff had the makings of medieval ink.' Bob counted off on his fingers. 'He'd got oak gall, iron nails, Gum Arabic and nib pens. I think he was into a bit of forging.'

'We might have a motive after all, Bob.'

'Indeed we might, Sandy. I should have spotted it sooner. I use ink pens all the time.'

'You did spot it. I wouldn't have.'

Bob shrugged, and opened his mouth to speak; he didn't get a chance to start the sentence.

'Damn! He said there were bits he'd never read before.'

'Eh!'

'Dr Keegan. He told me there were bits of information he hadn't come across before. No wonder, if Ratcliff was inserting them in the text.' Sandy scowled. 'I'm as dunderheaded as you seem to think you've been, Bob.'

'I'm worse than you think, he told us in this very room what he'd got, he said he'd got acacia gum. I just didn't think of Gum Arabic under that name.'

'Did you know that nearly caused a world shortage of Coke after 9/11?'

Both the senior men looked at Mark in astonishment.

He nodded. 'There was this rumour that Bin Laden had holdings in the Sudanese Gum Arabic production, and the

US wanted to boycott all products using it. Then Ukec, that was the Sudanese Ambassador to the US, he said he'd stop all imports and bring down the Western world, by depriving them of Coke-cola.'

'Good God, Mark, what will you tell us next.' Sandy shook his head sadly.

Bob was only half listening to Mark. 'Ratcliff even told us certain factions were against its export. My God, Sandy, the man must have been killing himself laughing at the thick coppers.' Bob frowned.

'Aye, lad. And now he's dead.' Sandy nodded at Mark. 'OK, Mark, take exhibits A and B and see what you can get from them.'

Mark nodded, carefully stowing the evidence bags and walking away to check on his team of evidence collectors.

23

THE BENT COPPER WAS having problems with his evidence collection. However, he wasn't too worried. He'd only ever collected it for Ratcliff, and Ratcliff was dead. The man had been as cautious as a hunter who feared to become prey. Now the only evidence he wanted was to be assured his own skin was safe.

It was a symbiotic relationship. At first he'd gone to Ratcliff with the suggestion that for a small sum of money he'd keep quiet about certain evidence that had come into his hands. Then he'd passed on information for further cash. Both had a hold on the other, and therefore both trusted each other, for a given value of trust.

He didn't like this audit though. Cases that should have stayed dead and buried were rising like Banquo's ghost, and he, like Macbeth, was in danger of losing his cool and betraying himself. He shivered in the evening air as he tried to contact the one person who could, and had, been complicit in his underhand dealings; and might be able to offer some reassurance. But they were out of range of his phone.

JAMES DOVE, ON THE other hand, was receiving reassurance that he would be protected from his underhand dealings by a very reluctant policeman. Nils Jakob was watching him carefully as he manoeuvred the small craft into the open water of the Solway Firth. There were several men secreted on board the skiff, dressed for the most part in diving gear.

Jakob leaned against the side of the cabin as he watched the competent way Dove handled the boat. 'You're sure they'll come tonight.' James dove was sweating lightly despite the chill off the water.

'I've allowed a few hints to be dropped in the right areas. They will be expecting Jenkins boat with Jenkins on it, out early this evening. We haven't allowed the news of his death to get into the public domain. Unless they killed him they can't know he's dead. All you have to do is take us out there and cast your line in the usual manner.'

Dove nodded, wiping the sweat off his brow with a clammy hand. 'If they know he's dead they'll know it's a trick.'

'Maybe, maybe not, they might just think you want to play with the big boys and take on his trade now.'

'But they might come after me.'

Jakob raised an eyebrow. 'They would have anyway, my lad. He was into a dirty business, and you were well implicated. They weren't going to leave a witness, you just be grateful we got to you first.' The laugh that accompanied this wasn't altogether pleasant to James Dove's ears, but he did recognise the truth of it.

The engine made a quiet phut phut sound as they made way across the water towards the distant sunset, and the Isle of Man in the distance. Jakob didn't speak again. Dove went about the business of dropping the anchor so that the boat faced to the North, putting out a line in silence, occasionally glancing at the wet-suit clad men on the deck.

Jakob had been watching the radar screen, the dots that represented his boats were now at their stations. Just after nine he raised his chin and, with a nod, five men slipped over the side and round to starboard, out of view of the Isle. Dove moved back into the cabin and sat down in the far corner. He hoped that no-one would know he was there. Jakob narrowed his eyes but said nothing. There was after all nothing to say that hadn't been said already.

HARRY WASN'T SPEAKING EITHER. She was looking at a very unrepentant Hugh as he sat at her kitchen table. 'I'm sorry, Harry. I couldn't stand it a minute longer. It's not as if they can do anything for me. They were going to discharge me tomorrow anyway.'

Harry continued to sit, just looking at him. She wasn't sure which she was more surprised at, the fact that Hugh had galvanised himself into positive action for once, or his appearance on her doorstep five minutes before or, worse, the overwhelming pleasure she had found in seeing him again so soon. She clasped her hands in front of her on the kitchen table and just kept looking at him.

Finally Hugh pushed back his chair with his legs and placed both hands on the table. 'I've obviously presumed too much. I'll go home.' He looked suddenly grim and very tired, and definitely all of the forty-five years he'd lived.

'Sit down, Hugh.' Harry shook her head. 'Before you fall down.' She moved and stretched out a hand, gripping his where they pushed against the table top. She offered a short smile and spoke gently. She watched him subside slowly onto the seat again. 'You are more than welcome here, Hugh. My concern is that you have discharged yourself from hospital. Not that you've come here.'

'I told you...'

'Yes, I know you did. But, as you pointed out yesterday, I'm an engineer and not a nurse. I'm scared that I wouldn't know what to do if anything went wrong.'

'You don't have to worry.' Hugh gave a small shake of his maltreated head and proffered an even smaller smile. 'I shall be fine.'

'Yes, I hear you.' Harry nodded, still gripping his hand. 'That still doesn't stop me being worried. I did get you in this mess in the first place.' She took a deep breath. 'Worse, I've spent so long imagining myself as a career woman that I'm not quite sure how to do this romantic stuff.'

'That's OK, I'll do that bit. I wasn't too good at it the last time around but *nil desperandum* as they say, we could learn together.' Hugh gripped the hands back and almost pleaded.

'But I'm clumsy, and somewhat fixated and I don't interact well, hence the imponderables. It keeps people at bay and stops them laughing at me, especially men.'

'You've interacted with me fine so far.'

'I've never met anyone I wanted to share with before and I'm scared that if I allow you too near we'll both end up hurt, Hugh.'

Hugh frowned. 'Ah.' He gripped the hands still holding his. 'You were worried yesterday weren't you? I thought I'd said something. I thought it was that damn list. But it wasn't. Thank God for that.' He grinned. 'I can be fixated too, Harriet. Especially if it's important.'

'But...'

'No, you'll give me a headache. And we don't want that.' He kept the grin in place. 'We'll take it one day at a time, because I do want you, Harriet.' He lifted the hands still holding his and dropped a kiss onto the knuckles. 'Now, I've brought all the paperwork home with me. So you shall read it, and then you will know what to do if necessary. OK.' He looked at her quizzically. 'I bet you've been avoiding men all your young life just in case...aren't I the lucky one.' He watched the blush. 'We won't fail from trying, my girl.'

Harry nodded slowly. She looked at Hugh watching her. Her lips curved into a smile, even though her eyes were misty with tears. 'If you try to fail and succeed, which have you done?'

'I know your secrets now, Harry; you can't cloud the issue with your blessed imponderables. I was a bit scared myself yesterday. I have tried and failed, but I'm sure now. I love you, so you'll have to make sure I don't fail again, won't you?' He stood up and walked around the table. 'I shall make us tea and you shall read the paperwork.' He glanced at the stove. 'Er, Harry. Why are you cooking a parcel?'

'I LOVE YOU. DID I tell you recently?' Bob stood in his kitchen watching his wife wipe down the draining board and hang the teacloth neatly on the rail. He'd just come in. His house radiated the peace found only after his daughter had been put to bed and there were no demands on any other member of the household.

'Not since this afternoon, on the phone, you didn't.' Jenny gave him a very wifely look as she came towards him and set her hands on his shoulders. 'I love you too.' She offered her lips and then took a hand and led him into the front room and pulled him down on the settee.

'I was propositioned today. It was a shock to the system, Jen.' He pulled her close into his side and sniffed at her hair as she turned her head in a rather startled manner and looked at him.

'What do you mean by 'propositioned' exactly, darling?'

'As in, 'you're a good looking bloke and I'd like to get you into my bed'.' Bob cocked his head on one side, looking at his wife's face; he thought her green eyes really were green. Then he gave a half smile, he was incurably honest with himself, he hoped she was a little jealous anyway. 'At least that's what the lady seemed to be asking.' He sniffed her unique scent again and pulled her tight for a long distracting kiss.

'Well, so long as that's all she did.' Jenny wasn't letting go of the subject just yet.

'I love you, pet. I couldn't be unfaithful if I tried. I can't function without my heart, love, and you've got that.' He offered a whimsical smile.

'Softy.' But Jenny gave him another kiss and snuggled down in his arms.

'It's been a funny sort of day really. We might have a breakthrough in our case.' Bob grinned as his wife squirmed a bit closer. 'I did some maths this morning and then went to the bank where the bank manageress came on to me.' He heard the faint chuckle, but carried on. 'Then I went back to the station and talked tactics with Sandy.' He suddenly stopped speaking, drawing in a deep breath and hugging her tight.

'Bob?'

He looked down at his wife as she sat up and looked at him. 'I was reminded today of how much I'd loved Beth, Jenny. And how I lost her. One of the young constables was talking about a case. Hit and run. He reminded me of all the frustration and anger I'd felt. I couldn't blame anyone except perhaps myself. God help me if I ever lose you, darling,' He gently kissed the mouth temptingly near him. 'The thought of losing you would drive me insane.'

'OK, how about sharing?'

'I just did.' Bob moved back a bit, looking very puzzled and slightly indignant. Jenny was always on at him to share his thoughts.

'I mean sharing me.'

He looked horrified. 'Jen! You're MY wife.' He tried to release her grip on his arm.

'For a copper you really can be dense. Sharing as in Caitlin and this.' She placed his hand on her tummy.'

'Oooh!' It was a long 'oh' and Jenny watched as her husband first went red then milk white. 'Oh, God, Jen, I love you.'

24

Friday

FRIDAY WAS AS BRIGHT and crisp as the freshly ironed shirt that Bob McInnis had put on his back. Both he and Sandy Bell had a feeling that the case was nearing a conclusion, though the evidence for that, as well as the case, was still very flimsy. As Sandy said, 'We've got bugger all, Bob. But what we have got might just help us to get a bit more.'

Sandy was seated in his shirt sleeves, at his desk. The air was redolent of coffee and deodorant, and men were moving about as if they had suddenly discovered a secret mission. Bob had scooted his own chair across to the front of Sandy's desk, and was nursing his first mug of coffee of the day. 'What do you want to do this morning then?'

'I think first a run through; when this bedlam has settled down.' Sandy cast a look at the scurrying constabulary around him with a scowl.

Bob nodded and watched with careful eyes as men set to work for the day. He noted the entrance of Michael Jorkvil and his partner and watched as they went over to their respective desks, talking rapidly. He became fascinated as the hand waving and low verbal conversation began to intensify. 'Hmm!'

'Eh, what's up, lad.'

Bob with a jerk of his head indicated the escalating argument across the room. Several men and women had stopped their own frantic hurry to watch, as Helen McKenzie continued to tear small strips off her subordinate. Her voice and pitch rising equally but unmusically, as her temper frayed like some badly played clarinet.

'What do you mean you've lost it? God damn it, Mike, audits are hard enough without you losing bloody files. If you put it on the desk that's where it should be. I don't care how many others you've done, we need that one as well.'

Mike was opening and shutting his mouth with absolutely no hope of getting a verbal foot in the doorway of her arpeggio.

Sandy listened for a few seconds more and then stood up with a scrape of his chair that seemed to echo around the suddenly still and silent room. Men glanced his way, and rapidly found work to do in other places, as he walked over to the arguing couple.

'Problem?' He spoke quietly behind Helen and she visibly jumped, stopping halfway through a word, before turning.

'Sorry, sir.'

Sandy cocked his head on one side and waited, watching her going red in the face.

'No, sir. No problem, sir.'

'It is from where I'm standing, lass. You're disrupting the smooth running of the workplace.' He gave a half smile which wasn't pleasant to see, indicating the rapidly emptying room. No-one wanted to be around if Sandy Bell was about to indulge in a tongue lashing. 'Mike, go and get yourself a coffee.' He ignored the two full mugs on the desk in front of him.

Mike, after a quick glance at him, nodded rapidly and left as if his heels had caught fire.

'Now, lass. Come over here and talk to me.' Sandy looked grim and Helen visibly swallowed. Bob watched the approaching couple and nodded politely. 'Won't be long, Sandy.' He left, and the dust metaphorically settled in an all but deserted area.

Sandy indicated Bob's empty chair. 'Sit down.' It was an order. He waited for her to sink onto the soft seat, and then took his own. 'Now, let's have it, lass. You can't go around undermining Mike in front of others, it's bad manners to start with, and bad morale to end with.'

'I'm sorry, sir.' She pressed her lips together for a moment. 'It won't happen again.'

'No, probably not, but you're a woman. I ken they're apt to be volatile in the wrong season. Is it that?' Sandy moderated his tone as he watched the flare of red climb her cheeks again, and flood the rest of her face. 'I'm not being nosy, lass. But you seem more upset than a lost file should account for.'

Helen nodded miserably. 'It's not...I...I had a row with Neil.'

'Aye, well, we all have marital problems, but you can't bring them to work, Helen.'

'No, I'm sorry, sir.' She gulped and Sandy pushed a tissue box across the desk. Helen blew her nose and shuddered. 'It's just he never rows with me, and then this week he's been sniping and arguing, and asking questions about Mike and me. Dammit, I love Neil. I'd never… But I have to work with him.' Sandy, sifting pronouns, nodded.

'I dunno what's wrong; he was fine Monday, and then Tuesday he started asking where I'd been Monday evening, and who with, and what we'd done. It was all work. But he wouldn't listen.' Her voice started up the scales again

Sandy nodded soothingly. 'So, tell me about Monday evening's work.'

Helen gulped again and wiped away a trickling tear, lowering her voice. 'We we're half way through supper, Mike phoned, told me he'd caught a burglar, wanted me to lend a hand. By the time we'd transported and booked, and seen the guy safely into his cell it was nearly half ten and Neil had gone on duty himself.' She sniffed inelegantly. 'Traffic's been a bitch lately, what with the build up of summer visitors. So I didn't see him. Tuesday he came to pick me up for lunch, only I'd forgot. We were off out on the case, and he was mad at me for forgetting, and it's just got worse from there.' She blew her nose again and looked with sodden eyes at Sandy.

'OK.' Sandy stood up and crossed the room, bringing back her mug of cooling coffee and setting it in front of her. 'Have a drink. Feeling better?'

He got a shy nod. 'Now as to the file. Mike told us it was gone yesterday, poor lad was beside himself. He checked all the desks; my guess is it's gone back into storage. Give records a ring and get them to go through things again, but everyone wants theirs so don't be surprised if they blow a raspberry at you and tell you to wait.' He offered a smile. 'I suggest you go and find your partner, and offer him as public an apology as you can manage, try the staff room. After that… well, go and get some fresh air the pair of you, and come back later.'

'Yes, sir.' She pushed back her chair and sniffed again. 'Thank you, sir.'

'And Helen...'

'Sir?'

'It's hard enough being a copper; try and find out what's bothering Neil before your marriage suffers any further.'

'Yes, sir.'

She pulled her skirt straight without looking at him, and walked over to the door. Pulling it open she found Bob lounging outside, effectively blocking the entrance, and using his mobile. He glanced at her, shook his head in reply to something on the end of the line and said, 'No, that's fine.' into the receiver, and clicked it shut, gave her a nice smile and went into the big squad room.

'Sorted?' Bob spoke quietly.

'Aye. For now.' Sandy shifted in his seat and pulled out his steel-rimmed glasses, perching them on his nose and looking over them at Bob. 'Now, let's reprise the case while we've got the room to ourselves.'

'Huh, I might have known you'd turn it to good account.' Bob grinned at Sandy's unrepentant face.

'Wee..ll we aw ha' ta' tak' the chances we can, lad.' Sandy turned his broad accent into a comprehensible one as he grinned back.

Bob sat down and flipped open the closed files in front of him, leafing through the pages. 'Where do you want to start, murder one or murder two?'

'Let's start with Joe Jenkins.'

'OK.' Bob swapped a file and pulled forward an A4 pad. 'Found out at Brownrigg…'

'No, let's go a bit further back, Bob.' Both ignored the slowly filling room as men returned to work.

Bob nodded. 'OK, Joe Jenkins, drug dealer. He spent the week before his death on the continent. Jakob confirms that he was in Belgium, France and Italy and then back to Newcastle and onwards to Carlisle. He visited Ratcliff on Friday night, bringing with him some dubious substances, among which was possibly fresh ambergris.'

Sandy nodded as he listened and doodled on the paper in front of him. Bob noticed with faint amusement that a blue whale was taking shape under his pen, completed with upturned fluke and spurting blowhole. Sandy looked up from his task to add, 'Later that night he went out in the boat with James Dove, where he disposed of some of his cargo of drugs.'

Bob nodded at Sandy's interjection and picked up the tale again. 'Meanwhile Jakob got wind of the deal and tried to catch him, only to find the bird had flown. Saturday, Ratcliff travelled to York for some undisclosed purpose. He demanded Jenkins attendance Saturday night, after a phone call on the way back from that trip. And I'm guessing at that connection, Sandy, but I think our 'mole' told him of the impending visit of the drugs squad.' He grinned and resumed. 'According to Fraser Wilson, he was 'put out' after that call. Later that evening he told Dove to sever his connection with Jenkins and, we assume, was waiting for the opportunity to sever it himself, agreed?'

'Agreed. Sunday, he gets busy, he needs to clean

house, and God help that man or woman when I find out who they are; because I can't think of a good enough excuse to give that kind of information away, Bob.' Sandy scowled ferociously, then shrugged at the quizzical expression on Bob's face. 'I know, concentrate on the case.' He offered a wry grin. 'But I will get him, Bob.' He added a few waves to his sea scene and then placed a seagull in the sky as he spoke.

'Yes, we will.' Bob's face had a matching grin, and it didn't reach his eyes either. 'Monday, Jenkins is found dead near Brownrigg, but probably knocked down in the vicinity of Ratcliff's house and from this we deduce... What do we deduce, Sandy?'

'That he'd been visiting Ratcliff for some unknown purpose, but possibly because of the phone call requesting his presence.' Sandy scowled, setting down his pen and looking at Bob across the desk. 'Fraser and James Dove both say they were informed on Sunday night that Jakob was to visit the next day. Perhaps Ratcliff finally got hold of Jenkins and told him to come round and talk.'

'Why not talk on the phone?'

'Maybe he was threatening or bribing, or wanted the man to dispose of goods he'd brought. I don't think we shall ever know that one, Bob. They're both dead and taken their secrets with them.'

Bob shrugged. 'So, Monday, Jenkins is dead and Jakob is visiting with his band of merry men. They find nothing, but then Ratcliff knew they were coming. So persons unknown killed Jenkins before that visit.

'Tuesday Ratcliff is dead. Different killer. Coincidence? His was slow poison, Bob.'

'I think that murderer might be the local who came a few times a year, Sandy. Mrs McGillivray's description is minimal at best. But 'ugly man and ugly dog'.'

'Aye.' Sandy sighed, and then became aware that they had an audience of two.

'I know of an ugly man and an ugly dog, sir.' Mike shrugged, offering a faint smile. 'We came back to apologise and thank you, sir.'

Sandy looked at Mike and Helen standing next to the desk. He raised an eyebrow and waited for further information. Bob looked over his shoulder at them.

'He lives near Mr Ratcliff's house but...

Bob swung the rest of his body around in his seat. 'I am strangely interested in this odd couple, tell us more.'

Mike opened his mouth and shut it again. He'd put his foot in it yesterday and didn't want to do it again today. Helen had no such compunction. 'I think he was a victim of our pick-pockets, sir. His wallet was returned on Monday, anonymously.' She held up a hand to stem the questions. 'Just a gut feeling. He didn't want a fuss made about the loss, said his daughter had been through enough after all the police activity last time, and he didn't want the whole business brought up again.' She shrugged.

'What whole business? How did you connect it to him?'

'Photo in the wallet. I recognised a picture from three years back. Neil was working traffic and I was doing my stint as uniform after I took my exams.' Sandy nodded; all 'plain clothes' had to serve time in uniform after the exams. Gareth was doing his time at the moment.

'Anyway, we attended a hit and run. Mother killed outright, child traumatised. Didn't catch the bastard. But I remembered the case. And when I saw the picture I went to see the man, Adrian Chappell.'

'Wasn't that the...' Sandy looked at Mike.

'Yeah.' Mike nodded. 'That was the file I lost yesterday, that's what made me think of him.'

'And he's an ugly man with an ugly dog.' Bob spoke slowly, and Sandy glanced at him but couldn't read the expression on his face.

'Yeah.' Both Helen and Mike spoke together.

'What's his occupation?'

'Chemist.'

'What!' Now it was Bob and Sandy who echoed each other.

Mike looked mystified.

'He couldn't be, could he, Sandy.'

'Nah, surely not!' Sandy shook his head. 'Where's the motive? Where's the connection?'

Bob shook his head. 'I want all the info you've got on this guy.' He looked from Helen to Mike 'And I want it now.'

Mike nodded mutely. Helen went over and brought her chair back to Sandy's desk and sat down.

'IT'S ARRANGED. WE'RE GOING to meet at the café about half one. Sit and have a chat, and then I can decide what we're going to do.' Jane smiled a bit forlornly at Dot. 'Alright'

'If that's what you want, Jane.'

'I'm coming too.' Fraser looked from one woman to the other. 'I won't interfere, mum. But I want to see what my father looks like. I'll sit in a corner where I won't be noticed, I promise.'

Jane bit her lip. 'I'm not sure...'

'I am. I don't want you hurt again, mum.'

'He won't hurt me. And he has agreed to talk to me, at least.'

'Yeah.' There was a hint of a sneer in the young voice.

'Fraser, he never knew about you. Don't go blaming him.'

'He never checked either. That you were alright, I mean.'

'I didn't give him the chance, love.'

'Hmm!'

Dot looked from mother to son. 'It's nearly eleven. I suggest we have something to eat, because we'll be wasting the coffee in the shop.' She spoke a a bit wryly. 'Half past one, you said. We've got time. I'll take us in the car. All of us.' She looked at Fraser. 'Alright?'

Fraser gave a nod, still watching his mother who sighed. 'OK, Fraser, but promise you won't speak to him until I say so.'

'I promise.'

'I'M GOING OUT. I'M fed up of doing nothing.' James Dove looked at the cook and shrugged his shoulders. 'I want to see someone anyway.'

'Please yourself.' Mrs MacGillivray looked at him. 'I should have a shave first.'

Dove pulled a face, it didn't improve his appearance. 'Can't be bothered. I'm tired.'

Mrs MacGillivray tutted, but carried on peeling carrots for the stew she was preparing. James Dove cast her a look of loathing and swung out of his chair. He was scared and bored and wanted the whole thing to be over. Indeed he wished it had never started. He didn't know what he was going to do when the solicitors had finished. He did know he would be out of a job and a home, with little cash to show for it. He supposed he could live on the boat…if the police let him keep it, or he wasn't in prison.

A short time later he dropped off the bus in the centre of the town and glanced at his watch before looking around; he still had over half an hour to fill. He began to walk down the street in the direction of the Cathedral. He supposed he could always drink tea while he waited.

The Café was fairly empty. The lunchtime rush had nearly dispersed, but Dove did spy a familiar face on the pavement. 'Hello, Fraser.' James Dove came to a stop next to the metal table and looked down at Fraser. 'Is this how you spend your time off?'

Fraser looked at the unshaven jaw and the brown eyes in the squashed in face, and nodded. He'd been examining every man who came in or out, or even lingered in the vicinity of the café entranceway, trying to guess if any of them might be his father. The thought that James Dove might be filled him with a kind of hysterical laughter he was hard put to suppress.

'Hello. I thought you were still a fixture at the house.'

'I had to meet someone here, so I took some time off. Not much I can do in that place until the police have finished anyway.'

'No, I suppose not.' Fraser shrugged, glancing quickly in the direction of his mother and Dot inside the café.

James Dove also looked inside. 'I'll get a drink. Can I get something for you?'

'No.' Fraser paused, 'Thanks.' He watched with horrified fascination as James went in. However, the man walked straight past Jane Wilson and over to the counter. Fraser kept an eye on him as he again passed within feet of Jane and came back outside, carrying a mug.

'Mind if I sit.'

'Suit yourself.'

'I need to find a job. I'm going to meet a bloke I know, he might be able to find me work. Do you want me to put a word in? I suppose you're looking too.'

'Yeah! I've been on the net. Checking out the job situation, but there's not a lot going. What there is out there, you're one of hundreds applying for.' Fraser tried to infuse a bit of thanks into his voice. It was a generous offer, but he was more than a little distracted at the moment. He nodded at James absently, as he picked up his own mug and took a sip, looking over the top as a man and pre-teen approached and wended their way through the barrier of chairs and tables to the open door of the cafe.

He sat up straighter as the man and child went over to a far corner and settled down without ordering anything. Then the man got up again and approached his mother. 'I gotta get a fresh mug.' He muttered the comment at James Dove and went inside with quick steps, heading for the counter and asking for a refill while keeping Jane and the man under observation.

Dorothy Skeat stood up and, refusing to meet Fraser's eye, went over to the young child and sat down on a seat at the same table. Fraser, looking at his mother and the man, opted to sit inside near the doorway. He looked at Mrs Skeat; she was speaking quietly to the child, who was watching her father with an anxious face.

He looked over and gave a smile and a nod, before turning back and facing Fraser's mother. Fraser could see the profile of what he assumed was his father. He'd thought James Dove was ugly, but this guy looked as though he'd had a fight with the spin cycle of a washing machine, and lost.

'Good God. What are you doing here?' The cultured voice spoke softly next to him. He looked up at the handsome face of Detective Inspector McInnis.

'Hello, Inspector.'

'Hush and sit still. In fact go away. Now!' The voice was still quiet, but Bob McInnis wasn't looking at him, he was focused across the room on Fraser's mum. Fraser got a sinking feeling in his stomach. Maybe whatever Mrs Skeat and his mother had been up to was coming home to roost.

Fraser looked about, the café seemed very full all of a sudden. One of those 'rush times' he supposed. He shook his head; he wasn't leaving his mum to face the music alone.

Bob frowned down at Fraser, and then checked around the room, noting the position of his men. He would have preferred to deal with this away from other citizens if possible. However, they'd been to the shop and had been directed to this café. It wasn't as if they'd got proof. Just a hell of a lot of coincidences, and one enormous hunch.

He glanced at Mike, who gave an imperceptible nod in the direction of their target. Bob nodded his thanks for the identification and jerked his head at the plain clothes men he'd brought with him. He'd got men round the back and in the street. He approached with a certain degree of caution. If he was right this man had killed with malice aforethought, but it hadn't been violent, so maybe the man wasn't. But you could never tell.

'Mr Adrian Chappell?'

'Yes.'

'I need you to accompany me down to the Police Station.' Bob got the words out, but the mayhem that ensued left him with a bloody nose, and a desperate desire for solitude, preferably on a deserted dessert island.

Chappell glanced swiftly at the warrant card being proffered discreetly for his inspection and rose like a grouse at the sight of the beaters. He brought his fist into contact with Bob's face. He pushed the chair back into the groin of the approaching uniform, shoved a palm into the solar plexus of a reeling Bob, who therefore impeded his own men as they tried to get around him.

Then Chappell straightened and made a dash for the door. For such a puny looking specimen he packed a hell of a punch, Bob thought. Bob wasn't about to let his man go without a fight though, and launched himself between two tables, grabbing the departing legs in a rugby tackle and bringing his quarry down, where he became the centre of a scrum.

Jane was by now on her feet yelling. 'Adrian?'

A child was shouting. 'Daddy!'

A man, who Bob later recognised as Fraser Wilson, was heading into the melee shouting. 'Mum.'

As the noise level rose, Sandy, following the last man inside, clapped his hands to his ears for a second before shoving roughly into the group and helping a bald headed uniform to get restraints onto Chappell's wrists.

'Be still. The more you struggle the more it will hurt. Stop it.' Sandy shook Chappell a bit roughly. 'Stop swearing, or I'll charge you with that as well.'

'Let me fucking go!'

'Not likely.' Sandy looked at Bob, who had blood running down his face, 'Charged?'

Bob shook his head and took a pile of napkins from a nearby table to stem the tide. 'I'd barely spoken before he made a run for it.' His voice came out a bit breathy. He was well and truly winded and had taken a mule kick to his stomach in the grapple.

'Get off me.' Chappell was still struggling.

Sandy looked at him with hard eyes. 'Why did you run?' Bob moved in to help hold Chappell still.

'Overdue parking tickets.' It was snarled as Chappell kicked out at all and sundry.

Fraser had gone over to his bewildered mother and was holding her as she sobbed into his chest. Bob noted the by-play as he tried to grab a flailing leg again. He was just about to speak when a small child hurtled through the surrounding men and started thumping him on the back. 'Ow.' He looked in astonishment at the small pigtail wearing girl.

'Leave my daddy alone.'

All the fight suddenly went out of Adrian Chappell. He stood still for a second or two, and then sagged in the arms of the constabulary. Bob turned, holding her firmly but gently between his hands, fending off the kicking legs of Maggie Chappell as best he could.

He glanced at Sandy with a comical expression of dismay on his face as she continued to shriek at him, her glasses tipping dangerously on her nose.

'It's alright, Maggie.' Chappell spoke a bit more sharply when he had no response the first time; 'Maggie!' and his daughter stopped hitting Bob and looked at him. Her lip quivered.

'Daddy?'

'It's OK.'

Bob looked frantically at Sandy; none of their plans had covered a child's presence.

Jane released herself from her son's arms. 'Adrian?'

He looked at her, looked at his daughter, and then spoke to the child. 'Be a good girl now. I want you to go and stay with that lady there for me while I talk to these men. OK?'

'But, Dad!'

'No, Maggie, do as I say. Now.' He frowned at her and Jane stepped forward and came over as the police made a path for her.

'Come over here, love, while your dad talks.' She took a small cold hand and steered the reluctant girl away from her father. Sandy nodded at her, then looked at one of his men. All the relevant detail would be ready for him when he got back.

'OK. Can we get this shambles sorted out? You,' he pointed at Adrian Chappell. 'I caution you that...' Sandy went through the preamble and then nodded at a sergeant. 'Get him transported, I'll be there when you are.' He turned away, noting that Bob seemed to have stemmed the blood somewhat and was leaning against a table dabbing his face. He took in the sobbing child clasped in the arms of Jane Wilson and that a young man who he vaguely recognised, was hovering around both.

'Thanks, Sandy.'

'Oh! I'll not let you forget this, Bob. Trounced by a slip of a thing.' A faint smile lit his face for a second.

'I'd no notion of shrenching him.' Bob spoke a bit thickly through the folds of the napkin.

'Of what?'

'Entrapping. I think we might have our man, Sandy, but I thought he would give us a bit more bluster before we could lay any charges.'

'Get yourself seen to, lad, and then come in.'

'I'm fine.'

'Aye, you look it.' Sandy's look was ironic, to say the least. 'Go see Jenny then, before you present yourself back at the office. That's an order.' He watched Adrian Chappell being walked out of the café, and looked at the chaos. 'Sorry.' He spoke to the young woman behind the desk, who appeared to be bereft of words as she surveyed her once neat coffee shop.

BOB STOOD IN THE small bathroom, shirtless, and voiceless. His wife dabbed witch-hazel onto a bruise and he winced. 'I don't suppose you'd get propositioned today, love. You've got the makings of a fine black eye. It's a pity I haven't got a leech or two.'

'No. It isn't!' Bob barely repressed a shudder. 'You can kiss it better. Is my nose broken?'

Jenny, looking up from her ministrations, grinned. 'No, just bashed. Stop fishing for sympathy, its not bleeding now.' She stood back and allowed him to pull his shirt back on, and then put her head on one side. 'How big was this bloke anyway?'

Bob sat on the side of the bath and rolled up his trouser legs. 'He was skinny and his kid was even smaller.' He surveyed the damage to his shins as his wife chuckled at him and knelt at his feet, the better to see to the damage.

'She got in a few good kicks, Bob.'

'Don't I know it?' He drew in his breath as Jenny laid

348

a damp flannel on the maltreated bone-work.

'This will be a nice colour too. Still, very little skin broken, just a few scratches.' She stood up after gently patting him dry.

Bob rolled down the trouser legs and pulled her close for a kiss. 'Thanks, pet.'

'OK. Downstairs and take a couple of panadol, and then you can return to the fray.'

'With my shield or on it, pet?'

Jenny took a hand and led him down to the kitchen. 'Yes, Bob.'

Bob sat down and waited as she poured tea and produced tablets. He held them in his hand as he looked at her sitting down next to him. 'You know Beth never got the hang of that. She was afraid for me.' He smiled. 'You are too, but you accept as well.' He clapped the hand holding the pills to his mouth and quickly washed down the medicine.

'You are a policeman, love.' She gave a faint smile. 'And, yes, I do worry, but I wouldn't change you.'

'Thank God for that.'

'Drink up. You've got a murderer to deal with.'

'Yeah, but I still haven't got a motive.'

'You're sure he did it, Bob?'

'Circumstantial as yet, and he bolted, Jen. Why would he do that if he didn't have a guilty conscience?'

Jenny offered a shrug. 'Who knows what drives people. Anger, grief, greed.'

'Yeah, well, we'll find out.'

SANDY WAS PILING UP paperwork when Bob got back to the station. 'Hah, you have returned. Just in time too. I was beginning to think I'd have to do all the paperwork myself.

'What, we've got a confession!'

'No, not a hint of one, Bob. I've got him sitting in the cells thinking about things.'

'The child?'

Sandy gave a half smile; Bob was always a soft touch for the children. 'Apparently he was there to meet his long lost love. Or, anyway, the woman he got pregnant twenty-three years ago. They had arranged a meeting to talk. He didn't know she'd had a son.' Sandy raised an eyebrow as Bob gave a very inelegant snort.

'He either couldn't or wouldn't leave the child behind. The woman, Jane Wilson, is willing to look after the girl for the present, but social services will have to get involved if we can prove he murdered Ratcliff, Bob.'

Bob sighed heavily and sat at his desk. 'I hate the fall-out, Sandy. They don't realise that it's not just one man killing another. Its two whole families grieving, murdered and murderer.

'Aye, you're right there. I've got a young Canadian in interview. Name of Charlie Reynolds. He's kin of Ratcliff. Nephew. He was literally on his way to visit and the copper on the door brought him down here.'

Bob looked up. 'Are we looking?'

'Got to check him out, Bob. His alibi isn't worth a bent nickel because those meds could have been planted anytime, and all he had to do was stand back and wait and gather the cash at the end of the day.'

'Form?'

'None so far, but I'm still waiting on our Canadian colleagues to get back to me.'

'Opinion?'

Sandy shook his grizzled head and pursed his lips. 'I misdoubt me he'll like the cash, but there's genuine grief there. He seemed shocked too. If he'd done it why not just sit and wait for the phone call telling him of death by natural causes.'

'OK. So you're not really looking, are you?'

Sandy shook his head again. 'Do you want to question him?'

This time Bob shook his head. 'I'll let the uniforms take the statement and wait for the Mounties to get back to us. Let's go and talk to Chappell.'

Adrian Chappell was brought up from the holding cells and shown into an interview room containing Sandy, Bob, a state solicitor and a large, black headed sergeant on the door. Sandy said Gareth ap Rhys always made a good door, and he was fulfilling this role more than adequately today.

Chappell was assisted into his seat and tried to relax. A task not made easier by the orange suit issued by the state, lace-less shoes and a pair of handcuffs.

He took a quick glance at the bruising beginning to

spread on Bob's face and as quickly looked away again.

Sandy began with name, address, time and place for the benefit of the tape and the paper trail, before starting to question in earnest. 'Right, Mr Chappell, perhaps you would like to explain why you saw fit to hit my colleague here, and run.'

Adrian Chappell looked at the solicitor. 'My client wishes to tender his apologies; however, that is the only comment he has to make.'

Sandy gave the solicitor a look of disgust, before transferring his attention back to Chappell. 'Do you know a Mr James Ratcliff?'

'No comment.'

'Have you ever visited his house?'

'No comment.'

Bob shrugged. 'Perhaps we should tell you that the cook is willing to state that you came round a few times to play chess and left your dog, who's she has also identified from photos, outside. The dog hairs, where you tied him up, have also been matched.' Or they will be thought Bob, as he looked at Chappell.

'No comment.'

'We have also matched your fingerprints to the underside of the window ledge inside Mr Ratcliff's downstairs bedroom.'

'That's a lie I...'

'You what, Mr Chappell?'

'Nothing, no comment.'

'If you have a legitimate reason for being there then say so, sir, and stop wasting our time.'

Chappell slid another sideways look at his solicitor, got a blank look in return and sighed. 'Look what if I visited. Nothing wrong with that is there?'

'So you admit you knew him?'

'Yeah.'

'We have a warrant here.' Sandy pulled the paper off the top of the pile and pushed it towards the solicitor. 'It gives us licence to search your home, car and work premises. It also gives us permission to take a sample of DNA.' The solicitor nodded and pushed it towards Chappell. 'We will be executing it within the next couple of hours. Is there anything you would like to say before said search is begun?'

'No comment.'

'Hmm. Sergeant, take Mr Chappell back to his cell.'

The two detectives waited until they were alone before Bob spoke. 'He's been coached.'

'Aye. Not much we can do, Bob. Just have to build the case around him. Do you want to go and do the search?'

'Yes.' They strolled along to the squad room and Bob walked across to his desk, picked up his briefcase, which had been left temptingly open, and gave a sly smile to Sandy. 'Riffled.'

'Good. Something good might come of this day yet.'

'I'll spring that trap, Bob, while you go check out the good chemist.'

Bob nodded and left the station. Sandy, meanwhile,

was striding along the corridor towards his superintendant's office.

25

THE CHAPPELL HOUSE HAD been relatively quiet until the forensics team arrived. As Bob turned the key he was greeted by a very familiar smell, and a hideous noise. 'Good grief! What the...' Mark Forester, deploying his team as he entered, wrinkled his face and stuck out his tongue as he said something that sounded like 'Awk!'

'If I make no mistake, Mark, that's Polly the parrot.' Bob raised his voice above the noise of squawking bird and barking dog.

Polly was sitting on a tree branch from the garden. It had been inexpertly nailed to some other pieces of wood to make a rustic stand. Under her feet were newspapers covered in droppings and two pots, of seed and water respectively.

'Right, Bob. It stinks.'

'Hmm! You could be right there.' He stepped over the floor and went to the bird. 'Hello, Polly. How are you, my friend?' Bob gently stroked the down bent head of the bird. 'Now, how do you come to be here?' The bird ceased her noise as he petted her. The dog, somewhere in the back regions, continued to bark, deep heavy woofs of sound.

Mark watched as Bob picked up a peanut and held it

for the bird. 'Well she left her feathers in the Daimler, maybe she hitched a ride.'

Bob stopped crooning to the bird and looked at Mark as if he'd never seen him. 'Say that again?'

'We found two of her feathers in the front seat of the Daimler, I told you, Bob. Even put it in the report.' Mark watched as Bob nodded, and his eyes developed a faraway look. 'So, you had a ride in the Daimler, Polly. That was enterprising of you.'

'Bob?'

'Whist. I think I've nearly got it.' Bob thought as he looked through Mark. 'No, that doesn't work, he was killed on Sunday and you were at home with your master on Monday weren't you, my pretty.' He continued to stroke the bird. 'Ah, of course. Mark, tell me what you found on the Daimler.'

Mark nodded, glancing at his team. 'Someone go and shut that dog up.' One of the men went off into the nether regions, and Mark watched as the rest spread out and began carefully going through drawers in various rooms. 'It had obviously been involved in an accident. Not the first either. I'm still waiting on matches, but visually I'd say it had been used to drive down a muddy road not a thousand miles from the one I went and looked at, over at Brownrigg.

'It had scratches consistent with the hedges there, and a few spikes of grass-leaved orache blossom. They mostly grow on the east coast, but you were right, Bob, there was a little bit just coming into flower down the path where we found Jenkins body. There was also a very lively specimen of *xerolycosa miniata,* Dune Wolf Spider to you; they don't just appear in the middle of Carlisle. Thank God for that.' He lowered his voice as the noise from the dog abruptly ceased.

'Either it's bitten him and is now eating the carcase, or Philip has found a friend.'

'And you say the car had been in collision?' Bob ignored the irrelevant comments.

'There were flecks of paint on Jenkins clothes that matched the Daimler. And an indent in his right knee which matched the fluted top surface of the radiator, according to Jonesy. There aren't that many Daimler Conquests around, Bob. I don't see how this ties in with Ratcliff's murder though.'

Bob smiled. 'You will. I imagine this bird belongs to the nephew, Charlie Reynolds. Won't he be pleased?' He grinned a bit wickedly. 'Wonder if he wants a dog too.'

'Shouldn't think so.' But Mark spoke to the departing back of his friend and senior. 'Hoi. What about the search.'

'You'll be fine, Mark. I'll see you back at the station.'

Bob climbed into his car and headed for Henry James Ratcliff's home. He just needed to verify one or two things. Hugh Keegan was in the specially humidified room, working his way through a steadily mounting pile of books and manuscripts.

He came out as Bob tapped on the glass door and smiled. 'Who gave you that?'

'No-one, I had to fight them for it.' Bob gave the stock answer as Hugh looked at the magnificent bruise blooming on Bob's cheek and eye socket. 'How have you got on?'

'Well, my girl is mad at me. She says I should still be in hospital or, failing that, at home in bed.' He gave a wicked grin. 'But I'm an honourable man.' He sobered for a minute.

'And I don't want to mess up again. Anyway,' he paused and turned while he spoke, going back into the room with Bob following. 'As requested I've looked at all the stuff I had been using, and yes, some of it, in light of your comments, will bear further scrutiny. I think someone has tampered with the texts. I also discovered a sheet that I'd gathered up with my papers last Friday. My god was that only last Friday.' He sighed heavily. 'It seems much longer,' he paused, frowned, 'or maybe shorter'.

Hugh pulled forward one piece of parchment. 'This one for instance. When I looked at it last week it had a splodge of ink just here.' Hugh gently laid a glove covered finger on the pristine page. It's gone. Cleaned up.'

'Are you sure?' Bob looked around the mounds of paper. 'It couldn't have been another one?'

'Nope. I know what I researched last. I can even show you the notes I made from this.'

'OK.' Bob offered a smile. 'Would you be able to spot the inserts or deletions?'

'It's been damn well done, Inspector. You're going to need an expert to go through it all. And, what's more, he was dealing in them. Buying and selling. God knows how many he's damaged and meddled with then sold on. They're out there telling tall tales about history.' Hugh looked both sad and angry.

'But it's written by the victors anyway, Hugh.' Bob spoke softly.

'Yeah, 'A fable agreed upon'.'

'Ah, Voltaire. History is a lie agreed upon.'

'Oh,' Hugh looked surprised for a minute, 'I thought

it was Bonaparte?'

'No.' Bob shook his head. 'My first wife was a researcher. She was careful with her quotes.' His lips twitched. 'And like you she hated it when the truth was bent for cash.'

'Was?'

Bob nodded. 'She died. Don't let your chance of happiness slip away, Hugh. Thank you for your help, but go home to your girl now. I'll get some experts in. In the meantime I'll lock the door.' He led the way outside the room, and suited action to word.

BACK AT THE STATION all was apparent frenzied activity as the change of shift swung into play. Sandy Bell was an oasis of calm amidst the chaos. Bob dropped into his own seat with a sigh of relief. He faced Sandy across the desk. 'The traffic's crazy out there, Sandy.' He surveyed his colleague. Sandy was sitting at his desk sipping from a habitual mug of tea. His shirt-sleeves were rolled up and his tie was at half mast. 'You look like the cat that got the cream.'

'Nay then, but I am the copper that got the crook though.' Sandy set his mug down and looked about at the mêlée going on around them. 'Do you fancy a spot of peace and quiet, Bob?' It was a rhetorical question as Sandy stood up and led the way out of the room and up to the roof-top garden. Bob following like some tantony pig.

They strolled over to the low parapet. 'Care to make a guess at our bent copper?'

Bob shook his head and pulled his jacket off,

standing in his shirt sleeves and allowing the breeze to cool his heated body.

'Neil McKenzie.'

'What?' Bob's astonishment was all and more than Sandy could have hoped for. 'But…'

'Aye, we were looking for flash. Or something like.'

'The cameras?'

'Aye. His picture's as clear as a bell as he goes over our desks and into your briefcase. He grabbed that envelope we planted among Ratcliff's papers. Like it was treasure trove. The super's got him tucked away pending a search of his bank details and home address.'

'Damn that's bad, Sandy.'

'Aye. Don't I know it, that wee lass is beside herself. I've sent her home with Mike. She can't go to her own home until we clear her.'

'You don't think she's complicit?'

'Nay. Do you?'

'No.' Bob shook his head. 'She gave us the info' to easily, and she could have hushed up Mike Jorkvil without any trouble.'

'Aye.'

'So how and why?'

'Don't know all the details, yet, Bob, and he ain't talking, he lawyered up as soon as he saw the game was up.'

Bob nodded a bit sadly. 'Yeah, that's sensible.'

'Aye, first sensible thing he's done in a long while.'

Sandy shook his head and ran a hand through his hair, rumpling the already wind-tossed locks further. 'Want in on the interview?'

'Try and keep me away. Has the news leaked?'

'Not yet, but give it another hour and it will. Men talk. Now tell me what you've got. You came back before Mark could possibly have finished?' He raised an eyebrow.

Bob leaned back against the low wall and looked at the bee-filled flower beds in the far corner of the roof. 'I must get some carnations for Beth tomorrow.' Sandy nodded but didn't say anything, he just waited.

'I think it went like this. Ratcliff was warned of Jakob's visit by McKenzie. Why, we don't yet know. But if we find evidence he's Mr Smith...' Bob put his head on one side for a minute. 'So Ratcliff warns his staff and plans to dump his illegals at the bank on Monday. He contacts Jenkins to warn him and pay him off too, because it's all getting a bit close to home. Fine so far.' Bob smiled a bit grimly. 'Only Joe Jenkins is knocked over by someone as he leaves, someone who knew who, or what, he was. They dump the body in the hopes it won't be connected to Ratcliff that quickly. Someone who hadn't got a car to do said dumping.'

'Why did they take the Daimler in the first place? We are talking about the Daimler?'

'Oh yeah!' Bob nodded. 'I'm not sure why whoever took it, maybe Joe Jenkins wasn't the only one Ratcliff warned about his dealings, and maybe there was more than just the new illegals to dump! Perhaps there was something in the car. I've got Mark going over it again.'

'Fraser Wilson?'

Bob shook his head. 'No, he's really is just the chauffeur.'

'Alright. So Jenkins is dead after his visit, and Ratcliff is dying by inches, even though he doesn't know it yet.'

Bob nodded, then paused. 'Do you think that…no…' he frowned in thought, 'Yes, that might work and it would give us…'

Sandy pursed his lips and focused on the hills in the distance, waiting for Bob to sort the puzzle in his mind.

'How about, Chappell knocking over Jenkins and dumping the body.'

'Why is he there?'

'Bringing the finished product for Ratcliff.'

'Why is he in the Daimler?'

'Mark said that the car had been in an accident before…' Bob spoke slowly. 'What if McKenzie, who is traffic, was blackmailing Ratcliff. It gives us a connection.'

'And the threat of Jakob visiting might be enough to cause yon man to want the car dumped.'

'Why not just sell it?' This time Bob played devil's advocate.

'Not enough time.' Sandy raised an eyebrow.

'Alright, why get Chappell to dump it? Why not Jenkins?'

'Didn't trust him enough?'

Bob nodded. 'Yes, that could work. So…We're saying Chappell accidently knocks him over. But he wasn't dead;

Chappell could have taken him to A&E.' Then he shook his head. 'But not if the car was hot, or he was drunk.'

Sandy nodded. 'He could have just left him on the street; Bob. Someone would have found him.'

'Hmm.' Bob nodded and gazed at the flowers. 'But he might have identified Chappell.'

'True.'

'So...McKenzie tells Ratcliff. Ratcliff gets Jenkins there and tells him to get going,. Ratcliff then tells Chappell, who gets the car from round the back to go and dump it. OK so far?'

'Aye.'

'Pure accident that the two collided? Maybe. But that car was back in the garage on Monday morning. So why didn't Chappell dump it as promised?'

Sandy scowled. 'I dunno.'

'No, nor do I. Yet. But I think all these comings and goings were through that dormer window.' He offered a half smile. 'Footprints up there, Sandy. And... I think Ratcliff had had a change of heart overnight. He told Fraser Wilson to fix the leak.'

'Aye, we're agreed on that too.'

Bob continued to frown at the flowers. 'McKenzie might have had a hold on Ratcliff, but surely Ratcliff had a hold on him. Blackmailers, if they're known, can be fingered.'

'Maybe it was mutual, Bob. Started as blackmail, 'I won't tell about the accident if you give me some money'. Or maybe the money was offered and just too tempting to resist. Then supplying info would net a bit more. Both are implicated, both benefit.'

'We need to test this theory, Sandy. Find out what accidents he was working.'

'Yes, lad. But it's getting chilly and I need to go home. So do you. They'll keep until we've got a bit more evidence.'

26

Saturday

THE NEXT MORNING SAW Bob and Sandy in the office with their jackets off before seven-thirty. Both had been hard at the paperwork for nearly an hour. The out-basket rising in direct proportion to the lowering level of the tea in their mugs.

'Right.' Sandy pushed back his chair. 'I'll go to the loo and I'm ready for interview. How about you, Bob?'

Bob nodded without looking up. 'Five minutes. Got Mark's report to go through, and I'll be with you.'

Sandy wandered away and Bob continued reading. A quiet cough at his elbow brought his head up. Mark, his blonde locks rioting over his head, stood grinning next to him. 'Congratulations, Bob.'

Bob grinned. 'Thanks, I think. What exactly am I being congratulated for?'

'I came up to give you one more result on the car. I hadn't got it when I dropped that off last night.' He nodded at the paperwork.

'You must have worked all night to get this much.'

'We aim to please. However, aside from the already mentioned bumps and bashes on the car there was a curious dint in the bonnet. I ran a few tests after you said to check out that other accident and discovered it had calcium and strontium in it.'

'Curious!'

'For what it's worth I would say that the dint was caused by a pair of front incisor of the human kind. And no, you'll not get DNA from it.' Mark grinned even while he shrugged.

'Thanks, Mark.'

Mark glanced around the empty room before he spoke. 'Is it true about McKenzie.'

Bob sobered. ''Fraid so.'

'God help his wife then. How's she gonna work here after that? Did he even think about that?' Mark glared fiercely at the empty desks around them.

'I don't know, but Sandy and I are about to go and ask him that among other questions.'

Sandy, walking in at that moment, nodded to Mark. 'Ready, Bob.'

'Yeah. Ready.'

Neil McKenzie was sitting in the interview room when they arrived. He had a police rep with him, and a solicitor in the corner. He looked miserable.

Sandy and Bob sat down, both looked tight lipped and grim to his weary eyes. Sandy read the details of the interview off and then sat back slightly and just looked at him.

'I'm glad I've been caught. I thought when he died I

could finally relax but...' Mackenzie shrugged.

Sandy nodded for him to continue; Mackenzie's voice started out slow but gained a bit of speed as he talked. 'I went to his house; Ratcliff's, a couple of years back. It was a car versus pedestrian. I'd finally tracked down a witness. I went to serve notice on him. He offered me five thousand pounds to forget it. We'd just moved into a new house, the mortgage interest had gone up and the recession was just beginning to bite. I walked away, but he sent the cheque through the post, it was on the doormat the next day, along with a demand from the bank to come and see them. I don't know how he got our address.

'I took the money. I shouldn't have.' He looked from one man's face to the other. 'After that, well, he'd got me and I'd got him. The money kept us afloat.'

'You had two wages coming in?'

'Yeah. And a previous wife and kids to keep happy, along with the CSA.' Bob could taste the bitterness, like the gall in the ink, black and sharp. 'I take it Ratcliff was driving?'

'Yeah, he quit. Used that major domo of his for a bit, then hired a chauffeur. He was a sick man.'

'The accident, that was Mrs Chappell?' Sandy looked across. 'That's why you took the cold file?'

'Yeah. God, it made my blood run cold, my wife turning up that file. I thought it was as dead and buried as the woman was.'

'So you let him know Jakob was going to pay a visit.'

'I had to. If I hadn't he'd have split on me. I'd learnt how ruthless he could be, and what kind of knowledge he seemed to be able to get. He knew all about my kids, the school and grades, and my wife and who her partner was. He let me know how much he knew.'

'And you told him we were going to visit as well.' Bob looked across the desk, his face devoid of all feeling.

'Same reason.'

'Yet it must have been a pure fluke that gave you that info, couldn't you have just told him you hadn't known?' The voice was arctic in its coldness.

'No. I don't know. I was bloody scared, don't you understand.'

'No.' Yet Bob did, he would protect his family too. He didn't think he'd sink to such depths, but he'd never been placed in that position.

Sandy nodded. 'Go on.'

'I let Chappell know, I told him the case might be opening again. I told him there was new evidence and he should watch his back. As soon as I saw that case file I knew things were going to blow wide open. I thought Ratcliff might, I don't know, do something to Chappell or the kid, so I warned him. Then I heard Ratcliff was dead and, dear God, I thought, Chappell had done for him because of what I'd said.' He paused. 'But I didn't tell him until Thursday and Ratcliff died Tuesday, so I relaxed again. Too bloody soon as it turns out. Now I hear you've got Chappell in the cells too. God, I didn't mean him to murder the bastard, no matter what I said.'

Sandy nodded. 'You've been very frank with us. I will be discussing the charges with the Superintendent. Perverting the course of Justice is only the start of it.'

'I know.' McKenzie sagged in the seat.

'Take him back, Sergeant.'

Both senior men watched him leave before they spoke. 'Poor bugger, with that hanging over his head for the past three years.'

Bob nodded. 'He still betrayed the uniform, Sandy.'

'Aye. But, 'there but for the Grace of God', Bob. Aye? Chappell next?' He looked up as Gareth came back in. 'Chappell, Gareth.'

'Right, Chief.'

Bob looked at the empty doorway. 'Mark says there were traces of teeth marks on the bonnet of the Daimler. Can't prove who, but can prove it was a human that hit.'

'It would suit Ratcliff's nature to make a mock of Chappell, Bob. He took great delight in making us look like fools. Imagine if he used the man to get rid of the car that had killed his wife. That would have been a real belly laugh for him.'

'And if Chappell knew and was exacting slow revenge, Sandy…?'

'Two wrongs don't make a right, Bob.'

'No.' He looked up as Chappell came in, followed by a solicitor. 'Mr Chappell, sit down.'

'We have nearly all the pieces now. Would you like to fill in the odd square we're missing?' Bob spoke pleasantly.

'Not really.' Chappell gave a cough of laughter. 'I don't fancy incriminating myself. Is my daughter OK?'

'You daughter is still with Ms Wilson and your son. She states that she will foster if the state allows and you are amenable.' Bob offered a faint smile.

'I never even got to see him.' He sighed. 'I suppose social services will be in to speak to me.'

'I should imagine so.'

'She's had enough upset, has my Maggie.'

'Is that why you took the parrot?'

Chappell's lips twisted upwards, you couldn't really call it a smile. 'She doesn't ask for much, and she's been reading Doctor Dolittle, the parrot talks for the others. I thought she might...' He stopped, abruptly aware that he'd given more away than he intended.

'Did you take it after you found him dead?'

Chappell shook his head. 'He wasn't dead, or not quite.'

Sandy raised an eyebrow and cocked his head on one side.

'The bastard was laughing at me, telling me he'd killed my wife, and I'd got rid of the evidence. So I took his bloody parrot, the only thing he was capable of loving. Only I hadn't got rid. I brought the car back the night before. I was going to dump it, but there was a couple in the damn lovers' lane. I told him and he started to laugh, then I told him I knew all along. His spray wouldn't do him any good. I left him alive.' Chappell looked at them. 'He took my wife and tossed away her life like she didn't count. Like I didn't count. Well, he didn't count either.'

'Unfortunately he did and does.' Bob spoke softly into the silence. 'You admit to tampering with his drugs. As a result he has died, and you are guilty of that death.'

Sandy nodded. 'You are formerly charged, by your own admission, with the deliberate murder of Henry James Ratcliff. Do you understand the charge?'

Chappell nodded. Sandy moved into official mode and the interview wound to a close. After Chappell had been removed to the cells again the two Detectives sat in the empty room and Bob sighed. 'You said there but for the Grace of God, Sandy. I don't know, would I have plotted revenge if I'd know Beth's killer? I hope not. But...'

'Aye, lad but...'

'Thank God I haven't been put to that test.'

BOB SAT WITH HIS daughter on his knee in their kitchen. The three year old was methodically demolishing a custard cream by pulling it apart and licking the cream from the middle. Sandy and his wife sat on the other side of the kitchen table and Jenny poured tea at the counter.

'It's all so sad, Bob.' Jenny spoke as she came over.

'Yeah, it is, Chappell killed Ratcliff because he'd knocked over and killed his wife. Apparently Dove had let slip the information about the accident one evening when Chappell was visiting and Chappell had put dates and times together and come up with the right answer. After that it was just a matter of time before he worked out a form of revenge.'

'What about your drug pusher?' Sandy's wife picked up her tea and looked at the brew. 'You said he was bringing in green tea or something.'

'Oh, more than tea, Sarah. As we suspected, Jenkins had been summoned to be warned about the police raid. Ratcliff wanted him to dispose of the car too. He'd been a passenger in it when Ratcliff hit Mrs Chappell. He kept quiet but Ratcliff was threatening him with exposure, claiming he, Jenkins, was driving. Chappell overheard from outside the bedroom window. He didn't deliberately knock Jenkins down, but he has even less liking for drug pushers and he wasn't exactly sorry.'

'This Ratcliff sounds a horrible man, Bob.'

'He was, it's difficult to investigate when the victim is as nasty as the villains.'

'I'm glad it's done with, love. Until the next time.' Jenny sat next to Bob and Caitlin slithered over onto her knee and proceeded to kiss her. Bob watched with a gentle smile. 'OK Munchkin, sit down and let mum drink her tea, she's gone of coffee.' Bob suddenly smiled it went from sly to singularly sweet and quite blindingly joyful, as he looked from Sandy to Sarah.

Sarah grinned. 'Oh I suspected...'

Sandy frowned and looked at his smiling wife and then the other two.

'Call yourself a detective, Sandy Bell.' His wife gave him a friendly poke in the ribs.

Sandy looked again at Jenny and Bob 'Oh! Now that takes the sour taste away.' He bit into a custard cream himself and it was open to conjecture whether he was referring to biscuit or baby.

About the author:-

The author began writing after employment in numerous jobs. Among other occupations there has been teaching, interpreting, nursing, stoker on a steam engine and shop worker. This variety has coloured the writing and informed the writer as all lives do.

Married with children, the temptation to commit murder has been firmly repressed, especially when family life has intruded into the time set aside for the enjoyment of solving the puzzle that is murder. And why men and women commit the act.

The author has lived in a number of countries including England, Scotland, Wales, and New Zealand and travel as they say, 'broadens the mind and the vocabulary'. If the occasional expression is new, the motives and causes of death are not.

Also by the same author:

Relative Dating. (2008) {e}
ISBN 978 1 9997425 2 2

Tree Dimensional. (2009) {e}
ISBN 978 1 9997425 5 3

Grave Doubts. (2009) {e}
ISBN 978 1 9997425 7 7

Diverse Distress. (2009)
ISBN 978 184386 558 2

Smokescreen. (2010)
ISBN 978 184386 649 7

Collide and Conquer. (2011)
ISBN 978 190349 048 8

In the Loop. (2011)
ISBN 978 184386 702 9

Timeline. (2011)
ISBN 978 184386 912 2

Enter Two Gravediggers. (2011)
ISBN 978 190349 066 2

Disreputable Truth. (2012)
ISBN 978 184386 829 3

Discarded Images. (2014) {e}
ISBN 978 184386 558 2

Entrapment. (2017) {e}
ISBN 978 1 9997425 6 0

{e} indicates also available in e-book form